Other

"My Texas Streak" (A Colorado Cowboy Romance Story)

Crystals of Syre Series

Awakening (Book 1)

Revelation (Book 2) Coming Spring 2020!

Assassins' Guild of Obseen

The Cost of Redemption (Sequel to Vision of a Torn Land)
[Coming Fall 2019!]

The

Assassins' Guild of Obseen

"Vision of a Torn Land"

Lindsey Cowherd

Acknowledgements

The Assassins' Guild books are my "babies", those I wasn't sure I would ever share with the world; however, thanks to those few souls who read this book and its sequel in their first stages and said, "These are different. I think you have something here…" thank you for that. The "AG" books are a world all of my own imagination and I enjoy being within them.

Next, I want to thank my parents and family. They support me through all the thick and thin and the waking up at nights to jot down another note. Somehow, they tolerate my obsession with writing on paper before I ever type a book up, cursive and all!

Another thanks goes to the teachers I have had in the past in martial arts classes. It started me on a path to have a "warrior's mindset" and a mind like a "hollow bone". I am forever changed by the ideas from the martial arts and the beauty of a truly masterful practitioner.

To the artist at SelfPubBookCovers.com/rgporter who made the cover of this book. It has the "stun" factor I was looking for. Thank you! And lastly, to the authors who have come before who have been a reminder to me that if we all love to write we should share it with the world!

Before you embark on a journey of revenge, dig two graves.

Japanese proverb

Character List

Clan: Las'wa

Seircor C'vail (Praic)

Kraiy C'vail

Zanishiria [Coursay'sora]

Art'or Coursay'sora

Tyen Evalaus

Cour'eysan (Coryu) Evalaus

Shy'ree C'vanil

Master Shay'renor

Master Tyracor

Taysor Training Center: Masters

Senior Master Sye Rainier (Kaumian)

Master Ranarro Dorsetti (Ghans)

Master Jeudeo Quinn (Baras)

Master Hiroku Yoshida (Mitoki)

Master Vidan Sunashi (Chars)

Master Corsetti (Ghans)

Master Roko Corbius (Shynor)

Master Hareoska (Ukati)

Master Shathahel (clan unknown)

Taysor Training Center: Students

Tarin Saerric (Neitiege)

K'sho Rease (Sinya)

Dăveed Quinn (Baras)

Emperor's Elite

Honored One Master Teera Sabina (Suez)

Davin (assistant to Teera Sabina; clan unknown)

Eric Sorey (Air'is Soreneay; Las'wa)

Xemin Cour'noum—Honored (Corez)

Shigge Autaro—Honored (Haukmen)

Tak'eth Sorēin—Honored (Suez)

Tath Enor—Honored (Corez)

Royals

Emperor Manscor (Royal-assassin)

King Paul Lapsair

Scarlett Novastone

Royal Qusairo Doz (leader Renegade Army)

Prince Anmero Doz

Asilisa Doz

Royal Aslén Doz (Renegade Army)

Captain Raynward (Renegade Army)

Captain Sieck (Renegade Army)

Major Calamas (Renegade Army)

Other

Alrik Kagar [Shadon] (Thereq)

General Landen (UEF)

Clan: Xsorian

Tá sharay Khan Torez

Tá sharid Page Torez

Tá sharid Lap Torez

con'trore Kee'van

Clan: Trayshan

Berris Tearrì Sinhail

Berzén Tyre Sinhail

Beynor Shane Sinhail

Backstory

There are no written records to help scholars and historians relive the human race's catastrophic downfall in the early era of the Star Date period, but plenty is known before then, in the A.D. years, and after the date 1073 S.D. The long gap is distorted by the awful breaking of humanity. Each story is colored in bias and discrepancies; this grey area will, therefore, remain a sort of mystery for those who lived afterward. As it is, the history I will lay before you may or may not be completely accurate. However, it is the most factually believed chronicle by historians all over the Abyss Solar System...

Entry One: The start of the end of Earth:

Humanity created itself into one large metropolis across the face of the earth. All its magnificence was seen in the great accomplishments of towering buildings, powerful engineering, and technologies. The energies of the wind and water were harnessed in hydroelectric plants created on floating platforms atop the oceans, allowing for much-needed room for the ever-growing human populations on the mainland. The human population smothered what little land was left.

It wasn't until much later that scientists realized what the effects of the mass-produced productions did to the earth. Their report thus stated: "the overuse of the oceans and soil is destroying Earth at a rate far greater than anything ever expected. Soon, it may become a race to stop the deterioration of Earth all together. If we wait, we may not have a planet to reside upon!" But the warning came too late.

In less than twelve years, the unstable elements of Earth shattered. Atmospheric build-up created massive thunderstorms that ripped across the globe, and lightning struck, engulfing flames that tore at the planet. In the water, enormous waves capped and crashed against the once-strong coasts to cut them apart. Human loss was substantial. A scream for salvation echoed across the continents of the world, showing how desperate humans had become at the severe losses.

Leaderships were unsure of what to do about the catastrophe, however. After months of hopeless debate, the Nations came together in one, last-ditch attempt to save the dying world. Unsure if any of the planet could be saved without serious intervention, the science fields and bioengineering hastened to invent ways to ease the earth's tolls.

(Back history). By this time, humanity had found a way to support human life on places such as the moon and Mars, but the devastations seen of Earth meant that most of humanity needed to leave the planet and not just the few hundred that called space home.

Entry Two: Creation of Space Stations

Under the great push, a committee was convened to create space stations—better known as colonies—to take up the slack. The space stations created within that year were predicted to an estimated 67% of the human population for fifty years before new resources would be needed to replace the shortages. This new system allowed for the colonies to become semi-independent from Earth, and would, hopefully, give the ailing planet some time to recover…

The peace that followed seemed fragile. In the fifty years of recovery, the earth did find a balance and began to heal. Relieved, a number of colonists were allowed to reestablish themselves on the planet; others satisfied with life in space stayed about the space stations.

(Back history). By this time in history there were fewer "world" powers—only the United Nations of the American continent, the Russian Empire, the Nation of Britain, the Unified Continent of Africa, the Republic of China (leader of the Unified Asian Alliance) and the Arab nations remained; however, these nations had come to barely tolerated each other and easily bickered over land and resources. It was only time before something would happen to break the tiny threads keeping the tensions in line.

Entry Three: The Last War

In the year 1857 S.D., the fragile peace was finally shaken apart. A negotiation between the United Nations of the Americas and the Republic of China went awry. Resentments began to build. Each side built up angry walls through betrayals and fear until on the eighteenth of August the first major thread broke: A United Nations envoy never returned from China. When asked about the disappeared persons, the Chinese replied that the envoy had killed some of their delegates and were being tried for their treasons. Three weeks later, all twelve of the U.S. envoys were returned to the Americas in boxes, the bodies mutilated. An angry United Nations' army was at China's doorstep within a week; however, the Americans' expectations of a swift demise to the Chinese were reversed. Instead, their attack on China roused the Russian and Arab nations, who quickly set up a defense around the Chinese domain.

The action triggered a war.

The colonies ignored the chaos below them for a short time, but, as the war blazed on, they watched in horror as Earth's people destroyed themselves and their precious planet for a final time. Thousands died daily and yet the war did not stop. In its third year, the war reached its climax. All forces, except the United Nations and Russia, were too damaged to fight, so the last two superpowers were left to bicker among themselves. The results were disastrous.

In a final effort to gain control of lands, an exhausted United Nations force risked all to plant seven nuclear bombs in Russian-controlled lands. When the bomb debris cleared, the area was void of any living lifeforms. Entire forests and bodies of water were evaporated away. Dust and nuclear radiation clung thickly to the air and traveled across the globe to destroy plants and animals as it settled over them. The war-torn Earth was slowly and officially dying.

For all the wrongdoings and hatred of the human race, was it worth killing the planet? This devastation shook the foundations of what life meant for human civilization. War was a plague. By the laws of nature, no human had the right to destroy all they touched but it took the destruction of Earth, in the Star Date year 1860, for them to learn this truth. By the time humanity really understood, there was no hope left for mankind; we had been our own doom.

Entry Four: Salvation for Humanity

Star Date 1868: a man named Devon Parc, a young half-Frenchman representative from the Swedish nationality of colony Angelholm first appeared publicly at the senatorial colony L3X008435-Thessalía to give the Nations some hope. At the time, Thessalía housed a mix of respectable American, Russian, African, Chinese, and Japanese people; it was the first colony to unify and pacify its habitants. Near the end of the planetary war raging below it, L3X008435-Thessalía's power was so great, that it was known as the leading pacifying force against the war. With the war concluded, colony Thessalía, and more importantly Devon Parc, stepped forward to take control of the chaotic aftermath.

Using foresight, Devon Parc began to organize advanced searches for life beyond known space—which at this time extended just past Neptune, a year's journey away—to look for habitable worlds outside of the solar system. In the Star Date 1894, Mars base received electrifying news: Devon Parc's search team had discovered a small system of eight planets only a twenty-six-light-year journey away (by the fastest star ship).

Parc's message was broadcast to all colonies a few days later. In elation the colonist heard these words: "Red base, we have found a home! Bring anyone who wishes to see our new land. Use the Solace and the World Maker from the United Earth Forces' starships. We will have a place prepared for those "pioneers" when they arrive."

Surprisingly, 2,187,483 colonists answered his message, though only half that number was allowed to board the two starships. Those first "pioneers" would reach their destination on November 18, 1921 S.D.

Entry Five: The Abyss Solar System

Eight planets there were, in what would later be called the Abyss Solar System. Most were many times larger than Earth, and all but one boasted at least three or more moons. There were also two asteroid fields that separated the planets from Sarius, the new sun, the very distant Neptune, and unknown space; these were called the Asteroid Base M2 and the Skurai Asteroid Fields. The space between the two asteroid fields, excluding any space taken by the planets, was called

"Skyreck Airspace". The importance of this airspace was for space-freighter passage and safe airways.

The first planet they discovered was named after the old science fictional world Planet X and was used as a research and industrial base for starships until the colonization began on the "newly" named New Earth six months later. Once New Earth was founded, all colonists were transported there to carve out an existence on a planet more Earth-like than any of the other worlds. Soon after, the Sentinal planets were explored and scientists began researching ways to make them habitable. Sentinal 1 was a lush planet that would not be used for civilizations; instead it was preserved and make into a place of serenity and religion, tended by priests and priestesses. Desert-oriented people moved to Sentinal 2, or the Tomb, where they created an existence similar to their past one on Earth. Finally, scientists started their bid to open up Sentinal 3 as a usable planet. Sentinal 3 proved difficult, for it was a gas giant, with similar layout to Venus, with a ferocious gravitational pull, but the scientists devised a large complex-dome—called Sycre Dome—that could lower the gravitational pull and protected people from the gases. Once completed, the dome covered one thousand acres of Sentinal 3's barren and mica-ridden ground.

The sixth discovered planet was called O'washia by its inhabitants. The gigantic watery world was home to an extraterrestrial species called the Hy'gual. At first, the scientists could not speak with the Hy'gual, but they soon learned that the marine-like species spoke a rough form of Korean. Once this was decided to be the easiest form of communication, it was simpler to coexist with the Hy'gual on O'washia.

Only a few years after civilization was established on the new planets, a sudden uprising of terrorists and assassins arose to torment the newly established United Earth Forces government. The uprising was quickly subdued, but the UEF was worried that another one was inevitable, so they sent the two groups to the two nastiest planets and made them prisoners there. The first planet, Al Tor, was large; so the large numbers of captured terrorists and "psycho/sociopaths" were sent there. It seemed the perfect place to send them, for it was closest to Sarius and was so harsh it was considered "barely habitable". The UEF hoped its environment would subdue the vicious terrorist nation.

Entry Six: Relevance to our story, The Assassins' Guild of Obseen

Meanwhile, the smaller population of "assassins", were sent to a small, out-of-the way planet near Planet X, called Obseen. Obseen was to be their last prison, for it hosted the most dangerous creatures ever known to man. Because of this, the UEF believed the assassins would not last long on the tiny, obsidian planet. To make sure that the assassins never left the planet again, the UEF assigned noblemen and kings, who were now frowned upon in society, to watch over Obseen. In return, the Royals were given the to-be abandoned Planet X and all its buildings.

However, the United Earth Forces would later learn that the assassins and terrorists could not be easily subdued or destroyed. In just over two thousand years, both would become major forces in the universe...

Forward

Year: 1921 S.D.

Many people have left the dirty, war-torn Earth in search of a new life on a handful of newly discovered planets past Neptune. Eight were found: New Earth, Planet X, the Sentinals (1,2, and 3), O'washia, Al Tor, and Obseen... A new government called the Unified Earth Forces took control of New Earth; its government would control how the other planets would be run. O'washia and the Sentinals were inhabited by many diverse cultures who wished to be separate from the UEF—and eventually they were able to attain their freedom.

Planet X was given to the control of kings and queens, so that the Royals could keep an eye on Obseen, the planet turned into a prison for the unruly assassins. Al Tor became the other prison planet; a place for those considered terrorists and "crazies".

Year: 4012 (Obseen)

The obsidian planet has once again been thrust into war. A Royal has taken over the planet, and a large percentage of the assassin clans do not want him as their leader. The Royal, now calling himself "Emperor Manscor", has sent his Royal guards and Honoreds to conquer the opposing forces, and he even went as far as massacring hundreds of assassins to prove his control of them.

By the year 4023, many assassin clans have quietly joined the Renegade Army in hopes of ending Manscor's reign. One such clan, called the Las'wa or Lakeans, has refused to become completely involved in the war, but they have given their support. The Lakeans have sent twelve assassin youths to the surface to stop Manscor...but they were deceived and hunted down.

Ending Manscor's reign seems impossible, yet, there is hope, even on this dark planet.

I have written this story so everyone will know of our strife. I pieced everything together after speaking with those involved in the Royals' War and hope many will learn from our situation someday. I give my thanks to those who helped me with the story behind the war—my friend and trainee Zanishiria, Senior Master Tarin Saerric, Seircor C'vail, King Lapsair, the Tà Sharay, Prince Anmero Doz, Princess Scarlett Novastone, Asilisa Doz, Berris Sinhail, and my fellow six masters at Taysor—for without you all, this story would not have been. Thank you.

Star Date: 4025

Written by: Master Quinn

Chapter One

There are two worlds to Obseen: the above, where most of the assassins reside, and the below, or underworld. Only one clan, the Las'wa, live in the underworld. It is a dangerous place filled with the most vile of Obseen's deadliest creatures. Too, it is a place of darkness, revealed only to the Las'wa by the use of lenses, called gamma lenses, taken from two creatures that live there: the preshair snakes and the creeshts spiders. To live in the underworld is to fight with death and terror daily. For such, the Las'wa have become legend in the assassin world. They are the leaders of all that is impossible.

A scream pierced the darkness. It was a scream of pain that echoed through the upper tunnels of Obseen. A void followed in its trail. The silence was even more disturbing than the noise that was dwindling down the long caverns of the planet.

A Las'wa youth of sixteen-years-of-age glanced over his shoulder in a futile attempt to see through the near-darkness of the long cavern he occupied to the eight-legged creatures that crawled somewhere behind. Worried they were not in sight but could still be heard, Seircor C'vail returned his attention to concentrate on running, following his sister, Kraiy, through the tunnels of the "underworld". He followed her deft footsteps as she led them through the maze of obsidian tunnels, following a secret path leading to the surface of Obseen.

The sudden clack of a close spider's leg coming down from the ceiling caused Seircor to duck involuntarily, causing the intended weapon to flash dangerously close overhead. "Clai!" [Faster/hurry!] He yelled to his sister as he caught his footing again. Kraiy increased her speed in response and disappeared around the corner into a side cavern, only to stop and moan in despair. "Oh, we don't need this."

Seircor slid to a stop beside his sister to survey the situation. Ahead, the cavern had somehow collapsed, barring their way of escape. "Creesht-áet!" [Roughly means: "spider spit"] He spat, "This is not a good place for a standoff." The ticking of a spider's legs on the cold stone caused Seircor to turn around. "Behind me, Kraiy, I think we've been found."

The younger girl followed his instructions with a look of despair. "I hope we aren't outnumbered, Praic." Seircor could only nod.

Five large spiders crawled into the small cavern and spread out along the walls, ceiling, and floor. The low luminescence of light from the lichen clinging to the obsidian rocks cast eerie glows of green-blue coloring over the arachnids' bodies. The spiders' sharp legs, which jutted out of their sides like twisted knives, were covered in strong, spike-like studs. Their exoskeletons, the color of the murky blue-black of the underground lakes, flashed menacingly from their smooth texture. The lead spider reared up, as if in victory, to flash his large "death-mark" symbol on his belly at the trapped youths.

Seircor slid his long creeshts sword from its sheath and held it in front of him. Behind him, Kraiy did the same. "These aren't normal creeshts, Ai'a. [Roughly means "with me" usually used for siblings/friends as endearment for close ties.] Their marks have been altered. No doubt they are servants to an assassin of the "man killer'."

Seircor's warning sent shivers down his sister's spine. "Then there will be more. They will not stop until we have killed them all or they kill all of us."

"Yes... I fear that we may not get out of these caverns alive. Certainly, someone is making an effort for none of us to. I hope..." He paused to choke back his terror at that certainty. "I hope one of us makes it through this day." A creeshts dropped from the ceiling behind them cutting Seircor off from his ponderings. "Creesht-áet! Take my back, Kraiy. I will take these four."

Kraiy's delicate, sweaty back settled into his as she took her defense. "We're surrounded, you know." Kraiy voiced her only concern before sounding more confident. "But I'm with you to the end, Praic."

Before Seircor could acknowledge his sister, three of the creeshts charged. Instinctively, Seircor ducked under his first attacker and, as he did, he brought his long-blade to bare. The creeshts blade kissed the spider's abdomen as it passed overhead, and the tip broke through the tough exoskeleton to the vital organs underneath. Glimmering blue blood began to drip slowly down the sword's blood groove, past the handle, and onto Seircor's arm. It felt warm and sticky, and tickled the sixteen-year-old distractingly as it wandered up his sleeve.

The creeshts gave a piercing scream of pain that pulled the youth back into focus. As if time had been made slower, the spider's large corpse began to fall on top of Seircor. Moving quickly, Seircor rolled out from under the looming mass before it could come to a crushing halt on top of him; however, his swift escape cost him his sword. The creeshts blade was lost, embedded somewhere deep beneath the dead arachnid. Empty handed, Seircor turned to face his other two attackers.

The second creeshts towered three meters above the young assassin, much larger than the first, and better equipped with hand-sharpened legs. Wary, it regarded its prey like a human would to squash a bug. "Come on you worthless bek'lee. [Senile or "without any brain"] I'll take your sorry ass down!" On second thought, maybe I should have a weapon first before making such statements.

Glancing around quickly, Seircor spotted a pile of rocks some four meters to his left—the only problem was that the creeshts was tracking his movements. The youth tried to let out a for-the-moment curse but had to cut it short as the creeshts tried to impale him with its right foremost leg. Still, Seircor managed to roll most of the way to the intended pile of rubble before another knife-like leg landed in front of him, barring his passage. The assassin barely jumped out of the way before a second leg drove into the stones near him. "Let me pass, you disgusting, brain-altered trep!" [Slang from UEF, trep= stupid/inferior] Seircor yelled in annoyance. The spider answered by trying to impale him.

A growl escaped the youth's lips and he turned about to face his nemesis. Still dodging the sharp legs, Seircor took note of where its saysora [heart] was. The brightness of the creeshts' heart was intense, showing that the creeshts was very aged, and that the exoskeleton was more vulnerable to an attack. "Ha! So, you're as good as dead, old vail." [Warrior] Seircor rolled away from another volley of legs. In five twisting moves, he managed to dance toward the rock pile until he was close enough to grab two hefty projectiles.

The creeshts reared in surprise when Seircor rolled underneath it. Glancing up at the exposed body, the assassin youth was able to glimpse the heart and aim for it. The saysora glowed a faint, blue globe through the spider's murky exoskeleton, making it an easy target. Seircor managed to throw one of his two stones at the large spot before a swinging leg caught him on the calf, severing deeply of the muscles and tendons. Fully shocked, he felt the tip go all the way to the bone of his shin. A hiss tore from Seircor's throat as the pain rocked him, and he collapsed to the ground.

Above him, the rock he had thrown pierced the creeshts' exoskeleton and logged itself in the saysora. The creeshts echoed its prey's cry and followed the youth's path toward the obsidian-stone floor. All Seircor could do was watch the enormous dying creature fall over him. With one finally thought, Seircor closed his eyes and whispered, "Oshay, Kraiy. Coursa'na shay lai. Kye moreay." ["Good-bye, Kraiy. I could not save you. I am sorry."]

A light draft of air caressed Seircor's face as he lay there, eyes closed, waiting for death. A moment passed with the sounds of Kraiy's struggles across the room tormenting his ears. In shocked realization, Seircor found he was not yet dead. Opening his eyes, he witnessed a lone figure standing next to him holding onto a rod that was keeping the enormous carcass from smashing the injured youth.

Straining with the weight of the creeshts, the girl spoke to Seircor through her clamped teeth. "Clai, Praic! Shay mora'lai." ["Hurry, Praic. Go save your sister!"]

Seircor pulled himself away from the creeshts as fast as he could bare and tried to find a handhold in the obsidian wall to pull himself up with. Finding none, he pulled his good leg underneath to take his weight and leaned against the wall. Seircor managed to stagger part way to his feet, though he began to black out as his injured left leg screamed at him with pain.

His rescuer was at his side in an instant, catching him as he swaggered about. "Sit back down, Praic." She ordered in basic, seeing the youth's situation. "I will go help your sister." Seircor let his body slid back down the wall, knowing better than to protest. He nearly lost consciousness as his left leg moved over the rough stone but he managed to stay the darkness enough to shift into a comfortable spot. His rescuer dropped a snakeskin pouch near his thigh, full of herbs that could staunch his bleeding. She, then, turned to launch herself at the remaining three creeshts.

Kraiy regarded the creeshts looming above her. The nearest one waved its left foreleg at her, its thrust managing to knock her sword from her hands. Kraiy gulped; she had not brought many other weapons, and many had already been lost to previous defenses. Suddenly feeling fear catching in her gut, she stepped away from the towering beasts. The three creeshts cried out a victory scream and scuttled near. Kraiy knew there was little more she could do against them.

Unexpectedly, the young Las'wa caught sight of distinctive, knife-like scales following a long, slender line. The flash of scarlet and ebony of the snakeskin whip surprised and relieved the now defenseless youth. "A preshair whip." She whispered reverently. [Preshairs are the large snakes of the underworld, the fiercest of all the creatures on Obseen. There are only a few Las'wa who have preshair armor and weapons made from these creatures as preshairs are almost invincible to defeat. The elite whip masters of the Las'wa are the only fighters who use the skins exclusively.] The terrifying crack of the distinguished weapon as it wrapped around the nearest spider, scattered the other creeshts and caused them to face this new attacker. The caught creeshts started to thrash around the cavern as it struggled with the whip that had lassoed itself around its neck. The whip's wielder flung herself atop the crazed creeshts and stationed herself on the creature's narrow back. In a panic, the creeshts flung itself around the small space, bashing itself against the walls to try and rid itself of its passenger. The girl tightened her hold on her weapon and leaned back on the creeshts' body, causing her whip to constrict even more. The sharp scales of the weapon bit deeper into the spider's exoskeleton. Blue blood began to drip past the wounds and fell to the floor in sticky masses. With a final, horrendous pull, the whip constricted to its maximum. A second later, the creeshts' head popped from its body, spraying blue crystals all over the place.

Kraiy choked back a scream as the head rolled into her view. High above her, the fighter jumped off the tumbling creeshts and landed beside the older girl. "I need you to stay back." She ordered. "My whip could catch you on accident. Here," She handed her one of her katanas, "You might need that." Then the whip-wielder was gone again, having launched herself at the final two creeshts.

The last two creeshts faced her predatorily as she landed between them. The one to her left attacked first, jumping at her in distraction. The second leapt mere seconds later, using its partner as a shield.

Anticipating the reaction, the lone fighter slashed her whip around to the left in a forward tri-double. Her last turn licked the whip's tail around the spider's front legs and pulled it off its feet. A moment later, she blocked the other's attack with a creeshts long sword, using it as a shield for her body. The latter creeshts roared in anger at being repulsed and backed away to attack from another angle. The girl smiled tightly and spun back to the first creeshts. "You two really are too predictable." She muttered as she flicked her whip off of the creeshts' front legs and readied it for another attack.

An obsidian stalactite caught Seircor's defender's gaze as she glanced upwards into the creeshts' nine eyes. Flicking her whip's tail at it, she managed to frighten the spider enough to back it away, giving her room to snag the whip around the pillar. Then she hurled herself at the creeshts' back. As she flew mere centimeters above the arched abdomen, the assailant stabbed a long-bladed sword through its tough spine, causing the arachnid to scream in pain. An instant later, she swung back around toward the creeshts' head and drove a preshair knife into its skull. The large spider fell without another sound.

Kraiy's agonized yelp caused the girl to turn back to where she had left the C'vail youth; the remaining spider had chosen to attack the other girl while the first was busy. Kraiy had tried to block the creeshts' many legs as they waved in front of her, but the creeshts outmatched her in speed and strength. With one mighty swish of its left most leg, it tore a nasty gash into the youth's abdomen. Kraiy's eyes rolled back in shock and she dropped the sword to the floor as her legs gave way.

"No!" The assassin-girl ran toward Kraiy and the spider. She angrily selected a throwing knife from one of the many on her belt and flicked it into the creeshts' belly. The spider turned on her in defense, but the five knives that followed finished him off, each lodging into one of his dark eyes. She then passed by the dying creeshts to where her friends were huddled.

Seircor was there already, having pulled himself toward his sister upon her collapse. Pain had shot up his leg, causing his vision to blur, but he made it to touching distance of his beloved sibling. In his panic over his sister, Seircor did not even noticed the death cry of the last creeshts as it died from the onslaught of the other fighter. All he could hear and see was his sister, who was dying in front of him. "Kraiy! Kraiy, Na'i kye re! Kraiy!" ["Kraiy...Do not leave me!"]

* * *

The obsidian caverns became silent once more as the dying scream of another creeshts disappeared into the depths of the caves. A seething assassin master stalked down a long cavern in her search for the few remaining Lakean children. [The Las'wa are called the Lakeans in common tongue (by surface dwellers)]. Trotting out of the darkness ahead of her came a young attendant of around twenty-years-old. He bowed in respect to his senior. "Master Teera, we have found twelve creeshts dead ahead of us. They may have all been killed by one Lakean youth; the marks on their bodies support this speculation."

Master Teera snarled. "One child could not possibly take down twelve adult creeshts. There must be more than one assassin at work here."

The young man shrunk lower at his master's crew tone and averted his eyes. "Master, I believe there is only one assassin. The weapon marks are all the same. There could not be another." In consideration he added, "Also, there are only three Lakeans left alive, if our source is correct. We have located two, but the third had evaded all our attempts at capture."

A lip on the master's face pulled upward in a sour smile. "Take me to the two brats. At least I have eight youths in our hands, even if all but two are dead."

"Yes, Most Honored." The assistant gave a quick bow and walked back the way he had come. Master Teera followed at a slower pace. She didn't bother to tell the lesser assassin that he was walking at a faster clip than needed. In truth, she basked in the fact that the man's hustle was due to her presence.

The man glanced back timidly, "Almost there, oh powerful master."

The Suez assassin-woman smirked and waved a hand to continue. "As you say, Honored, it will be so." The assistant just nodded and hurried along.

* * *

Seircor C'vail felt a hand on his shoulder. He looked up and, through eyes filled with tears, saw his rescuer staring sorrowfully into his face. Wiping his tears away before they caused his outward pride to deteriorate further, he bowed respectfully and stilled. "I thank you for trying to save my sister. I am surprised that it is you who came, seimora." [Seimora (feminine), seimore (masculine) = roughly prince/princess or high ruler.]

"Again, I ask you to not call me that, seimie." ["Friend"] The girl reminded gently. "And do not hide your sorrow to me. I, too, feel loss for your sister."

Seircor nodded woodenly and struggled to his feet, though the pain of his severed leg was tremendous. "Zanishiria, I can't get my leg to stop bleeding, the position doesn't allow me to get a good grasp on it. The wound is deep and I think a blood vessel is ruptured."

Zanishiria knelt down to inspect the damaged leg. "It is deep," She agreed, "And many muscles are severed, even the Achilles' tendon is partially injured, but you are not bleeding heavily enough to have glanced a large vessel." She kept her analysis short, though Seircor could tell she thought worse of his wound. His raven-haired friend took out a pouch full of fungus spores and patted the powder into his wound. She tried as gently as possible, but Seircor hissed in pain, nonetheless. "You have savya and florick mosses, so I will not give you mine, but take the rest of my spores in case you start to bleed again." She took out a wrap from her pouches and instructed Seircor to bit down on his shirt as she fixed his ankle in a neutral angle and bound it tightly. "This will have to do for now." She said. Zanishiria's attitude changed suddenly as her sensitive ears caught an echo through the caves. "I hate to rush you, Praic, but I feel someone is coming. With the sudden attacks, I've been avoiding all footsteps I can."

[Savya means life; but in this case it is the name of a plant found in the underworld with remarkable healing powers.]

Seircor nodded in response to his fourteen-year-old friend's assessment. Even he could hear the distant sounds of the invader's movements as they grew inside the tunnels. "We must go then."

Zanishiria paused for a moment, then glanced back at Kraiy's still body. "Kye moreay, Praic, sai lai'nom Ai'a sonon." ["I am sorry, Praic, but we cannot bring your siblings body."]

"Kye rei'un; she...is too much a burden to take with us." ["I understand"] Even to Seircor, his voice betrayed his true feelings.

His younger companion pretended not to notice the turmoil his words carried as she collected the creeshts swords and other weapons dropped in the fight. Handing them back to Seircor, she brought them back into the deadly situation they were in. "There is a tiny gap between the ceiling and the stones above us. The collapse must have been man-made to cause this. See if you can fit through it." Warily, she glanced back to the cavern entrance, guarding their backs, as Seircor went to inspect the rock pile.

With an agile grace, Zanishiria scampered up the enormous stone barrier and joined her friend as he finally pulled himself up next to the small gap. "You go first. I would like to know that you are through and safe before I am." Knowing better than to argue, Seircor fluidly slid his feet through the hole. Looking back at the seimora, he shared one parting thought with her, "Careful, seimie, the rock is slippery on this side." Then, he released his hold on the rocky lip and disappeared into the darkness beyond.

Young Zanishiria began to follow him, when a movement in the corner of her eye made her freeze. Slowly turning her head to focus on the shape more clearly, she realized she wasn't alone anymore. Standing in the luminescent light from the asrouc liken stood a young man with plain, light features and an assassin master of cruel aura. [Asrouc means light, it is the name of liken growing in underworld that puts off light when exposed to carbon dioxide.] Zanishiria's heart chilled as her instincts told her that the assassin master was the one killing her comrades. For a moment longer, she locked her eyes on the woman's stern face to memorize it, then as smoothly as she could, she released her hold on the obsidian stones and left the invaded room for the safety of the darkness.

The assassin girl's decent down the slick slab of obsidian was short lived, for about half way down the slide of stone had stopped, leaving her sailing through the air. Unable to control her feet-first flight, Zanishiria was forced to prepare to meet the obsidian floor that loomed ever nearer. As she sailed closer to her destination, a figure took shape. Startled, the fourteen-year-old realized that Seircor hadn't moved and was, maybe, unconscious. Grimly, she hoped her trajectory would throw her away from the other assassin.

The stone seemed to reach out to grasp her as she fell. All too soon, Zanishiria felt the hard impact she had known was coming. The force of the collision knocked the wind from her lungs and she nearly blacked out. With a fleeting thought that it would have felt better if she had, Zanishiria was forced to feel her body roll across the sharp cavern floor like a log and slam against the far wall.

A groan escaped her lips as Zanishiria pushed herself away from the stone. "Uh, that will leave a bruise," she complained as she felt her head where it had hit the obsidian. Suddenly, she remembered her friend and the image of his immobile body. "Praic!" Zanishiria clamored to her feet and experienced a wave of nausea with black dots in her vision. Groaning again, she steadied herself against the cool wall.

"Si'h." ["Easy"] Seircor was by her side in that moment holding her arm to steady her. "I would have warned you about the ending, but I was still recovering my breath. Did you hurt yourself? Your fall looked nasty."

"Kye rein." ["I'm all right"] The younger assassin straightened and brushed Seircor's hand away. "We need to be going. I'm not sure if the assassin saw me or not."

Seircor didn't ask about the woman Zanishiria had seen. "Crey." ["Yes"] He started to hobble toward the cavern entrance to their right when his friend grabbed his arm. "You should go back to Shairceeo lá Coursa." [The city the Las'wa live in underground, means "the jewel of the darkness"] Seircor opened his mouth to argue but the younger held up her hand to silence him. "You can't travel very fast with your wounded leg, and we still have five levels to travel up until we reach the surface."

"Kye rei'un." ["I understand (lai=you)"] Seircor turned his head away to bore his grey eyes heatedly into the cold obsidian stone, unable to voice his anger at his injury. "I would be a burden to you, seimora."

Zanishiria heard her friend's voice crack with emotion as he struggled to control his pride. "I do not send you away because of your injury, Praic." She glanced away to cover her own emotion from Seircor. "Many were lost today," She softly informed him. "I'm afraid that some surface dweller found out about our mission and came to massacre us. We..." Her voice stumbled and Seircor turned to look at her, "We may be the only ones left, Praic."

Seircor's eyes widened with grief. "All?"

Zanishiria took a sharp breath and nodded. "If anyone survived, they would have gone back to tell the council what happened. That is why you must go. They will need to be confirmed of this tragedy."

"But you still go?" Seircor asked.

Zanishiria's black-haired head bobbed an affirmative in the faint asrouc light. "Someone still needs to do this. And I don't want to go back anyway if Art'or will not be there."

"Kye rei'un." This time Seircor understood, for he too had just lost a sibling in the attack. "My parents will want to know about Kraiy, as will the rest of our people." Seircor laid his hands on Zanishiria's shoulders. "I will miss you though, seimie." Looking down at his friend, Seircor could have sworn he saw tears shinning in her slate eyes; tears that she would not let fall. He understood those too, for he also could feel them forming in his own grey eyes. "I guess I will see you again, seimora."

"Yes, I hope we do see each other again. I won't forget you." Her words echoed hollowly; their meaning of good-bye not lost on Seircor. "I go, as we were asked, to stop a war that has been going on for twelve years. It seems meaningless, a girl my age able to do such a thing, but the council decreed, so I go. I am sorry you will not be there with me, Praic, but you have a new mission now. Our paths may cross yet before the time of Eirhom-rei." [Rei= year, Eirhom= one cycle count]

"Yes, maybe it shall, seimora."

"Please," Zanishiria glanced up into her friend's face, "I wish you not to call me that, not anymore. I made an oath that disclaims my title. Any other name is now free for you to call me, seimie."

Seircor nodded. "I know your oath, Zan, but to me you will always be my seimora. Don't forget that."

"I won't." Zanishiria murmured then backed away into the shadows. "I need to go now. Be safe on your own way. Remember, too, that I will always carry your memory in my heart, but you need to forget about me, Praic." Seircor's nickname echoed softly through the cavern, staying long after Zanishiria had snuck away. Sadly, Seircor turned his back to her exit and made his way back to Shairceeo lá Coursa—alone.

Chapter Two

Dishonor to a clan is a serious offense. To do anything to damage it is reprimandable by any course the clan's council deems appropriate—including death or "defection" (banishment). Codes of respect and honor are followed to the letter to keep order. If such are broken, the assassin responsible must take the consequences that follow or take his own life. If one chooses death or defection (the highest of penalties) then they forfeit their sur-name and clan title. To become "defect" then means they are dead to the clan and unable to go to any other clan; they are outcast for life—unless new actions are deemed "worthy enough" to win back their status. Such "worthiness" has only happened twice, and is the rarest of occasions.

Master Teera made sure her feet pounded out confidently as she strolled across the stone floor. The sharp sound echoed down the hallway until it drowned away somewhere along the seemingly endless corridor. The few assassins that wandered along the hallway averted their eyes to the obsidian floor and bowed as the master passed by. Master Teera sneered at the less important Honored assassins. By the time she reached her destination, she had a wicked grin on her face from her gloating.

Davin, Teera's one most-efficient pawn, glanced up cautiously as Master Teera strutted in, the stone door sliding shut behind her. "Master." He murmured and bowed relevantly.

Master Teera passed him by, heading for the cell. Davin quietly, but promptly, hurried to keep by her side. "How are the prisoners?"

"The young girl we captured last is dead, Honored-one. The older youth is still unconscious."

Master Teera nodded approval at her subordinate's short response; unlike the other assassins, whom seemed to spout nonsense at her when she asked them to speak, Davin reserved his words for a quick council or opinion and refused to say more than what was important to the moment. "Then let me see him."

Davin bowed and hurried to unlock the door. Master Teera stepped past the threshold, her hand lazily resting on the sapphire-head of her fighting scepter. Beyond, lying motionless and nearly camouflaged with the obsidian stone, was a lone boy of about eighteen summers. The youth seemed lifeless except for the soft rise and fall of his breathing. A minute passed before Master Teera noticed a change in the boy's face, subtle but still a change. A moment afterward, the youth was lifting his head to glare at his visitors. Teera chuckled at the defiance she saw in the boy's eyes and turned back to Davin. "What have you learned about this infidel?" She stressed the word infidel to infuriate the youth some more.

"Nothing yet, master." Davin admitted with care, "He has spoken in Lakean thus far, but I cannot understand him. The linguists claim they are not educated in ancient Las'wa dialect."

"Oh, posh! Have them punished for idleness." Master Teera growled, clearly, she had had enough of the common excuses her people gave her. "Tell them it may not be basic, but Lakean, sure as hell, is not unheard of! Go call Sorey if the kutts can't do it themselves." [Idiots] Davin bowed with a "yes, master" and backed away with the message memorized; however, he lingered at the door knowing his master would call on him shortly.

Ignoring her inferior, Master Teera turned back to the captured Lakean youth. He glared at her again from underneath his typical, dark Lakean hair. His eyes, an unusual color of silver as bright and as piercing as a knife blade, leveled at the master before him, taking her on stare for stare.

"Cour'tray kiy lair syék?" ["What is your full name?"] Master Teera asked in his native tongue.

"Bi'ek trai, chreeshts-áet!" The boy cursed back refusing to tell her his given name.

"Well," Master Teera let go a laugh more suited to a lion, "Even I didn't know Lakeans had such sharp tongues. Amusing. In time you'll answer or else pay a justly consequence."

"I won't cooperate with an Honored." The boy hissed defensively. He stood then, and Master Teera realized he was taller than her, perhaps standing a close six feet.

"You would be doing no such thing!" Teera lied suavely. "I assure you, I am not among the Honored ones."

"You're their leader, the man killer's closest confidant, his morta". [Slang for whore] The Lakean argued knowingly.

"Then I am the best one for you to talk to get out of this mistake." The master tried to make her discreet, but false, offer sound sweet.

"Lai shée!" ["You're a liar."] The boy proclaimed. He spat on the floor in disgust and readied his stance for fighting.

Master Teera sighed at the youth's defiance and changed her inviting stance to a more commanding one. "I'll ask again, boy, tell me your name, or do I have to pound it out of you?"

"Creeshts-áet!" was all he answered.

Teera lunged herself at him then. The Lakean easily sidestepped her wild leap and lashed out with a well-aimed high kick to the back of her neck. The light force of his kick caused her vertebra to crack in protest but otherwise did no damage; however, it was enough to send the woman headfirst to the floor. Master Teera picked herself up quickly and spun around to face her opponent. The assassin youth looked like just a cautious boy once again.

"So, you are a skilled fighter. More so than many as young as you." The youth ignored her comment. Instead, he came at the master from her left side and suddenly dropped to a crouch on the floor. A rapid sidekick slammed into the back of Teera's knees to send her falling backwards. She relaxed into the fall and rolled away. Leaping to her feet, Master Teera tried to find an opening to counter the Lakean's next move. Across from her, the young adversary was already at arm's reach and closing the final gap. He came at her with such alacrity that his one-two-three punch combination followed by an ax kick surprised and stunned the master.

Master Teera fell for the third time in their short fight. That time, she did not move to get up. As an alternative, she leaned against the obsidian wall she had landed beside and placed her hands palm down in front of her on the cold obsidian floor. The youth eyes her warily from across the cell, but made no move to attack against an opponent who was signaling a back-down.

"I see you are a natural fighter and well trained." Teera commented again as she panted slightly from their exchange.

"You are much stronger than any of the youths your age, unnamed one."

"I am not stronger," The boy insisted without the haughtiness other youths showed in their victories, "I have merely been better trained and have studied long."

Master Teera was surprised at the integrity in the youth's words. He was very sincere and had the aura of someone who had been through many trials. "Perhaps you are right, but such skill is not usually seen in one so young. Even your clan has been unable to produce disciplined fighters—at least not for twelve years." No emotional response showed on the boy's face at the mention of the prior events that had happened to his clan. Annoyed that her ploy had not evoked a certain response, Master Teera stood back up.

Instantly, the boy was wary again, and he returned to his fighting stance.

"I'm not going to attack you." Teera assured him. "I've learned well enough what you can do. It would be pointless for me to test your proficiency again." She strode back to the doorway and motioned Davin over. "Davin, bring food and refreshment here. The boy might as well receive some kind of nourishment during his stay."

Her dark-haired attendant bowed. "Yes, Honored-one." Then, he backed away and hurried off to do her bidding.

Satisfied, Master Teera turned back to the situation at hand: the captive Lakean. "As you may know, I am Master Teera Sabina, Honored-one of His Excellency Manscor." She returned to her cross-legged position of the floor and waited for the boy to return the favor of his name.

"You are among the worst of our enemies, killer of many, and lover of the man killer. Why should I trust you with my name, oh Honored-one?" Teera raised an eyebrow at his harsh statement but said nothing. Even the tone of her spoken title had not shaken her into comment.

The two stared at each other then, one daring for exchange, the other demanding why such a high price—a name—must be given to the enemy. Only Davin's entry with a tray of refreshments broke them out of their trance. Thrown into uneasy diplomacy, the youth accepted a cup of tea from the kind assistant, though he refused to sip it until Master Teera drank some from the same pitcher. Still, no words were spoken. Done with his duty, Davin faded away to leave them alone again.

Teera picked up a Turkish delight piece and tasted it thoughtfully before eying her captive with a look if interrogation. "There were ten of you in the caves. Only you survived. There would have been two more of you to keep you company, but another young man refused custody and we had to dispose of him. The other, a girl of about thirteen or fourteen, I believe, died in her cell from mortal wounds. She fought bravely against our creeshts, however, and was quite commendable." Master Teera hoped her words sounded sincere enough, though she felt no remorse for the youths. A flicker of emotion did pass over the boy's face, though, when the master had spoken of the girl. Interesting. "So, only you survived. What you decide to do from here on out will determine if you follow their course or not. Though, such an action would not be beneficial to your clan, now would it?"

The emotion was gone and the boy looked passive again. "I was not sent to get myself killed. Nor was that my intent in the first place. I knew when the others were being hunted that I would not survive, so I did the one thing I could do."

"And that was?" She prompted.

"I was captured." He answered as if it should have been obvious.

Master Teera choked and sputtered on her drink. "You are a very foolish boy. No one wants to get captured by the emperor's men, especially by one such as myself; the only thing you'll get out of it is death."

"And yet I am still very much alive. And a threat to your man killer."

The assassin let out a pathetically loud laugh that sounded more like a roar. "Oh, now you're joking, Lakean! A threat to Manscor? Not even your great Coursay'sora leaders could touch him. Plus, young man, he is surrounded by honored assassins from the Guild, even if one was to get close enough, they'd be killed before a weapon could be handled."

"Nevertheless," The boy stood and eyed her regally, "the line of Coursay'sora has returned to extract revenge on those with the man killer. The emperor will meet his time."

There was something in his tone that made Teera's laugh die. The way he cocked his head, stood straight, and held her in his gaze, triggered a memory many years old. Without overthinking the complications such ideas would produce,

Master Teera could not help asking, "Are you related to the rebel Ze'is Coursay'sora?"

There was no hesitation in the youth's eyes now. With a look of pride, mixed with defiance, he answered, "I am his only son."

The announcement was great enough to send Teera to her feet. "His son!" How could we have missed this information? The Lakean scum had a back-up plan in case their leaders died. And I've got him right here! Manscor will be greatly pleased with this catch.

The Lakean youth suddenly looked dejected. He had admitted to something far greater than just a name; he had given his family name—a curse greater than death in his clan. He was shamed by the gross mistake. "Now that you know, Honored-one, you will kill me. Everyone knows the man killer despises the Coursay'soras above any other assassin line." He bowed his head to the ground, wrists extended in a posture demoting his arms should be slit and head severed.

"Kill you?" Teera asked in mock surprise. "And ruin all your long-thought-out plans? I think not. A youth as skilled as you has many ways to be useful. No, death is a penalty reserved for those of no valor or endowment. There are better uses for you." The Lakean youth looked up in ghastly shock to be left alive and asked for his service. The fervor in the Honored-one's eyes was wicked as she reveled in the sight. The plans were spinning in her head of what she could use such an heir for—once she broke him. "You are in my service now, young one. But, "she paused and looked the Lakean over as if considering, "'young one' is not a name for such a skilled assassin. Must I name you?"

The boy felt too defeated at his admittance to care about his continuing to hold true to his oath. "I have no name, as pledge has erased such, but if you must call me a name Art will do."

Master Teera could have crow with joy. "Very well, Art, I will meet with you again. For now I go to teach those less apt than you. Just tap on the door and Davin will provide you with anything you require." With that said, Master Teera left the room and locked the door. Davin hurried toward her. "Monitor this room at all times." She instructed him. "This Art has told me more than I thought possible! I must report to Manscor. You stay and watch him until I return."

"Yes, Master." Davin bowed, but Master Teera was already leaving.

Her slate-grey eyes flew open, and she surveyed her strange surroundings with sharp sight. The room was lavishly furnished in bright crimson and Royal purples. A window, made of stained glass in a mosaic pattern of a scene on Planet X, was glowing from the outside sunlight. Below it, a woman, her face turned from view, was invading a small dresser, adorned with a crystal lamp and pitcher of iced water. Sitting up quickly, Zanishiria regarded the intruder with narrowed eyes. Hearing the commotion behind her, the woman turned around with a warm smile on her face. In truth, Zanishiria realized the intruder was not a woman at all but a girl of around seventeen. And, the girl's face was familiar enough to remind the assassin where she was.

A day earlier, Zanishiria had finally climbed into the unusual warmth of Obseen's two suns. For the first time in her entire life, she had climbed free of the cool, darkened caverns of the underworld onto the surface that was, in many ways, abnormal from her enclosed home. The suns had been just one example of the differences from the blue-green luminous glow of the caves. Their odd yellow and white color, penetrating through the purplish atmosphere, had startled her enough to send her back into the safety of the darkness, until her pride convinced her she was acting foolish at such a natural phenomenon. A waterfall near the entranceway to the caves had been a mystery, too, for it was not the inky black but a startling crystalline blue. And there had been grass and trees! Something Zanishiria had only heard about. Obseen had been very different from how she had envisioned it.

The excitement of the new land had quickly worn off, for the flight and fighting Zanishiria had left had been trying on her. In exhaustion, Zanishiria had trudged only part of the way to the mapped-out Taysor Palace before she had to surrender to her fatigue. She had barely been able to pull herself into a tiny alcove among a pile of sharp, obsidian boulders before her eyes had closed. In her small hiding space, she had finally been able to rest after three long days escaping the horrors and being hunted in the caves. Still, even through her boggled memory, her senses were honed-in on approaching dangers. A quick as a wink, she had been awakened at the sound of light-treading footsteps. In the next instant, she had found herself looking into the deep grey eyes of a girl a little older than her age with similar features to herself.

The very same girl who stood by the ornate window. Smiling, the girl turned away to finish preparing a tray of breakfast items and drinks. Without her glancing her way, Zanishiria allowed her day-old memories to resurface again from their foggy alcove.

The two girls had stared at each other, one surprised the other suspicious, before Zanishiria had leapt to her feet and backed away from the stranger. The other girl had called out softly for her to wait. "I'm Scarlett Novastone. Are you one of the Las'wa we were asked to harbor?"

The title Las'wa halted the assassin from her escape. Cautiously she repeated, "Novastone," to herself. The name was familiar. Her master had told her that once she reached the surface, she was to search for a King Lapsair Novastone. He had promised her that the king would help her and give her sanctuary. "Lai shre vain'la Novastone, seimore?" She asked hopefully. ["Are you an associate of Novastone's, princess?"]

Scarlett hesitated before answering. "I cannot speak Lakean well. Let me see: kye aish mora là seimora Novastone Lapsair." [" I am the only daughter of Lapsair Novastone."]

Zanishiria forced her tired muscles to relax from their nervous tension. The king's daughter would not harm her. "Take me to Novastone then."

Scarlett nodded happily and traversed her way back down the boulder field. She paused near the waterfall, less for Zanishiria's sake and more for enjoyment. "I assume you know this is Taysor Palace's lands, though most are not owned by the emperor but by individual Royals. Back there," The princess pointed to a long canyon that disappeared behind an obsidian cliff, "Is Taysor Gulch. You can journey back to the underworld by either the entrance you used or one deeper in the gulch."

"I will remember that." Zanishiria had commented as she stepped up next to the Royal girl. "I do not know my way around up here. It is a very different place."

"Yes, it is." Scarlett had agreed. "But my farther and I can help you." She smiled broadly. "Let's get you back to the palace, though we will have to be careful not to tread too close to the emperor's section. Cover yourself with this cloak, too, because your clothes would stick out here." Zanishiria scowled in protest but took the luxurious cloak anyway. "I know it is not the same, but your snakeskin tunic and pants are too unusual, even for these days. You would blend in better with cloth robes and tunics. Unfortunately, assassins' tunics are less form-fitting than you light armor. It is something you will have to acquire a taste for."

Zanishiria had met with the king only briefly before being carted away to bath and dress in "surface-dwellers" cloths. She had then been led to a spacious dining room where an exotic dinner had been placed. Fully sated, the king had ordered her to bed to drift to sleep

Yes, Zanishiria remembered every detail from the other night; however, no matter how gracious the food and sanctuary, Zanishiria's heart was overshadowed with the dread and deaths the three previous days had wrought. The screams of felled creeshts and Lakean youths still echoes in her mind. They were painful enough to give her nightmares in her sleep. She remembered everything of the past seventy-eight hours; the assassin master's face who had caused such pain would pay for the deaths of Zanishiria's clansmen.

Scarlett walked over then, a tray full of delicious pastries and fruit and drinks of Mullen-berry. "You are looking better this morning." She said cheerfully. "You had better eat quickly and dress if you want to get to the Assassins' Guild training sessions. They started yesterday but some assassin trainees will arrive today and tomorrow."

Zanishiria knitted her eyebrows in annoyance. "Why do I need to be in the Guild? My mission is to attend to the man killer problem, not to get taught by a bunch of lousy masters."

Scarlett suppressed a grin. "As you told us last night, someone found out about the Lakeans' plans. If this is so, you will need to be protected until your superiors tell you to do your business. Until then, the Guild is the safest place to be for you. Yes, I know they are more like your enemies but the Royal guards will not look for a traitor among Obseen's best apprentices and masters."

"I guess that makes sense." Zanishiria muttered sullenly. "Yet, my identity would be a problem would it not?"

"We have that covered as well." Scarlett assured her. "Here put on these silk tunics while I talk. I had them tailored to your own tunics, so they aren't as free as they typically would be." Without pause, she continued talking as Zanishiria dressed herself and continued eating her breakfast. "My father had a false fabrication—well done I might add—by the Torez family of Xsenume. You are my cousin coming to train as a Royal-assassin. We had two ancestors that have done just that, so it is not like it is going to cause suspicion. Plus, you look so much like me that the ploy will work. So, from now on, you will be known as Zanishiria Novastone." She paused as if she thought of something, then commented, "You have a rather unusual name but I guess that there have been some weird Royal names before. Besides, we couldn't take away all of your identify. Your name is not known to anyone but your Las'wa, so there was no real need to alter it." Scarlett followed Zanishiria to the small dresser on the other side of the room. She watched Zanishiria fumble with her long, black hair for a moment before taking over. "I hope you don't mind all of this. We really are sorry you had to watch your kin suffer. The only reason we are taking so many precautions is that you had been attacked. Father, and others not associated with Emperor Manscor, are going to investigate the issue. They will find out who did this."

"I do thank you for all you have done, but the killer is someone of high authority, I believe. They will never be able to reach them, even if they do find out who it was." Zanishiria gingerly touched the beautiful braid Scarlett had woven into her hair.

Turning around to face the other girl, Scarlett realized she looked less like the confident assassin she had seen yesterday. There had been too much happenings too soon and they had taken a toll on the youth. Scarlett hoped the training sessions would rekindle the fire she had seen the other day, for more than Zanishiria's sake. "I'm glad you are to be my cousin." She smiled sincerely. "I always wanted a sister, until mother passed away, but a cousin will be just as well."

Zanishiria tried to mirror the other girl's smile. "I am pleased and honored as well." She turned around, once more, to study her new self in the mirror. No longer did she look like a Las'wa, though her features still had echoes of her past life. Instead, before her was a handsomely dressed young woman looking very much the part of an assassin-Royal coming to Obseen to be given instruction. "Unfortunately," she commented lightly, "I cannot make myself look like I have never been trained before, but I think I can down-play my abilities." The thought relaxed her nervousness for a moment and even lit a smile on her face. "Well, I guess I am ready. Take me to the training center."

Chapter Three

The training center of Taysor is host to the best masters on Obseen, sought planet-wide for their expertise. Youths that have proven themselves worthy of the Center receive their training from these esteemed masters for four years before they are given status as "assassins". Only youths of ages fifteen to twenty are allowed to train in Taysor. Rarely, youths of younger ages are allowed but only if they pass rigorous tests and agree to stay on longer than their older counterparts. All tests are taken on the "training square", which every clan has. So, to win on a square is to be recognized planet-wide as one worthy enough to be accepted to test out in Taysor's elite training center; however, even still, only five hundred students are allowed into Taysor every four years, making it the hardest martial arts school to get into on Obseen and in the Abyss Solar System.

Tarin Saerric jabbed his friend, K'sho Rease, in the ribs and nodded his blond head in the direction of a long bench reserved for newcomers. "Look, there is a girl among the newcomers. She's the first one I've seen apply this year."

"So, that's just one girl in a group of, what, seventeen newbies? She's probably here because she can hold her own." K'sho stated, with boredom heavy in his voice, and turned back to his reading of a war in 2436, Old Earth time. "Maybe she'll be like that Nalcian girl last year who didn't score high enough to make the Center's curriculum."

"Right." Tarin muttered sarcastically. "You obviously don't pay attention. She's already tested. They say her scores are the second highest yet today."

"Yeah? That's great for her."

K'sho was not listening to him. Tarin gritted his teeth in frustration and tried a different approach. "It's not good you idiot!" This time, K'sho lifted his eyes to meet his friend's demanding blue ones. "She's second to me. Me! I've got the highest score so far this year."

K'sho's interesting crimson-and-grey-speckled eyes widened. "Oh."

Tarin closed his eyes and suppressed his enraged emotions with a sigh. "On the intelligent scale today you're a two of fifty and failing fast." K'sho opened his mouth to remark that he wasn't worried about the preliminary scores, but Tarin stood to silence him. "I'm going to have a friendly chat with the new one. She must be an interesting Royal to be so talented— especially to get a score suited better for a fourth-year. Have fun reading about weapons, or war, or whatever you have today."

Tarin began to weave through the large crowd of trainees and masters to reach the new trainees' bench. Many students, all his junior, bowed their heads in respect and greeting as he passed. Tarin bowed in return. He knew he might be the most skilled student there, but no one, not even himself, should be so arrogant as to not show respect to others. Besides, they all looked up to him as a role model, so he should behave like one. With his greetings finalized, Tarin stepped in front of the new girl. By then, she should have seen him coming closer, but she pretended not to notice him as he loomed there, waiting. A moment passed before she tilted her head back to look up at Tarin with cool, near-black eyes. The older youth straightened his five-foot-eight frame, as if to look aloof. "You must be the second-rate student I heard about." He put an emphasis on second-rate.

The girl kept her features hard, even stony, though a frown began to carry up to her black eyebrows. A weary look entered her gaze, for the briefest second, then she glared up at him fiercely. Ever so slowly, she rose to her smaller height of five-foot-three, keeping her obsidian eyes locked with his. Tarin almost backed up from the intensity he felt radiating from her. Almost. "Second-rate? Then you must be a fairly wretched fighter yourself." Her eyes shown with amusement at the taunt. "Your score was only two points above mine. It was a poor showing really, from what I saw. Mine may have been shorter but better executed."

By then, the room had silenced as trainees and assassin alike paused to witness the confrontation between their known trainee leader and a newcomer.

Tarin felt the weight of his fellow trainees and knew his next words would be whispered along the corridors of the training center to the ears of all who were not there to watch.

"So, you seem to think highly of yourself. Around here such attitude is put to rest the moment it enters the front doors. But that has already passed, so I insist on a duel, to correct such thoughts of course." Tarin's eyes cast over to the main fighting square to their left.

"Free choice of weapons? Unlimited time?" The girl asked in inquiry, not missing a beat. Her enthusiasm hinting at why she had been thought of as good enough to enter the Guild's training program. Tarin nodded once to both questions. "Sau! Deal." She let a diminutive smile play across her lips as she stepped toward the square, following Tarin's lead, and halted in the indicated corner. The other assassin trainees crowded closer to witness as Tarin walked to his corner opposite his opponent.

The Senior Master of the Assassins' Guild, Sye Rainier, stepped out to the middle of the square and raised her hands for silence. "I declare this to be the first official duel of this year's advanced students' class, as well as the opening to our year here at the Center. In the left corner stands Tarin Saerric, our top student for four years now." She let the assassins cheer loudly for their classmate. Then, raising her cinnamon-sweet voice, she cut through the clamor. "And to the right," The room silenced at once, "Is newcomer, coming all the way from Planet X to learn our ways, Zanishiria Indigo Novastone." A semi-polite applause fluttered through the gathered body.

Zanishiria shifted fretfully at the unfamiliar name she went by. Yes, the Novastone names were what would protect her prestige in a place like the Guild's training center, but the foreign words seemed so bland when spoken after her Lakean name. It seemed, however, that no one noticed the unique first name. Breathing deeply, more to distract her from her past trauma then from nerves, she reached deep within herself to her center of calm and serenity. If they did not notice anything unusual about herself then she wouldn't—that was her Las'wa philosophy kicking in.

Across from the assassin-Royal, Tarin was studying the play of emotions on his opponent's face, or more precisely the lack of it. He could see the tenseness in her muscles, but the expression the young woman wore was not of apprehension but of battle-readiness. It was an unusual sign in one so young and untried in duels on Obseen. She is not what many would expect a Royal to be. Then again, if her master sent her here, he must have confidence in her abilities. *It's obvious she has at least had training in discipline during unfamiliar circumstances. What else will she know?* Giving a friendly smile to the other, he picked up a weapon, a blunted training sword, and swung it around expertly—in showiness and to test its feel. Again, he paid attention as Zanishiria bent to select a weapon from the provided stash.

Zanishiria, too, was watching her adversary. He had showed deftness with the sword he'd selected, so she wanted, not a weapon for close combat, as many would assume, but one for distance. Calculatingly, she drifted her hand over the whip and gauged the reaction of the young man. Tarin's eyes showed surprise at her selection, but the look was overcome with confidence. The whip has never been favorable in duels. It was too long for swordplay and too unpredictable for anything else. Not even a master would choose the weapon, unless it was the only choice. The Lakean caught the small smirk on the tall, fair-haired youth's face. With her own assurance sealed, she wrapped her slender fingers around the supple leather of the whip and stood. Their stupid whips have none of the features mine does. I guess that means I can't damage anyone either, which isn't exactly bad. The preshair whip would be too dangerous in a fight like this.

"So, the opponents have chosen their main weapons. As rules state at least two more can be selected for the duel. Fighters, do you wish this to be?" Sye Rainer's voice boomed sweetly above the crowd. Zanishiria's decisive nod prompted Tarin to agree as well. "Very well, at least two more weapons have been accepted into this duel. Choose now!" The choices came quicker this time. Neither opponent wished to change their main selections, so smaller, secondary weapons were taken up. Tarin supplied himself with hard-wooden, throwing knives and a dagger, while Zanishiria selected a three-meters-long training Dao and Sais. "Weapons have been chosen. This duel is officially begun!"

The two assassins stepped into the training square at the thunderous applause and bowed to each other.

"Let us get this over with, Tarin. I did not come here to entertain a bunch of amateurs on my first day."

"Very well." The taller youth assumed a forward fighting stance with his ten throwing knives in hand. "Shall we dance?" He asked in suggestion and readied a hand as a tester. As quick as a Shar cat, he released three in concession. Across the way, Zanishiria stood stone still as the knives flew toward her. Faster than lightning, her whip hand thrust outward in an arc. A loud, abnormal crack split the air in front of her, silencing the audience. Stunned, they all witnessed millions of wooden fragments hit the stone floor before the Novastone girl. None of the knives were identifiable.

"Damn." Tarin whispered is awe and glanced at his remaining seven throwing knives. Without another thought, he tossed them behind him, deemed useless.

"You have something better?" Zanishiria asked without smugness in her voice. Tarin nodded, speechless, and raised his sword in response.

A moment more passed, with Tarin coming to terms with a new outlook on the fight. Then, as if a word was spoken, the two fighters charged toward each other. Tarin raised his sword for a forward strike and brought it in a downward arc as he neared the other assassin. Zanishiria handily darted to the left of the blade and planted the Dao's end into the other's stomach. Her foot planted behind Tarin's, causing him to fall over it from the force of the hit on his stomach. Backing away nimbly, she allowed the fallen youth to pick himself up. Before he could think to retaliate, she leapt at him with the Dao raised in a transverse position. Her closing blow rapt his fingers harshly where they curled around his sword's hilt and served as a cover for another blow coming to his right. The end of the stick struck Tarin on the temple causing his vision to blur. Without respite, Zanishiria spun around the other direction and deftly caught the area above his right kidney. The blow smarted more than the one to his head.

Tarin knew he should be embarrassed. After all, this newcomer was using him as a plaything in front of the whole training center. The pain from his blows only fueled the anger welling up inside. But one look at the girl before him subdued the impulse to strike out in rage. She looked serene, the perfect illustration of mastery. What she was doing to him was no less than he deserved. He had fought better than this; it had just been a long time—and she was there to remind him of that fact. "You have a weakness somewhere don't you?" The question sounded feeble.

Zanishiria's smile was calming and gentle, and the first Tarin had seen. "Everyone does. You just have to find it." Then quietly, a song-like language flowed from her mouth to his ears alone. "Real'yé mernon ar'eya lair vanor. Sa'van saysora varei bèn'ya. Laus eim'ano, va lai è'iro vanora-anen. Focus your mind; your opponent is your only concern. Let your heart guide your motions. Use all you know, and always use your surroundings as an advantage." The words she spoke had been from her past. A link to her one, true master. They were as clear to her now as they had been the first time she had trained. Her master would be proud to know they would be heard by another. "And always expect the unexpected."

"Very well, Zanishiria Novastone. Perhaps I will do just that. Shall we begin again?" By the crowd's reaction, the suggestion couldn't have come at a better time. They wanted to see what the unknown girl would do next.

* * *

Master Teera paced heatedly in the back of the room. She watched every occasion she could, when the crowd permitted, as her apprentice was easily knocked down by Zanishiria Indigo Novastone. "She's toying with him." She hissed to Senior Master Sye Rainier. "You see it. Why don't you just call this duel void?"

"No." Sye answered calmly. "This is good for Tarin— and her." She, too, had been watching the progress of the duel, but where Teera saw her apprentice being tossed around like a rag doll, Sye saw an opportunity for Tarin to become better. "With these advanced students, Teera, it is best to let them teach each other. Tarin just hasn't had the competition to do that yet, so, in truth this is the perfect opportunity." She watched again as Tarin and Zanishiria exchanged some conversation out on the square. "No," she repeated, "I am not ending this training session."

"But it's one-sided." Teera argued further.

"Why would you, of all people, care about that?" The Senior Master glanced over at the other with a shrewd look. "Just watch, Master, your apprentice will find his own stride."

Just then someone shouted, "You've got her, Tarin!"

Master Teera stepped up beside Sye Rainier to glance through the throng. Tarin and Zanishiria where stuck in a struggle of strength in the center of the square. The older youth was obviously stronger, and he proved it by pushing the small girl backward a step.

"He found a weakness!" Teera crowed in victory.

Sye nodded contemplatively beside her. "Yes, it seems. Though the Novastone is holding fairly well. This will be an interesting outcome."

* * *

Tarin and Zanishiria stood locked in place. The older boy closed his fingers around her delicate hands and tried to force her back one more step. In response, he could feel Zanishiria using all of her strength to keep Tarin where he stood.

Then, Zanishiria glanced up at Tarin with her stunning, dark eyes and pushed harder against the taller assassin as he forced her to give up a foot. She was not going to give him another. "You might beat me in strength, Tarin Saerric, but you are not going to win by that. Holding me is a grave mistake; one you should not make again." To prove her point, she suddenly lashed out with a kick to the blond-haired youth's groin. Tarin began to crumple over to escape further injury, but Zanishiria closed her hands around his wrists and caused his weight to shift forward. She fell to her back and raised her legs to kick her opponent over her. Tarin crashed into the stone floor with a solid thud, all the air knocked out of his lungs. Zanishiria found her feet in an instant. She eyes Tarin as he gasped for air, but made no move to close the distance between them.

The room became void of sound as everyone waited to see if Tarin would get up or call the fight drawn.

Finally, though cautiously, Zanishiria dropped her prepared arms to her sides, collected her discarded weapons, and stepped to Tarin's side. With all senses on alert, she prodded him with a foot and fingered her retrieved training stick, just in case.

Tarin opened his eyes and found himself staring into the solid slate ones of Zanishiria Novastone. The young girl took a tense step away and stared back. With a groan, Tarin sat up. "What do you call that little ditty?"

"Thinking." Zanishiria stepped forward and extended her hand. "My master wanted me to be good at hand-to-hand fighting as well as weapons. Just another way to get out of a bind. "

"And because we're assassins, we should be good at that." Tarin agreed with a small chuckle then flinched in pain. Recovering quickly, he lit a grin on his face, a devilish smile to hide his intentions. Resisting Zanishiria's pull, he tried to haul the other off her feet.

Zanishiria allowed herself to hit the floor but expertly rolled away from the other, who clearly wished to continue their confrontation. A slight smile crossed her lips. "You are a worthy opponent, Saerric. And amusing in your minute attempts. I heard you were better than this, unless you have gone past your prime?"

The remark did more than irk the youth. Humiliation and anger were building up slightly under his calm physique. He knew her last comment was not a play at undermining him, but still it stung nonetheless. Straightening his tall, willowy frame, Tarin prepared himself to go all out with all of the training he knew. "My people, the Neitiege, have a saying." Zanishiria cocked her head as if listening, though Tarin knew she was really just interpreting the sudden energy flux radiating from him. Raising his sword, Tarin finished what he had been saying, "We say, nys'iar tésouk resai ne'soum! Meisak neaxoum syom, traxuc kamein tyi'reaum!" ["Honor and strength I bring to this fight! With it, all others will be vanquished by my sword!"]

The Neitiege rushed the assassin-Royal with his sword in a forward-defensive position. Zanishiria paused, as if confused as to what attack the youth was using, but she managed to bring her training stick up to block just as Tarin brought his word sweeping down at her head. A loud crack followed the impact of the metal on wood, then the Dao snapped in two. The dark-haired girl barely managed to dodge the sword as it flew, uncontrolled, through the air where the Dao had been. Tarin, too, seemed stunned at the incident. The training center's weapons were usually not supposed to break, unless an inhuman force hit them. That the Dao had broken would be a matter the Guild would look into, perhaps for sabotage.

Zanishiria recovered from the shock soonest. She did not know that weapons weren't theoretical supposed to break, and she had had incidents, of the like, happen before. Repositioning her hands on the two broken pieces, she readied herself to wield them like twin kodachis. Spinning around, she clubbed Tarin in the back of his head, while he was still distracted. Whirling to face the girl, Tarin composed himself. In a moment, they were continuing with their fight. Tarin parrying with his sword as Zanishiria blocked his advances with her two wooden short-swords.

They danced their way across the floor. Both managing to nick the other in an arm or leg as a guard was dropped for a moment to try for a hit. The two spun through some movements and halted in others. If one was to watch, the two opponents were in more of a choreographed dance than a dangerous duel. Then, one of Zanishiria's kodachis when flying from her hands. She futilely blocked with the other one and managed to hang onto three more minutes before the other was also knocked from her hand. To escape, the young girl back flipped away, but Tarin ran after her. When she paused, he was there to thrust the sword at her face.

They paused then, waiting for someone to call the duel. The answer that can from the Senior Master was surprising, however.

"The duel is a stale-mate!" Sye Rainier cried out.

"What?" Tarin exclaimed as he glanced at his sword thrust very close to the other's face. "It's clear that I've got the ending blow."

Zanishiria, who was mirroring Tarin's hard breathing smiled in amusement. "Perhaps, young Neitiege, you should reassess the situation. My whip is around your neck and a Sai to your belly."

With a quick glance, Tarin realized what Zanishiria claimed was true. At the last second, she had pulled her whip out, and one of her Sais was held ready, waiting for another move. If the duel had been for real, they would have both died: Zanishiria from the sword thrust and Tarin from the constriction of the whip, or being impaled on her Sai, as Zanishiria fell away. "Damn, woman, you were taught well to have pulled that off."

Zanishiria smiled at the compliment. "It was more an act of reflexes than from any skill, I'm afraid. You would have had me."

"Well whatever it was, Zanishiria Novastone, I welcome you fully to Taysor's training center." The two youths stood to a round of wild applause. The first duel at the Center had been a thrilling one that promised more excitement to come. Tarin bowed to the Center crowd and indicated his opponent should do the same. Then, as the crowd thinned, the Neitiege offered the newcomer to join him and his friend for brunch.

After some thought, Zanishiria accepted the offer. Tarin beamed a smile that usually had young women's hearts skipping a beat. The thirteen-year-old just blinked her slate eyes and replied neutrally. "I will join you to learn more of this place and how it runs. You seem to be someone who knows your way around here well."

"I was raised here in Taysor most of my life." Tarin agreed. Tarin had been Master Teera Sabina's apprentice for most of that time, too—a fact the young Lakean had learned from a student more than gushing about the handsome Neitiege as he had performed his test. Here was someone Zanishiria knew would be a close tie to the one person she had need of keeping close tabs on: the woman who had killed her fellow preshans.

Little did Zanishiria know, however, that by accepting Tarin's offer she would become not just acquaintances but close friends with the two boys from the Center; (but that is a story for another time); and a complication the young preshanen had yet to calculate into the work she had yet to do.

The days of war were yet to come to Obseen's capitol city, as they were distant squabbles from the day-to-day life of the assassin youths within the walls of the training center; however, the days were numbered on how long such serenity could last at the training center of Taysor. After all, within their walls was an undercover agent of the Resistance; Zanishiria was their loaded gun concealed in plain sight for events yet to come...

Chapter Four

[One year later, Star Date 4024...]

There have been many battles on Obseen; the worst of them during the last war, the Royals' War. The incident with the twelve Las'wa youths, who had been sent in secret to assassinate the emperor, was marked as a horrible downturn during the war. The Renegade army, having relied on the victory of the secret group of preshans, were at a loss on how to proceed with their agenda to assassinate the emperor. Still, the resistance continued on, hoping that there would be some way to take down the Emperor Manscor without the Las'wa. They would bid their time, and continue to hack away at the Royal-assassin's forces from afar. One year, they felt, would be the time to make their final bid for freedom—for better or for worse.

One year to find a new angle to attack the emperor...

The Royal spaceship glided effortlessly through the greasy, brown atmosphere of the polluted and near-abandoned city of Starlight, one of the oldest relay station probes near the asteroid M2. Its silver lines contrasted greatly against the trashed brown soil of the once-beautiful central park. The ship rotated on its repolsarlifts before settling on a landing port.

Two robed figures stepped lightly down the boarding ramp and proceeded through the abandoned out-buildings of the park to the littered streets beyond, the taller form leading the way through the canyon of skyscrapers. Along the way, they passed the few-hundred human residents still living in the city; most just lined the cracked asphalt streets to glance blankly at the two strangers, only mild interest in their deadened eyes. Others, more daring than the rest, looked hopefully, or with mal-content, into the hoods of the two passersby in search of food or something else of value.

Zanishiria stared silently back with eyes of stone, daring these people to try anything untoward her. She continued on passed without a word, following the robed form of her cousin as the Royal woman wove through the maze of buildings. Scarlett stopped wordlessly at a three-story building that was just as run down as the others around it and motioned for Zanishiria to step ahead of her to check for ambushers. Zanishiria disappeared inside the building, then, a few minutes later, peeped her head back outside to wave Scarlett in. "It's empty. Not a dust particle out of place."

Scarlett joined Zanishiria in what looked like the kitchen. She glanced around in partial disgust. "You're right about it being vacant. I'm beginning to think Royal Qusairo gave us the wrong coordinates. His son couldn't possibly live here."

Zanishiria heard the slightest creak of a floorboard and spun in defensiveness toward the sound. The assassin walked warily to the next room and peered inside. Her keen eyes noticed a shift in the dust that layered the floor. The assassin-girl bent down and touched the floor with her fingertips. She felt the wood beneath the grainy feel of the dust. Lifting her hand, she sniffed her dusty fingertips and frowned. "Scarlett, someone has been here."

"What?" Her cousin came to stand beside her. She surveyed the room. "I don't see anything."

Zanishiria scowled and stood. "I know there was someone here. I'm going to investigate the cellar."

"I thought you had checked everything?" Scarlett hurried after the assassin.

"I thought I did, but there were a few closets and such that I didn't bother to check out. "

"Still--."

"If someone lives here, they would know where to find good places to hide." Zanishiria replied with a glare back at the black-haired princess. "I just want to be completely sure." With that, she started down the steps leading down into the gloomy cellar, confident that her preshair gamma lenses in her eyes would help her see into the darkness. Scarlett hesitated against the impending blackness, unsure if she should head down without a light, before following Zanishiria, less finesse and stealth in her step.

The air below was mustier than above, but that wasn't what attracted Zanishiria's senses. It was the smell of human sweat and fear that hung in the air. Zan heard a shuffling from a closet near her. Tensing, she grabbed a knife from her belt. Quickly, Zanishiria threw open the door. Someone jumped out at her with his arms outstretched. The assailant wrestled with the assassin on the floor for a moment before Zanishiria managed to pin the man and get her knife to his neck. The attacker immediately stopped his struggle. Zanishiria looked the man over.

The young man looked like the average street orphan. His dark, chestnut hair fell down in a draggled mess around his burly shoulders, looking unkept and shaggy. The man's torso was very muscular, though, and lean, speaking to both strength and athleticism. There were smudges and scars running all over the guy's arms, legs, and bare torso. However, there were a few details that made Zanishiria realize who the assailant was. The deep, piercing green eyes and sculptured face were just like Royal Qusairo's.

"You are Anmero." She stated calmly.

The young man's eyes widened in surprise at the knowledge of his name. Wordlessly, he nodded his admittance to her statement then glanced nervously at the knife the assassin held to his neck. "I-I'm Anmero Doz. Ah, could you, um...Who are you?"

Zanishiria realized she was still pinning the prince in place, her full body weight perched over the man's muscular and half-naked frame. If she had been capable of a blush, she might have at that moment; however, without caring to show such reactions, she brushed aside the slight fluttering in her stomach and backed away from the young man.

"We're terribly sorry." Scarlett apologized to the prince. "Assassins are always this wary with strangers." Zanishiria scowled at her cousin but the princess ignored her. "I am Princess Scarlett Novastone and this is my cousin, Zanishiria Indigo Novastone."

Anmero stood up and brushed the dust from his body. "I think I understand now." The prince replied. "You must be the people my father told me were coming, are you not?"

"Royal Qusairo spoke of us to you?" Scarlett murmured, wondering how the Royal had been able to get a message to his son in this abandoned place. Waving away her thoughts, she answered, "Yes, we are the very ones. May we speak upstairs, in the light?" She asked, ready to be out of the din. Scarlett followed Anmero as the prince led the way back up to the kitchen. "Your father wants us to bring you back to Obseen."

Zanishiria waited until the two Royals had disappeared up the stairs before brushing off her own dusty cloths. "Well, so much for needing me along. He's not even the slightest bit worried over this." Sighing, the assassin bound up the stairs two at a time and found the others in the kitchen. Scarlett barely acknowledged her cousin's return, but Prince Anmero turned when he heard her arrive. "I assume you will be wanting to leave as soon as possible?"

Zanishiria nodded and headed for the door, as if his question was order enough to leave. "I have no need to stay here any longer than this. We have acquired you, after all."

Scarlett chuckled at her cousin's attitude. "She is anxious to return to Obseen." She explained to the prince. "We have been away searching for you for three days, and that is two days too long for her. She hates to miss out on any days to train."

"Oh, well, in that case, I guess there is nothing for us to do but go." He had intended the reply be for Zanishiria but the assassin-girl had already left the building. He shrugged helplessly at the princess and waved her to the door. "After you, then. I have nothing here I need to take with us, so might as well head away."

* * *

Master Quinn glanced out his window at the seemingly endless tarol tree forest that covered the expansive valley that made up the territory of Taysor, trying to act like his attention was not really on the impatient woman staring at his turned back. Behind him, Senior Master Sye Rainier, his former apprentice, cleared her throat, anxious to speak with her master. Master Quinn turned around reluctantly, knowing only too well what argument his student was likely to have. He rose an eyebrow questioningly.

"Zanishiria has left without my consent. Again, Master. I really should punish her severely this time." Sye tossed her long, cinnamon-colored hair behind a shoulder and made an expression that ruined her pretty face. The pout made the thirty-eight-year-old Senior Master seem like a teenager again.

"Should you?" Master Quinn countered. "Punishing such a promising apprentice—especially when it worked so well the last time—doesn't sound like a solution to me." Master Quinn walked to his study table and picked up a decanter of mipa fruit juice to pour for himself and his apprentice. "Zanishiria has never broken any of your "important" rules before now and is highly unlikely to do so again. So, do you really think making an example of one little incident, especially when it is a family one, is worth your relationship with her?"

"One minor incident?" Sye shook her head in frustration. "She has broken three rules by taking on her uncle's assignment. Three! And they are not minor! There is nothing little about this."

Master Quinn handed his apprentice a glass of juice. "Three rules broken, my dear? I don't see how that is possible."

Sye retorted irritably, "Of course three, Master. First, she accepts a mission without counseling me about it. Then, she leaves the planet without a word to myself or anyone in the Guild, and, third, she has taken weapons from this Center without the proper paperwork on them or permission to use them. The second two incidences are grave offenses!"

Master Quinn smiled in amusement. "I think you are overstating this issue, Sye. As I recall, I had my own apprentice whom was fond of taking off on her own "missions", and I did not punish said individual for such actions then." An embarrassed flush colored Sye's cheeks. "As for the other two incidents, I believe that there are times when some things should be given a blind eye to, especially when you know what the consequences are for such indiscretions." As the Senior Master of the training center, Sye Rainier knew all the penalties that could be awarded for wrong-doings. Her eyes tensed as she recalled how severe the punishment for the second two transgressions was. "See? As Zanishiria's master, you can cover for the girl's mistakes. You are in a position to."

Sye clenched her jaw at the thought. "As the Senior Master, I should be keeping the laws better than anyone else. My apprentice did wrong. I should not dismiss it. With her, there is always the possibility of a worse offense."

"You do not really believe that." Quinn responded quietly. Sye had to glance back to her master to hear him. "Sye," Her elder master gave her a look that seemed almost pleading. "Do not go through with this. Zanishiria will be back here very soon and everything will return to normal, you will see. Do not do something you will regret later."

Sye let her drink down resolutely. "Master Quinn, I respect you for your wisdom and all you have endowed me with, but I must uphold the laws. I will need to report this to the council. If ill comes from this than it is as it must be. My apprentice or not, I must follow the rules of the council. If at such time they feel Zanishiria is called forth for a punishment, whether that be slight or all the way to the status of defect, I have to do this."

Her master's sigh seemed sad. "Alas, my dear, you are indeed the Senior Master; I cannot dispute that. But, perhaps, you should consider what such a title means. You have the control that overpowers the counsel in its entirety. Remember that, if ever there comes a time you can use it."

Sye Rainier gave her master one last hard-mouthed look. "Thank you for your counsel, Master. I will call on you again."

* * *

Scarlett instructed that the starship be landed at a small spaceport in Creed city, in the Chartar territory. The capitol city lay in a large crater nearly three quarters of a mile across. Zanishiria and Scarlett had debated on the issue of where to land for the whole day previously, finally settling on Creed city for its distance far away from the Royal capitol, Taysor, which would allow them to get the prince onto the planet without too much attention.

Cautiously, Zanishiria disembarked from the ship and studied the surrounding spaceport, looking for anyone who might prove to be a concern later on. Only a handful of assassins walked around, however, and none seemed to give the Royal ship a glance. On closer inspection, she was able to note that every person present was from the Char clan that lived in Creed; there was no one around whom would send word to the emperor that a Royal had slipped onto the planet using unusual protocols. Satisfied, the assassin-youth turned back to the ship and motioned for Prince Anmero to join her.

The handsome prince walked down the gangplank, his green eyes taking in the new sights around him. Changed out of his "street clothes" into a practical tunic and assassin training robe, his hair trimmed down, he looked more the part of a Royals' son...perhaps a little too obvious but the assassin-girl wasn't going to comment. "So, this is Creed." He muttered as he took in the one-story buildings that stretched across the crater. No much told the prince what the Char clan was like, for the spaceport was pretty nondescript. Anmero directed his gaze to the girl beside him. "How long until we reach Taysor?"

Zanishiria shrugged. "That would depend on how fast you can travel, but don't expect to reach the capitol any time soon. It may not look it, but we are at war with the Emperor Manscor. Creed city is one of the few cities that has remained neutral between the Royal-assassin's forces and Renegades; though, it would not be wise to remain here long. You'll find it safer below ground, in the coursa [underworld], where I can get you to Taysor safely."

"We're going underground!?" There was a hint of alarm in the prince's voice. Apparently, he was privy to the knowledge of what creatures lived in the tunnels of Obseen. Zanishiria gave Anmero a small, mocking smile.

"Don't worry." Scarlett consoled the prince as she came to stand beside them. "Zanishiria is the best guide you can find to traverse the underground. You can trust her to keep you safe and alive on your passage."

"That doesn't make me feel any better." Anmero muttered. "Not with what stories my father told me about the snakes and spiders that call those said tunnels home."

The two Novastones ignored the prince as they said their good-byes to each other. Scarlett gave her cousin a quick hug. "Hurry back to us, Zan. Father and I will be constantly worried until we hear of your success at delivering the prince to his father. Be careful, cuz. "

"I will be." Zanishiria replied and stepped away from the beautiful princess. "You just stay safe yourself, and I will see you on the other side." The raven-haired assassin bowed respectfully to the Royal and turned away. "Come, Prince Anmero, we need to leave the city quickly."

Prince Anmero had to run after his small companion as she fell into step with the rest of the population in the streets. He huffed his annoyance at not being waited for but managed to follow the girl as she wound through the other assassins, slipping quickly and smoothly through the throng. Anmero followed the assassin across an intersection to a side street and down many winding alleys until they came out at the side of a country road, leading away from the city proper.

Large, purple-trunked tarol trees lined the road heading from the city, creating a peaceful canopy to walk without the direct glare of the three suns. Beyond the line of trees lay open prairie, made of blue-green grasses that changed to a violet shimmer in the wind. Anmero gaped in amazement, but his guide did not pause to allow the prince to enjoy the exotic view of the Nalar plains. Zanishiria strode forward purposely, leaving the young man to hurry after her once again. Anmero jogged to her side. "Is it okay if you would slow down? Or, is there a reason for us to be traveling so quickly?"

"It is safer here so you can talk freely; however, I will not slow down." Zanishiria informed him blatantly. "We will travel off-road. Follow closely." She didn't announce to the prince her suspicion of having been followed through the streets of Creed; hence her reason for choosing a wandering path until they lost their tail. Such a detail would not help her duties in any case and would come with unnecessary questions.

She suddenly cut to the left of the road and studied the ground there. "The sooner we get to the caves, the safer you will be." Zanishiria took ten more steps up the roadway then jumped over a tarn shrub.

Anmero sighed and stepped around the shrub only to give a low groan as he saw the Las'wa assassin running across the prairie ahead of him. "I'm not in shape for this type of activity." Nevertheless, he took off after the assassin.

When Anmero finally caught up with Zanishiria in a small clump of tarol trees thirty minutes later, he let go a loud groan and sat down on the ground tiredly. The only words he could get out between intakes of air were, "I really hate you."

Zanishiria gave a knowing smile and began to walk through a pair of trees, intent on continuing onward. "You'll hate me more when you see our destination." She only waited to make sure Anmero was following before she headed off, at a fast-paced walk. Behind her, the prince drew in a sharp breath and trod after. The two of them walked on for two more hours, neither speaking about much of anything, just making as much distance disappear behind them as they could. Finally, though, Zanishiria indicated that they could stop and take a break. As Anmero neared the girl though, he wished he had stayed farther behind, so as not to see what was next. In front of them, a massive, vertical wall of obsidian stone stretched a good fifty feet upward into the sky. The black stone had a smooth, glassy face, with little to no handholds for which to climb the obstacle.

"We're going up this?" Anmero sighed helplessly.

"I'm going to climb up this and toss you down a rig so you can climb up easier."

"Oh, yeah, that's a great help." Anmero grumbled sarcastically. "I appreciate it."

Zanishiria ignored the prince. She paced the wall, studying it. "Wait and rest here." With a turn of her wrist and tap of her heels, she released the preshair clamps in her wrist-guards and boots before grabbing a jutted piece of rock along the face to the left. With easy deftness, she began to scale the wall, unerringly climbing up the stone all the way to the top. Anmero shook his head in amazement at her speed and reserved his energy to grab the rope he knew would be soon descending to him.

It took the prince twenty minutes to climb up the rock face. When he finally reached the top, fatigued and breathing hard, he found Zanishiria meditating. "I'm so glad to see you were watching out for me." He muttered sarcastically as he fell in an exhausted pile beside the assassin.

Zanishiria gave a small, barely perceptible smile. She stood then and proceeded to recoil her rope. "I knew you would be fine, prince."

"Oh, thanks for the vote of confidence. You know, every prince has been trained in expedition trekking and rock climbing, not to forget, they have been tested in every way to get killed. So, I guess today is just another day at work."

An amused expression flitted across Zanishiria's serene face. "Glad to see we agree." His sarcasm not lost on her but Zanishiria wouldn't acknowledge it. She passed a jug of water to the prince and waved her hand to the rocky landscape beyond. "We'll take a half-an-hour break then we will continue. The boulder field ahead of us is a part of the Xsor Plateau. We're a few hours away from our destination."

Anmero drank greedily from the canteen and worked on getting his breath. From what he could see, their journey was far from over. Stealing what minutes he could, he finally pulled himself to his feet before the assassin-girl gave their okay to continue. "Okay, assassin, we can go now." Zanishiria rose an eyebrow skeptically before shrugging and finding her feet. She was quick to pick up their previous pace.

Hoping from boulder to boulder, she led them deeper into the plateau of obsidian. Reaching a rise, she motioned Anmero to rest. The prince sat down immediately, knowing better than to argue about any respite he was given. Brushing his damp, chestnut hair away from his eyes, he gazed out at the solid landscape. To the left of them, stretched the Nalar Plains. Its beautiful grasses a stark contrast to the obsidian plateau that towered above it. Everywhere else Anmero looked was the solid obsidian stone, unchanging like an unscathed piece of ice. In random places the obsidian rock jutted upward in sharp slabs. Nothing seemed to grow on the black surface. "It's kind of barren." He commented lightly.

The assassin girl nodded once to the statement. "The city is stunning, though. Only the Taysor Palace, which was designed by the Xsorians, rivals the buildings in Xsenume. Both are completely made of this obsidian stone; however, the Xsorian city is a masterpiece of pictures and designs. "

"A city made entirely of stone is beautiful?"

"Hold your skepticism until after you have seen Xsenume. I think you will be very impressed." She hopped off the boulder she had occupied and started walking. Anmero hurried after. "We will reach Xsenume City by nightfall.

Chapter Five

There are fourteen "territories" on Obseen, and the natural boundaries that define them, give rise to the ten region that make up the topography of Obseen. The capitol of Obseen, and seat-head of Emperor Manscor and the Assassins' Guild, is in the Taysor Valley, a seven-miles-long tarol tree valley that drops from the land around it. Bordering it, are the territories: Balthnor, Nyhore, Bialthioum, and Ghaystouw. Respectively, these territories are made of four "vegetation" types, giving rise to the names of these region. Balthnor and Nyhore are made mostly of obsidian plateaus, like that in Xsenume, called the Xsor Plateau, however, Balthnor also boasts some tarol forests, called Chareim, like those also seen in Chartar, Takato, and Tatauku territories; those three south-westerly territories also boast the Nalar Plains that run the entire width of their northern borders and the western area of Edis'daln. To the east of Balthnor, is the Naieej, a rugged region of plains and arroyos that butt up to the Shatray region in the territory of Traygor. West of Balthnor and Taysor, in Ghaystouw, is a region made up of the Ghantaur Plains that then run into the Zaphara Desert of Edis'daln—the center nicknamed the "Smelter Lands" because the area becomes so hot—and the territories of Imari, Imak, and Karnak to the north. Lastly, south of Taysor Valley is the territory of Bialthioum, hosting the largest region, called the Hills of Bialthioum. These strange and unique territories and regions of Obseen are host to the Seventy-two established clans of the Assassins' Guild.

Zanishiria continued to push their strenuous pace, and by the time the first of the suns was setting, the towering shape of Xsenume city came into view. Zanishiria gave Anmero one last rest break, using the tantalizing silhouette of the city to spur the prince into one last push of effort. The Royal was not without reward. As they entered the beginnings of the stone city, Anmero had to pause, dumbfounded. The stone city was spectacular! As far as his eyes could see, intricately sculpted buildings, carved into delicate patterns and images ranged from a translucent whitish-grey color all the way to deep, rich ebonies and interesting inky purples. Following Zanishiria deeper into the heart of the city, Anmero was welcomed by hundreds of elaborate still-life monochromes, depicting events and everyday life of Obseen. The city was a living history of the Assassins' Guild.

They came to an intersection and Zanishiria stepped off of the chiseled cobblestone road to sit upon a stone slab carved in delicate Xsorian script. Anmero was about to join her when he looked down at his feet. "Whoa!" He exclaimed, startled by what was beneath him. Zanishiria rose her eyebrow questioningly. "They have a steam running underneath the sidewalks!"

The assassin chuckled. "It's an illusion, Prince Anmero. The architects shaped the stones in such a way as to imitate a rushing stream. It's a brilliant idea." She lazily waved her hand to the sky. "The three suns helped to make the illusion possible."

"Oh," Anmero stepped away from the stream sheepishly and joined the fourteen-year-old on the bench.

Twenty minutes passed as the two companions sat. Anmero shifted boredly, glancing over at the assassin, as if she would give him some kind of indication as to what they waited for. The assassin leaned against the stone wall behind them, looking calm and in no hurry to move. If Anmero hadn't known better, he would have even guessed her to be asleep; however, as a Xsorian walked close by, Zanishiria's delicate hand moved to a weapon hidden under her outer robe.

The Xsorian stopped then and turned to her. "J'e sheì serapt tá assassin cor Taysor?" ["Are you the assassin we wait for fro Taysor?"] The man asked. Zanishiria gave a subtle flick with her hand. The Xsorian glanced around with an unconcerned expression and waved to another man across the street. The other returned the motion with an imperceptible nod and disappeared around a building. The former man turned back to Zanishiria. "Tá sharay shí bai sie." ["The Tá sharay has been waiting."]

Zanishiria lifted her head proudly and bowed to the man. "Kye kar'oum." ["I am ready"] She motioned for Anmero to follow her; a command the prince was getting well familiarized with. Staying a few customary paces behind their contact, they headed down the street.

The Xsorian led them through many side streets and hidden doorways. Anmero soon became lost in the never-ending maze of stone. He was so overwhelmed that he didn't notice the slightest changes in the stones around him, more elaborate and filled with important scroll work. Suddenly, their Xsorian escort stopped, and they were joined by eight others. The leader pushed through to the two visitors, bearing the black stripes of high rank. The tall, white-haired man stopped in front of Zanishiria and bowed. "Kie mourak lai—we welcome you. My name is Kee'van, con'trore [right-hand man] to the Tá sharay. I was unable to introduce myself to you last you were here."

Zanishiria bowed in return. "Itai. Tá sharay á shor kye." ["I see. The Tá Sharay made mention of you to me."]

"Qu'e sha." ["Very good."] The con'trore turned to the contact and gave him a cue to proceed.

Zanishiria and Prince Anmero were led through two large doors and into a spacious courtyard. Very few Xsorians occupied the space, and, those who did, bore the stripes of the Tá sharay's protectors. An older man stood near a stone water fountain. His hair was a shocking white that brought out the sharpness of his features and deep-green eyes. The man's features were typical Xsorian, Anmero knew, yet the clothing the man wore were those of a master of Taysor. There was an air of lordliness about the man, though Anmero could tell that the person was not of Royal blood.

This man turned to address them as they approached. He smiled warmly at Zanishiria and placed his strong hands on the assassin's shoulders affectionately. "Of all the assassins on this planet, only my favorite had to wander today. How happy I feel, Zanishiria, to be gifted with your presence."

"The honor is mine, Tá sharay." Zanishiria returned the smile then waved her hand at Anmero. "You know of Prince Doz, do you not?"

The Tá Sharay paused to look Anmero over. A smile of realization took over the man's face. "Indeed? King Qusairo's son? I would not believe you to be the man's escort." He nodded as if something quite agreed with him over the thought. "It is good news that you have gotten him planet-side without alerting the emperor."

"For now." Zanishiria said. Her grey eyes wandered over the courtyard. "If you do not mind, Tá sharay, I would feel better if we finished our discussion on Taysor or this prince in a less open area."

The Tá sharay took the hint with grace. "Very well. Let us move inside. I am sure you are exhausted from whatever journey this young lady dragged you on." The leader's words were directed to the prince.

Anmero couldn't agree more. He may have kept himself in decent shape while in his seclusion, however, he had not been prepared for the pace the young assassin-girl had pushed him to all day. His muscles were screaming at him for rest and his stomach growled in hunger. Eagerly, he followed the Xsorian and Las'wa into the Tá sharay's residence.

* * *

Zanishiria took in the quarters the Tá sharay had given them, memorizing the placement of the furniture and what items were in the room. The beautiful architecture, common to Xsenume, was evident in the walls and floor. Simple golden-plated chandeliers hung from the high ceiling casting adequate light against the coming night and softened the harshness of the dark stone. Vibrant colors, in contrast to the obsidian, made up the rest of the features. Plush chairs in a rich blue and gold-studs were placed in a comfortable square around a rare, oak-wood table. The rest of the furniture, plus the cabinets and bookcases pressed against the walls, were carved of obsidian so thin that they were nearly opaque. Two sofa-beds were separated from the rest of the room, in an alcove set just off the main room, to provide some privacy.

"Thank you for providing us a place for the night."

"I am glad you are satisfied." The Tá sharay replied. His words were meant to include more than just the offering of thanks. "I have asked my cook to bring your food here." Zanishiria acknowledged with a nod. The Tá sharay sat down in one of the plush chairs and motioned for his guests to do the same. "You are in need of something, Zanishiria? Or, are you, perhaps, in trouble again?" There was a spark of humor and concern in the leader's voice.

"Yes." The assassin responded, not clarifying to which question she answered.

The Tá sharay motioned for Zanishiria to come to his side. As she settled to a comfortable position on the floor in front of the Xsorian, he took one of her slender hands between his and locked eyes with her. Instantaneously, the two assassins' minds were connected telepathically, a talent all Xsorians possessed.

"What has gone on?" The Tá sharay asked, concerned.

"As I am sure you have guessed, Tá sharay, Prince Anmero is here without the approval of the emperor or his council. King Lapsair promised Qusairo we would smuggle his son in, but this has left me in an awkward position."

"You did not tell you master, did you?"

Zanishiria's emotions skirted quickly through guilt before settling back into calmness. *"Indeed, Tá sharay. Master Rainier would not have approved my going had I asked her. She is too shackled to the council and its control from the emperor. I could not risk her involvement if I was to help Royal Qusairo; any admittance to involvement with the Renegades will have me sent straight into the man killer's hands."*

"So, where does that leave us, then?"

"No one knows of the prince's presence here, except myself, you, the Novastones, and Master Quinn. Even the other leaders of the Legion have not been told. Master Quinn and I believe it foolish that Qusairo wishes his son here." She paused briefly, unsure if she should have thought so rashly to the Tá sharay. The Xsorian leader nudged her to continue, though. *"The Renegades have prepared themselves for a final push into Taysor. Soon now, they want to bring the war to the emperor's doorstep, no longer from the distance. Royal Qusairo will be in the thick of it. I doubt having Anmero so near the fighting will be a wise choice, but I follow the orders I've been given."*

"That is all you can do, Zan." The Tá sharay squeezed her hands in a fatherly gesture. *"What do you need from me?"*

"I would, first, like the use of your entrance to the caves. I am, after all, still Las'wa at heart and feel I can travel quickest in the coursa. It may keep the prince from harm's way for a few more days."

"And the other favor?" He asked knowingly.

Zanishiria's eyes hardened resolutely. *"In place of Royal Qusairo or King Lapsair's say, I would ask personally that you would help support the Renegades attack on the capital. This may be the only chance to take down the emperor; there may not be another opportunity once my identity is sprung. I know you have not officially fought in the resistance since the Battle of Barashi, but I know how much you and your people could help. Please—."*

"Stop there." The Tá sharay ordered gently. Zanishiria closed her eyes against the strong command. *"Zan, you do not need to feel obligated to ask me. I would fight for Obseen's freedom any day, especially with the daughter of one of the greatest men I have ever known. I will be there the day the Renegades storm the capital. You have my word."*

"Tá sharay." Zanishiria bowed respectfully and with gratitude.

"All that can be done, will." The Tá sharay broke there contact and stood, going to the door to wave the servants waiting outside to carrying in the guests' dinner trays. The three servants quickly set up the food on the oak table and left the room.

Prince Anmero, who had occupied a chair beside a window, was still turned away, unaware that the two assassins were done talking. He had been confused at their exchange. It had seemed odd to him that that they would look into each other's faces so intently, as if they had been speaking. Unnerved, he has let his attention drift to the courtyard seen beyond the thin obsidian windowpane. Below, he has witnessed two Xsorian youths, one around age of seventeen, the other fifteen, dueling each other with twin shayswords. Both boys looked lithe and athletic, boasting strong limbs and handsome features. Their white hair fell half way down their backs, tied neatly by matching thongs that were the same shade as their deep, green eyes. The vigor that they dueled each other was both mesmerizingly beautiful and deadly, leaving Anmero awestruck that they did not hurt one another. As if they sensed they were being watched, the two boys turned their striking eyes up to the window in one motion. Then, just as fast, they were running toward the entrance of the residence and lost from Anmero's view.

"Hungry?" Zanishiria asked, coming to Anmero's side. She saw the youth startle and blush.

"Yes, very much so." Anmero answered back and followed the girl back to the chairs. He picked up some meat and bread and began to eat ravenously. His vigor seemed to amuse the assassin girl. Realizing his rudeness, Anmero gulped down his last bite and bowed his head toward the Tá sharay. "Thank you for the meal and lodgings. It is very courteous of you to take us into such a beautiful city."

"If you think this city is beautiful, then you will be especially pleased with our Cathedral of the Winds." The Tá sharay replied. Anmero looked back in polite curiosity.

Zanishiria provided information on the place. "The entire building was built in such a way that when the wind blows through its structures, they create songs, much like those played on a flute. The melody is never the same but always masterful. There is not another building like it in the entire Abyss system."

"Hm. That sounds intriguing. I will be eagerly awaiting my visit to the place."

"Yes. Tomorrow, you will get a chance."

Just then the door opened and the two youths from the courtyard came through. The Tá sharay smiled warmly at them and motioned them to seats. His casual acceptance of their intrusion informed Anmero that they were not just regular clansmen.

"You know my sons, Page and Lap Torez, Zanishiria." The Tá sharay introduced. "Boys, this is Prince Anmero Doz." The youths bowed politely to their father's guests. Zanishiria returned the respect and nudged Anmero to do the same.

Lap Torez, the younger of the two, grinned broadly at the Lakean and took her hand to kiss it gently on the knuckles. His reward was a slightly shocked expression that was quickly covered by a cross look. The Tá sharay's clearing of this throat warned his son to not do so again, and Lap quickly released her hand as if stung. "Zanishiria I apologize for my behavior. It's just that we were on good terms last time you were here and I got excited to see you again. I will not offend you again."

"Just so, do remember, Torez, that next time I will not be lenient…. you may end up with a bruise for such an action." Zanishiria smile was mischievous as she promised about a reprimand the next time the older boy tried to woe her.

"I will not forget." The boy promised.

More reserved, Page repeated his bow to the Lakean and offered her a small gift of a fruit he had snagged from the kitchens on their way up, her favorite. "We are very happy to see you again, Zan. Lap and I could not wait to come meet with you. I hope our interruption does not tire you for future endeavors." The assassin girl snorted as if the last comment was absurd. The telepaths heard her retort mentally but ignored the chance to respond. To Anmero, Page said, "And it is very nice to finally meet Royal Qusairo's son. You are welcome to our city any time you like."

"Ah, thank you."

The Tá sharay suggested that they finish their dinners and reminded them that Zanishiria and Anmero had need of getting a good rest before heading off to Taysor. The leader and his sons left shortly after the meal was over, to leave the two guests in peace. Zanishiria motioned for Anmero to take sleep in one of the fold-out beds, while she settled herself comfortably into the plush chair she had occupied. Hearing Anmero lay down, she called for the lights in the room to darken. In the blackness of the room, she finally relaxed from their long journey and closed her eyes.

* * *

The room was quiet, except for the steady breathing from the sleeping prince. The sounds from the rest of the residence, however, could not escape Zanishiria's trained ears. She heard most of the movements of people walking or talking, or even the occasional snore. Fully awakened by the early-dawn movements of the building, Zanishiria rose from her chair and slunk through the room to the alcove where Anmero slept. The nineteen-year-old's sleeping form stood out mutely from the other shadows; the steady rise and fall of his chest seeming peaceful.

Peaceful, Zanishiria thought. *I have never had a peaceful moment since the death of my parents all those years ago, and, now, even this sleeping prince will have no peace— now that he is on Obseen. It is a shame that he has been drug into this war. I hope he is strong enough to bear what may surely come.* With an inaudible sigh, Zanishiria turned away from the sleeping prince and walked to the large window. The courtyard below was cast in shadows and moonlight from the twin moons. The large water fountain's contents glittered magically from the center of the yard. There was a great comfort in the night, which calmed Zanishiria's restless soul. Torn between the two feelings, Zanishiria turned away from the window and returned to her chair. Forcing herself to meditate, she demanded her body try to get what little rest was left for it, especially since she was not sure how long it would be before she would get another respite.

Concentrating on her breathing, she was able to slip away into the rhythm of her heartbeat.

Prince Anmero woke a while later. His eyes immediately adjusting to the darkness of the room. He was disoriented, for a moment, in the ordered surroundings so unlike the place he had been hidden, but as the moments passed, he was able to recall just where and why he was in the place he was. Brushing the sheets aside, the young man stood and cautiously made his way back to the familiar surroundings of the chairs and table. As he approached, Anmero became aware of Zanishiria's still form. Hesitantly, he shuffled over to her chair and paused in front of the "sleeping" assassin.

For the first time since they had met, Anmero was finally able to get a good look at the girl who was leading him. The fourteen-year-old looked to be three years more aged, with a face that was hardened by the trials of war and loss. However, in the darkened room, her features looked less stern, more youthful. Without the hard train of her eyes on him, Anmero actually found that he liked the soft curve of her mouth and the delicate cheekbones that lead the eye across her delicate face. In a few more years, the prince predicted that Zanishiria would be a beautiful woman.

Almost without a thought, Anmero reached his hand out to brush a stray lock of the assassin's raven hair away from her face. Suddenly, the girl's hand was lashing out to stay his motion. The prince gasped and felt himself stumbling back at the abrupt movement. Zanishiria's piercing, grey eyes locked onto his green ones, recognition shining in them as she became aware of what her automatic response to danger had done. Quickly pulling Anmero back to a steady posture, she released her strong grip on his wrist and leapt off the left side of her seat to the floor. "My apologies, Prince Anmero." Zanishiria averted her eyes and gave a slight bow. "I did not mean to harm you in any way. You just startled me."

The prince willed his racing heart to slow and rubbed his aching wrist gingerly. "It was not your fault, Zan. I knew better than to bother a sleeping assassin." His sheepish smile seemed to calm the strung-tight girl a little. "I... should have kept said hand to myself. Your reaction was quite impressive, though."

"Be lucky that it was not a knife I pulled on you." She answered. Her words implied that she could have done much worse to the prince. Anmero noted it dutifully.

With both of them awake, Zanishiria began a customary inventory of her weapons, and even gave Anmero two knives to keep with his person. By the time the first sun was rising, the assassin-girl had cleaned and checked all her weapons, brought Anmero up to date on the happenings of Obseen, and made sure both herself and the prince had eaten a decent breakfast.

In the end, there was nothing left to do but meet with the Tá sharay one last time and begin their journey to Taysor.

Chapter Six

Obseen is comprised of a mixture of similar-minded peoples that strive to have separate identities. The seventy-two clans may be connected through their arts of fighting and a code of ethics, however, each clan boasts a look and feel that is all their own. Once such way the clans expressing such differences is through their architecture.

Most buildings on Obseen are made of the obsidian rock that forms the planet. Though the dark stone seems threatening and dreary to outsiders, many of the clans have found it to be well-suited to architectural designs. The Xsorian clan, in particular, has adopted the cold, dark stone in the construction of it cities, creating elaborate pictures out of the dark glass. Some of their gorgeous structures are seen in their capitol city Xsenume, though their greatest works are found in Taysor at the Royal Palace and the training center. Xsenume and Taysor are only a few of Obseen's beautiful architectural ingenuities, however.

Three other major clans are also known for their intricate structures. The Palace of Ar, in Imak, is the Suez clan's greatest achievement. Nicknamed the "Palace of Gold", it is created from a mixture of black obsidian stone with a golden-like alkaline substance found in the rocks of the Zaphara desert. The result is a golden-bronze roof and trimmings on an ebony-walled palace that seems venerated by the glare of the three suns. The Trayshans, likewise, have mixed the obsidian with a mineral called traznic, an indestructible mineral found in the mountain ore of Traygor. Just like their famous swords, their traznic buildings are carved with the elaborate symbols of their clan that will never lose their vividity. The last of the great buildings of Obseen is the council chamber in Koro, Nyhore. Built of tarol wood and stone, it has a feel of ancient roots mixed with an earthen background. Though it is the smallest and least intricate of the structures on Obseen, it is the oldest, being the first council house built on the planet. It is a testament of the unification of the Assassins' Guild and a symbol of its strong-rooted foundation.

"Davin reported seeing the Novastone girls at Creed City earlier this morning, Majesty." Master Teera bowed low in greeting to her leader.

The handsome ruler, still well into his prime, turned away from the picture window he was at and flipped his long, near-black ponytail over his shoulder. The emperor strode over to his throne and sat down arrogantly. "Where are they now?"

Master Teera hesitated. "Scarlett has returned to the Palace, My Liege. Zanishiria was reported heading westward from Creed, presumably to Xsenume—though our contacts are not completely sure. Once she left the city, she may have headed to Traygor instead."

Manscor scowled, his chiseled features taking on a menacing air. "I do not want assumptions, Teera. I want that prince! Royal Qusairo is my strongest enemy. If I cannot get to him, then I want his only son. One of them will pay for the Doz family's defiance. Having them both out of my grasp means that the Renegades are one step closer to convincing the assassins unhappy with having an emperor as their ruler to revolt. I cannot have another Barashi on my hands."

"I understand, My Liege." Master Teera averted her eyes to the floor. "I am working to make all your wishes come true. We will make sure to get to the Doz family."

Manscor stood heatedly and began to pace across his dais, his mind still spinning over possibilities. "This Zanishiria...she is a cousin of King Lapsair, trained as an assassin-Royal here in Taysor?" He mused. "She intrigues me. I have heard some rumors of her at the Center, how she has created a stir by being good enough to join the highest rankings, though she is still quite young. That she is involved with the Doz family makes me suspicious." The emperor spun on Master Teera, his brandy eyes narrowed. "King Lapsair had never undermined me, playing the perfect subordinate. So, why then is a blood-relative of the Novastones and his daughter helping out the Dozes, when they must be well aware of how the betrayal reflects on King Lapsair? I want to know more about the assassin-girl."

"Indeed, sir." Master Teera responded. "But, My Liege, she is less of an issue than other posing matters. I ask that you dismiss her from your mind. If you wish her investigated, I have an easy solution that will allow you people to not be burdened with this... tedious assignment." Manscor stopped his pacing to listen to his woman. "My apprentice, Tarin Saerric, is a good friend to Zanishiria Novastone. I will ask him to pry into his friend's past. After all, it is always easier to get an answer from a trusted friend than a stranger; he may get information not otherwise available."

The Emperor's eyes seemed to brighten at the thought, then they darkened. "But, Zanishiria is not here to ask. Her friend--."

"She will have to return, Majesty, do not doubt that. Zanishiria is well aware of what codes she has broken by her leaving the training center unannounced. She will come back to make amends. She always does, that perfect bitch." Teera spoke sweetly, but her face showed how disgusted she was with the Royal girl. "You will have all your answers."

"Very well then, my Honored-one." Manscor purred charmingly. "I will let you and your apprentice handle everything. I assume then, my dear," He stepped forward and down the three steps of his dais until he was able to wrap his arms around master's slender waist, "That you will have the counsel sorted out to my liking very soon."

"Yes." Teera allowed for the emperor to give her one quick kiss on her cheek before she pushed away. "Though, with your seal declaring me as the Senior Master in Sye Rainier's place, for her apprentice's disobedience, I can do so so much easier." Her hint was less than subtle.

"Of course, Teera, I can grant you that." Manscor shot her a seductive smile and turned away to his small table to write up a correspondence. He quickly stamped his seal on the parchment and walked back over to hand it to Master Teera.

"Thank you, My Majesty." Master Teera said suavely and bowed deeply, keeping eye contact with the emperor enticingly. "I will have the counsel within the next two days."

"And, you will join me for dinner to celebrate our victories."

"Yes, My Liege." Master Teera bowed once again and turned on her heels and strode down the long throne room to the hallway beyond. Only when she was two hallways away did she let go a sinister laugh. "Victory, indeed, My Liege! Now, I have control of the head counsel of the Guild and title over that cowering skepht, Sye Rainier. Hah! Very soon now, Manscor, it will be only you and me, Empress and Emperor of Obseen. All who oppose us will be dead. We will be powerful!"

      The Cathedral of the Winds was grander than Anmero had expected. It had been obvious that the group had been nearing the large structure, for the music that had filled the air was very breathtaking and intricately rare in its composition. Hundreds of melodies and harmonies wove into each other to disappear and begin anew. The beautiful sound led the visitors right to its doorstep. The Cathedral of the Winds towered seven stories above the rest of the city, covering two acres at its base and tapering to multiple points at the top. Though it was made of the same obsidian as the rest of Xsenume, there was something otherworldly about the walls that made its observers believe the cathedral was a figment of the imagination. Anmero had never seen anything like it.

      Inside, there was more to amaze. Thousands of mirrors, made of thinned crystal, spanned the high ceilings, creating a maze. As each note was played, a color would come through the holes in the walls where the wind had entered and struck the mirrors, creating a light show of red, orange, yellow, green, blue, and purple that changed with the music. The dance of the music and the lights was mesmerizing.

      "Quite shunning, isn't it?" Lap asked as he stepped over to the prince. "It seems mind-blowing that such mastery can come from wind and light, but there you have it."

      Anmero was still glancing around, dumbfounded. "Just how long did it take to create this place? I can't even imagine what it would take."

      "Only about three years." Lap answered sincerely. Anmero's eyes widened in disbelief. "That's slow considering most of our buildings are created in six months to a year. We work had to finish one building at a time."

      "Only." Anmero whispered. He remembered all the complicated architecture he had seen on his walk through the city. To think that each of those buildings had taken less than a year each was inconceivable. He followed the group through the Cathedral.

      The Tá sharay lead the group through the maze of ever-changing colors. It was hard to tell which way they were going or where they had come from, yet the Xsorian leader never hesitated. He finally stopped at a large, mirrored wall and motioned for his eldest son. Page walked over to a smaller panel hidden to their left and beamed a laser at different intensities onto a small keypad. The panel flashed through colors of red, blue, purple, and green. The large mirror in front of the Tá sharay became opaque, then dissolved into a bubble-like substance. The Tá sharay stepped through the odd portal and disappeared into the dark beyond. Page and Lap followed, with Kee'van right behind.

Zanishiria motioned for Anmero to go first and waited as he hesitated at the doorway. The prince reached out tentatively to touch the surface, feeling his hand slide through the substance as if it was not there. Wondering if it was only an illusion, the youth felt he was confident enough to walk the rest of the way through. Zanishiria watched the prince disappear beyond the portal. With a last look around and a small nod to the final Xsorian behind her, she stepped over to the doorway and walked through.

The other side was a stark contrast to the Cathedral of Light. The room the portal led to was made of rough obsidian, like most buildings were, but this room held little light, only being illuminated by the natural asrouc in the stone. The small room led away into the darkness, the walls slowly taking the natural shape of the underworld. The slight musk of the caves floated up to the Las'wa and she breathed deeply of the place she had called home for most of her life.

Page stood by another panel, which he used to reactivate the mirror once Zanishiria was through. "The others have continued ahead." He informed her. Zanishiria bobbed her head and waited for the Tá sharid to finish up with his business. Together, the two assassins moved noiselessly down the darkened room to the stairway beyond. The footsteps of the others below drifted up to their ears, but neither hurried to rejoin the group. Reaching out to stop Zanishiria, Page offered the younger assassin a bag of herbals and food. "I think you will be needing these where you are headed."

Zanishiria glanced quickly through the bag to inventory the items and chuckled softly. "I knew you would think to give me something as a departing gift, Page."

"Of course, Zan, it is our custom." He said, referring to the three times the two of them had met. Each time, the Tá sharid had made sure to send Zanishiria away with a parting friendship gift; after all, the young assassin girl was well known to get into trouble by her random excursions across the surface of Obseen. Page had insisted that such a reckless girl should never be without certain items. "Oh, and the carving, flint, and hemp are from Lap. He was too embarrassed from his performance yesterday to give them to you himself." Page have a fond grin as he thought of his brother.

"Well, thank you both for your gifts."

Page nodded. A distant look appeared in his eyes, showing that he was probably talking telepathically to Lap. Zanishiria waited, knowing the look well. Only Xsorians could speak to each other without touching, which sometimes made it hard to know when they were talking to someone else or just daydreaming; however, Zanishiria had learned to read the Torez brothers well enough to know when they were communicating with each other. Page's eyes cleared and he grinned once more at Zanishiria. "Lap is happy to hear you are satisfied. He says they have reached the entrance to the caves. Shall we go join them?" He waved her ahead of himself courteously.

The Tá sharay had stopped at a metal doorway and had waited for his eldest son and Zanishiria to meet back up with them. When the two assassins reappeared, he stepped over to the door and touched the control pad to open it. The heavy door made a soft hiss as it equalized with the different air pressures on either of its sides before it slid into the wall. What lay beyond was a darkness so complete that it had Anmero's nerves tingling.

Zanishiria felt her heart beat faster as she looked into the caverns beyond, the gamma lenses in her eyes allowing her to see into the inky blackness and make out all of the shapes and fissures of the cavern walls, ceiling, and floor. Beside her, though, she sensed Anmero was ready to panic. "Well, we must depart now, Tá sharay." Zanishiria turned to the Xsorian leader and his sons. "Thank you for your assistance. Until we see each other again."

"And you as well." The Tá sharay and the assassin girl bowed to one another. "Shy mor'grea shie kye." ["My wishes go with you."]

"Eigh krey'grea shie kye." ["And, mine go with you."] Zanishiria bowed to the Torez brothers then walked over the threshold of the doorway. "Come, Anmero, we need to reach Taysor with much haste."

"I'm coming." Anmero answered weakly. He followed the assassin as she stepped into the cavern. To his relief, Zanishiria took his arm and lead him across the blackness of the room. It seemed strange and a little awkward to walk without sight, but Zanishiria's confident steps never stumbled or miss-stepped. Anmero could almost believe that the girl leading him could see.

"We are entering the main tunnels." Zanishiria whispered. She walked the prince thirty more steps before stopping and guiding him to a seat. "Sit here, and put these lenses into your eyes." She ordered gently, continuing to whisper. The assassin waited until the gamma lenses were in his eyes before she continued. "I'll be back soon. I just need to check around." Anmero reached out to keep the assassin from leaving his side but the girl easily slipped through his grasp.

The prince could not hear her as the assassin-girl moved about the cavern. All sound seemed muted in the dark abyss. Minutes passed by with Zanishiria not reappearing. Soon, Anmero's nerves were getting frayed and every sound made him jump nervously. Without warning, Zanishiria showed back up by Anmero's side. Her quiet voice cut through the blackness, like a knife. "Tell me when you can start to see shadowy shapes in the darkness. It may take you some time, but you should be able to make out something. There is enough asrouc in the rocks to cast some light."

"Zanishiria," Anmero could not keep the quiver from his voice, though he tried to put on a brave face, "I have never done well with the dark. In Starlight, if you fell asleep at night in the open, you would be attacked, or worse." Some nightmarish thought came into his mind.

Zanishiria could sense the fear of it in the young man's musk. The young assassin knelt in front of the prince and laid a reassuring hand on his shoulder. "I will not let you get hurt down here, I promise you, Prince Anmero. I know this land well and all its secrets are open to me."

"You aren't afraid of anything, are you?" Anmero asked to keep his mind from certain thoughts.

Zanishiria let go a dry laugh that was as soft as her words. "When your whole life is comprised of fear, you learn that there is really no such thing. And, by saying so, it becomes so." She sat down next to Anmero and fingered something in her hand. "I have always trusted the dark, because the dark was the only home I knew. To me, it was the sunshine that seemed scary—at least, at first." She chuckled at the admittance. "As I said, you will be safe with me, prince."

A sound from deeper in the underworld startled Anmero. It seemed that someone or something had screamed. The sound sent icy chills across the prince's skin. "Zanishiria? Ah, don't you think we should get going now? I would hate to be here too long."

The assassin was now on her feet listening to the noises from somewhere in the tunnels. "Not until you can see. The tunnels are too dangerous to travel without sight."

"I can!" Anmero stood up and joined Zanishiria. To prove he was not just reacting out of fear, he pointed out a rock formation to their right. "There is a three-meters-long fissure along that wall and a pile of stones over there in the corner. Above up, I see five stalactites."

Zanishiria nodded in satisfaction. "Very good. Well," she handed the prince the stone she had held in her hand, "We should go, then. Take this stone. It contains asrouc, a mineral that glows when it comes into contact with carbon dioxide. It will help guide your way in places you have trouble seeing."

Anmero looked at the smooth stone in his hand. Its worn surface didn't look like much. "Is there some trick to get this thing to work?"

"Breath on it." Zanishiria replied shortly and began to pick her way across the large cavern. Her eyes were always moving, always watchful, as she flitted across the uneven ground. She paused for Anmero to catch up before entering a large tunnel leading to the right. "We head east until noon, then turn northeast. If we are not given any trouble, we should reach Taysor by noon in two days' time."

"How do you know which direction we are going or what time it is, for that matter?" Anmero asked skeptically, making his way less gracefully across the stone floor.

Zanishiria threw a secretive smile over her shoulder. "Some things you will just had to take my word for, Prince Anmero."

Chapter Seven

Gamma lenses, taken from creeshts—or in Zanishiria's case, a preshair eye—are the most useful of all the discoveries of the Las'wa clan. The lenses allow humans to see fairly well into the darkness of the underwold and through other situations where sight is hindered. Creeshts lenses have to be removed daily for cleaning—like contact lenses worn to correct eyesight; however preshair lenses are shaped to the individual's eye size and kept in. Over the period of a month, these preshair gamma lenses grow into the natural structures of the eyes, never needing to be removed and even create a heat-censoring ability in the human eye. Since preshair lenses are so rare, as only harvesting fresh lenses from a recent preshair kill is the only way to procure them, they are only worn by preshair whip wielders or by the rare few others who are gifted them by a whip wielder. To be given a preshair gamma lens over a creeshts one is a gift worth its weight more than gold.

Tarin parried K'sho's sword and thrust his own at his friend's torso. K'sho was just able to block Tarin's attack, but the taller assassin quickly swung his weapon at a difficult angle in the opposite direction, taking advantage of the Sinya's weaker side. K'sho missed his friend's blade all together. Tarin stopped his swing just short of K'sho's neck, and the two stood in silence, eying each other. The sound of the two fighters' breaths echoed off the obsidian walls of the small fighting room. The rich, purplish light from the setting suns set the golden line, which outlined the fighting square's boarder, alight. A soft breeze swept across the room from the window in the western wall, taking the musty smell of the boys' sweat with it.

Suddenly, K'sho began to laugh. It slowly grew and vibrated off the walls. Tarin grinned and dropped his sword. "Well, you got me, again."

"You would have lasted longer if you didn't hesitate so much." Tarin instructed as he walked over to the paneless window and sat down on its sill. K'sho joined him a minute later, handing his friend a clean towel. Tarin wiped the sweat from the back of his neck and face and leaned back against the stone sill, his gaze wandering to the tarol forest that covered the valley and hills around the training center. "How do you think Zanishiria is?" Tarin asked, finally, his voice distant.

"How? Well, she is taking her precious time gallivanting across the planet this time around, which means she is probably having the time of her life. However, when she returns, she will be in a shit-load of trouble for leaving and taking unauthorized weapons with her and all that." K'sho ran his fingers through his dark hair to help it dry. "She knows what kind of trouble she's in. She always knows…I just hope she's okay. I heard she is helping smuggle in the Doz's son, so she's in quite a bit of a scandal against the Emperor. However, in my opinion, I'm glad she's doing what she's doing. It's not good to keep families separated just because the Emperor wishes it." Bitterness crept into K'sho's voice as he spoke.

Tarin glanced at his friend, concerned. "I didn't know you had a disliking for our leader."

"Don't say anything." K'sho begged his friend quietly. "I have my reasons." Tarin continued to study K'sho's face, waiting for his friend to confide in him. "Look," K'sho started, "Keep this to yourself..." He looked away to the sunset, distressed. "My...mother. She was taken by the Emperor's Honoreds five years ago, when they found out she was a supporter of the Renegades. My family has not heard from her sense. It is suspected that she was killed, along with the rest of those they rounded up at Nyashio."

Tarin's eyes crinkled in sympathy. He reached a hand out to clasp K'sho's shoulder. "You have every right then, my friend. The matter is dropped. We will speak of this no more." Pushing the matter to the back of his mind, Tarin pursued his former conversation. "I still hope Zan's all right, though. There's too much going on right now with the war between the Emperor and the Renegades. I'm worried she'll end up in the middle of it, as she's wont to do—especially if she is associating herself with the Doz family."

This time it was K'sho's turn to look inquiringly at Tarin. His sharp eyes took in the handsome sixteen-year-old's face, seeing the lines of stress around his eyes. "There is something bothering you, far than you've said." He prompted. "About Zanishiria? She's been on your lips a lot these days."

"Hm." Tarin nodded and closed his blue eyes. "My master has asked me to have "inquiries" about her past when Zan get back."

"But why? We all know she is a cousin to King Lapsair, trained privately on Planet X since she was three. What more does Master Teera need to know about Zanishiria?"

"She wouldn't say, but somehow, I get the feeling that the order comes from higher than even my master. Someone thinks Zan's past is worth looking into. Or, perhaps, it is more about the Novastones. Nothing they have done has been in opposition to the Emperor, until this recent assignment for the Doz family. Is my master concerned that they are going to betray the Emperor?" Tarin stopped and sat up straighter, knowing he had just stumbled on the answer—or at least part of it. "That's it! Master Teera must be worried that King Lapsair is planning something; it isn't over Zan at all!"

"What?" K'sho raised an eyebrow skeptically. "Why would King Lapsair do that? He has been nothing but loyal to Emperor Manscor. And, why would Zanishiria follow her uncle into a scheme that crazy if he were? She knows the consequences for going against the emperor." K'sho looked worried. "Tarin, please don't say what I know you're saying. Zanishiria is not in on a scheme against Emperor Manscor."

Tarin's expression was distant as he was lost deep in thought. "I want to trust that Zan is smart enough not to, but there have been whispers about that something big is going to happen on the Renegades' side. However…I do not want to make any conclusions until I speak with Zan myself."

"Yes, yes, until you speak with her make no assumptions." K'sho warned his friend to caution. "Zanishiria is our friend, Tarin. Keep remembering that."

"Yes, I know." Tarin let his features lighten, so as to stop worrying his friend. He even let a charming smile pasted onto his lips. "She's our friend." However, a shadow of doubt was beginning to color the Neitiege's thoughts. There was too little he, or anyone else, knew about Zanishiria, and, though she had always been endearing and talented, there had been a bit of mystery about her, too. Tarin was beginning to feel anxious to see his friend again, just so he could speak with her. And get the truth.

* * *

It had seemed like hours of wandering had passed in the shadowy caves before Zanishiria called a stop to let Anmero rest. The prince glanced around the large tunnel tiredly, looking for a place to sit, but his eyes, still unaccustomed to living entirely in the darkness, could not clearly distinguish rock formations in the obsidian. By now, the prince had been able to regain a great deal of his night-vision but the ability to place gross details in the dark rock but minute nuances were still beyond him. Anmero began to pick his way across the uneven floor.

Suddenly, his foot stepped into thin air and Anmero felt himself falling into nothingness.

Zanishiria whirled around as she heard Anmero's surprised yelp. Her heart turned to stone as she watched the prince fall beneath the floor. "Creesht-áet!" She cursed and rushed over to the large hole the prince had fallen into. Without a second's hesitation, she jumped in after him, her hand already going to her preshair whip.

Anmero landed none too gently on a hard shelf of obsidian rock. His asrouc stone slipped from his grasp and tumbled deeper into the cavern, where it continued to cast a surreal bluish-white glow. Anmero sat up slowly with a groan and glanced around. As usual, he could not see overly much, but what he could distinguish was that the large cavern spanned a very large distance beyond his sight. More importantly, it was laced in a strong, thread-like latticework that looked strikingly familiar. A shape scuttled across the floor somewhere beyond the asrouc light. It was followed by more noises, and, suddenly, a ghostly greenish-blue creature wandered into the light nine meters in front of the prince. In frozen terror, Prince Anmero watched as the largest arachnid he had ever seen stepped farther into the light and stared at him with its beady eyes.

The spider and Anmero stared at each other for what seemed like an eternity.

Unexpectedly, the arachnid reared up and disappeared into the blackness. A moment later, Zanishiria landed softly beside Anmero. The assassin narrowed her grey eyes and studied the cavern critically. She heard the tapping of the creeshts' feet as they scuttled around the room. Silently, she counted the different beats and estimated six creeshts in all. *I think I can take them.* Zanishiria turned to the young man beside her and touched his shoulder. "You all right?" She whispered. Anmero nodded mutely. He murmured something inaudible and glanced back at the area where he had seen the spider. Zanishiria followed his gaze past the asrouc to the shadows beyond. A large shadow could be made out among the darkness.

The assassin-girl took a few steps toward the shape and slowly unraveled her preshair whip; the scaly leather scraped against the obsidian stone causing more movement beyond the dim circle of asrouc. Zanishiria moved the whip around more, letting its scrapping grow louder. The sound caused unrest in the small creeshts nest, and a few of the creeshts wandered into and out of the light in their nervousness. Anmero watched as Zanishiria stood up, straight and still as a hunting cat in the slight cast of asrouc light. The Lakean did not move but he could bet she was listening to the spiders as they moved around unseen in the dark. Unknown to the prince, Zanishiria's preshair gamma lenses allowed her to take in every detail of the cavern. Though not able to see quite as clearly as if it were day, combined with her heightened hearing and taste, she could get a fairly accurate picture of the cavern and the creeshts within it.

A creeshts moved closer to her right. Zanishiria's eyes shifted to the shadows there and she readied her whip. A second later, the creeshts lunged out at the girl. It swung its large front legs at the assassin, trying to pierce her. Zanishiria dodged the large limbs. Soon, the arachnid and the assassin were locked in a harmonious dance across the cavern floor. Other creeshts wandered out into the light to join their nestmate's chase. The young warrioress soon became lost in the clump of greenish-blue bodies.

A moment later, the intricate dance was broken as two creeshts fell down dead, blue blood dripping from wounds behind their heads. Zanishiria reappeared in a flurry of quick spins and whip lashes. She jumped onto one of the dead creeshts and hurled herself at another. Her whip lashed out around the creeshts' neck, as Zanishiria landed on its back. She took out a preshair knife from her belt, and, hanging on skillfully as the spider raced around in a crazy frenzy, she took careful aim. Thrusting true, she thrust the knife point into the spider's head, the exoskeleton breaking like butter beneath the deadly blade. Zanishiria allowed the knife to embed itself until half her arm was inside the creature's head, making sure that the creeshts was very much dead. Blue blood squirted out onto her arms and face, but the assassin kept a tight hold on her weapon. Pulling the preshair knife back out, she leapt off the dying creature. Zanishiria landed near two other creeshts as the nest tried to scatter from their companion as it fell down. She threw her knife instinctively at the closest one. The blade penetrated above the creeshts' eyes and disappeared.

The two remaining creeshts turned in unison and, with an odd scream, charged Prince Anmero, who was standing near the wall on the opposite side of the cave where he had fallen. Zanishiria rushed to block the attack, her hand on a preshair sword, while her other stayed ready on her whip. Yelling at Anmero, the assassin threw her sword at the Royal and turned to fend off the rushing arachnids. Behind her, Anmero fumbled with the unfamiliar weapon, finally getting it into a defensive position.

The first creeshts launched itself over Zanishiria's reach and landed on the cavern floor behind the girl. It continued its mad dash toward Anmero. The other spider reared up at the assassin. It let out a loud shriek and slashed out with its sharp legs. In reply, Zanishiria uncurled her whip and sent it flicking around the spider's front legs, to noose then together. She jumped to the side as the creeshts' legs touched the ground and pulled. The spider's legs were instantly sliced out from under the heavy creature and the spider tottered; however, using its second pair of legs, it managed to hold itself upright. Wasting no time, the assassin girl hurled herself at the creeshts. Again, the creature reared up, albeit unsteadily. This time, though, Zanishiria reached for her two preshair tooth daggers. Running underneath the towering creeshts, she forced the two daggers into the large "death-mark" on the spider's exposed belly.

Blood flowed out of the wounds and dripped onto the cavern floor and down Zanishiria's arms. The creeshts screamed painfully, its loud cry so shrill it almost deafened the assassin. The horrible sound was muted soon after, however, as the slick blue blood covered Zanishiria's head. Slashing sideways, though she was blinded by the sticky wetness that had sloshed all over her, Zanishiria managed to open the arachnid's belly. More blood and intestines pooled out onto the floor. Rolling out of the way, Zanishiria crumbled to the ground a safe distance away as the large spider fell into its own puddle of blood and insides.

Blue blood slowly dripped down the Las'wa's body to the obsidian floor. It dripped off enough to uncover her eyes so she could see, and, a few seconds later, her ears unclogged, as well. A blast of sound exploded though Zanishiria's skull as the last remaining creeshts angrily reverberated its loss. In that instant, the young assassin was on her feet, knowing she had only seconds to save Anmero.

The prince was struggling to wield the creeshts sword, yet, somehow, he had managed to not incur the slightest injury. He jumped out of the way as the enormous spider swung its legs at him using what skills he knew from hiding out on Starlight to help aid him in his fight. Mistakenly, though, he tried to block one leg that flashed too close. The strike sent him flying backward into the hard rock wall, where he landed with a sickening thud. The creeshts gave a victorious scream and sauntered over to its unconscious prey.

It was at that moment that Zanishiria reached the creeshts. She flung herself upon the creature's back and slashed at it with a dagger. The spider reared up and let loose an agonized scream. Zanishiria felt herself start to slide down the creeshts' back until her whip's scales caught in the tough exoskeleton. Using the whip as an anchor, she swung off the left side of the creeshts' body; her full weight on the whip constricted it around the weakest area behind the spider's head. With one final, sickening snap, the whip dissected the creeshts head from its body. Silence followed as the creeshts fell.

Zanishiria landed beside the creature, crouched. She straightened and wound her whip up before turning and hurrying to the unconscious prince. Zanishiria checked Anmero over and took out a small vial of smelling salts to wave under his nose. A few tense seconds later, Anmero's eyes fluttered followed by a wrinkling of his nose. With a groan, he pushed the vial away and slowly say up. "What's that awful smell?"

Zanishiria gave an inward sigh of relief and recapped the vial. "I'm glad to see you are all right."

Anmero looked up at her and winced. "I feel like a sledge hammer hit my skull."

"Obsidian can do that to you." Zanishiria responded lightly and helped the prince to his feet. Anmero swayed and grasped the assassin's shoulders for support as his vision threatened to go black. "Take it easy." Zanishiria cautioned with a frown. She was instantly concerned that the prince had a concussion. "I wish I could let you stay here and rest, prince, but it is not safe here by a creeshts' nest." She glanced around the cavern to get her bearings. Nodding toward the left, she helped

Anmero to the entrance of another tunnel and set him down to check out the cavern beyond. She came back a minute later and had to poke the prince out of his stupor. "If I remember right, there is a large pool a few caverns ahead. We'll head that way after I collect my weapons. I need you to stay awake while I do." She handed him the smelling salts. "Use these again if you feel you're starting to get sleepy." Anmero gave her a disgusted look but took the vial nonetheless.

Zanishiria hurried to collect her weapons. It took some moments to dig out her knife and daggers from the two creeshts, a very wet and gooey process, but once she had the three weapons, she did not waste another second getting back to Prince Anmero. Luckily, Anmero was still awake when she returned to his side. "Let's go." She prompted, helping the Royal as he limped down two long tunnels. A half an hour later, they finally reached a spacious cavern that smelled moist and warm.

Water steamed down the slick, dark walls to fall into a shimmering pool, lite by asrouc. The pool was about nine meters wide and stretched the full twenty meters of the cavern. Zanishiria walked the prince over to a large, flat shelf of obsidian stone overlooking the water. She helped Anmero sit down then hurried away to a large patch of florick moss that grew near to the tiny waterfalls dripping from the top pool into its deeper section. She used a preshair knife to hack off a section of it. She gave it a thorough cleaning in the water and walked back to Anmero's side.

"My head is still ringing." Anmero touched the back of his head gingerly. "At least I haven't found any blood."

"Don't get too excited about that." Zanishiria warned as she separated the long, silver strands of florick moss from the clump she had collected. She held up a few in front of Anmero. "Eat this; it will diminish your pain and prevent a hemorrhage."

Anmero eyes the moss doubtfully but took the silver threads. He hesitated but finally stuffed three of them into his mouth. "Hm, not too bad." He admitted as he chewed. "Kind of like a nut of some kind."

Zanishiria smiled at the comparison and rolled some strands into a ball for herself. She chewed on the moss while she reviewed the mental map of the underworld in her head. Anmero glanced over at her from time to time while he continued to consume the florick moss, but he kept a respectful silence as the assassin thought, his own mind wandering on its own train.

Again, the Lakean seemed to be as cold and mysterious as the underground caves they occupied. Both seemed too complex to understand and neither gave out much of themselves to onlookers. However, despite the feeling of distance that seemed to cloak the assassin, there was also an allure of beauty and serenity within the girl that called for attention. The clashing of the two sides only added to the mystery of who Zanishiria was. The Las'wa finally seemed to realize that the prince was studying her. Turning to him, she narrowed her eyes slightly at the offense but kept her tone neutral. "Is there something you need, Prince Anmero?"

Caught off guard, Anmero managed a, "uh, yeah," while he searched his mind for a decent question. "How long will it take us to reach Taysor now that we have fallen deeper into the caves?"

Zanishiria's eyes softened. "We have been thrown back a day or two, maybe more. It is more dangerous at this level than the previous one, but that's not what worries me."

"Then what does?" Anmero asked, not sure if he really wanted the answer.

"There had been a few cave-ins in the main tunnels of this level—or at least there were a year ago. If we come upon one, we would have to backtrack, which costs us time."

"Oh, that could be a problem." Anmero mumbled. "I really have no desire to stay down here longer than I have to."

"I know." Zanishiria's smile was teasing. "Don't worry, prince, I won't try to keep you here too long." She stood and stretched. "Rest here. I'll be in the next cave over." Anmero kept his eyes of the assassin as she deftly made her way around the pool's edge to the connecting cavern. She disappeared into the gloom beyond.

Many minutes passed, until Anmero found himself both curious and anxious that Zanishiria had not reappeared. Standing slowly, he followed the wall she had taken earlier.

The second cavern was smaller than the first but held similar characteristic as its counterpart. The pool here, though, steamed as if trying to breathe itself into a living form. The warm, humid air eased the chill from the underworld. Near the edge of the pool lay Zanishiria's clothes, washed of blood and left to dry on the warm stones around the pool. The assassin herself was submerged in the water up to her chin. She turned around as she heard Anmero enter. "I see you could not rest."

"After the incident earlier I'm not entirely comfortable going to sleep without you to guard my back." Anmero stepped closer to the pool and dipped his hand into the warm liquid. "It's quite warm." he commented.

"Yes." Zanishiria replied shortly. She swam over to the prince and grasped the obsidian ledge while she spoke. "This is one of a number of underground hot water pools. Supposedly, the water comes from Edis'daln, the territory with the hottest humidity and lowest precipitation on Obseen. Nothing leaves there without being thoroughly cooked." Her eyes seemed to dance in amusement at her words. "Would you like to join me? The water feels great after a hard day."

"Ah..." Anmero blushed at the thought, knowing Zanishiria was naked, and a naked girl with a nineteen-year-old young man made a bad combination.

Zanishiria chuckled, eying the prince knowingly below his waist. "Like I would let you do anything so untoward me, prince. Now get in here and relax. I'll turn away until you are in." She turned her back not waiting for a reply and swam to the other side of the pool. Unable to really argue with Zanishiria, Anmero took off his clothes and quickly lowered himself into the hot water, finding he was very satisfied to be in the pool. His delighted sigh told the assassin that he had gotten in. She turned around and leaned back against the obsidian wall, also content.

"I would never have guessed in a million years that anything so crazy would happen to me." Anmero started a few minutes later, thinking out loud.

"Crazy?"

"Yeah, crazy. I had thought that as long as the Manscor controlled Obseen that I would never be able to be with my family. My father did not want to live on Planet X, you see, feeling his cause was here, but he was also very worried that I would be used by the emperor to punish my father, which is why he sent me away, to "safety'." Anmero huffed and brushed his chestnut hair from his eyes unconsciously. "This planet has always seemed so foreign and untamed compared to my home on Planet X. The few times I've come here have always led to some debacle or another. I guess, I should just expect it by now."

"Obseen has a way of testing its people, no matter how familiar they are to its patterns."

Anmero wasn't sure if Zanishiria was sympathizing or imparting an odd form of Las'wa wisdom. "Falling down a hole into a den of spiders is certainly one way I wish to never be tested again."

"Indeed, I hope you do not have to suffer that one again either." Zanishiria replied, "And, I'll make extra sure that you will avoid such a fate. Once we are free of the caves, you may never have to venture here again, if that is your wish. Though I must warn you, until this war with the emperor is over, you may find your incident with the creeshts to be the least of your "debacles"."

The two of them lapsed into silence then, the hot water making them very relaxed and sleepy. Anmero dozed off for a time, leaving Zanishiria alone with her thoughts. The assassin herself was slightly troubled, though she had refused to admit such openly. One year was a very long time for her to not live in the coursa and she was not sure what changes had taken place in her absence. It had not helped that Anmero had fallen into a nest of creeshts their first day within the caves; the reminder of past events with such creatures had continued to haunt Zanishiria's dreams every night since. Treading water restlessly in the deeper end of the hot water pool, the young girl forced her mind from wandering over the dreadful topic. Finding herself too uptight, she finally swam over to the side where her clothes were laid out and pulled herself onto the rocks next to them. She basked on the warmed obsidian, drying off, until she was able to put on her under layers without overly wetting them. Being properly covered, she walked over to Anmero's side and leaned down to shake the Royal awake. "Come out now. We should get some sustenance down before you nod off too deeply."

Anmero groaned at the interruption to his wonderful nap but was able to get himself awake enough to stand up against the ledge. Zanishiria politely averted her eyes from the naked prince, making the movement look like she had meant to turn away and find a spot to lay back on the warm stones. Anmero didn't even notice as he came the rest of the way out of the pool and grabbed his pants. He pulled them on, grabbed his shirt and came to sit next to Zanishiria. "I feel much better."

"That's good." Zanishiria replied lightly as she squeezed out the remaining water from her long, black hair and started to braid it back. Anmero could not help staring at her lovely features, so nicely framed by her raven hair. His staring was quickly found out by his guide, who glared at him with dark, slate eyes. "What had you so interested, prince?"

"Ah," Anmero cleared his throat and busied himself putting on his shirt. "You're very good at braiding your hair. I was just admiring your skill."

"I'm sure you were." She responded knowingly. "That's what most boys your age are peeping at."

"You are very confident with yourself, aren't you?" She replied with a look that said, "well, duh". Anmero grinned charmingly. "I can't wait until I know you when you're of age. I bet there will be plenty of young dandies around you."

Zanishiria's face soured and she stood up. "I'm afraid, Prince Anmero, that you are treading into some very dangerous territory. And, as for my person, I doubt I will be with any "dandy" any time soon. I have too much to do to be bothered with such trivial pursuits."

"Oh, you say that now, miss.....ah, how old are you?"

"Fourteen cycles." She replied shortly quickly donning her preshair snakeskin armor, which was both very light and supple and able to withstand almost any attacks. She hoped Anmero would drop the subject if she began to ignore him.

"Miss fourteen-year-old." Anmero continued without a pause. "When you are just a little older, you will be very interested in men and all they have to offer."

"Which is?" She just couldn't help asking the question, though it was given sarcastically.

"Oh, attention, protection, love, stability...."

"And I would need to get those things from another person because?"

"Well—." Anmero hurried after the assassin as she made her way across the misted obsidian stones mindfully. He had slipped in his inattentiveness and Zanishiria had to reach out and stabilize him. "Yes, I see that men are very capable." Her cutting words stung. Anmero righted himself abashedly and followed after in a more subdued manor.

They sat down next to the few bags and heavier weapons Zanishiria and Anmero had left by the cooler pool and the girl sorted through her larger bag for food items. Anmero waited dejectedly, though his emerald eyes couldn't help watch the assassin as she moved. He took the offered food silently and bit into it. He also accepted another dose of florick mosses, having found the plant to not be repulsive in the least. Zanishiria set aside her bag and leaned back against the cool stone to eat.

The moments stretched into uncomfortable silence, save for the steady water droplets falling from the ceiling into the pool.

Finished with her meal, Zanishiria rose and walked over to the pool to lean down and cup her hands into the mineral water. She sipped deeply of the liquid, enjoying the sweet taste of the waters she had always known. Sated, she turned to the prince. "Would you mind staying on guard for thirty breaths counts? I would like to get some rest in before you doze off again." Anmero nodded, still subdued. "Very well. Wake me if there is anything unsettling."

"Such as?" He asked.

"You'll know. Anything that has you jumpy or nervous."

"That's everything." The prince muttered.

Zanishiria studied the Royal for a long second before going back to her bags. She shuffled around again and pulled a small, leather bound book out and handed it to the prince. "Read this a while. It will help you pass the time and keep you less worried about what lurks in the dark. Not that you should be." She added quickly, "Because the creeshts and such avoid pools as well lite as this one. Too bright for them."

Anmero knew the last words were probably said just for his peace of mind, though he did feel somewhat comforted by them. Settling himself as comfortably as he could, he opened the small book she had given him and began to read of the careful, hand-scripted print. Some time passed and the youth began to feel thirsty. Setting the book aside, he made his way to the water, following where Zanishiria had gone, and dipped his hands into the luminescent pool. He sipped as quietly as he possibly could. Some of the droplets fell between his palms to the pool below, sending circles playing across the surface. The sound of the droplets falling became the only noise. An odd feeling came over the prince, like he was being watched, and he stilled. Unnerved by the raising of the hair on the back of his neck, Anmero quickly hurried to the assassin girl's side and touched her. Her eyes flew open instantly and her hand came to the preshair dagger by her side.

"Easy." Anmero whispered, now afraid of the assassin as much as he was of the shadows.

Zanishiria did not move but he could see she had picked out the oddness of the silence as well. She cocked her head slightly to hear into the cavern better and waited. A shuffle, barely audible, echoed quietly from just beyond the cavern. The girl searched the shadows for any sign of a darker shape looming amongst the darkness. A shuffle came again, and she knew, instinctively, that the movement had been done on purpose. It gave Zanishiria some comfort; the intruder was human. Yet, Zanishiria's past training made it hard for her to trust an unrecognized face. Not knowing if the watcher was a threat, or not, made her defenses surface like raised hackles. She waited, poised, where she had just been sleeping, daring the person to move again.

Once the watcher moved, this time toward them, Zanishiria launched herself at the shape. The clash of two daggers resounded throughout the nearby tunnels and faded away. Zanishiria jumped back, preparing for another attack. Her opponent disappeared into the shadows again, becoming lost even to her gamma lenses. She hissed and stayed poised.

A gentle, baritone voice floated out to Zanishiria and Anmero. "You still have a mirthless attack style, I see, seimora."

Zanishiria lowered her dagger slightly. "C'vail?" She whispered. "Praic."

"Glad you haven't forgotten your closest friend in one year." Seircor teased as he stepped out of the shadows.

Anmero was completely shocked and befuddled at the sudden change in the two assassins, one minute fighting each other, the next joking companionably; however, the tall, sinewy man surprised him the most. Seircor had sharp, dark-steel eyes and short-cropped black hair typical of the Las'wa. He looked both dashing and threatening in his black-and-red-scaled snakeskin armor (a gift from Zanishiria two years back); the neckline of the piece was lined with the black pelt of a chatar cat making it stick up wildly around his nape and hair giving him the look of a dangerous lion. His weapons, visible from their places at his belt and across his back, made Seircor look ready for any danger that might come his way. Anmero gulped, intimidated.

Seircor walked over to Zanishiria and looked his younger friend up and down critically. "You look terrible." A moment later, the seventeen-year-old's face broke out in a smile. "It is good to see you, Zan."

"And you, Praic." Zanishiria allowed a small smile of joy cross her lips. The two assassins stared at each other for a long moment, taking the other in. Then, Zanishiria broke away. "I wish we were meeting over better circumstances, Seircor."

The older Las'wa immediately sobered at the use of his formal name and followed Zanishiria over to where Anmero was still gaping. "Prince Anmero Doz I give you Seircor C'vail, a friend of mine."

Seircor bowed respectfully and Anmero hurried to follow suit. "Prince Doz, it is good to make your acquaintance."

"Ah...likewise."

Formalities over, Seircor returned to the unspoken matter at hand. "What is it that you need, seimora? Perhaps, I can help." For Zanishiria to be there at all showed she was in some sort of trouble.

Zanishiria's smiled, though the look did not show in her eyes. "I greatly appreciate that, Praic. As I'm sure you are aware, seimie, having Prince Anmero on Obseen will cause quite a stir. I'm escorting him to Royal Qusairo. After that--."

"All hell will break loose." Seircor finished the thought. "Yes, the seimreal [Las'wa council] has called everyone into session. It is rumored war is upon the Guild, again. I was asked to go ahead and see what I can learn of it."

"The Renegades wish this to be the last battle. Everything is being put into this final stand. The fighting will be pushed into Taysor. It is then that I will hit the emperor."

Seircor nodded in understanding. "So, you have decided to continue with the mission."

"I would make no other choice; the man killer has taken too much from me and from Obseen. His time is up."

"Then I will go with you, seimora."

"If you come, then I would ask you to help keep Anmero safe." She glanced at the prince whom listened from a respectful distance. "I promised to have his returned to Royal Qusairo alive. It seems I have split myself into two duties."

"As usual, Zan." Seircor teased. "Then I will do as you need, seimora. Just tell me what to do when."

"Kye mureak." ["Thank you."]

Chapter Eight

The history on the assassins of Obseen has been rift with strife. From the start, barriers between the many clans has been the cause of a series of four civil wars. The Royals, their nursemaids, could do little to stop the bloodshed. It took almost eighty years for the planet to come to an unstable resolution. Slowly, Obseen molded itself. Using relations with the Royals, the Assassins' Guild build up their people's assets and arts and cooperated in creating new technologies. The assassins became notorious for being as tough as they come and very intelligent, proving valuable to the Royals of Planet X for their skill sets in espionage, hacking, and fighting.

Setting aside past grievances, the assassins created a society to be reckoned with, feared especially by the United Earth Forces. Yet, this amazing force could also be used unjustly in the wrong hands. Prince Xi, son of King Chiang Xi, a high-standing Royal, saw the amazing power of the Assassins' Guild as an untapped weapon and made plans to use it against his enemies. He slowly worked himself into the Assassins' Guild, gaining respect through their customary and intricate martial system. On the eve of the year 4012, he used his influence to gain support from a large handful of assassins and Royals and took control of the Assassins' Guild for good. Within the first year of his takeover, he massacred hundreds of opposing Royals and assassins to gain control of the two planets. With total control of the Guild, Prince Xi, took the Neitiege name Manscor, or "man killer".

However, Manscor's reign would not be without unease.

For the twelve years of his reign, a resistance, first called the Las'wa Resistance and later reemerging as the Renegades, have continued to battle against the rule of one emperor. Always staying just beyond the reach of the Royal guard, they bypass plots from the emperor and continue to gather support across the planet. In this year, 4023 SD, the Renegades have finally decided on a final, all-out effort to take down the emperor once and for all.

The landscape was red, blood red. Bodies of waring clan members dotted the hillsides. Night was just falling, but a few skirmishes still remained. These warriors would fight all night if allowed, yet it was not necessary. By now, the Royal guards had been forced to retreat into Shaytyar (Taysor). The Renegade clansmen were that much closer to the capitol, that much closer to Manscor. These fighters were among the growing number of Renegades that opposed the emperor. They had fought alongside the Royals for nearly thirteen years, fighting the opposition of Manscor's guild. Now, this group controlled most of Obseen, militaristically, but the control of the Assassins' Guild, based in Taysor, still remained with the emperor.

A messenger run up to one of the tents lined up next to the tarol trees bordering Shaytyar. He paused at the entrance, panting, then pushed the flap away and entered. Royal Qusairo glanced up as the young man walked up to his table. His wife backed away from her husband, who she had been bandaging up from his injuries he had acquired during the fight. Qusairo spun in his chair to address the runner. "What is it, lad?" He asked.

The young man held out a thin piece of obsidian sheet and bowed. "A message from King Lapsair, sir."

Qusairo accepted the thin sheet and motioned his wife forward. "How about getting this young runner something to eat, eh?" He waited for his wife and the messenger to leave the tent then switched on a light so he could read the tiny writing on the stone.

Qusairo, my friend, I hope this comes to you in good circumstances. I regret that I could not give you the news in person, but business over here keeps me occupied. I have kept my end of the bargain, now you keep yours...My "adopted" niece returned three days ago with your son and is on her way to you. If all goes well, she will reach Taysor in about two days, so there is the time you have to work with. Keep safe until then, my friend. Say hello to Asilisa for me.

--Paul Lapsair

Qusairo laughed at his friend's excuse of "business". He knew better than to believe Lapsair worked. The fact was that Lapsair was keeping Manscor busy with major distractions in the Guild, using the secret Legion of Leaders that were based in the capitol to cause trouble. "Manscor won't ever admit that he's outmatched, which makes it easier for us to disable him. However, I fear there will still be some time before we take the emperor down...just too much damn time." The Royal stood up and wrapped the obsidian in a cloth before stuffing it into a pocket. He then proceeded outside, to the large mess tent.

Entering the tent, smells of the night's repast and the sounds of chatter bombarded Qusairo. Some of the soldiers looked up and saluted. Qusairo returned the gesture and wove his way around the room to the long table at the front. There, he collected a bowl of soup, some bread, and eating utensils. Glancing around, he spotted his wife and the messenger eating with a small group of assassins and commanders near the left side of the tent. Again, he wove around the dining army to reach his wife, sitting down beside her.

"How is Paul?" Asilisa asked, glowing up at her husband.

"He is well." Qusairo answered and nodded a greeting at the others at the table. "He wants us to move into Taysor before two days are up. What are your opinions?"

"That seems like a good time frame." Captain Sieck replied. "It could be a little difficult getting to Manscor in that time, though."

"I agree." Major Calamas, the taller man beside Captain Sieck said.

"We are only needing to get to the Palace." Qusairo told them, to calm their concerns about the emperor. "There is another plan in place to challenge Manscor. We will deal with his army and the Royal guard."

Another captain, named Raynward, an older veteran of war nodded. "Our fighters are ready to take on the Royal guard and the Guild in Taysor. They're fired up for it."

"That is what I need." Qusairo met the eyes of his leaders in turn, ending with Shy'ree, a raven-haired, grey-eyed assassin woman. "And you?"

Shy'ree glanced up from her meal. "The assassins are ready for your signal, Royal Qusairo."

"Good." The Renegade leader leaned back in his chair. "Now we just have to make it to Taysor."

* * *

"We have made good time. Let's stop here." Zanishiria said as Seircor lead them up to the next level. Having run into the older Las'wa had proved most beneficial, as he knew which tunnels to take to avoid the numerous rock slides. Seircor nodded in agreement and allowed his pack to slip off his back. Zanishiria turned to the prince. "How are you holding up, Prince Anmero?"

"Better." He searched the ground carefully before finding a seat on the obsidian floor, his last adventure making him more mindful of where he tred. "My head doesn't hurt anymore."

"That's good news." Seircor commented as he took out a slab of cooked and salted meat and cut it into pieces. "A concussion can be serious without monitoring, but the florick moss really helps with the swelling and prevents bleeding." He handed Anmero and Zanishiria their lunch and continued. "You're also really lucky to have Zanishiria with you. She's the best guide to have down here in the caves and certainly one of the best fighters, too." The Lakean smiled broadly at his best friend and gave her a hand signal.

Anmero watched as Zanishiria returned the motion with one of her own. Both seemed to understand what the other said, though Anmero had no idea what they were saying in siihshe sign language. Anmero felt he was left out of something, just as he had when Zanishiria had spoken with the Tá sharay. He shifted uncomfortably as he waited on the two assassins.

Zanishiria became aware of Anmero's discomfort and gave one last signal to Seircor before turning back to the prince. "No disrespect is intended, Prince Anmero. I was just telling my friend how good it is to be with him again. We will discontinue with the siihshe so you may not feel so left out." She paused, seeming to be lost in a thought. "I almost forgot. I had asked Praic to teach you some self-defense skills and how to use a blade. You should know at least enough to keep you alive before we reach Taysor."

Anmero looked like he was going to protest, so Seircor added, "She wants me to teach you because I am a more patient teacher than she and I enjoy swordsmanship more."

"Oh, I see…Well, if you think it best, I will give it a try." The prince stood up again and followed the Las'wa to a flatter area. Seircor scoped out the site to make sure it was safe and adequate before nodding to Anmero that he was ready to begin.

Zanishiria watched for a bit as Seircor explained the different defensive positions of the sword and some common blocks in hand-to-hand combat. She was very grateful her friend had agreed to teach the Royal because Seircor was a very patient and instructive teacher. He also excelled at the sword, making it his choice weapon, though he had been able to choose from a number of disciplines.

After some time, Seircor called her over to help him with his lesson. "Zan, could you come demonstrate to Anmero what it looks like with all of this together?"

"Crey." ["Yes."] Zanishiria walked over to Seircor's side and unsheathed her preshair short sword. "What would you like me to do?"

"I have been trying to explain how to be on alert for changes to opponents instead of just following patterns. Prince Anmero has been very apt at learning the forms but he lacks a bit of spontaneity." He grinned to lessen the severity of his critique. "I was wanting him to see what it looked like to "dance" through a dual."

"Remember water." Zanishiria told the prince as she stepped back to perform. Anmero looked at her confused. "Water is the ultimate substance of change. It is fluid and ever moving. Just like water, you must be able to allow yourself to adapt to changes in a fight. Watch and you may see what I mean." The young assassin nodded to her friend and signaled him to come at her. Anmero watched as Seircor closed the distance between them, his sword raised offensively. The taller man suddenly stepped farther to the right, at the last second before engagement, and he let loose some kicks into a spin combination, all of it still moving into a swing at Zanishiria's left shoulder. His smaller opponent easily followed the movements, seeming to meet ever thrust and parry and kick as if she already knew where it would be. Changing to a new direction, Seircor influenced the tempo of the fight, with Zanishiria easily following.

For three minutes, the two assassins kept up their dance until Zanishiria managed to skip her sword into Seircor's space. They froze with her blade at his throat, then she calmly stepped away and bowed gracefully. She came up to the observing Royal. "All is fluid, all is like water. The movements take on the energy of the form, adapting to any and all nuances. Within every form, there is the non-form. By knowing the first, you can become the second. All you need to do is let the forms take you until all you need to do is react. Study the forms you have learned and you will begin to see where these changes occur."

"That was absolutely mesmerizing." Anmero replied. His mind was spinning with the visions of the two assassins fighting. Awe came to him as he realized he had just learned every move the two of them had gone through. They were the same movements Seircor had just taught him. "You know, I think I'm beginning to understand now."

"Good." Seircor walked over and handed back the sword he had given the prince to borrow. "Then we will start where we left off." He paused long enough to thank Zanishiria. "Kree eis shi'tai. Kye mureak, Zan." ["You make a great teacher, I thank you."]

Zanishiria bowed in thanks and stepped away to leave Anmero alone to his lesson. She returned to the pile of belongings they had set at their lunch spot and picked up a leather bag from her belongings before heading over to a tiny, flat-topped outcropping overlooking the two young men. She sat down cross-legged and opened the small pouch. The long, scales-smoothed-down whip, in natural black with red tips, dropped into her palm and onto the obsidian stone. Just the sight of the powerful weapon stopped Zanishiria's breathe. She carefully ran her fingers down the familiar snakeskin scaling, knowing caution was needed over the sharp edges. She finally wrapped her hand around the smooth handle, feeling the weight of the nearly-twenty-foot-length. Feeling the need to dance with her deadly weapon, she stood and released its coils.

If one has never heard the sound of a preshair whip, they will never forget it again. Its sharp crack echoes menacingly down the obsidian tunnels, and the sound of the scales scraping against one another sends a chill down a human's spine, as they mimic the actual sound of a preshair as it hunts its prey. Zanishiria knew these details intimately and when she swung her whip around she was careful to keep the noise to a minimum. Yet, the distinctive crack still caused Anmero and Seircor to jump in surprise.

Seircor felt his muscles bunch as the sharp sound of the whip caused his already heightened senses to double. For just a moment, he was afraid that the very creature who the sound mimicked was in the cavern, but, just as soon, Seircor was able to rationalize what he had heard. Slowly, he forced himself to relax and looked up to where Zanishiria's silhouette stood out against the black obsidian wall. His young friend stood poised and haloed in the essence of her own prowess atop a towering outcropping. For that moment, Seircor marveled at how changed and confident Zanishiria appeared. Her true self seemed to come forth.

Anmero, however, shook next to Seircor, still enthralled by the sharp sound of the whip as its crack continued to echo against the walls. The Lakean reached over to steady him. "The sound of a preshair whip is to be feared." Seircor said, still glancing at Zanishiria. Anmero followed his grey gaze to where the girl stood. "Take a good look, Prince Anmero, for this will be the only time you may see the preshair whip when it is not being used on our enemies."

A quiet knock resounded on the master's door. Master Quinn glanced up from the book he was studying. "Now who would that be at this hour?" He mumbled as he stood and crossed over to the door. The knock came again, more urgently. By then, Master Quinn had reached the door and was unlocking it. He it and glanced out into the darkened hallway. "Oh, Roko, Sunashi, please come in." Master Quinn ushered his fellow masters in and closed the door after them, after checking down the hallway. "I assume you have something important to say if you're here at three-ten in the morning?"

"We do, Quinn." Master Roko replied. The smaller, spikey-chestnut-haired assassin glanced around Master Quinn's quarters before sitting down on his bedroll. "We bring news on the Renegade army." He paused and waited until both men sat down before continuing. "It would seem that the Renegades have overtaken the Royal guards at the border between Shaytyar and Bialthioum. My sources tell me that they will be making a final push into Taysor tomorrow."

"We do not quite know when, though." Master Sunashi continued. "There hasn't been any reason for them to come into Taysor so quickly. Before, they had planned to move at a pace that would enable them to take away the guards' positions strategically, but this time, it seems they want to forgo caution and attack the capitol directly. There is some unseen deadline we are unaware about?" Sunashi noticed that Master Quinn seemed unconcerned with the change. Irritated, he said, "This isn't a humorous situation, Quinn."

Master Quinn rose an eyebrow. "I'm not laughing."

"Then look a little concerned." Sunashi berated. "You know that with the council as fragile as it is, that even as a part of the Legion, we will not be able to help out our allies. If they still are our allies. Why were we not informed on this new development?"

"It is not just the council that is close to breaking." Master Quinn reminded gently. He leaned back against the wall and looked at the other masters calmly. Sunashi shifted impatiently across from Quinn, as Roko, the exact opposite, sat meditating. "I'm sure that you both know that Manscor is becoming increasing agitated."

"Of course, Quinn. He knows the Renegades are at his doorstep ready to take him down."

Master Quinn frowned at Sunashi. "I am not talking about the Renegade army. King Lapsair has been causing enough problems here at the capitol that he has caused the emperor to deal with the fires he has created—which have no direct ties to the Royal king but are from him nonetheless. Manscor cannot find reason to implicate Lapsair but he certainly wishes to."

"I am surprised Manscor hasn't sent orders to assassinate Lapsair." Master Roko said.

"Yes, I am as well." Quinn agreed.

Master Roko smiled slyly at Quinn. "Corsetti tells me that there is another distraction, too."

"There have been many distractions to--."

"Oh, do tell." Roko interrupted. "I have known you long enough to tell when you are keeping things from us."

Sunashi seemed to liven up. "Ooh, the great Quinn must have become a defect." [Defect= tear away from the Assassins' Guild, in this case opposing the Emperor (and the Guild's rules).]

"Sunashi," Master Roko glared at the younger master menacingly. "Master Quinn has not defected. He is too smart to do that." He glanced back at Quinn. "But, I bet you are protecting someone who has."

"Really?" Sunashi eyes Quinn expectantly. "Do tell, do tell."

By now, the usually calm master was getting irked. Master Quinn risked a look at his clock and saw that eight minutes had passed. Silently, he was cursing himself for letting Sunashi in and then he was angry at himself for being mad. Realizing the two masters were still waiting for an answer, he straightened and allowed his eyes to meet Roko's "It is Zanishiria, and, no, she has not defected." He glared at Sunashi. "She has just gotten herself mixed up in something I knew she would not be able to evade forever."

Roko nodded in understanding. "She could not escape the fighting between the Royals, since she is a Novastone. I'm sure that you know as well as I, that now that she is involved, she could very well be called a defect by the council. If she is, it would mean a certain banishment from the Guild."

"I know." Quinn said softly, though he withheld the truth of the matter. Master Quinn was privy to Zanishiria's real identity, and she was far more important than any Royal to the cause of Obseen. "But, she is far too good a fighter to simply ignore like that. That is why I have been telling Sye to hold off on the finger pointing, at least for now."

"There is more." Roko coaxed.

Quinn frowned. "There has been unrest in the council. I fear there is more amiss than we know. I am sure you both are aware that Manscor has given Master Teera the permission to overrule a decision made by the Senior Mater. If Sye cannot stop or counteract Teera, there will be more than just a petty squabble amidst the council members. The council will be divided, and I am sure all hell would break loose."

"Yes, yes." Master Sunashi agreed.

"Interesting," Master Roko nodded. "Young Tarin said the same thing to me earlier. He had come by because he feared his master was doing something of the sort. He believed the council will revolt and cause chaos amongst themselves." On a second thought he added, "He also said he fears for Zanishiria."

Master Quinn straightened considerably. "What about Zan?"

"Tarin informed me that his master told him to "deal" with his friend." Master Roko glanced away from Quinn's piercing gaze. "He didn't tell me much on that subject, but what he did express has me concerned."

Master Quinn was on his feet in a second and was already reaching for his door. He was gone just as quickly, leaving a bewildered Roko and Sunashi behind. He turned left down the hallway and strode purposely down the steps to the lower levels. Quinn continued across the enormous training areas of the Naitiege section and entered the highly-decorated halls leading to their living quarters. Master Quinn walked to the end and stopped at Tarin's door. He rapped twice and waited for the groggy young man to open the door. "May I come in a moment?" He asked softly.

Tarin blinked away the sleep from his eyes and waved the master through. He glanced quickly at the clock above his window and turned irritably to Master Quinn. "Master, what do you want at three-forty-five in the morning?"

Master Quinn took a once-over at Tarin, seeing the weariness in the tall, blond haired youth's chiseled features. He decided he would be brief. "I just need to know what Master Teera told you to do about Zanishiria Novastone."

Tarin's blue eyes cleared completely at the mention of his friend. "She didn't tell me much."

"Then just repeat what she said, if you would." Master Quinn coaxed.

"I guess I can do that." Tarin sank onto his bed roll and offered the master a seat at his study desk. He picked up his shirt and slipped it on before starting. "Master came to me yesterday with the order to "learn more about Zanishiria's past" and to "question her to find out if she or her family have defected from the Guild's codes"." He paused and glanced down at his balled-up hands. "She told me that if I were to see Zan again and find out that she has indeed defected to the Resistance I am to either take her captive or kill her, depending on how Zan responds to orders of being taken infront of the council." This last little bit of information was forced. Tarin continued. "Master Teera has never liked Zan, but this is absurd! She cannot expect me to do this to my best friend all because she is concerned that the Novastones are in on some plot. Which they aren't, I strongly hope." Tarin glanced up at Mater Quinn with hard blue eyes. "I can't make an enemy of Zan."

Master Quinn sat back and thought over what the young man had said. "So, she does think Zanishiria—or more aptly the Novastones—are a threat to Manscor." He mumbled. "Tell me, Tarin, did Teera say anything of this to the council?"

Tarin knitted his eyebrows in thought then nodded. "She seemed pleased after her talk with the emperor. It seems Manscor has given her authority over something, though I do not know what that might be. If she had enough power, she could easily convince the council that Zan has done something very wrong—and that the Novastones are in it with her." Tarin paused, unsure if he wanted the answer to the question in his mind. Finally, he asked, "Do you think my master has that kind of power, Master Quinn?"

It took a moment for Master Quinn to realize Tarin had spoken. He had been too busy digesting everything the Neitiege had said. "Master Teera is the Emperor's Honored-one, as you already know, so she has always had greater power than most in the Guild; however, if she were given a position of control over the Guild greater than she wields now, I fear she could do much worse to any she sees as an enemy. If your master sets her sights on Zanishiria, your friend would have no power against her if Sye Rainier is ousted from her position as Senior Master."

"Can Senior Master Rainier really be taken down like that?" Tarin asked, shocked. The Guild-head position was given by vote of the Seventy-two high clansmen and never before by a single person (though that had been before Emperor Manscor had taken control of Obseen).

Master Quinn studied Tarin warily. He was very reluctant to tell the youth anything. "You cannot get involved with any of this. If you learned something your master did not want you to know, she will not hesitate to torture or even kill you for information."

Tarin kept his face calm, though his eyes betrayed his concerns. Tarin's countenance shifted, and he stared back at the master. "It is a risk I must take. I need to know what is going on. I have gone about my life sheltered within these walls and following what I was told. I have reached an age where doing such leaves me a bumbling, ignorant apprentice not worthy of serving my master let alone the Guild."

Master Quinn felt his respect for the young man grow at the admittance of his flaws. He didn't say this to the other assassin, however. "Ignorance is one thing; loyalty another. It seems to me these orders your master gives splits you in two."

Tarin nodded and his blue eyes looked distant. "Zan...she isn't really involved in the Resistance, is she?" He said the words more as if he was trying to not believe them but suspecting they spoke the truth. Quinn knew better than to affirm or deny that truth. "She told me once, when I first met Zan, that 'she is the only one who can save her people from the evils of this world'. The statement was a little nonsensical, but I believe she believed what she said back then." Tarin sat up straighter, gathering strength. "But Zan is a Royal. What evil could she possibly be referring to? Manscor? The Novastones have only ever been loyal to his rule." He shook his blonde head tiredly as his mind worked through everything. "I don't know why my master is suspicious of Zan but if I can protect her from some unjust wrath from Master Sabina, I will try to do so."

Silence followed and settled between the two assassins. The clock above the window changed to four and movement from the hallway signaled the waking of some of the older assassins. Tarin's gaze shifted to the window where the first traces of dawn lighted the distant tarol trees in an orchid hue. Red splashed the orchid, turning to crimson. "Bloodstains" is what Zanishiria had called them. Today, they were darker, more ominous.

Master Quinn let go a breathy sigh and stood. "I see you are very set on this." Tarin stood as well and nodded. "I do not have to tell you this will not be easy, as you are caught between two loyalties. However, I have seen you to be a man of honor. You have shown that you can walk fine lines and still keep the truth in order. If you are indeed ready to leave your sheltered life then I would have you learn the sides of it you have yet to know. Take this book," Quinn reached into his robes and pulled out a small, leather-bound codex. "It is a journal of mine. In it, I have written about the wars of Obseen that I have lived through. It is from my perspective of it, but from a view you have yet to come across. This Royals' War has been the most gruesome in our history. Learn of it and its people from my eyes and glean from it what you will. Decide for yourself where you belong within it."

Master Quinn rose and settled his robes about his person. "Now, though, I must be elsewhere. There has been rumor that the Renegade army was spotted just hours from Taysor Valley." He gave the youth a direct, serious look. "If this is true, you need to be ready for the Guild to become a madhouse." Tarin's eyes widened in shock at the information. He opened his mouth to ask what the elder master knew but the Baras man turned away, unwilling to trap Master Sabina's apprentice in such entanglements. Master Quinn paused at the doorway and turned back to Tarin. "Come to me in one hour if you have questions about my journal and I will tell you anything you are ready to hear." He lay a hand on the youth's shoulder. "But be careful, young Saerric. These times will become more difficult than you can imagine."

Master Teera left the council chamber with an evil glint in her eye. She let loose a harsh laugh that echoed sinisterly even to the shadows. The Suez stalked away. Master Teera finally found Senior Master Sye Rainier in the large garden behind the training center's back entrance. The younger woman sat on a finely sculpted border around one of the fountains.

"Oh, well isn't that a pretty spectacle." Master Teera said with little gaiety.

Sye Rainier glanced up and gazed back at the woman blankly. "Pretty isn't in you vocabulary."

Master Teera raised her eyebrows in mock surprise. "Oh, you're absolutely right. Would it be better if I had said bloody, instead?"

A sour look passed the senior master's lovely face. "Drop the act, Teera, it's not working."

"Act? I'm not acting but whatever I'm doing it seems to be working on you quite well."

"Enough, Teera." Sye stood, fingering a small dagger in her hand. She played with the weight a moment before aiming it at the other master's face. Teera caught the weapon just before it touched her skin. "I've already heard what happened today in the council chambers. All you came to do is rub you victory in my face."

"I came here not just to rub my new position in your face." Master Teera threw the dagger into the fountain and sat down on the marble ledge. "The decision concerning your apprentice has been resolved." Sye glanced at Teera from the corner of her golden-brown eye. "She's a defect, as I'm sure you've known. If she is seen again, she'll be told to enter the caves. If she does not take to her banishment, then she will be killed on the spot. I want you to be the one to tell her, Senior Master."

Sye Rainier's eyes widened in astonishment. "Me! Tell my apprentice that she is banished? You're crazy. And, how do you expect the Royals will take one of their own being cast into the deadly bowels of Obseen? There is sure to be discord over this."

"You're the Senior Master of Taysor. Just consider it one of your duties you're still allowed to impart. Use your superior negotiating skills to smooth things over on all ends." Master Teera started to walk away. "Besides, Zanishiria only listens to you." She called back over her shoulder.

"Yeah, right." Sye scoffed to herself. "If only that were true. Zanishiria doesn't take orders from anyone, least of all myself, as proved hundreds of times this year." The Senior Master gazed into the pristine waters wishing there was a simple resolution to the situation; however, no matter what she thought, it seemed there would be anger and betrayal any which way.

They exited the caves just as the first of the suns topped the valley hills. They came from the waterfall entrance farthest from the city proper in Taysor Gulch. Anmero was surprised at the water's thundering veil that plunged twenty-feet-down from the slippery ledge they stood on. It started another twenty-five feet above them and crashed to the small lake far below.

"Come this way, Anmero." Zanishiria called up from her place far below. The assassin had almost reached the bottom, and her Lakean friend was not far behind.

"I'm coming." He shouted back. "If I don't kill myself first." He began to make his way down the slicked surface, praying softly that he would not slip on the wet stones and plunge to his dead. With Anmero muttering to himself, he didn't realize he had reached the base of the falls until Seircor handed him a water pouch. "Thanks." Seircor murmured an "uh huh" and turned away from the prince to speak with Zanishiria.

"Shay, Praic, shre lai na'ey cor?" Zanishiria said in Lakean, with her back turned from Anmero so the prince would not see them talking. [Shayso=hello, shay=hey; "Hey, Praic, are you allowed to come up here?"]

Seircor lay a hand gently on her shoulder. "Osho, lá seimreal lei kye'er." ["No [it's okay], the council sent me] for knowledge."]

"Itai." ["I see."]

"Hey, what are you two whispering over there?" Anmero asked. "Didn't we agree to no more conferences without me?"

"Yes, your highness." Zanishiria waved the prince over. "Do you see that palace barely visible down the gulch?"

"Ah, yeah." Prince Anmero squinted at the tiny palace in the distance.

"That is the Taysor Palace where the Royals stay. King Lapsair is waiting for us there. We need to make it there within an hour, which means you need to keep up. We cannot linger if we are to avoid detection."

"Hey, don't worry. I've kept up this far, haven't I?'

Zanishiria gave a skeptical look to the prince and leapt off the ledge. She began to run, or hop more precisely, down the boulder field. In seconds, she had left the two men behind.

"Oh, well that's a different story." Anmero eyed the boulders doubtfully. "Well, if I kill myself, you won't have to be concerned with me anymore."

"That won't happen, prince. Let us go." Seircor kept pace with the Royal as they hopped down the boulder field. In little less than an hour, the threesome met at the end of the gulch. The young assassin had waited in the crack of a large boulder, keeping watch for danger as the two young men came her way. Then, Zanishiria led them through a maze of boulders and tarn bushes until they reached the shiny crystal-and-obsidian-stone walls of the near side of the gigantic palace. Seircor pressed against the side next to her with Anmero on the other side.

"Is it safe here, Zan?" Seircor whispered.

"Yes, for now." Zanishiria glanced around. "We are safe on this side of the palace. Manscor lives of the north side, and his forces do not patrol over here very often."

"Are you sure?" Anmero asked.

"Yes. You could live in Taysor Palace for a year and never run into all its occupants, unless they live in your quarter of the palace."

"A quarter?" Anmero glanced along the intricate palace face.

"I'll explain another time." Zanishiria glanced around one last time. "We're clear." She motioned them forward to a large, sculpted door and slowly pulled it open. She squeezed through and checked around. "Come in, quickly." The assassin waved them passed. "King Lapsair will be waiting."

* * *

King Lapsair smiled broadly as his visitors filed into his private study. "Welcome back, Zan. I see you have brought the prince safely."

"Well as safely as expected traveling the caves." Zanishiria bowed. "This is Prince Anmero Doz, Your Highness and this other man is my Las'wa friend, Seircor C'vail."

King Lapsair stood up from his jewel-adorned chair to shake Anmero's hand. He then turned to Seircor. "Oshay, Seircor C'vail. Lai syhom ay'sh." ["Hello, Seircor. Your presence is welcome here any time."]

"Kye reyh'or." Seircor bowed. ["I am honored."]

King Lapsair returned the assassin's bow then returned to Zanishiria. "A lot has happened in the week you have been gone. The Renegades will surely reach Taysor by nightfall. Manscor had hurried an assembly of his guards to counter them, but they may not amass quickly enough."

"And what of the council?"

"The news is not good, I'm afraid." The elder king's face grew sad. "You were right to think that Manscor would grant Teera Sabina the power to override the Senior Master. She had forced the council against you as well. You have been deemed a defect and are to be banished."

"It is no less than I would expect." Zanishiria turned away to walk over to the large picture window to gaze out at the waking city beyond. "The day has come, Your Highness."

"Zan..." King Lapsair's voice trailed off.

"We cannot wait any longer, King Lapsair. I was sent here for a reason, now I must fulfill my mission." The assassin turned back to the others. "If I do not, more assassins and Royals will die under Manscor's rule. The attack on the capitol will give the emperor all the reasons to massacre entire clans, so we need to make sure everything we do today does not fail."

"Seimora." Seircor stepped forward. "May I accompany you?"

Zanishiria knew Seircor's reasons for his request. He had been one of the original preshans after all; however, she did not want to see her friend put through the cost she feared coming with her would bring to him. She shook her head resolutely. "No, Seircor, you may not." She used his formal name to emphasis her point. Seircor's eyes twitched in surprise but he kept his face blank. "I need you to do something more important to me, Praic. You must protect Anmero. If he dies, than the hopes of the

Royals' future will be damaged as well. Too many Royals are fighting against the emperor. We need at least one Royal to live through this. Also," Zanishiria lay a hand on her friend's forearm. "If I do not survive my encounter with the emperor, then you must continue the mission in my place."

Seircor's jaw clenched but he held his tongue. "You will not die, seimora." Softly, he whispered. "You mustn't die."

"There are no guarantees in a battle to the death. Fate does side with the emperor half way." Zanishiria replied bluntly. She felt her friend's hand tighten over hers. "Kye moreay, seimie, sey vermon resoum lei seim'kye tor'na." ["I am sorry, my friend, but if that is to be my destiny then nothing can stop it from happening."]

"Please, do not talk of destiny, not now." Anguish filled the Las'wa's voice.

King Lapsair ushered Anmero out of the room and quietly shut the door. It only felt right that he give the two friends some time alone. Besides, he himself was feeling the weight of the situation coming down around his shoulders like a cloak. It didn't seem right that a young, fourteen-year-old girl be used as a weapon to kill the emperor, especially when the king had found the young assassin to be quite an exceptional person; however, nothing had been right with the Royals' War.

"What is going on?" Anmero demanded. "Tell me, please. Assassins do not just fall apart like that. What mission were they talking about?"

King Lapsair lay a calming hand on the handsome prince's shoulder. "Easy, boy. I will tell you." He paused and steadied his wrenching heart. "Zanishiria was sent here by her people to kill Emperor Manscor. She has been here for a year gathering information on the emperor and preparing herself. Now, the Renegade army is attacking Taysor, as a decoy, to give Zanishiria the opportunity she needs to go after him."

"She believes she will die, doesn't she?" Anmero asked.

"She is prepared for such an end, if she becomes injured enough. Fighting the emperor will not be easy. He is a seasoned fighter; however, Zanishiria has been trained for this since she was three. She will do whatever is needed to take him out."

"But she doesn't have to throw her life away like it's nothing!" Anmero knocked the king's hand aside and backed away.

"This is the assassin's way, Anmero. These people live by the rules of the fighting square. Duels for superiority are a normal. That was how the emperor gained his power in the first place. Zanishiria will challenge him on the square as many have done before. However, she is going to give up everything to make sure the emperor does not return from this fight…she knows that such a feat will not come without great cost to herself. She has had the time to come to terms with that."

"It's a suicide mission, then, and she knows that! How stupid that is, to throw her life away as if it is worth so little. Zan doesn't have to do that; there are other ways, many other ways, for the emperor to be taken down. It doesn't have to be her!"

The king looked sad. "She made this choice, Anmero. All of her family was killed by the emperor. She is the only Coursay'sora left. This was her promise to them, and to the future assassins of this planet, to take the emperor down. It is all she desires now."

Anmero growled at the insanity of her logic. "No. She may have made the choice, but I will not believe it is the only one, or the right one, for her to take. I see that there are those who would not wish her dead. Can she not see that? You should be asking her to live, not die. That is what you and she should desire."

"Anmero—."

The prince wasn't listening. The thought of the talented assassin going willingly to her death had his blood boiling. Angered, Anmero turned away; he didn't know where he was going, but he knew he did not want to stay where he was. He would not stand there quietly as the events began to unfold. Finally he chose an empty bedroom to reside in and slammed the heavy door in his anger and anguish. Vehemently, he flung pillows setting on a long couch against the walls, venting his frustration before falling in an exhausted pile on the floor. "Stupid assassins…. selfless martyr…."

Some time went by before the door opened quietly. Anmero did not look up to see who had come in but he had a guess. A gentle but steadying hand touched his shoulder and squeezed in sympathy. Zanishiria lowered herself to a sitting position next to the prince. Softly, she began to sing in Lakean. Her voice was so soothing and pretty that it startled Anmero out of his reverie. The words were unknown to him, but the whispering, calming sounds were alluring. Finally, Anmero straightened and met the assassin's eyes. "That song...it's beautiful."

Zanishiria let her voice fade away and smiled. "It is called "The Flowing waters" in Las'wa. I used to sing it all the time when I was a little girl."

Anmero saw a wistful look cross the girl's serene face. "You must come back, Zanishiria. After all, there are many who are here wanting you to live. If you do not, then your mission fails."

"No, not failed, prince. You and all those I hold dear, and many innocents of this war will still be here. That is why I took this mission—to save this world more pain. No more should have to suffer as I have." Zanishiria forged ahead before Anmero could say anything. "I'm not planning on dying, prince, but I have to be realistic. Not many people go against the 'man killer' and live. Yet, he needs to be taken down if Obseen is to live free of such tyranny. I must try, Anmero, for everything that I hold dear..."

Chapter Nine

Sa noreay lâ taysor
Reneiy re saigh'nlay
Shey ne rye so'me
Sa norey lâ saysor
Tashay lâ shorie'ya
Shy'ne lâ taysors
[So flows the river> running with swiftness> through the
stony caves>
So flows the waters> colors of crystal> down the
waterfalls.]

Saysors norey nore kye
Tashay shaw kye re renih'norey
Slai kye shaw lai renih'norey
Là re rye coursa bei
Ar'she là traicors
Va sevyei na shasor.
[Waters flow over me> colors tell me a story> Come, I'll
tell you a story>
From the darkness deep> that speak of dangers> and
secrets untold]

For over thirteen years Manscor ruled Obseen with impunity, yet... opposing assassins and Royals devised plans to overthrow the emperor. Finally, they concluded that an army of elite warriors could be the answer to taking down the ruler. The resistance sent word to the Las'wa clan to create these assassins, then they left the Lakeans alone to create these weapons.

The Las'wa high council picked thirteen young—some even only five-years-old—children and began to run them through intensive training. Eleven looked promising, while two others died from illness and injury, the last did not complete his training. The seimreal knew that picking two more preshans to replace the deceased would take too long, so, though it was considered a bad omen, they did not search out other protégés.

However, one of the masters, Mater Tyracor, had his own apprentice, a young girl, and sister to one of the preshans. This girl, trained in the rare techniques of the preshair whip, was accepted to the preshan group just a few weeks before the small group was sent off to the surface. Making the preshan assassination force number twelve, the Las'wa youths were sent forth as new weapons to aid in the war against the emperor.

With the crimson dawn came the spilling of yet more blood; Royal Qusairo knew this well and, for once in his life, he wished he could will the dawn to come slower. Asilisa stirred from her sleep next to him, her green eyes glancing up into his. "You didn't sleep well."

"No, I didn't." Qusairo tried to force a smile that refused to come. He lifted a hand to touch his wife's beautiful face before letting his eyes drift back to the approaching dawn. "I was thinking: do you think Anmero is safe from this chaos I've created?"

"You did not create this." Asilisa enervated his words. "And, you know that the Las'wa are the best bodyguards, so our son will be fine."

"I know." Qusairo sighed and ran a hand through his dark hair. "I just have a bad feeling about this upcoming battle."

Asilisa sat up and hugged her husband from behind. "Foreshadowing isn't something to think of. You'll be fine. I had a dream last night that you and the Renegades were victorious; your flag hung over Taysor."

"I hope you're right, sweetheart." The Royal leaned back against his wife for a moment, savoring her scent and love, before reluctantly pulling away. "I must go now." The Dozes stood and Qusairo readied himself for battle. Asilisa personally handed him his scabbard containing his prized sword. They kissed once, long and lingering, before Royal Qusairo turned and headed out to meet his forces.

The Renegade leader strode purposely through the numerous tents, pushing aside his doubts. He topped the hill and the sight of Taysor Valley spread out before him. His commanding assassin officer, Shy'ree, joined him quietly. "Is all well?"

"Yes, Royal Qusairo." Shy'ree bowed her head, her long black hair hiding her face. Soon, it would be tied back in a braid, but for now she left it free to feel the wind blow through it. "All that is needed has been prepared, sir."

"Then I won't keep them waiting." Qusairo joined his large army, with Shy'ree at his side. His soldiers stood at ready, awaiting his orders. "We will strike out with the sun growing behind us. Tonight, we feast in Taysor!" A yell arose from the fighters and the many units began to disperse. The army would move with caution, fighting where ever they encountered the Royal guard or Honored assassin forces. With luck, they would make the palace by nightfall.

The ground around her feet was red, as was the sky above. A scarlet pool was to her left. In her dream, Sye Rainier walked closer to the pool. "No, it's not water!" She realized in horror. "It's blood." And there was a lot of it. It flowed steadily from the cliff above, forming a waterfall. Sye gulped and hesitantly began to climb up the cliff to see where the blood was coming from.

Sye froze in terror at the spectacle in front of her. Hundreds of corpses piled on top of each other dripped blood from their wounds. The dark liquid formed a stream toward the cliff. The Senior Master started to look away, trying to keep herself from retching. Her eyes caught sight of a man standing above something curled at his feet. Curiosity overcame Sye's fear, and she crawled closer to the man.

The man turned then and thrust his sword into the ground beside him. Sye shivered. Emperor Manscor stood there, gloating. The "man killer" raised a gleaming knife above his head and brought it down on the thing, no person, below him. The person writhed for a moment in pain then went still. Manscor turned to Sye, as if he had expected her there and waved her forward. Sye wanted to scream but no words reached her throat—and yet her feet moved on their own accord toward the evil man.

As she neared, the person who Manscor had stabbed took shape. The girl was barely recognizable but Sye realized whom she was. With horror, she blanched. Zanishiria's face was bruised and bleeding from numerous cuts and the skin on the right cheek, from her eyebrow to ear to chin, was peeled away to reveal the structures beneath. Blood dropped into Zanishiria's grey eyes, filling them with red and soaking her clothes like tears. Her clothes hung in tatters, revealing more wounds beneath. The young assassin's right arm was nearly severed and her legs had been shattered. Sye's eyes lingered over the sight of her poor apprentice before she moved higher to the knife that Manscor had used to stab Zanishiria's heart with. Somehow, the girl's heart still beat!

Zanishiria lifted her left hand and reached out to Sye, crying, "You could have saved me, master, but you didn't even try! You could have stopped Manscor, yet, as always, you are too late! I hope you suffer for eternity!" With her last cry, she twisted the knife in her chest and yanked it out. Zanishiria discarded the still thumping heart from the blade and prepared the knife to throw at her master. Sye backed away screaming her innocence, but Zanishiria stood up and stalked her. The girl continued closer, stepping on ankles unable to support her weight. "Die!" She cried and threw the weapon at her master.

Sye screamed loudly and willed herself to sit up. Her muscles finally moved and she was able to wake from her nightmare. Red light from the dawn filtered through her window, lighting her sheets in its color. Panicked still from her dream, Sye pushed her sweat-soaked sheets away as if they were cursed. She pulled her knees to her chest and hid her face until her heart stopped its crazy beating. Sye finally stood and walked to her window. The light of morning could not stop the Senior Master's shivering, however, and Sye picked up her black robe to pull it close around herself.

The sound of running feet in the hallway turned Sye's attention from the window and ventured her to the door. A knock sounded at that the next instant, startling Sye. Quickly composing herself, she pulled the door open. Her master stood outside already dressed and wide awake. Master Quinn glanced over his apprentice with a critical eye. Rarely did he miss anything going on with his former apprentice. Did he see the fear still in her eyes? Sye blushed under her master's stare and wrapped her robe around herself tighter, covering up her wet and clinging clothes.

"What is it, Master?"

Master Quinn had the look of being preoccupied, yet he answered Sye's question. "All assassins have been called to the

main room. The Resistance is attacking the outskirts of the city."
Master Quinn shifted anxiously, ready to be away. "I just
thought you would want to know."

Sye immediately forgot her nightmare. "I thank you,
Master." She turned to re-entered her quarters, but paused at the
threshold. "Master Quinn," She called after her elder. Quinn
turned back to his apprentice. "What of Zanishiria? I know you
keep track of her. Is she here?"

Master Quinn hesitated, then smiled and shrugged. "She
is where she is supposed to be."

"She's a part of the Resistance, isn't she?" Sye declared.

"No..." Master Quinn countered. "She fights only for her
own people. She will not take part in the battle with the Royal
guards and the Renegades."

"But she will fight."

Master Quinn turned away. "She has her own part to
play in this war. That is all you need to know."

Sye watched as her master disappeared down the
hallway. Slowly, she became aware of the other assassins who
stared at her as they passed. Disgruntled, she pulled her robes
around herself tighter, scowled at the onlookers, and pushed
through the door into her quarters. "Quite tight-lipped today,
aren't we, Quinn?" She grumbled as she pulled a tunic and pants
on. "I have a right to know where my apprentice has run off to,
you know." She stopped dressing as she recollected her thoughts.
Only then did the Senior Master go over her conversation with
her master. "What part does Zan have in this war, then?" The
question nagged at the edge of her consciousness until, suddenly,
it wandered into her thoughts. There was only one place in the
war Zanishiria could be of most use to the Royals and
Renegades. The prospect chilled Sye. "I need to stop her!" She
thought desperately. Sye scrambled to finish dressing and
collected her weapons. She ran out the doorway in a panic.

The nightmare followed her, making her plight even
more desperate. Even still, it refused to dissipate at Sye's will.
Sye rushed though the winding halls and spacious training levels,
always heading for the northern entrance, knowing that she
needed to intercept Zanishiria before she reached Taysor
Palace—before she reached Manscor. How she would stop her
was another matter, but Sye was only thinking of the former
problem. She surmised she would do whatever it took to stop
Zanishiria from reaching the emperor.

* * *

The sound of a distant battle echoed through the buildings of the great city as Zanishiria led Anmero and Seircor through its maze. She kept to the shadows and away from the fighting, circling around to reach the Renegade army. Finally, she stopped and motioned Seircor to her side. "There is Shy'ree." Zanishiria pointed out the assassin fighter in the mist of the battle in the square in front of them. "She is Qusairo's protector. She will lead you to the Royal."

"I will have to wait for the fighting to move up the street." Seircor analyzed.

"Yes," Zanishiria agreed. "The Renegades prefer to have two waves. They attack first and pull back so another group can take over. They should change soon. You can go then. Shy'ree will know why you come if you use siihshe." Zanishiria knew she was supplying more information than her friend needed but it was more for the prince's benefit, anyway.

The three watched as the battle continued. Shy'ree's forces easily pushed back the Royal guard. Only a few of her forces fell to enemy fire, yet the other side suffered heavier losses; the Renegades showed to be more superior. For every man killed by the Royal guard, eight of their own would fall. In a short time, the Renegades had the guards pushed back to the edge of the square. Only half of the guard was left. It was then that the dark-haired assassin woman lifted her hand in signal to retreat, and her fighters quickly pulled back. The second wave came in like shadows of the main force and took up the vacancies. The switch was complete and effortless and took only a matter of seconds.

"Go now." Zanishiria whispered to her companions. Seircor was standing instantly but the prince hesitated. "Remember your promise." Anmero whispered in Zanishiria's ear. Before she could protest, he wrapped his arms around her in a quick hug before hurrying after his assassin bodyguard.

Zanishiria watched Anmero go. A soft fondness came to her eyes as she watched her two companions reach Shy'ree's side and shuffle away with the woman. "May you both survive and live a life you have always wanted." Sadness overcame the young assassin and she tore her gaze away from her friends. "Be safe, always. Good-bye, my friends. Good-bye."

* * *

The higher-level trainees were ordered to the main fighting square. They gathered around the room and listened attentively to their instructions, given by the Assassins' Guild leaders. Weapons were distributed throughout the group. Tension fell heavily in the room, suffocating the young assassins. Everyone was acutely aware of what was going on, but the prospect of fighting other assassins, some that may be from the same clan or even family, was not easy to stomach.

Tarin Saerric unsheathed his Neitiege sword and studied it critically. His sword had always been his own, created specifically for himself when he was born. It was still as sharp and strong as it had been eighteen years ago, on its creation. Tarin stared at his reflection and noted the silent despair that shadowed his eyes. His talk with Master Quinn earlier still played in his head, making him feel like a trapped animal. The journal had made matters worse. Such atrocities the Baras master had witnessed seemed surreal to the life he had been witness to; they were lives cut from such different cloth Tarin almost didn't believe; however, it had made him understand why K'sho had pleaded for his friend's silence. What Tarin was about to do worn at his nerves, but he knew he had to do it for K'sho's sake. The young Neitiege resheathed his sword and glanced over to his companion. K'sho Rease was silent next to his taller friend; he has not said a single word all morning. Now, he played with the hilt of his sword as if to distract himself from something. "Are you all right?" Tarin asked, uncomfortable with silence between them.

K'sho glanced up as if surprised with the question. "Of course." He did not embellish. Tarin continued to eye his friend until K'sho resigned. "So, I am not all right."

Tarin usually did not press anyone for details, but he could tell that now was a time that he needed to. "You are troubled." He prodded gently.

K'sho glanced around the room cautiously. If it had not been for the fact that they were at the back of the room and away from eavesdroppers, he probably would not have said anything of his thoughts, but Tarin was his friend. "I have already told you of this before."

"Your disliking of our leader?" Tarin guessed, trying to keep from saying the emperor's name out loud where others would hear.

"Yes, that." K'sho fiddled with his sword again, nervously. "I've thought long and hard about it. I can't go on following the orders of a blood thirsty, spoiled rotten..." he didn't fill in the word. K'sho paused. Tarin strained to hear his last words. "Therefore, I've decided to join the other side today."

K'sho glanced up as if he was expecting Tarin to gasp at his audacity or call out to the others in the room that they had a deserter. Tarin did neither. His handsome face was filled with a different, surprising look. Was it relief? K'sho was not sure. Tarin closed his eyes and gave a diminutive, thoughtful smile. "I thought you would do as much, and I'm pleased with your decision. It was never right or honorable for you to fight against your own people or serve the man whom killed your mother."

K'sho was struck with relief at his friend's words. Could it be some outside influence that Tarin had come to realize how malicious the emperor actually was, or was Tarin just being very thoughtful to his friend? Tarin was the first to speak, as if he had read his friend's mind. "Master Quinn came to me early this morning. He filled me in on some history I was not aware of..." Tarin looked out into the crowd without seeing the others there. "I have thought about this for days now, since our talk, and have come to the conclusion that we must all fight where we believe we are supposed to...and not ordered to be." Tarin's eyes cleared and he glanced back at K'sho. "Zanishiria has her own part to play, of that I have become certain. For why else would she be gone from this Center when events are playing out as they are? Despite that I am torn between duty and friendship, I want to help her, if such a path is available to me without damaging my oath to my clan and the Guild..." He paused and said quietly, "As for you, my friend, I will take you first to the Renegade army. Then, I will go find our friend and ask her what I need to know."

K'sho gaped in surprise. He nearly dropped his sword but quickly recovered it. "You would go against your master?"

"I am not going against my master." Tarin straightened and motioned for K'sho to follow the stream of assassins out of the training center to fight against the Renegade army. "I'm keeping my loyalties to my friends and to the Guild." He finished. Quietly, he motioned for the tarn bushed and the two friends snuck behind them. Surprisingly, other assassins had done the same, and Tarin heard a few mention they were meeting up with the Renegade army as well. Silently, he signaled for K'sho and himself to follow the others.

The small band of assassin trainees crept their way through the empty back streets of Taysor slowly and side stepped the few skirmishes they came across. One boy, in particular, seemed to have a good sense of where he was going and even motioned for Tarin and K'sho to catch up with him. Once the two friends had, he waved them through a small side passageway that opened out to the outskirts of the city. An enormous cascade of blue, crystalline waters hid the entrance way from the main street, which was empty save for three assassins that hurried toward the waterfall. The lead woman of the newcomers had the symbol of the Renegade army on her emblem of rank. Her two companions followed behind purposely, though neither bore a rank or marking of any kind.

"That is Shy'ree." The one boy whispered to the gathered trainees. "She is Royal Qusairo's second-in-command." He motioned for the others to wait at the entrance. Shy'ree immediately turned to the youth. The two assassins signed something to each other, then the boy turned back to the bunch of trainees and waved them forward. Shy'ree surveyed the group with a critical eye and nodded her approval at the large numbers whom had come. "I'll take you to Qusairo." She informed them shortly and continued deeper into the hidden passage without waiting to see if anyone came. All the assassins followed without comment.

Shy'ree led the procession to another waterfall. This one stretched a full one thousand feet from cliff face to cliff face and thundered into a pool with a force strong enough to mute all other sounds. The assassin commander picked her way across the line of rocks at its base, with one of the companions following deftly behind. The others followed slowly, finally crossing the span of stones with only three trainees getting the slightest bit wet. Again, Shy'ree only nodded approval and made her way to a hidden entrance of a cave that was covered in a sheath of strong water. All the trainees hustled passed the falling water and found themselves in a damp cavern. A passage continued out of sight. Continuing into it, the group entered a cavern that stretched a good fifty meters across and was well lite with lanterns.

This was where Royal Qusairo had made his headquarters.

The Tá sharay stared out of the large, thin stone window to his beautiful city beyond. His gaze did not take in its splendor, however, as he was deep in thought over the situation on Obseen. It had been four days since Zanishiria had left with Prince Anmero, and he knew they would have reached Taysor. The Tá sharay was worried. Zanishiria had told him of the troubles at the training center, as well as, the Renegade's final attack plan. That information, plus the emotions she had transferred with them during their mind contact, took up all of the leader's attention. "Not all is what it seems." The Tá sharay felt. Zanishiria had left something out, which had seemed unusual; however, the Xsorian had a fairly good idea what that detail was.

It had been over one year since the Las'wa clan had communicated with the Xsorians. The same time since the young Lakean preshans had been deceived, hunted down, and killed. The Xsorians had been told that none had survived the massacre, but Khan Torez suspected that the information had been false, to protect Zanishiria. The Tá sharay believed she had been one of the few to survive and the only one to make it to the surface. Khan knew that, if it had not been for his telepathic abilities, he would not have suspected Zanishiria's background. To the eye, she passed quite convincingly as a Royal, even glamoring herself with fancy clothing and fancy hairstyles, so unlike the Lakean assassins, who preferred to be practical and conservative.

The Tá sharay turned away from the window and summoned his eldest son with his mind. Page Torez materialized suddenly out of the shadows and stepped to his father's side.

"Yes, father?" Page asked quietly.

"Have you come to any conclusions about Zanishiria's report?"

"Yes, father."

Khan nodded his approval but didn't ask for his son's opinion. Instead he asked another question. *"What can you infer from your finds on Taysor and the Guild?"*

"The council is indeed in turmoil. Emperor Manscor has given authority to override the Senior Master's decisions, giving

Master Teera Sabina the privilege. The council is uneasy with this change, as Teera had not received the position the normal way, and distrust runs rampant. Those in the council are afraid to stand up to Master Teera. It will only be a matter of time before the Guild lies in ruins. Betrayals have shown up throughout the Center, a large number have quietly defected, and it is hard to tell which assassins are loyal to Manscor and which support the Renegade Army. This only divides the council more. The bigger problem lies elsewhere, though. It is not just the training center that is divided. The whole planet is not sure which side to be on. This causes a great number of problems. Do you think that is why the Las'wa have withdrawn all traces of their existence on the surface?"

The sudden question startled the Tá sharay for a moment. *"Maybe. It is something to look into. Do so when we are done here."* Page nodded beside his father. The Tá sharay continued. *"The palace is sure to be in turmoil."*

"Indeed," Page agreed, *"King Lapsair had continued to gain support from the assassin clans and creating disturbances in the capitol. I am slightly surprised that Manscor has not tried to assassinate him yet, though."*

"Don't be," The Tá sharay thought gently. *"Manscor will bid his time with Lapsair. Right now, the emperor has his attention cast to Royal Qusairo and his son Anmero."*

"Why is the prince so important?"

"Because he is a threat to Manscor. If he continues the legacy his father is creating, he could become a greater opposition than Qusairo. Manscor cannot risk that."

"So, Manscor will try to stop him while he is still young and not influential." Page concluded.

"Exactly. He is trying to kill two seeds with one stone. And, as for that first seed, he may well accomplish that."

"You are saying Qusairo is vulnerable."

"The emperor has many Royal guards to bring to bear against the assassin-Royal, and one, at least, could kill Qusairo during the battle, as long as the man insists that he must be on the field with his Renegades."

"That is only speculation, but, yes, it is very easy to kill a single man during battle. More turmoil will result if the Renegades fail."

"Then they mustn't." Khan Torez straightened as he came to a decision. "I will gather up my guards and go to Taysor to support the Renegades."

Page blinked in surprise, first over his father's rapid transition from telepathy to verbal conversation, and secondly, for the suddenness of his father's decision. Then, his countenance changed as he realized the full extent of what his father's actions meant. "Will I be allowed to accompany you, father?" He asked, keeping his excitement hidden.

The Tá sharay was already shaking his head. "No, you and Lap must stay here." He rose a hand to silence his son's protest. "I know you are seventeen and old enough to decide your own actions, but you will be more useful to me here, where you can hack into any computer base."

Page frowned. He knew his father's real reason was because he did not want his sons involved in the Planetary War. Yet, because he could read his father's thoughts, he did not feel that his father was being selfish. After all, Khan had been through one other planetary war. What had happened then was not a sight the Xsorian wished on his sons. Even now, Page could feel a chill and cold barrier in his father's mind where those memories resided; he never would share what he had seen with his two sons. Finally, Page allowed his anger at being left behind diminished.

The Tá sharay felt his son's anger drift away and laid a hand on his son's shoulder. *"I'd take you with me if I could."*

"I know, father." Page allowed an inward smile to grow before becoming serious again. *"What is it that you want me to investigate?"*

"Take care of your brother, Page, and help us find the truths behind all the lies. That is all that is required for now."

"Yes, father."

"And," The Tá sharay continued, *"Don't tell Lap what is happening. He may be fifteen, but he is safer if he does not know everything about this war."*

Page hesitated at that but finally nodded in understanding. *"Yes, father, Lap will not know."*

"Thank you." The Tá sharay headed for the door with Page following close behind. They walked down the hallway together and stopped at Page's private quarters. *"Have the information you collect ready for me on my arrival"* The Tá sharay instructed, becoming the Xsorian leader once again. A

secretive smile was shared between the father and son. *"I am very interested to learn about our Lakean friends."*

Page brought a fist up to his chest in salute and watched as his father disappeared down the carved hallway. The white-haired youth finally let out a disappointed sigh and pushed open the door to his room. With another sigh, he sat down in front of his computer and turned it on. With fingers flying, he bypassed the planetary security until he was deep into the Royal guard's top-secret files. What he was looking for, he was not entirely sure, but he felt that there was something he could learn...

Three hours later, long after the Tá sharay had left for Taysor, Page stumbled on some files that held surprising secrets. Some of the names in the document were familiar to him, yet the information within the files were different than what they had been reported as. "Q'a shik!" [Expression like "holy shit!"] Page cursed in surprise. "This can't possibly be true." But, it was. He had stumbled into the heart of the Emperor's plans, and Page did not like what he found.

The Royal guard hurried to the throne room door and waited nervously until the guards there opened the ornate doors and waved him inside. The man scurried to the emperor's dais and dropped to one knee at the bottom of the steps. "My Liege."

Emperor Manscor rose from his chair and stepped to the edge of the dais. "What is it now?"

The guard kept his gaze to the floor as he answered. "We have spotted Senior Master Sye Rainier heading into the city, My Liege. We are preparing to follow her."

"It is as I said it would be, Emperor." A voice, low and husky yet not at all unpleasant, sounded from the shadows behind Manscor's chair. The emperor turned his eyes to the shadows there and caught the chilling reflection from the man's look. The gamma lenses in the man's dark eyes lighted like a cat's as the midday sunlight filtering through the large window to the left of the dais struck them. The man continued, "She is going to find her apprentice, I expect."

Manscor nodded and turned back to the Royal guard, who gulped in fear at knowing someone else quite dangerous was there. "Continue to follow her, but keep a distance. Let the master and apprentice meet before you capture Zanishiria Novastone. I want that girl alive. Stun her if need be."

"Y-yes, My Liege." The Royal guard bowed again then hurried away.

"I love the way they tremble in fear of me." The lurking shadow chuckled vehemently.

Emperor Manscor scowled. "It may entertain you, but I find it distracting. If you wish to scare my minions so much, then try getting a rise out of Teera the next time she is here."

"You would like that wouldn't you?" The man moved out of the concealing shadows to reveal his handsome, yet disturbing, self. A scar ran from the man's forehead, across his right eye, and ended at the bottom of his chiseled high-cheekbone. His long, black hair was neatly pulled back with a leather thong and fell to his slender waistline. An evil glint in his dark purple eyes dared anyone to try and fight him—for he knew he would win indefinitely.

Manscor ignored the assassin. He stepped over to his large window instead and glanced out at his city. The Taysor Valley spread out for miles around the capitol city, surrounding it in its powerful, wild clutches. Manscor smiled inwardly. The beautiful landscape had been his since the beginning and it was because of his father's love of the blessed beauty that it had fallen into his hands so easily. "I will need someone as a witness if your plan is to work, Eric."

Eric Sorey took a step closer to Manscor at the emperor's sudden request. "I have already thought of that, Your Highness." Manscor turned to look at the assassin. "Whom better than Master Teera's apprentice."

"Tarin Saerric?"

"Yes." Eric hissed. "The boy is honest and he is Zanishiria's best friend."

"What does them be friends have to do with any of this?"

"It has little importance. It is more of an added bonus, really." Eric grinned evilly and cloaked his sinister face in shadow. "No, he is best because he had a good mind for perspective and good instincts—and, he is the apprentice of your dear Teera. The best part is that Teera is planning to admit him into the council after this war is over. You will have complete control over him. Especially, after he sees your might and proficiency in battle."

Manscor nodded at this, and a satisfied smile spread over his face. "That would be perfect."

"Yes." Eric hissed again.

"Will you get Tarin yourself?"

"I will if the emperor wishes it."

"I do."

"Then, I will go now. I already know where the boy is, in fact. At this moment, he is heading for the Renegade Army with young K'sho Rease. He does this so his friend can fight against your guards." Manscor narrowed his eyes in anger though he trusted Eric Sorey to have the information right; it was why he kept the once-enemy man so close. The former Lakean clansman was so gifted in espionage and in torture that he could replace the entire Honoreds force single-handedly.

The look on the Emperor's face made Eric's smile grow larger. "Yes, there are many who would rather die with the Renegades than for you, as has always been the story." Eric stopped his goading there and turned away from the now steaming Manscor. The Emperor's shadow knew when to quit while he was ahead of the game he and the ruler always played. Eric Sorey was the only man alive—to Manscor's knowledge—who could best the emperor in a duel. However, the Lakean man had no desire to rule. He preferred the freedom his position granted him as left—or shadow—hand to the Royal-assassin. "Tarin will not join the enemy, though. He would never go that far. After all, the kid would not directly disobey his master, who is very loyal to you." Eric slipped back into the shadows. "I will be back here shortly, Your Highness. You will have your "witness" long before you have your enemy in your grasp."

Chapter Ten

There were five planetary wars on Obseen. Aptly named the "Bloody Wars" by scholars, these wars were usually long skirmishes and power struggles to exact dominance on the small, secluded planet. Mostly, these fights seemed meaningless, just clan turf-wars, and only the fifth, and final war, was considered to have any significance.

The "First War" started eight-hundred-and-two years after the assassins has been imprisoned on Obseen. Clans, now formed and growing larger by the year, fought against one another intermittently for sixty-seven long years. The main cause for this fighting was to establish boundaries and territories that each clan could hold. Finally, the war dimmed down, the clans exhausted of the long squabbles. Seventeen High clans, whom had proved their powers supreme, came together and laid out the boundaries for fourteen territories and gave to each clan their own city within the territory they most supported. United, the seventeen High clans began to set up what would later transform into the planetary "laws" of the Assassins' Guild.

The "Blind War" followed the "First War", nine years later. It came about when one lower-class clan revolted against the control of its lead high-clansmen. During this time, a disease called the stone-blindness plague, was running rampant through the northern territories of Obseen. This plague, though originally from Sentinal 2, had been carried to Obseen by patrolling UEF soldiers. Without the proper medicines to counteract the disease, many lower-clansmen were either killed, the usual result, or permanently blinded. Many of the lower-class clans were unable to receive necessary medicines to treat this disease and the high-clansmen did not come to their aid. Outraged, many of the suffering clans took up arms against the other clans in hopes that they could steal the needed medicinals to heal their people.

Resentments carried over from the "Blind War" simmered under the placid surface, until, finally unable to be held back, the lower clans massed together to start the "Dark Revolution". Lasting five years, the angered clans revolted against the others, spreading across the planet until not a single city was left untouched by the fighting. However, the seventeen High clans were not leaders for nothing. Their superior powers, finally united on the eve of the fifth year, allowed them to subdue the population. Knowing there was a possibility of more wars, the High clans sought a different way to equalize the powers of the seventy-two clans. In the star date year 3990, the Assassins' Guild was created and the council at Taysor, established because it was the only territory not held by a high-clan, was created. The capitol city, held by the Royals as a gesture of friendship, was deemed equal ground to all clans. Four seats were given to each clan, to be held by elected members for a five-year term. The power of the seventeen High clans was lowered so that the lesser clans could take an equal part of the laws of the Guild.

The fourth was, in a way, a continuation of the "Dark Revolution". It began nine years after the creation of the Assassins' Guild. Most called it the "Power Struggle" war, for indeed it was more of the same type of bickering that had ensued during the last wars. Though this war was the smallest, lasting only one year, it was by far the most important. It tested the strength of the new Guild, as clans that were still skeptical over the new system tried ways to break apart the Assassins' Guild. The battles proved to be less than bothersome and were quickly and efficiently counteracted. The Guild had proved its strength and structure was strong enough to hold together despite the lack of trust. The new government, as that is what it now was, unified the clans and turned their attentions away from pointless wars to more important matters, those of culture and skill.

The "Power Struggle" ended and was followed by twenty-one years of calm and growth. The Royals from Planet X, who had left the assassins to their squabbles, found new reasons to unite with the assassin people, finding the assassins to be apt at starship building, construction, hacking, the arts, and, above all, the art of war. The "babysitters", as the Royals jokingly called themselves, found their children were in little need of mediation. The new Assassins' Guild was a force to be reckoned with.

One Royal-assassin understood this new power and took advantage of the assassins' strength and government. Prince Chang Xi had grown up in his father's enormous palace in Taysor and had learned how to fight from the assassins that lived there. After King Chiang Xi"s death in 4011 SD, Chang took up his father's position as the head Royal in Taysor. Thus, began his bid to control the Assassins' Guild from the inside out. In less than a year, King Xi—whom had taken up the Suez name Manscor ("man killer") —had asserted himself at the head of the Guild. With his new power as both a King and an assassin head, Manscor was quickly able to amass enough support to control the capitol. In short time, he asserted himself as emperor and began to conquer the rest of the planet. Thus, opened the "Royals' War".

The "Royals' War" started in 4012. It began when Manscor's forces clashed with an opposing force, led by a large percentage of the Legion of Leaders, at the city of Barashi. The Battle of Barashi was a turning point in the war. During the fight, a number of influential assassins were killed, enraging many of the clans. In anger, many clans rose out of their stupor and joined the Renegade Army to oppose the Royal guard. Then, in the year 4021, the Renegade Army began to push the Royal guards back toward the capitol. By the next year, half of the planet was reclaimed by the Renegades. During this time, two Royal families, Novastone and Doz, made covert plans with the Legion of Leaders and Las'wa in hopes that the unification of the Royals and Guild could bring down the emperor and his supporters. The underground-dwelling Las'wa clan, whom had disappeared from the war since the Battle at Barashi, promised to release a small band of specialty trained assassin youths to be planted in the Assassins' Guild at Taysor. It was supposed to be with the Royals Lapsair and Qusairo's help that the Las'wa could get the students into the training center at the capitol, right underneath Manscor's nose. Unfortunately, some leak ruined the plan of the day of the preshans' journey to Taysor, and none were reported to have survived the attack. Yet, the Renegades continued with their own battle and succeeded in pushing the Royal guard back into Shaytyar.

This is where our story brings us to now. The stardate 4023. The stage has been set for one final hurrah. There must be an ending to this "Royals' War"; somehow, the Renegades must win or the efforts to keep this planet assassin-ruled will be in vain. All of the opposing forces have been sent to the capitol. Now, by some miracle, the emperor must be taken down. Or, there may no longer be an Assassins' Guild.

Master Quinn

Senior Master Sye Rainier was so intent on finding her apprentice that she did not notice she was being followed. Sye searched through the many, empty streets of Taysor City looking for Zanishiria. She was wandering down one such deserted street when she met up with the first of some of the wandering Resistance.

A group of young Renegade fighters were wandering aimlessly through Taysor when they happened on the same street as Sye Rainier. It only took one of them to recognize the Senior Master's emblem and yelling, calling her a traitor, for the rest to follow his lead. Their attack was uncoordinated.

Sye turned tail and sprinted back the way she had come. The five youths were quick to chase her, running with a loud whoop. Sye ran through four long streets before she began to tire. The younger men began to gain their ground. Sye ducked into a side street before she had realized she had taken a dead-end. With a disgusted growl, the cinnamon-haired woman turned around and took out her twin Kaumian deah-knives as her five attackers entered her street and stalked forward.

The first fighter to catch her jumped closer and fainted an attack, giving another a chance to leap in and slice through the master's right sleeve. The other three, emboldened, circles around until Sye was surrounded. Sye cast her gaze around frantically and forced herself from panicking. She was THE Senior Master at Taysor after all! Silently, she cursed herself for not being as skilled at fighting multiple attackers at one time as she needed to be for that moment. Clenching her teeth, Sye prepared herself and rose her deah-knives in defiance.

Unexpectedly, however, a lone assassin jumped from a rooftop near the dead end and landed behind the Senior Master, placing themself between the master and the three youths. Sye whipped around in panic to slash at the person, but the attacker was already moving to take on the attackers. Surprised and uncentered, Sye turned back to her two remaining enemies and rose her weapons threateningly.

Behind Sye, the unknown rescuer continued to push the three fighters deeper into the alley. They tried to catch this new opponent off guard but to no avail. The attacks were easily turned aside and the assassin turned them back on the fighters. One, angered, rushed the newcomer only to have his sword parried and twisted out of his grasp to land far behind him. The lone attack sliced the unarmed boy's ribs and thighs, rendering him useless. After, the boy was kicked aside to fall in a heap of pain. The other two fighters backed up to regroup. By then, they knew success would not be won by running in recklessly. They spread out to take on their new nemesis from opposite sides, but, unbeknownst to them, this tactic only made their enemy's counterattack easier.

Meanwhile, Sye's opponents had spread out as well. These two fighters continued to flit around the Senior Master, striking and fainting their attacks. Sye began to feel like a mouse being toyed with. The analogy annoyed her. In sudden anger, she changed her stance and took a very serious slash at her taunters. Her renewed vengeance won her some deliberate and well-aimed blows. Her deah-knives connected with flesh and blood began to flow from the wounds.

The fight became chillingly real.

One deah-knife punctured a youth's arm and left a gory hole all the way through the shoulder. That one screamed and scrambled away to clutch his wound against the far wall. The other rushed to defend his friend just as Sye raised her knife to perry. The weapon bit deeply into the youth's back and Sye released her hand as if she had been burned. In horror, she watched the youth drop to the ground beside his friend, anguish written over his features. Sye trembles as the seriousness of the situation hit her; she had nearly killed a young assassin fighter— never in her life had she given a killing stroke! Shuddering, Sye backed away from the two injured youths.

A loud eerie crack caused Sye to jump out of her horror and turn toward the sound. Her so-called "rescuer" had the deadliest looking whip Sye had ever seen in her hand. Its leathery, lithe body glistened maliciously, gleaming a scarlet and ebony color in the late afternoon sunlight. It was a whip that was for certain, but Sye had never seen the likes of its kind before.

The fighter lifted her hand and began to swing the whip in a circle. The two fighters hesitated, unsure of how to proceed against the weapon. Finally, though, they charged—or more aptly tried to charge—the lone fighter. They came on full force, their weapons held at ready. The lone assassin stood calmly against the rush and, in one fluid turn of the wrist, unleashed the wraith of her whip. In seconds it was all over. The preshair weapon sliced deep into the two assailants' bodies like scissors to paper. The two boys stopped in pain, their eyes wide in shock. Then, one and the other, they fell to the ground, very dead.

Sye Rainier was paralyzed in shock as the previous few seconds swept through her mind. She stared almost blankly at the lone assassin's turned back. The person seemed to be blankly staring down at her victims, as if there was no emotion to the act. How could someone kill like that? How? Quietly at first, then louder, Sye croaked out, "H-how can you do that?"

The lone assassin tensed at the words, almost as if she had forgotten the Senior Master had been there. Slowly, the assassin turned to face the Senior Master. The expression on the girl's face was cold and her eyes were deep and depthless. Senior Master Sye Rainier felt herself gasped in horror as she came face to face with her apprentice, Zanishiria Indigo Novastone.

No longer did the fourteen-year-old look like a Royal. Those grey eyes, so sharp and piercing, and that form-fitting preshair armor took on an older facade, one of a Lakean preshanen. The very essence of the young girl had changed. The feel of her chilled the Senior Master as details finally clicked into place. Her apprentice had been so apt at the training center because Zanishiria had already possessed all the skills she was taught. Only someone well-trained in the arts of deception could have pulled off the front.

"How, master?" Zanishiria responded expressionlessly. "I was created as a weapon. I am what they have made me. What else can I do but be their puppet?"

Royal Qusairo looked at the large group of trainees warmly. He stood up from the rock outcropping he considered his chair and walked over to the young boy who had led them there. Smiling, he embraced him. "I am glad to see you have made it safely, Dǎveed."

The young man bowed solemnly, so much like his sire. "My father was very clear with his directions to this place."

"Then I will have to tell Quinn I am grateful when I see him next." Qusairo turned then to the two youths who had accompanied Shy'ree.

Anmero Doz gave a broad smile at seeing his father again and rushed to meet his warm embrace. The father and the son stayed like that for a long moment before hesitantly breaking apart. Anmero then remembered his father had never met his protector and motioned the Lakean forward. "Father, I mean Royal Qusairo, this is Seircor C'vail."

"Seircor?" Qusairo took in the tall man's sharp features, black hair, and grey eyes.

"Kye'sh Zanishiria seimie." ["I am a friend of Zanishiria's".]

Qusairo was unfamiliar with the language and his confusion showed on his face. Shy'ree stepped forth and held up a hand to silence the Royal before turning to Seircor. "Shre lei là coursa. Lá seimreal lei kye'or?" ["Have you come from the underworld? Did the council send you?"]

"Crey, kye'or vearoum." ["Yes, I am and they sent me."]

"Itai a'y. Sie'kye salla." ["I see. Let me relay that."] Shy'ree pulled her leader aside and whispered in his ear whom Seircor was, what clan he was from, and why he was there. Qusairo's eyes widened in surprise and he whispered back fiercely. "Why didn't you tell me you were Lakean? As you look just like this Seircor." He added to Shy'ree's sharp look. "What happened to Zanishiria?"

The Lakean woman turned back to Seircor. "Ai'y laus'oum Zanishiria?"

Now everyone but Anmero turned to study the Lakean assassin at the mention of their fellow trainee. Seircor gazed back unfazed and guessed these other assassins must be from the training center. "She split off with us after we joined you. She had other things to tend to, so she sent me on with Prince Anmero in her stead."

"What other things?" A tall, blond-haired and beyond-handsome young man about Seircor's age pushed his way to the front of the group and came to stand right in front of the Lakean. The two youths stared eye to eye in a slight challenge. "Tell me." Tarin Saerric whispered forcefully. "What is Zan doing? I swore I would protect her but I need to know where I need to be."

Seircor immediately disliked this man in from of him. Especially since he seemed to think himself to be very important to Zanishiria; the Las'wa did not need protecting. "I will not say anything about Zanishiria."

Tarin's blue eyes flashed angrily. "Zan is my best friend. I have the right to know where she is."

Seircor's dislike deepened. He didn't like the fact that Tarin had said Zanishiria's shortened name instead of her full in public. If this man was her friend, he would have respected her by using her full name. "You will refer to her as Zanishiria from now on, and I am not telling you anything about her."

"I've called her Zan from the day I met her and will continue to do so." Tarin countered. The two men glared daggers at each other, unaware of the scene they were making from their confrontation. They were just about to go at it again when Tarin's friend stepped in.

"That is enough, Tarin." K'sho whispered forcefully to his friend. "It is obvious this guy is also a friend of Zanishiria's and he has probably known her for years." Tarin glanced at Seircor doubtfully but backed off just the same. K'sho turned to Seircor before the Neitiege could say anything more. "We apologize for any disrespect shown, though I think there are some misunderstandings here. You obviously have different...customs than we do."

Seircor glanced cautiously at K'sho for a tense moment then nodded. This guy is not so bad. "My name is Seircor C'vail."

"K'sho Rease." He returned Seircor's bow then pointed back to his friend. "That is Tarin Saerric. You two are probably Zanishiria's closest friends, so I suggest you two should get on more even terms."

Seircor glanced back at Tarin and stared as if he was reading the other's soul. The Neitiege glanced back unblinking, and both mirrored the other's doubt. Mistrust, annoyance, and a slight bit of jealousy toward the other man kept them distanced, even at K'sho's words. Neither moved, still unaware of the tension they created.

Finally, Anmero could not take it any longer and deliberately placed himself between Tarin and Seircor. "Enough! Put your feelings aside. We have more important issues at the moment." Both men turned their attention to the young prince. "Do not continue this confrontation. Or, are you so wrapped up in who's more Zanishiria's friend that you have forgotten we are in the middle of a war?"

The Lakean backed away first and quickly regained his composure. "I apologize, Prince, Royal Qusairo, please forgive my flippant behavior. Zanishiria would not have wished it of me."

Prince Anmero nodded his acceptance of the man's apology then turned to the Naitiege youth. Tarin backed away from the prince's powerful stare and muttered his unhappy apology. Anmero turned back to his father, causing the others' eyes to wander there as well.

Royal Qusairo nodded his thanks to his son then began his instructions to the new recruits without preamble. "I am not pleased to be putting you all in this war, but there is little choice anymore. We are in need of all the fighters we can get if we are to push back the Royal guards and put a stop to the "Royals' War". All of you that dare to take up arms against the emperor will go with Shy'ree now. Anyone else must leave."

No one moved for the longest time, then Tarin stepped away from the others. "You will have to excuse me, then." He said warily. "I helped my friend get here safely, but now I must fulfill my promise to Master Quinn to protect Zan."

Seircor gave a miffed look but K'sho's glance gave the Lakean pause. K'sho excused himself from the others and walked with Tarin to the waterfall entrance. The Lakean followed, like a silent warning. Once they were alone, the young man spoke. "I won't deny that I still dislike you." His words caused Tarin's mental defenses to come to the fore. "But, I cannot let that stop me from sympathizing on a cause concerning Zanishiria. She is very important to me, as well as, to our clan." He hinted to the Neitiege that there would be hell to pay if anything happened to the young assassin girl.

"She is important to me as well." Tarin threw back at him.

Seircor bit back a retort, choosing instead to study the blonde-haired man. "Zanishiria didn't tell you much, did she?" Tarin's eyes flashed briefly showing he had been rankled by the jest, then he shook his head. Seircor dropped the mocking smile he held. "You should be careful then. Zanishiria's sole purpose here was to end Manscor's reign. What she had to do to blend in here, I have no idea, but she is not what she pretended to be. In the next few hours, the outcome of the war will be upon us, and very possibly the fate of Obseen's future. Neither you nor I will be able to help Zanishiria during her task. So, if you are trying to be some valiant savior, you should kill that thought right now." The Lakean paused, unsure if he should say anything else. By the way Tarin waited, Seircor could see that the Neitiege expected him to say more. "Zanishiria will fight Manscor. That is the only way to end this war. You will find her where ever the emperor is; that is, if you are still too stubborn to not heed my warning to stay away."

Tarin understood. A calm enveloped him. The pieces of the conversations he had had with his friend fell into place and Tarin knew then what Zanishiria had tried to say to him countless times before: she wasn't a Royal, she was an assassin under cover for the Renegade army. Yet, he knew, too, that the relationship he and the young assassin had had over that last year, hinting on something more, was not his imagination—or had it been his imagination? No matter, Tarin felt strong emotions toward his friend, and if going to her, even if it meant that he may be imprisoned by Manscor and labeled a defected, he wanted to go to her and hear her tell him in her own words what she was about. "I am going to Zan."

Seircor gave a distasteful look that said he thought the other man a fool. Finally, though, he shrugged as if indifferent. "Suit yourself. If you do manage to meet with Zanishiria, tell her that Prince Anmero made it safely." With the little favor asked, Seircor turned way and disappeared down the passageway. Tarin watched the Lakean depart before giving K'sho one last good-bye and departing himself.

Seircor watched from the shadows as the Neitiege left. The other assassin hadn't noticed that the Las'wa had doubled back to ensure that he departed. Satisfied, Seircor turned around and strode back to the cavern, confident that K'sho would find his way back through the short passage. Only Royal Qusairo and his son were present, the others having headed for the battlefield. Anmero turned as the assassin approached and nodded in acknowledgment. "I take it you have more to ask of me?" Seircor asked Qusairo.

The Royal leader nodded. "I do. I am grateful that you took over Zanishiria's care of my son. She picked wisely." Seircor smiled slightly at the words. "Yet, as I am sure you know, this war is far from over, and my son will not be safe until it is. Therefore, I ask that you continue to protect Prince Anmero." Qusairo used his son's title to stress the importance of the task.

"Then I will do so, sir." Seircor bowed respectfully. "No harm will come to him."

"Yes, I know I can trust in that." Royal Qusairo rose up to his full six-foot-three height and clasped a hand to the Lakean's shoulder. "May you both stay safe."

Master Quinn paced anxiously passed the tiny window. He and the other six assassin masters that made up the small portion of the "Legion of Leaders" in Taysor had taken refuge in a now-abandoned one-story house across from the Sorey River, near the training center. There, they watched as the older, more advanced trainees had streamed from the Center to join in the fighting, none happy with the emperor's orders. They had slipped away that morning while everyone else were preparing for the battle. Now, the group of masters waited in the empty house, also defying the emperor, and tried to determine their next course of action. On request by Master Quinn, Master Ranarro Dorsetti had gone in search of Royal Qusairo to learn where the Renegade Army stood, and Master Corsetti had traveled to Taysor Palace to speak with King Lapsair. As of yet, neither had returned, meaning the others had to sit tight.

Master Quinn forced himself to stop his pointless pacing. He knows it would do no good fretting over circumstances beyond his control. Instead, he thought of other thing; things from his past, like the "Legion of Leaders".

The "Legion of Leaders" had been formed during the First War by thirteen assassin masters. None had been from the same clan, but all had been friends. They had vowed to protect the other assassins from oppressions of any clan or leader. The Legion worked well for years, giving advice from points of view not biased toward any one clan and not associated with any councils. In its history, the Legion had been a powerful force used for the greater need of the assassin nation as a whole, but, without warning, it had been dissolved at the start of the "Blind War".

Master Quinn had searched for information on the Legion years later, after he survived the moon blindness plague and during his campaigning in the "Power Struggle"; however, very little had survived to tell the tale of the "Legion of Leaders". Dissatisfied, Quinn continued his search, to no avail. As the years had gone by, Master Quinn had continued thinking about the long-dissolved group. It wasn't until a year after the fourth war was over, however, that Quinn brought up the issue behind the Legions' disappearance to his companions, Roko, Corsetti and Hareoska. The four masters decided to form their own legion, but only as a secretive union. The few leaders they later invited into their group included Hiroku Yoshida, Sunashi, the Berzén and Berris of Traygor, the Coursay'soras, Khan Torez, King Lapsair, and three masters from Syltha, Barashi, and Utako. No other members had been added to the Legion since, though Master Quinn had been hoping to one day induct Zanishiria to her deceased parents' places, if she proved worthy, as well as the possibility of the Tá sharay's sons and Quinn's own son.

The Legion had agreed to keep their group secret to most assassins, however, including their own offspring, until someone showed true promise, to ensure that the Legion of Leaders would not be dissolved again. The confidentiality of the group was very important if the Legion was to have an unadulterated influence on Obseen.

—And, help they would, Master Quinn knew even if it meant going against the Assassins' Guild that he had helped form years ago now under the control of the emperor—.

A movement outside the window alerted Master Quinn to the arrival of Corsetti. The other master pushed through the house's back door and came over to Quinn. His older face was flushed from running all the way from Taysor Palace and his wispy, dusty-blond hair stuck to his sweaty head. Yet, Corsetti was in great shape for his age and recovered from the exertion quickly. "Quinn." He smiled and stopped beside the other master. "That run felt good."

Master Quinn offered a smile of his own and a chair to his friend. "So, what did King Lapsair have to say?"

"Hey, have patience! Can't an old man have time to recover?" Master Corsetti reprimanded in mock annoyance. He took a sip of water from the jug Quinn offered him and sat back. "Lapsair sends his best, by the way." The younger master chuckled before eying Corsetti expectantly. "All right, all ready." He took a big swig of water before continuing. "Zanishiria had returned this morning and met with Lapsair. Prince Doz was with her as was a Lakean boy. They left a little before noon."

"And?"

"And what? Lapsair just said she was ready to finish her mission." Corsetti looked straight into Quinn's multicolored eyes. "She will finish what the Las'wa sent her here for. There's nothing else to say."

"Sorry." Quinn raised his hands to soothe his friend. "I don't mean to sound miffed, it's just that that I expected him to say more."

"I know." Corsetti waved the apology away with his hand. "We're all on edge as this war begins to wane. It is to be expected." He picked up a mipa fruit and bit a large chunk out of its topaz rind. "Has Dorsetti returned?"

"Not yet." Quinn sat down across from Corsetti and watched the scenery outside through the tiny widow. "He could be having a hard time finding Qusairo through all the battling."

Silence fell between the two masters and continued even as the other four masters joined them. The suns rose and started their decent in the sky, and still Dorsetti did not come. Master Sunashi tried to crack a few jokes but those were quickly silenced by Roko and Yoshida. Wise old Hareoska finally suggested they take a short nap while they waited, since they did not know how long it would be until their next one. His suggestion was easily taken, and in minutes most of the masters were in a light sleep. Only Master Quinn remained awake, thinking over everything again, including the plans from over a year ago that were to be executed by the Lakean preshans in retaliation against the emperor.

It wasn't until late that evening, when the third sun was setting, that Dorsetti returned. He came from the west, using the suns to hide his approach. Master Quinn heard the door open and dismissed his previous thought. The black-haired master climbed out of his chair, his shifting waking the other masters, and went to meet Dorsetti in the other room.

Master Dorsetti looked up wearily with his mysterious amber-colored eyes. The younger master did not look at all good to Quinn and his concern for the other man showed clearly on his face. The Ghans's clothes were tattered in places and speckled in blood. Cuts were clearly seen on the master's hands, neck, and face, but it was the limp arm that concerned Master Quinn the most. Dorsetti rose the other hand to silence the older master. "I'm fine. I found Qusairo." He allowed Quinn to lead him to the chair the Baras had occupied before and sat down. Accepting a drink gratefully, he continued, "Coming back, I was attacked by some Honored youths. There's quite a few who'll attack anyone they meet no matter which side they're on. I got lucky." His smile held little joy, just dry sarcasm. "My shoulder was pulled out of the socket, but I managed to pop it back in. I won't be able to use it for a few weeks."

"At least you're alive. That's all that matters." Master Hareoska reminded thoughtfully and gently put the injured master's arm in a sling. "No fighting for you for at least three weeks, though, and find some perin berries to ease the pain."

"Yes, doctor." Dorsetti joked and gulped down some bread and mipa fruit.

"Whoa, show down there or the doctor will have to do the Heimlich on you!"

"Quiet, Sunashi, and let the man eat." Hareoska reprimanded the youngest master. "You'd think that by your age, you'd be less childish." Sunashi pouted his protest.

After Dorsetti replenished himself, he told the others what he had learned from Royal Qusairo. "The Renegades advancement had gone well. They are deep into the city and the Royal guards are being pushed back easier than anticipated. Yet, they have been able to hold the section near Taysor Palace. The Emperor's main force is concentrated there. Qusairo is worried they are trying to set a trap, but he cannot be sure. There is another good development that had come about," Dorsetti let his tone become cheerful. "It seems that the Lakeans are helping us after all, and not just Zanishiria, as we had expected. Shy'ree and another named Seircor have also declared their clan allegiance to the Las'wa. They say others are being sent to support the Renegades. It may be the largest number of Lakeans on the surface that we have had in over twelve years. I suspect that they have been on the surface for some time, but we were unaware because they had changed their identities to protect the clan."

"So, Zanishiria announced herself as a Las'wa?" Master Roko asked.

"No. Not officially." Dorsetti turned to the small, spike-haired master. "Qusairo confirmed her identity through Seircor. She was among the preshans sent last year, and the only one to make it to the surface after they were betrayed."

Master Quinn gave a satisfied grin and leaned back against the wall with his arms crossed. "I knew the Las'wa wouldn't abandon us. We were just too short-sighted to notice."

"Yes, we were." Yoshida nodded his agreement. "We should not be so quick to judge the Las'wa next time. After all, they are still the best fighters among our clans and brilliant tacticians."

"Agreed." Master Hareoska stood up. "Now, we really need to decide what we're going to do. Going after the Royal guards is out of the question." His last statement was said to keep Sunashi from suggesting it. The young Chars had been griping about the guards for months, saying he'd go after them one of those days.

"I'll second that." Dorsetti agreed from his place under the window. He gingerly touched his injured shoulder.

"Glad you all agree." Master Quinn turned their attention on him. "I was thinking we would go sabotage the emperor's private shipyards. I heard that after this battle, Manscor was planning on conquering other planets, somehow, or at least wreak havoc. I would like to see what arsenal he has planned to do that." All six masters agreed to the plan, and as darkness began to fall over Taysor Valley, they headed out to the spaceport near the Nyhore-Taysor border to the west. In a few hours, they would reach the border and Manscor's exclusive star ships.

Chapter Eleven

As with all cultures, certain etiquettes and customs must be acknowledged when visiting or interacting with different people. For the Las'wa, the importance of titles and names—and the correct usage or formal/informal titles—is imperative. Not only does saying the wrong name a horrible insult to the Las'wa bearing it, it is also considered a grave offense in public. In private, around friends, nicknames or shortened versions of the clansman's full name can be accepted to show friendship, trust, and intimacy. However, in public, saying either is very disrespectful. Using these "intimate" titles can show the speaker's ignorance to custom or their rudest intent. Only the full name, in public, is showing the deepest respect. So, when in the presence of a Las'wa, it is always best to opt for the usage of the assassin's full name or title only to avoid any disgrace to the intended.

The second sun was just setting, its light casting long shadows through the stone buildings of Taysor. Its white tendrils reached the lone backstreet to put the two assassins there in the spotlight on an empty stage. For many long, agonizing breathes neither master nor apprentice had spoken or moved; however, the setting sun reminded the student she needed to move into action.

Zanishiria shifted and Sye shuddered as her student stepped away from the two dead youths to the injured one. The boy cringed as the girl neared. He threw up his hands to ward off the touched but Zanishiria persisted until a hand came to his injured knee. Her eyes must have looked very profound for it subdued him. Zanishiria then proceeded to bandage up his wounds with stripes of her shirt until she had used up both of her sleeves. By then, the youth helped by using his own clothing. After they were done, he stood, pain etching deep fissures into his face. Still eyeing his attacker, he backed away. Zanishiria waited until he had disappeared into the shadows of another side street before she turned to the Senior Master—her master.

Sye was just recovering from her earlier shock when Zanishiria faced her. Her apprentice's face immediately formed into stone and the eyes took on that deathly cold glare again. The Senior Master felt a chill down her spine. For a moment, it froze all of the thoughts of why Sye had searched out Zanishiria in the first place. Then, the image of the fight that had just taken place crossed her mind with a jolt. Sye straightened in anger and met Zanishiria's gaze. "You malicious cold-blooded crip! I can't believe you just killed those two youths so ruthlessly. I—."

"Yes, I killed them." Zanishiria interrupted tonelessly. "And, I had no pleasure in doing so. I will not deny to you that I was trained to kill like I just did. I have been for most of my life. That training at the Center…its kids' play compared to what I've been through."

Sye gasped inwardly as she realized what that meant; it was a warning that Zanishiria was capable of much more fighting prowess than she had shown—and she had already beaten many advanced trainees and masters that year! If she was truly only toying with them, as the girl boasted, then Zanishiria was indeed powerful. Definitely more so than Sye herself. "I don't believe you." Sye managed to get out. "No one as young as you is capable of that."

Across from Sye, becoming hidden in the growing shadows, Zanishiria let a cold smile play across her lips; however, she banished it quickly. "It is possible, master. It is vital that I be if I am to defeat the emperor tonight."

"You will do no such thing!" Sye commanded, though she knew the order fell on deaf ears. "I won't let you."

Determined, Sye raised a deah-knife. She hurled it at her apprentice. Zanishiria took one, well-calculated step to her left and watched as the blade imbed itself in the ground directly beside her foot. The Lakean girl gave her Center master a bored look. Sye threw her other knife straight at Zanishiria's head. If she couldn't stop her by making her submit then Sye would have to seriously wound the child. However, with unfathomable speed, Zanishiria brought a wrist up to deflect the deah-knife. It bounced up into the air above her and the assassin-girl caught it as the blade spun back down. Sye gasped and backed up slightly.

"I will not fight you." Zanishiria declared quietly. "You are not the enemy I seek. Stand aside!"

"No!" Sye recovered her composer. "I will not let you fight Manscor. No one is capable of beating him, least of all yourself. It is certain death!" Sye clenched her fists, activating the releases there, and three hand blades appeared above her knuckles. She rose her hands to cross the six blades together threateningly. "I will stop you here."

Zanishiria sighed and thrust the deah-knife into the ground beside its twin. "I refuse to fight you." She pleaded quietly once more. "But, if you give me no other choice, then I will defend myself. Heed me, though, if you will, when I say that you may not walk away from this."

"You mock my skills?" Sye growled angrily. She refused to listen to the fourteen-year-old girl in front of her. "What do you know of fighting? You're too young to understand." Without waiting for her apprentice's reply, she leapt toward Zanishiria and brought a hand back ready to release a glancing blow.

The young assassin did not even flinch. With a sure quickness, Zanishiria brought a preshair dagger up to block her master's attack just as the blades came a hair's breathe away from her neck. The Senior Master's other hand swept upward and her apprentice blocked those blades with another dagger. Master and apprentice stood, locked together, and glaring into each other's eyes. Then, they broke and Sye attacked again. Zanishiria easily deflected the blow. Sye swung again and thrice more noting that her apprentice was content to just block her attacks with a calmness she had lacked over the past year.

Anger boiled out of Sye Rainier. Anger over her apprentice's chilling calmness, over her deception, and over the young girl's choice to defy her orders to stay away from her imminent death at the emperor's hands. The angrier she became, the better she seemed to fight. Across from Sye, Zanishiria was the complete opposite, cool and collected. The Las'wa felt no attachment to the fight at hand, it was not the one she had been saving up for. Her actions came automatically after years of training and, as the Senior Master became more furious, she felt the peaceful center inside of herself spread to her entire being.

Sye's hand flashed past her belt and came up with four suraik darts. These she hurled at intervals between swipes at Zanishiria. The poisoned darts could paralyze a human in a matter of minutes, yet, they seemed to be of little significance against the preshair knives that easily knocked them aside. Slowly, Zanishiria advanced toward the Senior Master. And yet, she allowed her master to jump away now and then. The distance, unnoticed by Sye, got smaller and smaller until the young girl made a great lunge at the woman. Zanishiria landed and jumped back just as quickly—a feint.

Yet, one preshair knife had been thrown to pin down the Senior Master's cloak to the obsidian street. Sye took a step forward only to find herself rebuffed. Glanced down, she finally realized the weapon holding her in place. Sye tugged anxiously at her clothing but the preshair knife was imbedded to the hilt and would not budge. Close to panicking, Sye Rainier did the only sensible thing she could think of: she unfastened the tight clasp at her neck and slipped out of the cloak, wasting precious seconds to untangle her person from the voluminous fabric. Just in time, Sye managed to avoid another blade as it was thrust at her shoulder.

Sye brought up a hand to ward off the oncoming blow but she froze in shock as her hand blades were suddenly spliced in two. A breath later, the other blades were also demolished.

Weapons now useless, Sye backed away from her apprentice. She looked up at the girl's face just in time to see Zanishiria's hands return empty from her waist, having just returned her whip there. The two stood motionless, regaining their breaths and studying each other. Both awaited the other's move to a new weapon.

"I will say it again, master. You will not win this. Back away."

Tarin Saerric glanced back just once at the large waterfall to see if Seircor was watching. Once he was confident that the Lakean was not following, he surveyed the surrounding area and headed toward the looming shadow of Taysor Palace. By the time he had left K'sho, the second sun was setting over the cliffs bordering the valley, and an evening chilliness wandered through the deserted city streets, with the heavy promise of rain in its wake. Even the sounds of the distant battle on the outskirts of Taysor seemed muted in the quiet of the inner city.

Dark clouds, heavy with moisture, hung ominously over the city of Taysor and quickly obscured the few remaining rays of light from the third sinking sun. Without warning, a sheet of bone-chilling rain blasted Tarin in the face. Caught unprepared, the young man struggled to protect his vision with the long, draping sleeve of his thin training tunic. Tarin squinted through the torrent of water in search of the large shadow that marked the location of Taysor Palace. He found he could not and groped around instead for the nearest wall. Finally, the Neitiege, youth felt the smoothed face of an obsidian stone building against his palm. He wandered ahead, blinded, for several long minutes before the rain lessened and the palace took shape once again. Tarin shivered in his dripping clothing and glanced back at the sheet of rain as it continued its pass through the city. "The blasted weather." He hissed defiantly. "It's too unpredictable, but that storm will, at least temporarily, slow the fighting."

Tarin was less than two blocks from the palace when the sounds of shuffling and interplay of shadows began. The sounds echoed off the buildings, making their origins unknown, and the shadows seemed to come from everywhere and nowhere at the same time. Usually one to stay calm, Tarin was getting a bad feeling about the situation. He slowed his pace and reached toward the short sword at his belt. Glancing around cautiously, he continued forward.

A skittering of tarol leaves to his right brought Tarin around, but on closer inspection, there was nothing there. Tarin started to turn back toward the palace but froze as his eyes came across the robed figure of a man that stepped out of the shadows of a building overhang further down the street. Quickly, he brought his short sword to bare against the unknown assassin.

"What a foolish boy." The husky voice did little to assuage Tarin's coiled nerves. "Haven't you learned to never accept or provoke an attack from an unknown advisary? I thought your master taught you that? Oh, but I guess Teera never really did teach her students the fundamentals." An amused laugh followed the man's loud mutterings. Tarin watched as the man lifted the cowl of his robe away from his face. The glint of purplish-eyes stunned him and kept the Neitiege from moving with their hypnotic effect, yet, the man's scarred visage paralyzed Tarin the most. "You find my appearance surprising, perhaps." A smile that looked better on Master Teera spread vilely over the assassin's lips. "The scar was from a creeshts spider, boy. I was forced to kill it with my bare hands." Tarin gulped and glanced around for a place to escape. "Ah, you won't be running anywhere, young Saerric. I have orders from your emperor to bring you in."

It was then that Tarin understood the nature of the assassin before him. This man was an Elite; the one known only as the emperor's "shadow". He was the one who served the emperor only when he felt it served him and killed for the pure pleasure of the victim's pain. Tarin abandoned his training and went straight to instinct. He turned and fled as fast as his long legs could carry him.

Eric Sorey allowed Tarin a few seconds of freedom before he ran after the young man. He came on silently, a deadly intent in his stride. Oh, how he wished to see this boy's reactions before his death, but, no, he knew he could not do that. Not if the emperor's plan was going to work. Saddened by the fact, Eric resigned himself to the fact that he would at least get to see Tarin's terror.

Tarin ran blindly through the streets too panicked to think clearly. He could not hear his stalker following, but that gave him no incentive to slow down. Pushing on, he hoped he could outdistance the other assassin. So intent was he on running that even the slight burning near his right shoulder blade did not slow him down. It was only when Tarin started to see dots in his vision that the young assassin became alarmed. By then it was too late.

Eric watched as the Neitiege youth crumpled to the stone street as the suraik poison worked its paralysis on the boy's muscles. After he was sure Tarin was immobilized, he pulled out a syringe filled with florick juices meant to counter-act the poison and keep the youth's heart beating. After all, he could not bring back a dead witness. Once he was sure the antidote was working, Eric tossed the boy's unconscious form over his shoulder and started the trek back toward the Taysor Palace.

Sye shook away her growing panic and replaced it with anger. Stubbornly, she refused to back away from the fight. Deep down, however, the Senior Master could feel dread building itself to a breaking point. Zanishiria's skills were what pushed her emotions. The girl she thought she knew was nothing of her imagination. Silently, Sye cursed herself her weakness. *I can't let her go to Manscor. I couldn't bear her death!*

Zanishiria watched her master with eyes of stone. She knew she had the fight; it was a bones-deep knowledge. However, the assassin-girl refused to think much of the fact, for, even if she won this fight, her battles would not be done. The remembrance of the massacre one year before stirred to the fore of her memory, making the harsh reality at hand come into clear focus. This fight needed to finish; time was running out!

With a measured quickness, Zanishiria grabbed another weapon, a creeshts short-sword, and launched herself at the Senior Master. Sye barely reacted as Zanishiria closed the distance. Seconds ticked by as the youth neared, with the short-sword pointed at Sye's heart. She held her breathe, expecting the woman to react, but there was no comprehension in the master's eyes. Next, there was impact and Zanishiria continued passed the woman.

Sye stood, stunned, still shocked at what had just happened. Rich, red blood began to drip down Sye's right arm. The Senior Master became aware of the piercing pain in her shoulder and realized she was not mortally wounded. *She missed me on purpose! Damn it!*

But she needed a weapon to respond with. Sye turned her head and caught sight of the preshair knife next to her right foot. She stooped to pick it up and spun to face her apprentice, who still had her back turned. Yet, as the sound of the dagger being pulled from the stone, Zanishiria's head twisted around enough to show her left eye to the Kaumian, apathy in its dark glare. "You will either fight me or let me go. No more of this useless standing."

Sye straightened. "You didn't kill me! Even though you had the chance, you did not end it!"

The young assassin turned to face her master and held the short-sword to her side. "A person who is not here is not an enemy. Your mind was clearly elsewhere. I will not fight you under such conditions." The voice was soft, compelling, and lacked its usual mockery.

"Then Manscor will certainly kill you." Sye spat vehemently. "Don't you think your life is more valuable than that?" Zanishiria didn't answer. "That is what disgusts me! I thought I taught you to value your life."

"My life isn't what I value. My people are what I value."

"It's not worth much when you are dead."

Sye attacked her apprentice again. The two Lakean weapons collided, parted, and then collided again. Sye thrust low toward Zanishiria's left hip then arced it around the girl's counterattack to her right shoulder. Zanishiria pulled her body away just in time and spun around to cast a blow to the Senior Master's right thigh. The young assassin then spun back around to round kick the Kaumian in the stomach. Zanishiria took a step away and thrust toward the master's injured arm. Sye parried once, then twice, as Zanishiria aimed for her shoulder, then torso, and ended with a punch to the master's face. The last attack sent the Senior Master's head about. Sye recovered quickly enough to kick at her student's side, forcing Zanishiria to back away and come at the Senior Master from a new angle. They met again in a flurry of thrusts and perries.

A chilling sheet of rain suddenly came down obscuring the fighters' vision. Sye stood, unmoving, in the onslaught of water, squinting fervently for any sign of her apprentice. The rain was so thick that Sye could not even see her hand in front of her. Worse, it was so cold that it felt like it bit deep into the body to freeze her very soul in eternal frost. In slight despair, Sye realized she was deaf and blind to any attack from Zanishiria—if the youth knew where she was.

Unbeknownst to Sye Rainier, Zanishiria could see just fine through the barrage of water. Her gamma lenses allowed her greater eyesight in not only the dark but through other restrictions, too, including rain. Though not as clear as a preshair's eyes, the gamma lenses allowed a limited amount of ultra-red censoring in certain occasions. Through the rain, Sye's figure became a purplish outline against a crystalline-blue background.

The fourteen-year-old's next attack came from the right flank. The sting of the short-sword through the cloth of Sye's shirt was like fire. Sye spun toward the attack to find Zanishiria already gone. The next front came to her right again, and, once more, the sword left a stinging cut on the master's side. For the third time that day, Sye felt like she was being toyed with. Only this time, there was little she could do about it.

The rain lessened just as quickly as it had begun, and through the light drizzle, Sye finally caught sight of the young assassin. Immediately, the Senior Master launched herself at the girl. Zanishiria parried the preshair knife just as swiftly and blocked a kick aimed at her ribs. They began a series of thrusts and launched into rounds of kicks and punches, their weapons momentarily forgotten. Zanishiria blocked a right-handed punch and issued her own sudden forward kick to Sye's torso. Her master buffered the blow to her side, ignoring the harsh throb in her arm, and let loose two quick punches followed by a kick-punch-punch combination. Zanishiria back flipped away from the last attack, landed, and spun, kicking out to hit her master in the neck. Sye hissed in pain and dropped to one knee. The younger assassin landed away from the elder and placed her hand on the hilt of her creeshts sword, ready to use it.

"Attack me, heksa!" [Kaumian= "inferior/infidel] Sye hissed as she looked up furiously. "A fight with Manscor is not done until defeat or death is admitted. Now attack!"

Zanishiria rushed her master then. With veritable speed, she whipped out her blade and swept it downward toward her master's head. Sye ducked and knocked her student's legs out from under her. Sye managed to throw the preshair knife at Zanishiria as the assassin-girl rolled away. The knife spliced through Zanishiria's leg, leaving a deep gash. As Zanishiria hit the ground, her sword fell from her hand and slid away on the slick stone.

The young assassin rolled onto her back and just happened to look up to see Sye Rainier raise her hands, ready to bring down a deah-knife at Zanishiria's exposed chest...

Chapter Twelve

There were no assassins so talented and so ruthless that the Emperor Manscor kept close except two: Teera Sabina, his lover, and Eric Sorey. The first was his leader of all the assassins loyal to him, his Honored-one; the latter was his hand of shadows and death. Eric Sorey told Manscor little of his past, other than he had been (shockingly) a Las'wa defect, but his abilities far outmatched any other assassin in the emperor's employment. Over the course of eight years, Eric proved his worth by undertaking jobs others found unsavory. If the emperor needed someone interrogated, he called on Eric; eliminated: Eric, investigated: Eric, even information-gathering and espionage: Eric. If Teera Sabina was the Emperor's right hand, then Eric Sorey was his shadow: dark, effective, and ever near.

The rocks were slick with moisture and the air still clung with the recent rainfall. Dew and water droplets dripped off leaves to drop into tiny pools below. The rippling of the water broke the placid reflection of the third sun as it made its descent behind the horizon. Its bright, white rays fell on the backs of the small fighting force, hiding them from the view of anyone looking toward the sun.

Khan Torez, the Tá sharay of Xsenume, stood looking down on the enormous valley of Taysor from his spot near the cliff edge. Even from there, distant sounds of the battle drifted up from Taysor City. The sounds were like a deadly promise of what lay ahead for the Tá sharay and his small force of protectors.

"We won't be able to reach Royal Qusairo before nightfall." Kee'van, Khan's protector, pointed out.

Khan turned to his con'trore. *"I wasn't expecting us to. I figured we would get here around dusk and I presumed right."* He turned back to the view of the sprawling city below them. *"Qusairo will need our help tomorrow for the fighting is sure to be comparably worse than today. We'll need to keep the Royal guard occupied until Manscor has been defeated."*

Silence stole over them for a moment before Kee'van spoke his mind. *"Are you sure it's wise to trust all our freedom to a fourteen-year-old girl, Tá sharay?"*

"I don't know, Kee'van." The Tá sharay finally admitted. *"I just don't know."*

Grayness. Pain. Both were eminent to him as he began to regain consciousness. He was being carried, but by whom or to where, he didn't know. Distant, obscured voices buzzed faintly in his ears, but he could not understand them. He tried to move, to open his eyes, but nothing would respond. *Poison!* Even that thought came slowly. Yet, he could recall easily his encounter just moments before. *I'm being taken to the Palace.*

Tarin was thrown unceremoniously through a doorway and landed on the cold, stone floor of the room. *No, not a room, a cell.* No pain coursed through his paralyzed body from the fall, though he was sure he had bruised himself most thoroughly. But, at least, he could still open his eyes. A blank, black wall was all that welcomed him to his destination.

"You got lucky, kid. This is the last suite vacant on the Royal Block." The man's mocking voice sounded muffled in Tarin's ears, but his intent was evident even to the Neitiege's muddled head. Tarin groaned and tried to say something or move; but his mouth tasted like iron and was dry, his muscles were still numbed. "Oh, don't be complaining, young Saerric, we'll be needing you. There's no way we will be killing you. Yet." The man walked into Tarin's view and knelt down next to him. "Manscor has need of you as a witness for his duel against the seimora. You know who that is? Of course, you don't. The seimora là coursa is none other than your dear friend Zanishiria. Oh, but her name isn't Novastone, not that you would know that either. Didn't know you weren't messing around with the legendary Coursay'soras' only daughter, eh?" Tarin muddled the words through his head, still unable to understand what this man was saying. He had said a lot of words. Tarin recognized the man now as the assassin who had come after him. This man could be none other. The purple eyes, scars, and black hair were unmistakable. The barely contained malice in the man's voice was also familiar. "Not so long now, you'll be joined by

Zanishiria." He stood back up. "The seimora will surely die this time."

The words chilled Tarin. He tried to speak, to ask what the man meant, but his voice still failed him. The assassin walked back out of Tarin's range and left with an ominous laugh still echoing off the obsidian walls.

The shadows were as foreboding as ever, though the gamma lenses in his eyes were able to cut through the blackness. A drop of water fell from the high cavern ceiling above his head to drop into the enormous mirror of water. The master watched it fall and break the perfect surface of the lake. He stood at the edge of Lake Shaisor that lay around the large stone island that was Shairceeo là Coursa.

The old master stood with an unhappy frown over his worn features. His preshair armor glistened dully from being worn for years and hung limply over his beginning-to-thin shoulders. It had been one year since he had let his apprentice go with the "chosen" preshan group, heading for Taysor. He wondered how the young assassin fared among the surface-dwelling clans. He had tried hard, pushing her far beyond her normal limits. Using the harsh reality of her life to mold her into a weapon, he had made her ready far sooner than any of the other assassin trainees. Zanishiria had been skilled enough to go to the surface and become the Las'wa's weapon against the evil emperor.

Now, though, the aging seivier wasn't sure he had done the right thing in letting his best student go so soon…

The familiar, hollow tapping from a tarol wood cane sounded evenly behind Master Tyracor, but the master didn't turn toward the sound, even as it neared. The hunched, gnarled form of Master Shay'renor appeared beside his towering apprentice. Master Tyracor ignored his master. The elder man had great patience—anyone who was over the age of one-hundred-and-eight and kept alive and healthy from florick mosses and savya could afford to be. Tyracor used to enjoy his master's presence, back when he himself was a beginner at the preshair whip, but differences in opinion over Zanishiria's training had caused a rift in their friendship. Even now, there was a large space between them, greater than the vastness of O'washia's oceans, as they stood next to each other.

"She'll never survive this, you know." Master Tyracor didn't move even at his master's malevolent statement. "The emperor will kill her, and then where will you be? You are too old and incompetent to train another apprentice."

Master Tyracor made an imperceptible flicker of anger in his eyes. "You don't know Zanishiria very well to say such about her."

"I know how to train assassins and when they are ready to go on their own." Shay'renor growled back. "You were foolish to release her from her training at so young an age, as you did. Now, not only will we lose our last trained prev'aron [preshair whip wielder] but also the only chance that our style will be continued."

"Zanishiria gave up everything—her people, her title, and her identity—all so the planet can be rid of the dictator Manscor—that same "man killer" that killed her parents and many of us [assassins]. Do not ever question what she is doing!" Shay'renor just gaped in surprise at his apprentice's reprimand, but Tyracor was not done unleashing his anger. "If Zanishiria is to prove she is more than qualified to be our next whip master and seimora of the coursa then she has got to follow this path. The fight with Manscor is her destiny. She is required to face him to save us and our future. It's what she was trained to do. She will not back down."

Master Shay'renor was silently seething from all the insults his apprentice had thrown at him. He stood like a transfixed statue against the torrent of words he should have issued at the offense, yet he felt no shame for not saying them. He let an uncomfortable silence hang between them. Then, he continued the conversation that would undoubtedly lead to more insults and rude comments. "The council had finished their debate on Zanishiria. They feel there is little more that can be done—if she dies, she dies. And, she was too young to have been called to this. We were foolish to think otherwise; therefore, the council is leaving her to her fate."

"Bi'ek trai rekai!" Master Tyracor cursed loudly, his voice echoing through the enormous cavern. "She is a mere child, yes, but also our only living seimora. Why? Why!" He stalked around in angst and furry. "They had sworn before to keep her protected, was that not the promises they sent the other preshanen up there with?!"

"She had cast all help aside, as well as, cast away her name, as all the preshans did. She no longer follows our codes." Shay'renor stood calmly in place as his apprentice seethed.

"Damn, the codes! She is important."

"More important than the clans?" Master Shay'renor asked "She is but one person, while we are many. The council has done all it can for her. It is she that has shunned their help away. There is nothing more they can do."

"Creeshts-áet! You do not know that she did not accept their help; they may not have given it! There is always more the seimreal could do." Master Tyracor suddenly changed course and turned to the path leading back across the stone bridge to Shairceeo là Coursa.

"And, what do you plan to do?" Master Shay'renor yelled out to him. "You will never reach her in time."

"Better late than never! I will never abandon her like you did me. She will need me when it is all over."

"You're a fool, my apprentice!" Shay'renor called out. "That is why I left you, and that is why the seimora will die."

Master Tyracor muttered a truly incredible curse that stabbed deep into the old master's soul as Tyracor strode away without a backward glance.

The deah-knife froze mere inches from her face then was dropped; the young assassin dodged the deadly blade as it fell beside her. Sye Rainier's hands went to her throat, as Zanishiria rolled away from the sharp Kaumian blade. The young assassin hurried quickly to her master's side. Sye's hands clutched desperately at the whip that had constricted around her neck in a vain attempt to loosen it. Zanishiria sank to the Senior Master's height and brushed her master's cut and bleeding hands away from the preshair whip. Carefully, she removed it from around the woman's neck, trying unsuccessfully to keep the truth from her eyes.

"Stop" Sye croaked and grasped Zanishiria's hands. "I can tell that it is hopeless to try and save me."

"Not hopeless." Zanishiria tried to soothe but her voice trailed away, for she knew that most people would die from the deep preshair wounds in Sye's neck.

The Kaumian could see the truth in the girl's depthless grey eyes but was relieved to see emotion there as well. "I'm glad I didn't lose you." Zanishiria glanced away sadly, her eyes filled with much shame. "You must believe your life is valuable, Zan." Sye whispered. "You cannot help others if you cannot first help yourself. Never become emotionless, for emotion is what makes you human. It does not matter if you are a made-assassin or not, you must have emotion." It seemed Sye Rainier would say more, but her breath failed her and she lay back, exhausted. She lay there, groping for air, beside her apprentice of only-one-year for many long, agonizing minutes, then, she took a long breath.

"Master, I never meant to do this!" Zanishiria urgently told her.

"I-I know. But, you had to if you are to defeat him." Her last word hung on a long moment then faded to silence. Zanishiria searched her master's face and wished for her master to say more, but the silence continued unhindered. A single tear fell from Zanishiria's dark eyes and landed on Sye's forehead. Slowly, it dripped down the master's calm face and disappeared into her cinnamon hair.

Zanishiria stayed, bent over her master's body for a long time. The last sun had set before she moved again. It was then that she became acutely aware of the Royal guards in the shadows of the buildings. They stayed motionless around her, afraid of what she could do to them. Zanishiria glared coldly at each in turn and stood up slowly, as if burdened by a heavy task. The guards backed away nervously and cleared a path to the Taysor Palace. The young assassin walked by without a second glance; her sadness turned to anger which she then directed at the one man in Taysor who had caused her to live the life she had: Manscor.

The Lakean youth strode down the deserted streets of Taysor, followed at a distance by the Royal guard. Only when she reached the final landing of the steps was she stopped. A word in Las'wa froze her in place at the enormous arched entryway of the southern entrance to the palace. Zanishiria turned to the shadow there not surprised nor glad to see the man.

"You will not enter, Zanishiria." Eric Sorey hissed as she stepped out of the shadows. He pronounced her name correctly, rolling it lightly off his tongue like honey.

"Air'is Soreneay." Zanishiria acknowledged, saying his Las'wa name bitterly. "Even you cannot stop me. I do not acknowledge your authority here. You are an outcast of our people. I will never linger on your word."

"You, like the others I left behind, are stupid and weak. The Las'wa care not for the power to be gained above ground. That is why they sent you, a mere fourteen-year-old girl, to stop the most powerful men on this planet."

"A man such as the likes of you is not worth my time." Zanishiria threw an insult back.

Eric let go a mocking chuckle. "Oh, do spare me. You may have scared the Royal guard, but you do not quiver even a hair on my head. You see, I control even Manscor, and he is nothing compared to what I have become. You would be foolish to go after him, for even if he dies, I would still control Obseen."

"You think too highly of yourself." Zanishiria retorted. She turned away and reached for the carved handle on the enormous door.

Eric pulled out his prized weapon—his own preshair whip—knowing any Las'wa would understand its potential. "You will not take another step. If you follow what I say, you may live to another day."

The assassin youth turned her head to gaze at the whip, staying unaffected by its presence—an interesting reaction that Eric noted; even Las'wa clansmen found the weapon disquieting, except by the less-than-a-handful that wielded them. A bored look glazed over her eyes. "You would gain nothing by killing me here, Air'is."

"Nor would you by your death." Eric pointed out. "Now, you can either take what I've offered or take the slashing. Which do you prefer?"

Zanishiria dropped her hands and allowed Eric to bind them. "Don't you know using a preshair whip in such a way is a cheap, unskilled way of proving you really are just a want-to-be prev'aron?"

Eric rose his eyebrows at her goading but then he smiled, becoming amused. He chuckled as he pulled open the door and pushed her through ahead of him. "I heard you were good at tossing mocking words around, or maybe it was just that you understood reason, aiy?" ["Which is it?"] Zanishiria did not respond that time as Eric pushed her down one long, stone-sculptured hallway and down another; however, she could sense her silence had the other Lakean checking her out and making assessments. Her instincts were rewarded when Eric finally stopped her at a blank metal door and pressed a button beside it. As the door whooshed open to an empty black-walled room, the scared-faced assassin-man spun Zanishiria around and took one last, assessing glance at her person. His eyes passed briefly at the preshair whip around her waist. "Want-to-be prev'aron, ey? Says one who is the same. I should have suspected sooner that a girl as young as you had to be a whip-wielder to make the seimreal think her capable of taking on the Emperor."

"Seivier was the one to think me capable of the task."

"Seivier?" Eric repeated.

"Tyracor." She said the name of their shared teacher with a knowing look in her eye. A black eyebrow twitched at the name. "Seivier told me a brief bit about you." Zanishiria continued. "You were the clan's greatest disappointment."

"Only a disappointment? Such a boring word for all I have done." His eyes narrowed as he tried to gleam more information from the young Coursay'sora girl. When Zanishiria didn't add anything, he gloated. "Tyracor told you very little then. I guess I was his best apprentice, after all."

"He only had three of us and you aren't his best." Zanishiria taunted.

Eric rolled his eyes in response to the girl's badgering and thrust her inside the cell. He closed the door with a final harsh laugh.

However, once the door had slid shut, Eric's haughtiness evaporated and his purple eyes gleamed in thought. Did Zanishiria know who Air'is Soreneay was? Eric's full identity had been fully repudiated from all Lakean records upon his betrayal to the clan. Tyracor had vowed to his former apprentice that none would remember who Air'is Soreneay was or what he had done for the Las'wa, not after all the heinous acts Air'is had performed for the Emperor. In return, Air'is had vowed to let go all his ties to the Las'wa, including his name, for the dishonor he had brought on the clan. Their parting, nearly fifteen long years ago, had been melancholy. Yet, if Master Tyracor had continued to honor such a vow, as the man was one to think highly of such contracts, then he would not have given his last apprentice such details. Why else would Zanishiria use such a bland word as disappointment unless she didn't know more than that?

Eric glanced back one last time at the cell he had thrown the young girl into. Certainly, Zanishiria was not the kind of preshanen Eric would have guessed the seimreal to place their bets on, hence why he had not suspected her to be Las'wa until he had laid eyes on her coming up toward the Palace dressed in preshair snakeskin. The girl was too young and too cocky to be anything but naïve for the job. Yet…Tyracor thought her capable of taking on the emperor? Even Air'is, after twelve years of training solely as a prev'aron, had barely the skills to oust Manscor. It hadn't been until Eric had thrust aside all convictions of morality that he had been able to beat the man. *And they send her?* Eric shook his head at the nonsense. *Just what was Tyracor thinking?* This was why he was on the side he had chosen; the Las'wa were on the losing end, as usual.

* * *

Zanishiria ducked a shoulder to land hard on the stone floor. She cursed her still bound hands and pulled herself up the best she could. A groan escaped from someone across from her, causing Zanishiria to freeze and look around the room calculatingly. It was then that Zanishiria noticed the figure hunched up in a fetal position by the door. The young man was very familiar. "Tarin!" She hurried over and worked on the slipping her hands from the bindings.

Tarin thought he was hallucinating, yet Zanishiria sounded right in front of him, seeming so real. "Zan." He croaked. A cool hand touched his cheek—oh, this hallucination was much too real! His name was said again. *Zan sounds like she is sorry to see me.* Tarin felt strong hands pull him to an upright position, and he thought he was next to Zanishiria. *I could never be this close to Zan in real life.* But then, she began talking again, and her voice was too clear to Tarin to be anything but real.

"Come on, Tarin. You need to snap out of it." Zanishiria pulled Tarin's torso onto her lap and rocked him gently. "Creesht-áet! You must have been paralyzed by suraik poison." Zanishiria knew what that usually meant. Without the proper antidote, the victim would die. *No! I cannot lose him, too.* The loss of Sye Rainier was still too great in the assassin's mind and caused unwanted emotions to swell up inside of her. A single tear escaped from her eyes and landed on Tarin's lips.

Tarin felt the wetness on his mouth. He pressed his lips on the droplet. It tastes like salt water. *No,* Tarin muddled through his cloudy thoughts. *It is a tear. Is Zan crying? Why would she cry? She never cries!* With much effort, Tarin lifted a hand and touched Zanishiria's arm clumsily. He felt Zanishiria balk at his touch and felt slightly guilty for startling her. "Zan?" He called softly and felt her lean closer. "I'm fine, Zan. I'm here; stop cryin'. Once th'anti-dote's workin' I'll be good."

Zanishiria paused to comprehend the muddled words Tarin had spoken. "Antidote? Who gave you an antidote?"

"Do'know. Someone wi' purple eyes an' scares on 'is face."

"Air'is." Zanishiria's blood froze. "Manscor must have ordered him to keep you alive. But, why did Air'is listen…?"

Tarin felt the numbness recede a little more from his lips and throat and felt he could say more words. "Th' man said he was after me so I could be a witness."

"Witness to what?" Zanishiria asked, though in her mind she already knew the answer.

"Fight against the seimora." Tarin whispered and exhaled sharply as he struggled to clear his mind. "You have a secret to tell me, eh?"

Zanishiria froze, Tarin could feel the tension in her body. Still hesitant, she sat back and gave her proposal. "Yes, I have something to say, I do admit, but, let us wait until you are functioning before I begin."

"You sure you want me functional?" Tarin attempted to joke. "I could be worse when I'm thinking straight."

"No, I want you thinking clearly." Zanishiria averted her eyes to the blank obsidian wall opposite of her. Her seriousness was almost chilling. "There is much I am sure you wish to discuss." Tarin could feel her emotionally pull back from him as she admitted she had lied to one she called "friend".

The honesty stung, but Tarin knew it was something he had been preparing for since the Lakean Seircor had glared at him next to the waterfall. "Yes, I do."

Chapter Thirteen

When Zanishiria became a preshanen, she gave up everything, her sur-name, people, and life, so that she could try to end the war against the emperor. She had been born the second offspring to the seimore, but she never knew the position she had come into. [Chosen leader of the Las'wa, seimore=masculine, seimora=feminine] At the age of two, her parents were killed in a rebellion at Barashi in Imari. Alone, Art'or, himself only six, found himself needing to take care of his little sister. Uncertain, scared, and without relatives to take them in, Art'or accepted Master Reyh'nor Sei'air's invitation to train under him in the ways of the ancient secrets of assassination (He is one of only two assassins of the Las'wa to follow their ancestors' trade.)

Three years later, the left out Zanishiria caught Master Tyracor's eye and the girl found herself under the aged man's tutelage. He trained her intensely on the techniques of the rare preshair whips, hoping to give her a chance in the harsh underworld. As the girl's skills improved, her seivier [master] began to petition the council to accept Zanishiria into their preshan group—to no avail. It was only fate that intervened on the girl's behalf, sending a preshair to attack the city before the preshans were to leave for the surface. In an unbelievable display of skills and persistence, Zanishiria took down the terrifying beast, proving she was indeed ready for the mission to the assassinate the emperor. Her path was set.

With her first steps into the light, she denounced herself as a Las'wa and knew she would have to rely on herself alone to keep out of the emperor's watchful eye. There were some things Zanishiria refused to let go of, however, the preshair weapons of her trade, though these she hide with the utmost care, her preshair armor, and her thoughts of revenge for her parents and her brother. For her, as long as she had those items, she still had a link to who she was and what she fought for. For her, that was enough...

The rain came down fiercely against the men as they climbed the steep cliffs surrounding Taysor Valley. It bit painfully against exposed flesh and ran in torrents around their hand and footholds in vain attempts to wash the trespassers away to a terrible death. Yet, even in all its fury, the rainstorm couldn't persuade the determined travelers to turn back. The seven poorly-cloaked figures reached the top of the cliffs and huddled close to each other to discuss their route, and to try to conjure up as much warmth as their aging bodies were able. Rain dripped in streams down their hoods to drip to the slick obsidian stone underfoot as they huddled futilely.

Master Yoshida glanced back toward the sprawling city of Taysor that was barely visible through the rain. "We have to get off these cliffs soon! If that next wall hits us, the rocks will be too slippery to hang on to."

Hareoska nodded in agreement and yelled out in turn, "The Gulch of Shaynuar would be the quickest path to Nyhore."

"No," Corsetti argued, "Shaynuar is too dangerous in this weather. The Daunshay Ravine would be safer!" Hareoska shook his head and opened his mouth to disagree, but a loud clap of thunder sounded close by startling them all.

"We have to leave now!" Roko warned from his place next to Dorsetti and Quinn. "Shaynuar is closer, so we will take it. Sunashi," The short master called to the youngest of them, "You know the way the best."

"Yes, sir." Sunashi wiped rain droplets from his eyes and pointed in the direction of the gulch. "It's about eight minutes' walk from here, but I must say, I disagree about this. Dorsetti's arm won't be able to make the climb."

"Oh, don't worry about me, boy, I can handle that climb even if this arm was severed off."

"No, you couldn't, Dorsetti," Master Quinn nodded at Sunashi. "Sun's right. We'd be better off taking the Pass of Kennon or Daunshay Ravine as Corsetti suggested. Both are only a little farther than Shaynuar, but they take us closer to Nyashio."

The six masters lapsed into silence as they contemplated what Quinn had just said. Finally, Hareoska broke the silence. "I'll agree with that. The Pass of Kennon would be more exposed right no, but I feel that it is safer than Daunshay." The others nodded their agreements and in seconds they were moving again with rain hitting their backs in sheets. The twelve-minute trudge through the rain was spent groping for the cloak of the master in front of each walker, so they would not lose each other in the heavy downfall of water, and to keep their dwindling hopes that Sunashi knew where he was going in check. Alas, Sunashi brought them to a halt under a small overhang. Beyond was a bare cliff side that glistened with water droplets. The cliff dropped gradually into the Nyhore plain twenty-five meters below.

"Well, here's the Pass of Kennon," Sunashi turned his back against the rain.

Dorsetti eyes the pass doubtfully "It doesn't look much like a pass to me."

"It's not." The younger master chuckled slightly. "But, the crip explorers thought it was. I'm just glad I wasn't the one to name the place."

"Yeah, you'd probably call it cliff face number two," Dorsetti jested as he fixed his make-shift sling. The master wrapped it carefully then knotted it tighter against his chest. "All right. I think this thing'll hold. Just get me off this rock and back on safe ground again."

The masters began their decent, following Sunashi's lead. They descended slowly, for the rocks were slick underfoot from the pounding of the waters. There were few crevices and ledges to choose from making the way more hazardous. As they climbed downward, the storm released in a greater fury, as if in an attempt to kill the trespassers who invaded its domain. In one such attempt, a loud crack of thunder startled the already precarious hold of Dorsetti's hand. The master floundered for purchase on the rocks but his fingers slipped of the tiny ledge he clung to. A startled yelp warned the masters below that a man was sliding down. Yoshida and Sunashi pressed themselves tightly against the cliff face and watched helplessly as the wounded master flashed past, still groping for a handhold. The group watched as Dorsetti's body lost contact with the cliff face and fell eight feet until it pitched against a pointed outcropping, where he slid over it clutching for handholds, and disappeared below.

There had been no time to register the man's plight to rescue him.

Hareoska swore and urged them to climb faster, and much to their benefit, the rain slackened its barrage and allowed them a quicker decent. They found vines below the outcropping and used them to climb down. It was near the bottom of the cliff that they found Dorsetti dangling from a vine overlooking a fourteen-meter-drop.

"You had better hurry up! I can't hang here all day, you know." Dorsetti growled as his arm strained and his grip began to falter.

The others chuckled in nervous relief at seeing their friend safe. Sunashi and Corsetti lowered themselves closer to Dorsetti and grasped his tunic. "Alright, you can let go. We'll haul you up." Corsetti instructed and helped Sunashi pull the wounded man away from the edge. Once Dorsetti was away from the drop, the rest of the masters helped him to a large ledge that allowed everyone but Yoshida to stand together.

"Shoot, was that a killer!" Dorsetti exclaimed as he released his breadth. He leaned against the rock face gratefully until he realized just how much his arm hurt. He inspected his shoulder gingerly and found a tiny fracture with his fingers as he probed an open gash on the top-most point of his shoulder. He gritted his teeth in pain as he pulled his fingers free of the wound and wiped the blood on his now tattered tunic. "Well, my arm's broken, I'm pretty sure," he announced, "You know, that smooth piece of ground below looks mighty appealing right now, if you ask me. So, by all means, can we get down and meet it?"

"He's all right." Sunashi joked, "A broken bone or two never stopped him any. Oh, and look! There is Pass #1. I knew it was around here somewhere."

"Will you just get moving!" Yoshida growled from his dangling perch on the other side of the ledge.

"Right, right, I was just going to." Sunashi turned away and grabbed a vine to test his weight on. "See you all at the bottom!" And, with a cheerful wave, Sunashi slid down the plant all the way to the ground.

"Trŏv, that kid's crazy!" [Closest translation: "shit!"] Hareoska grumbled as he grasped the vine and started his descent. The others followed suit until only Yoshida and Dorsetti were left standing on the ledge.

"I'll go first so I can help you, if you need." Yoshida offered.

"Nah. I'm good. I'll just take Sunashi's lead and fly down." Yoshida opened his mouth to object but Dorsetti waved him to silence. "You don't get to be my age without learning something, you know." Dorsetti smiled ruefully and showed

Yoshida his palm. "It's a little trick I showed Sunashi when he was still my trainee."

"Tarénik scales." Yoshida recognized the Stikes weapon easily. "To protect the skin from being burned when sliding down ropes but to stop a fall nearly as easily, like a creeshts can when climbing walls. Impressive. I guess I'll be following you down." [Tarénik = lizard of Nyashio, large and dangerous.]

Once Dorsetti and Yoshida joined the others, Master Quinn took a moment to inspect Dorsetti's shoulder and apply a thin coat of mica plant ointment over the wound. "All right, already! Quite worrying about me. We have more important business right now." Dorsetti swatted Quinn away and stood up. "Lead." He ordered Sunashi.

Sunashi started to lead them to the left, where Nyhore's main road came out from the north, the direction to Kauxazoum in Bialthioum, but Corsetti grabbed his shoulder and turned his around. "The spaceports are south."

"Oh, right. I knew that." Sunashi didn't miss a beat as he changed his direction, acting as if he had never made a wrong step. "Don't worry. We should be there before nightfall."

Roko rolled his eyes. "Yeah, who's worried, Sunashi's leading."

The paralysis had worn off but the numbness of the situation had not. His only companion had not moved since they had last spoken and the chill from her words still lingered in the air. Tarin shifted, something he could do now, in an attempt to attract Zanishiria's attention. The young assassin merely glanced over at him then away without a word. "I'm ready." Tarin croaked out in hopes that she'd break the awkward silence.

Zanishiria glanced back with an assessing look, causing Tarin to want to look away, but his stiff muscles wouldn't respond fast enough. "How much of the truth can you stand, my friend?"

Tarin mulled over the question slowly, finding his mind would only process so fast. "If it is what I need to know to understand then I will handle whatever you will give me...you have always known how much I can tolerate."

"I'm not sure on this case." Zanishiria looked away wistfully. "But, there is too little time to be delicate with my words." Tarin chuckled at her wording. Zanishiria was never delicate when it came to speaking the truth. "I may take a while to get through all the details but do you feel like you can listen and hear me out?"

"I will listen but I may ask questions."

"Ar'sé. [That's fine.] But you must listen carefully." Zanishiria paused and drew a deep breath to gather her thoughts. To Tarin's surprise, she started off telling him of Obseen's history before Manscor's take-over, some of which he had read in Quinn's journals. It was not the direction he had thought the young-assassin to take. "The Royals' War, as you know, was brought on by Prince Xi's domination. The opposing assassin clans, that despised his dictatorship, pulled together to form what was once called the "Lakean Resistance". Their revolt officially started the war four months before the written date of 4012.

"Manscor's first act to ensure his power by taking over our capitol city, Taysor. Unnerved by the emperor's closeness, the Naitiege attacked the capitol, hoping to wrestle it away from his control; however, they failed and Manscor's Royal guard stormed Nyashio. The Naitiege retreated to Koro at the Nyore-Imak boarder—though they were pursued by the guard. The Suez refused to assist the Naitiege in any way, save to give them passage through Imak to Imari and to call for aide; it was later found out that Imak's refusal was because they had decided to side with the emperor.

"The Xsorians quickly came to the call of the Neitiege and helped fend off the Royal guard long enough for a small group of rogue fighters, led by Ze'is and Mei'cor Coursay'sora to join them at Barashi. The Royal guard then attacked with its full force. The fighting lasted from four o' clock that morning until twenty-three-thirteen that evening—right before the last sun set. The fight was hopeless... and orders were given to retreat at will. All did but a handful of assassins who stayed behind to cover the retreat. It was Ze'is and Mei'cor who held the last stand at Baeriant Square. In the end, they were the last to be killed on that unfortunate day. Their deaths dealt a fateful blow to the resisting clans who had amassed behind them against Manscor. It seemed the war had been lost before it really began."

"I have never heard of those two leaders, Ze'is and Mei'cor. Who were they and why were they so important?" Tarin asked.

Zanishiria turned her head to glare as him, though he
was not sure what he had said to offend her. "They were great
leaders of the Las'wa, superior fighters whose abilities in battle
and as leaders were uncontested by the Guild to be the "best". It
was they who started the resistance, their opposition of the
emperor being acknowledged by most of the Assassins' Guild.
Their deaths were a great loss for the clans."

"You are Lakean as well." Zanishiria stilled beside
Tarin, causing him to glance up at her stiff body. "Your friend
Seircor said he was a Lakean and that you were important to the
clan, so I put two and two together with little thought."

"So, they made it to Qusairo then."

"Yes. Prince Anmero is safe, as is K'sho." Tarin paused,
hesitating to admit his and Seircor's dislike of each other. "They
wished me to assure you that they are fine; however, I think I
have taken you off the subject…So, what happened after the
leaders were killed?" He did not have to say he was ignorant to
the resistance's history, as he, being one of the conquered
Neitiege, had been kept under the emperor's watch. At least it
seemed to coincide with the notes in the journal.

Zanishiria eyed Tarin, wondering about his pause, but
she had little time to tell Tarin what she could as it was, so she
continued. "The Resistance began to break up until King
Lapsair, the Tá sharay Khan Torez, Master Quinn, and Berris
Tearrì Sinhail reformed the pieces of the army."

"The Berris? Isn't she the High Lady of Traygor? I did
not know she and the Trayshans had any part in this war."

Zanishiria sighed unhappily at the constant interruptions.
"She is the high warrioress of the Trayshans, yes. More
importantly, she and her husband were close friends with Ze'is
and Mei'cor Coursay'sora. Now, stop asking so many questions.
What happened then has less importance than what happens
now."

"Fine."

"Fine…With the deaths of the Coursay'soras, the Las'wa
vanished, wanting to distance themselves from this war;
however, they found they could not remain silent forever, not
when their enemy still lived—and a traitor to their people could
lead Manscor to their hidden city. That man who captured you
was once a clansman." Tarin face looked shocked at the news.
Zanishiria ignored him as she kept talking. "The Las'wa
promised the resistance that they would create thirteen warriors

to personally assassinate Manscor. Seircor, whom you met, as well as his sister, and my older brother were among those selected." Tarin glanced up again, this time in surprise at finding Zanishiria had had a brother; she had never mentioned anything about her family before—not that she had a chance faking to be assassin-Royal. This time, though, Tarin managed to keep his mouth shut. "I wasn't one of the preshanen selected but I watched my friend and my brother train on occasion, wishing I was with them. The training was the most difficult our people have ever seen. Three died in the first year…" Zanishiria's dark eyes took on a distant look and she paused at the thoughts of those who died. She stirred after three-breadths-counts. "Not a year and a half ago, the council finally deemed the preshans fit to head to Taysor. That was when my master, Tyracor, stepped up to the council with one last plea for me to join the preshans. He told them I was ready. The council was doubtful still but they finally agreed to give me a test that would prove my abilities. When I succeeded, I was allowed to join the others in bringing an end to Manscor's reign."

"Wait, back up a sec." Tarin struggled to sit up "What was your test about?"

Zanishiria helped the Naitiege youth into a comfortable position then sat back and stared indifferently at the never-changing black wall across from them. "You wouldn't believe me, even if I told you."

"There are many things I have come to see differently in these past few months, Zan, most of them about you. I am willing to listen now to even the most incredible possibility."

His friend could not help an ironic smile at the young man's honesty. "I had to kill a preshair if I was to become a whip master. It is a rite of passage every whip wielder is opted to go through but most don't attempt. I was desperate enough to try."

Tarin's eyes grew wide. "A preshair." He whispered as if it was a curse. He ran his tongue along his dry lips and felt his clammy skin freeze along his back at the thought of the sharp, knife-scaled snakes that ruled the underworld. "That is an instant path to death to engage with a preshair."

"Yes, but I had to do what I could to be allowed to go with the preshans."

Silence engulfed the room as the truth of Zanishiria's life became clear to Tarin. The Naitiege wondered if he really knew her at all; the young assassin he had come to know was a Royal-born, and not some crazy, preshair-killing Lakean-born. If what Zanishiria now told him was true, not only was she not related to the Novastones but her skills were unsurpassed by most in the Guild, let alone the planet. And, if the history of her training was any indication, Tarin felt he understood what her mission entailed: her battle with Manscor would claim her life if it didn't claim the emperor's first.

With the realizations, he signed in defeat and slumped down to the floor again. "Seircor was right. I am so stupid! I had no idea what I was getting myself into when I promised Master Quinn I would protect you." The Lakean rose her eyebrows at him muttering. Tarin thought he needed to protect her? What had ever given him the idea she was in need of protection? Master Quinn? Tarin then let go a hollow laugh at the gloomy epiphany of his predicament past. "Hey, I never had a chance, did I?" Again, Zanishiria just stared at him, waiting for clarification. After Tarin's last comment of making a "Vow of Protection" she wasn't quite sure what the Neitiege was referring. "Our rematch from our very first fight at the Center. I never had a chance."

"No, you didn't." Zanishiria agreed quietly but without any arrogance coloring her words.

"In all the nine hells!" Tarin cursed and met her eyes. "So, what are you capable of exactly?"

"As a fighter? I am not sure." Zanishiria grew quiet and very still. "You will find out very soon, I think."

Tarin sat up quickly and spun around to clamp his friend's shoulders in desperation. "So you were going to fight Manscor?"

"I still am." Zanishiria met Tarin's blue eyes calmly.

"You're thrown in the Emperor's cell block." He pointed out the obvious.

Zanishiria kept the fact that she could easily get out to herself. "It is what I was trained to do—kill the Emperor Manscor. Call it revenge, if you would like. Revenge for the loss of our greatest leaders." *My parents.*

"But Manscor's the best fighter on Obseen right now! No one's beaten him in a duel since his very first year as an apprentice. You'll die if he ever actually lets you out to duel him. Damn it, Zan!"

Zanishiria touched her fingers to Tarin's lips to silence him. Tarin quieted and sat back as his younger companion gazed at him with a placid countenance. "Manscor has never been against anyone like me before. I cannot guarantee that I will beat him, but I believe I can. My master told me once that I was the emperor's equal in battle. The victor will be whomever wants to live more..." Zanishiria was going to say more when the door slid open and two food trays were slid into the room. The door hissed shut in their wake. "Oh, how thoughtful of them." She said sarcastically and stood up to collect the trays. She set them down next to Tarin and straightened back up.

"You should eat too." Tarin motioned for the second tray as he picked up a mint roll.

Zanishiria shook her head. "Not now, but don't let me stop you. I have to prepare my weapons first." Tarin rose an eyebrow questioningly, so Zanishiria took out a preshair knife. "My weapons need to be inspected and sharpened."

Tarin was surprised the guard had even allowed her to be captured without taking away her weapons. It was unusual but perhaps for the best, as Zanishiria would not have given them up without a fight. As he ate, Tarin watched her inspect and care for her two preshair knives, creeshts short-sword, then katana sword, her two wrist blades, eight shuriken, and set of shée fans. "I can't believe they didn't take your weapons." He finally stated out loud.

Zanishiria shrugged, unconcerned. "Their mistake. Air'is probably thought this cell could keep me in, so I am not a threat right now."

"You know this Air'is well?"

"He is a traitor from our clan." She answered coldly and preoccupied herself with her final weapon.

"What kind of weapon is that?" Tarin asked curiously, not really seeing what was in her hands.

"A preshair whip." Zanishiria held its lithe body up where Tarin could see its slender but menacing shape. Even after more than two years of use, the whip was shiny, every scarlet-tipped black scale oiled to perfection and sharpened to a deadly pointedness. Awe filled the Neitiege's eyes as he looked upon the weapon he had only heard distant rumors about. "See, young Stikes, I really did take on a preshair." Dumbfounded, Tarin could only nod his head and finished his food in silence.

Zanishiria waited until Tarin had curled up and fallen asleep before collecting her weapons and sitting down in the corner opposite the door. She took out a handful of florick moss and mykco herbs and chewed them slowly. As the juices started their work, she bandaged her preshair knife cut she had required from fighting Sye Rainier and then checked her body for other wounds, which she applied a savya ointment to. Finally, when all was done and her pain was diminished, she drifted off to a dreamless half-sleep.

The Xsorian youth pressed the off switch on his computer and watched as the image in the air disappeared to cast the room in shades of grey and black. Silence blanketed the room allowing Page to hear the distant sounds of others moving in the great mansion of stone. He allowed his turmoiled mind to pass through his fellow Xsorians until he came to his brother's peaceful presence. The quietness of Lap's mind was like a sharp wall against Page's solicitous one, and caused Page to immediately break the contact and rub his pounding temples. "Well, at least he's asleep." The tá sharid glanced back at his computer before standing up and heading for the door. *Father needs to know all this right away. I'll just have to leave without waking Lap.* Page was out the door then, slowing only to swoop up his long coat, and stalked down the dark and deserted hallway to the garage.

The winding staircase was dark and silent and a cool breeze blew upon Page's face as he descended it. Only the hollowness of his footsteps echoed around his ears causing him to wish for the plush carpeting of the hallways that could mute his passage. The stairs ended on an open platform leading to a walkway over a running stream. Page strode across it but paused at the end to glance back to make sure there wasn't a shadow out of place. His eyes saw nothing, so he scanned the dark buildings of the city, catching their ethereal beauty of lines and shapes before turning back to his destination.

The spacious garage was empty except for the eight-or-so vehicles parked in equal spaces across the bay. Page wove his way through the assortment of machines until he came to his small racing hover-car. He ran his hand over the sleek metallic green body admiringly before hopping over the side into the plush driver's seat. His fingers automatically pressed the security code into the computer and the hover-car thrummed to life. The stealth mode kicked on immediately and masked the sound of the engine thrusters.

As the hover-car rose off the ground, Page reached out with his mind for his brother's but found nothing there. Frowning slightly, he stretched his awareness to the many corridors of the mansion with little success. A frustrated growl escaped his throat as he widened his senses outward. "I never should have taught him the evasion technique. He mastered it too well."

"I mastered it too well." Lap's voice taunted in Page's head.

Page's head twirled to the right and his eyes glared disapprovingly at his brother sitting in the back seat. "Get out! I can't take you with me. Now!"

"No." Lap retorted and crossed his arms defiantly "You're not leaving me this time. You always go gallivanting off and I miss all the adventure. Not this time."

Page sighed, exhausted by what he had learned and from the time of night, and found himself annoyed that he was losing another argument with his brother. "We are going into a war zone." He said to try to persuade his stubborn brother. Lap just stared expectantly back. "I could sleep while you drive, I guess." Page admitted. "But," he interjected at his brother's flash of glee, "If you leave so much as a scratch on this baby, I will kill you...very slowly."

The brothers went through the process of exchanging seats and Lap eased the hover-car out of the garage. He whizzed it through the city in silent speed then brought up the night vision on the car's windshield. "So, where are we going?"

Page looked to be asleep but he responded immediately. *"To Taysor where else?"* Page felt his brother's mind freeze. He opened one green eye to glance over at Lap's boyish figure. *"Where else did you think I was going?"*

"No, I suspected." Lap hesitated, "But I am in trouble now...we will be meeting father there I expect."

"Hey, I warned you," Page closed his eye and relaxed into the plushness of the heated seat, *"It's no longer my problem what trouble you get into with father."*

Lap glared at his unsupportive brother "You're in more trouble for allowing me along." He said sulkily and pushed the hover-car to its top speed and began to dodge rock outcroppings with the hope that Page might not sleep well during the trip; however, he didn't keep at it for long. Lap could feel the exhaustion radiating off his brother. It was the only reason the older Torez hadn't made much attempt at an argument. No way had he been in a position to drive. *"I hope whatever you found for father will be worth ignoring his orders."*

Starting to drift, Page answered slowly, *"Me too."*

Lap gave a quick glance sideways to see Page slumped against the seat, already dozing off. The fatigue on his face stayed there despite him already lost to sleep. Lap frowned in sympathy and focused of their road and pushing the hover-car to maximum speed. *Father makes you do too much, and, as his obedient heir, you would do anything until your heart gives out. I hope father recognizes that.* Lap gave one last glance to Page's form and pulled his brother's overcoat around him tighter. *I won't let you do it alone.* He vowed as he returned to his task. *Not if it's something I can do in your instead, brother.*

Darkness descended quickly over the valley of Taysor. It brought with it a silence that was sullen and layered with a sense of doom. To one and all, it seemed as if the world was taking a deep breath preparing for what was to come.

In the vastness of the halls and lavish rooms in the emperor's quadrant of Taysor Palace, the deadened quiet blanketed everything; not a single person was presently daring the halls. Only the emperor himself, preoccupied by the prisoners in his cell, was awake in his quarters, pacing away on the floor.

"You would best to get to sleep, My Liege, or you will be in ill condition to face Zanishiria tomorrow."

Manscor whirled toward the voice to his right, a weapon appearing in his hand. "You know not to sneak, Teera."

"I do not sneak, Manscor." The Suez master rebuked suavely. "But, I do keep an eye on the condition and health of my leader." Teera stepped away from the enormous window she had come through and eyed the richly garnished room with mild distaste. "I see you have still not added more weapons to this clutter of finery." She commented darkly then stalked over to her leader. Manscor watched her carefully as she stepped around behind him and sat on a corner of his bed. He had heard the assassin woman's criticisms of his rooms before. She liked to spew off her mouth at how, for all his training and time on Obseen, he still clung to his former Royal ways, not adopting the less refined furnishings the assassins preferred.

"What brings my most dangerous adviser to me tonight?"

Teera allowed him the pleasure of a small, genuine smile before she stood up and stepped toward him, seduction riddling her footsteps. "My Liege, I am not your most dangerous adviser. I am your most trusted."

Still there was slight caution in Manscor's eyes. He was not easily swayed by the advances of his favorite assassin woman. "You never come without reason Teera; this I know well."

"So, I cannot come to see my lord as I please?" She asked teasingly, her voice husky and pouty. "No? Sad, I wanted to see you." She sighed theatrically. "But...I did have a reason for coming. First, though, you must take off those uncomfortable clothes, change into something more casual. You overwork yourself on the eve of a day that is sure to be a turning point in your victory over the Assassins' Guild." Without waiting for a reply, Teera ran her hands over his muscular shoulders and lifted the stately robe off of his body. Deftly, she threw it onto the back of a chair nearby and was already undoing the leather laces at the neck of his shirt. They loosened and she pulled the shirt over his head. Teera turned her back to Manscor to collect his night robe, giving the leader a chance to pull off his boots and pants. She turned back and helped him into the robe, stepping to the front to tie its silk belt together.

Manscor studied her beautiful but hardened face as she concentrated on his belt. Finally, he could stand it no longer and he reached out to touch her dark brown hair. Teera glanced up at the emperor with a smile and allowed him to kiss her passionately. When they finally broke, she pushed back gently to look him seriously in the eye. "You must hold off for a little while, My Liege. We have things to discuss first."

Manscor sighed and went to sit on his enormous bed. "You are right, of course." He gathered himself up and gave her all of his keen-eyed attention. "Well, my confidant?" He asked, now back into his role as emperor.

"First, I am displeased of your using my apprentice so."

"Tarin will not be harmed in any way, Teera."

"You cannot guarantee that, you know, not during war time. I swear I will kill anyone whom harms the boy."

"I will keep him in the best of care." Manscor promised. "Now, tell me why you've really come. I know your feigned care of your apprentice is slight at best."

Teera strode over to the bed and lowered her voice. "King Lapsair needs to be dealt with."

"Oh? What can you convict him with, my dear? The clans would rebel fully if we arrest him on no charges."

"They are already rebelling." Teera replied. "With the war going on, arresting Lapsair will be the easiest of tasks. Why do you hesitate so? Just arrest him quietly and be done with it."

Manscor smiled and reached for Teera's hands. "I like the direct way you handle things. It makes decisions that much easier." The Royal-assassin tried to pull Teera closer but the Suez woman refused. "What, not the answer you wanted?"

"You can't blow this off so quickly. Make signed orders so that I can arrest King Lapsair. I will then go to his quarters before the suns break."

Manscor paused to consider then he turned away to write some orders on a thin slab of Xsorian-designed obsidian. "You have my permission to apprehend King Lapsair; do so at your own discretion."

Teera accepted the orders and tucked them into a pouch at her belt. She still refused his gentle pull, however, so Manscor lay his rakish frame down on his plush bedspread and turned so he was looking at his articulate ceiling and the indolent way the support beams met the crystalline walls. Finally, the silence gnawed on him and the Royal-assassin adverted his gaze to his still assassin adviser. "You have more to say, I assume?"

"I do." Teera stated icily and yet she allowed the silence to grow. Manscor eyed her impatiently, his brandy eyes dark with anger at the master's insolence. Master Teera's visage let slip a diminutive grin of satisfaction at her leader's glare. "The marks on the Senior Master are from a weapon we have no information on."

Manscor let go the breath he had been withholding and chuckled. "For a moment, I thought you were really worried about something."

"This is a serious matter!" Teera growled, her thirty-seven-year-old body coiled in her anger. Manscor snapped his mouth shut. "She's a Lakean for sure. Only Lakeans have weapons more powerful than any we possess. You would be wise to study everything Eric Sorey gave us before you face Zanishiria tomorrow."

"I've already studied his files." The emperor sighed and sat up. "Ever since we discovered the Las'wa were sending specialized youths to try and assassinate me, I have made it my business to know them. However, none of the weapons we were informed about match the wounds on Rainier's neck. Zanishiria is carrying a weapon that is not in Eric's files."

"So, why haven't you searched her?"

"Eric threw her in the cell with Tarin still fully armed. Because of that we went to Plan B."

"Plan B?" Master Teera narrowed her steely, topanish eyes. "Did you poison her food?"

"No," Manscor shook his head, "I couldn't risk killing Tarin, so I ordered my guard to add sauleen to their meal."

"And what if Zanishiria suspected that?"

Manscor shrugged. "I don't think that will happen but if it does, I will just have to be extra cautious tomorrow. She may not ask for a square face-off, anyway, in which case I will not be obliged to fight with her."

"She's had special training; training made to go against your own. Of course, she will want to fight you. And, do not assume you are the better fighter. She will know there is sauleen in her food and that you do not know what weapons she is carrying. She has the upper-hand." Teera paused to study her leader's face. "Why are you so calm about all this?"

"If I was to panic, Zanishiria would have the advantage; besides, I planned for the possibility of the girl not taking my bait. Eric has set her a trap."

"Well thought, My Liege. I apologize for doubting you; you are always better than I ever estimate you. I am intrigued at how you will outplay me next."

"I enjoy our game of cunning just as much as you, my love." Manscor purred, sensing a change in the slender woman as she swayed provocatively toward him. "Does this mean I have answered all your concerns now?"

Teera leered at her leader, her topanish eyes sliding over his well-formed frame hungrily. "I will always be concerned of you, my lord. But, yes, I am quite ready to make you go to bed. You've kept me from it for too long."

Chapter Fourteen

Sauleen is one of many drugs that are tasteless and well-versed to the assassin's trade. From Sentinal 2, this spice quickly puts a victim in a state of sleep not unlike being put under for surgery; however, Sauleen does not need the monitoring of surgical anesthesia and quickly surpassed the ages-old drug used for operations. For the assassins of Obseen, it is an illegal substance they obtain through the Royal's black-market business with the nations of Sentinal 2.

For a room with thick walls, it wasn't very quiet. To Zanishiria's trained ears, there was a constant noise thrumming through the cell from voices or the footsteps of the Royal guards outside. She sighed inwardly, having already given up on sleep, and listened tentatively to the murmuring voices in the hall. Hours passed until it was well into the night, and still sleep eluded the young assassin. Finally, grown restless, and a little annoyed that she could have a chance to sleep if she only ate the cold food given to them by the guards, Zanishiria sat up and fiddled with her preshair knife. "Air'is did me a favor by allowing me to keep my weapons."

Zanishiria stopped playing with her knife to think of the significance of that fact. *"So, why do I keep myself here?"* A year ago, she would have already cut out of her cell with the dagger. She eyed the wall and weapon calculatingly. "But, Air'is knew that when he threw me in here...this is a trap... Creeshts-áet!" She hissed and rolled onto her back again to play with the knife some more. "However, I'd much rather fill my time scouting out the palace than sitting here waiting for the emperor to decide to bring me to him." She growled at her reluctance to play the game Air'is Soreneay obviously wanted her to join. With a final frustrated huff, Zanishiria stood and stalked to the door. She studied it to some length before deciding to hack into the wiring system.

An easy stab into the metal control panel pushed the knife up to its hilt. Another slice across made a right angle and downward finished the other side of the triangular section she had decided to cut. A final stab in the center of the cut section and a quick twist and pull had the metal piece out and on the floor. Zanishiria studied the wiring inside and in less than five minutes, she was able to figure out which wires went where. The door whooshed open another minute later.

Not a single warning was issued against her as Zanishiria slipped out of her prison cell. In fact, there wasn't a guard close by, which sent the youth's mind on instant alert. She skulked quickly down the long prison hallways, finding only a handful of soldiers, until she came to the large, eastern-block door. With surprising skill, Zanishiria navigated through the emperor's security system, even finding a map that showed her to the tech room twenty-nine rooms beyond. Every room the Lakean assassin passed was empty, but there was sign of habitation—like the well cleaned rooms, that told the girl the rooms were well used. Zanishiria kept note of every detail in the hallway and rooms she passed, keeping watch for suspicious areas and quick exits. By the time she had reached the tech room, she had a pretty efficient escape plan in place.

There were three occupants in the tech room. Zanishiria found one to be a Royal guard and the other two to be computer technicians. They were laughing at some joke and not paying any attention to their monitors. There were four long tables and thirty-five computers between Zanishiria and the three workers, but the youth crept over to them in mere seconds. In a flash of scarlet and black and the small spray of blood, the three people fell to the floor, dead. None had seen the assassin sneak up upon them, so not a sound had been raised.

Zanishiria stepped over the fallen bodies lamentably but, once she was at the main computer, she was focused on her business. She surveyed the security monitors carefully before bringing uploaded files of Manscor's onto the largest screen. Zanishiria bypassed the emperor's security codes quickly and began to survey the documents. Her dark eyes swept the files, catching every major piece of information with a critical swiftness. A low snarl formed in her throat as she read the last file. "How dare he! I swear I will stop him for good this time."

She demolished the computer system in a slight fury and stood up. A movement of the security screens averted her attention. Eric Sorey was striding down the hallway toward the tech room. Zanishiria stalked to the door and slipped into the room across the way to wait. Eric's footsteps paused in the tech room then hurried as he saw the dead technicians and guard. Zanishiria fled silently as she heard him curse at the inoperable computer monitors.

The well-thought-out route Zanishiria had prepared earlier took her past an empty mess hall and through a series of luxury-adorned rooms until she reached a large, empty training room. Enormous Suez-designed pillars connected the obsidian floor to its marble-ceilinged partner. There were fifty similar pillars in perfect rows across the room, showing Zanishiria the spaciousness of the place. *This is a good a place as any for a face off.* Zanishiria thought as she proceeded into the room. Behind her, Eric's angry footsteps echoed down the halls, reminding the younger Lakean that he knew how to track her.

Zanishiria ducked behind an enormous pillar just as Eric's shadow fell across the doorway. She watched as the man's purple eyes swept the room keenly. Eric stalked cautiously into the room. "I know you're in here, seimora, I can smell you." Zanishiria could see that Eric did not know where she was hiding, so, though she wanted to strangle the traitor's throat, she waited where she was. "Or should I call you a Royal crip then? Abandoned the assassin ways for a life of luxury, have you? If it was your brother, he'd have attacked me by now." Zanishiria still didn't respond to Eric's words, despite the fact that she was reeling from the mention of her deceased brother. "But, I guess you've become soft with your year up here. After all, everyone is pampered in a way you never knew." Zanishiria heard him pause and thought the sound of scraping scales followed. Warily, she peeped her head around the stone pillar and caught sight of Eric across the room with his back turned to her; in his hand was his own preshair whip.

Zanishiria slipped to another pillar, being careful to not make a sound, and paused to look back at Eric. The one-time Las'wa had turned his head slightly to the right to show the long scar that stretched from his hairline, across his eye, and down to his chin. Zanishiria knew the story of how he had gotten the scar, but to her, it wasn't anything valiant. She continued to watch the other man carefully; though, the weapon in his hand was a real threat to her.

"You know Tyracor created me to be the best preshair whip wielder of all time." Eric continued his muttering as he scanned the room. "So how then do you think a little girl that was the one-time daughter of the seimoré would have a chance with the apprentice he spent the most time on? He gave you the perfect fairy tale story, perhaps? Hm? Of how the orphaned daughter of an acclaimed leader could be taught to wield the most dangerous weapon on all of Obseen and avenge her parents' deaths?" Eric turned as he thought he saw Zanishiria skipping around behind pillars. "But...you are too young to understand what a preshair whip can do. To you it is just a tool to swing around, but in my hands, it is used as it should, a weapon!" Eric struck with his whip at a pillar and lavished at the loud crack it made as it wrapped around the sturdy poll. No sound of pain followed, however. Annoyed, Eric marched around the pillar and found nothing there. "Chreeshts-áet! Where are you, you cur!"

Zanishiria flinched slightly at his loud voice like she hadn't at the whip's noise. She had flitted away from the pillar just as Eric had unleashed the weapon and was now not five feet away. She knew it would be only a matter of time before Eric found her, unless she faced him first. "You have no right to use a weapon such as that." She finally replied and quickly stepped away as the preshair whip wrapped around the pillar where her head had been.

"I swear I will get you! How dare you, a fourteen-year-old sighp, tell me how to use a preshair whip! I'm more worthy of it than you."

Zanishiria dodged another attack. "You are foolish to say that. The preshair whip can only be used if you have proven yourself. From what I heard, that isn't you. You would be wise to take that into account." Zanishiria spun and blocked the next whip strike, the two whips coiling around each other. A loud crack echoed dangerously thought the room.

There was a chilly wind blowing that resulted from the already come and gone rainstorm. Its cold tendrils pulled on the tight tent fabrics, causing them to pop loudly. Soldiers all throughout the camp were lying awake, unable to sleep from the sound. Every time the winds died down and they would start to drift to sleep just to be startled awake again from a roaring breath of air.

"This is a nasty turn." Seircor muttered as he glanced at the ceiling of Qusairo's large tent. "My first real night above ground and I am unable to sleep because of the wind."

Both Anmero and K'sho rolled over to look at the Lakean. It was Anmero who answered first. "Indeed, this squall is a tad too ferocious. It makes me wish for the calmness of the underground...I wonder how Zanishiria is faring in all this."

Seircor glanced over at Anmero in his calculating way. After a moment his eyes warmed enough to answer. "I am sure she is handling herself well; she was always good at surviving on her own. And, I am sure she would be honored that you show her concern; though she would never say so out loud. Zanishiria...is not one to show her affections easily."

"She seems to voice them well to me and Tarin." K'sho countered quietly from his place across the way.

"I would be surprised if she actually spoke what was close to her heart." Seircor turned his attention to the other youth. "Zanishiria was not one to even show her affections to her brother or to myself, her dearest friend since childhood." K'sho shied away from Seircor's hard voice, causing the Lakean's eyes to soften. "Kye moreay, I am sorry. You knew her differently than me. It is not for me to judge her as I do; perhaps, she did indeed open up to you more, as you are very different from the life and people she grew up with. In all honesty, it would be nice if she has changed and become more open because of you."

K'sho brushed away Seircor's apology in a way the other man could not help admire. "You are her dearest friend, Seircor, so I am certain your assessment of her is accurate. I have only known her one year and know that that is not much time to truly know someone. You are right to caution me on my conceived notions of her as a friend; I merely have seen her as being honest and open."

Anmero watched the exchange and noted the easy way the two assassins negotiated their differences. It was very different compared to the way Seircor had faced-off with Tarin. Then again, K'sho was much more diplomatic than he had judged his tall Neitiege friend to be. Seircor turned back to Anmero, interrupting his thoughts. "As for the calmness of the underground, Shairceeo has been a little tense lately, with the war and all, but it is the council that is the most on edge. So, it is really a false sense of peace below." He paused as one of the other fighters groaned from his bedroll and rolled over. Seircor continued in a whisper, being respectful to the men whom had finally found sleep. "Las'wa do not venture above ground these days without giving up their names—it is a rule of ours—but I was asked by the council to come here under the special circumstances...." He paused as if considering how best to explain the seimreal's "special" orders. "I....was asked because I had been one of the original preshans. I am Zanishiria's back-up, I guess the term is, and also her "evaluator". The council was concerned Zanishiria had turned. I was sent to see if she was sticking with the clan's plans or had exposed us to Manscor."

"Exposed?" K'sho asked, sounding surprised at Seircor's choice of words.

"I was to evaluate how effective Zanishiria had been living here for one year. If she had given the emperor or the Honoreds any hint that she was Las'wa, I was to eliminate her."

"By eliminate you mean "kill" right?" Anmero asked, alarmed. He had not expected such horrible measures be placed on a clan's own.

Seircor motioned for the prince to quiet his voice. "Yes, but only if I deemed it necessary. The secrecy of Zanishiria's identity was imperative to keeping the emperor from being tipped off that the Las'wa were still in the war. Seeing as none, not even her closest friends, knew who she was means Zanishiria kept herself from being discovered."

Anmero nodded in understanding, or as much as he felt he could considering how little he really knew of the assassins of Obseen. He knew better, though, then to press further on an inquiry into the secrets of a clan that held such tight measures on keeping itself hidden; therefore, he changed the direction of the conversation. "I have heard that there are strained relations between Obseen and New Earth."

K'sho immediately spoke up, eager to talk about history. "There have been tensions, yes, but not with New Earth. It's the UEF of New Earth that the conflicts reside. You are aware of the UEF, yes?" Anmero nodded. The United Earth Forces, New Earth's military, was considered the main defensive force in the Abyss Solar System. "The government tries to interfere in other planets' affairs, causing resentments among the populace. If they would leave each planet to its own fate, then none of us would see them as a dictator group, but, alas, they love meddling in others' affairs, ignoring their own."

"You are the son of Redair of the Universal council, are you not?" Seircor asked quietly. K'sho nodded, though he looked uncertain of why the Lakean would ask him such a question. Seircor turned to Anmero without expounding of his question. "The Reases are a distinguished family among the Sinya clan. They are the ones who have direct relations with the UEF and the other planets." He turned back to K'sho. "I apologize for interrupting, but I have heard of all your family has done for Obseen in negotiating for our freedoms and trade. My greatest respect to all your efforts."

K'sho averted his eyes to the floor in embarrassment. "My father has made a name for himself that doesn't, or shouldn't, pertain to me. I have done nothing compared to what he has done. Your praise should be said to him."

"Nonsense!" Seircor countered, and the two were off on a discussion of their accomplishments for their clans.

Anmero sighed, feeling left out yet happy to be since the conversation wasn't something he could contribute to. He rolled onto his back and glanced up at the ceiling. *I don't really envy these people. They didn't have a normal youth like I did...what with the wars here on Obseen and clan tensions and all. They don't even know what they are missing. It just seems like the wars and the harsh lifestyle has beaten the childhood right out of them.* Another inaudible sigh escaped his lips. *But who am I to judge? I was Royal-born and raised on X for most of my life. Then hidden on M2 to protect me from the Emperor and his spies... I wonder how Zan is doing right now.* He smiled. *She is probably off sneaking around the emperor's palace causing trouble as she sees fit. Too bad she found me a burden; it would have been an interesting show watching her pester the Royal guard.*

Chapter Fifteen

In all of Obseen, there are five unique weapons that are revered above all the others. The first is the Trayshan katana. The sword was created by the toughest metals on the planet, traznic, found only in the harsh mountains of the Trayshans' home territory. The secret of the metal's strength is unknown, for the Trayshans never say how they make their weapons—which has made them highly valued. The katana is the smaller and narrower than the Trayshan broadsword but it is prized for its better weight and sharpness. A good traznic sword will never rust or dull and is engraved in intricate Trayshan symbols. The oldest swords are carried by the Trayshan leaders, the Berris and Berzén; the pair being over a thousand years old.

The shée fans are nearly equal to the Trayshan katana and these well-crafted weapons are used as both ornamentation as well as defense, making them useful in places where weapons are banned. Originally a weapon of the Las'wa, its popularity spread throughout the clans. However, with the rise of Emperor Manscor, the Las'wa disappeared to the dangerous underworld, taking the craft of the shée fans with them. Afterward, the Trayshans, whom forged duplicates of the fans, stopped producing the weapons, so that the Emperor would not have access to them. Thus, they became a rare, sought after weapon.

Made of obsidian and an unknown metal in Edis'daln, the Nalcian hand blades, became the go-to choice for both offensive and defensive combat. Popular also with the Trayshan and Kaumian clans, the hand blades were designed to look like claws that came out above the knuckles and extended up to eight centimeters past the longest digits on a grown man's hands. They are crafted large enough to work as a shield against swords or pole weapons while still being light and strong enough for quick, close attacks.

Taken from the teeth of a feline-like suraiks, the Ghans were able to make darts, as well as arrowheads, equipped with natural poisons for quick hunts and assassinations. The Ghans, themselves, preferred the needle-like teeth over many other weapons and solely base all their techniques around them. The suraik darts became popular during the Royals' War as a tool for under-handed attacks.

Last of the weapons unique to Obseen, is the preshair whip. Though rarely seen or used, its name speaks for itself. Only the Las'wa seiviers have found a way to kill the believed impenetrable preshair snakeskin. Being that the whips are made from the same tough, deadly scales as the snakes of the underworld, they can cut through any substance known to man and easily take out an opponent with a single, constricting coil. Of the five weapons, the preshair whip is the most unique and the most feared, which is why it is rarely utilized, even by the Las'wa. By 4012, only four living whip wielders exist on Obseen.

The tremendous crack of the two whips meeting resounded throughout the enormous training room and disappeared down the many exiting halls. With its passage, came the feeling of cold dread and doom of a promised end. The echo came back to the room and carried over the two assassins there. Both stood rigidly across from the other and waited for the next movement. Eric smiled wickedly as he took in the gleaming whip in Zanishiria's hand. "So, you take up your prized weapon after all, and first. Isn't that against your "rules of engagement", as your master taught you?" Zanishiria just glared at the traitorous assassin and tried to snap her whip away from Eric's to untangle them, to no avail. "Oh, temper, your lowliness. You know as I do that Tyracor dislikes such behavior. What would he think?"

That I am being dishonorable to the clan. He, like everyone else, would be appalled that I almost let go my mission for the friendships I have procured—and the emotions I have let myself feel. I have no right to be called the seimora; I have lost a sense of myself and my mission. Yet, Zanishiria did not say these things to Eric, for it would only do to prove his words had irked her.

"Silent as a graveyard, are we?" Eric continued to prattle on, even while he waggled his preshair whip at the other Lakean. "I don't believe you've become a mute since I've last seen you, but I guess anything's possible... Hey, did you know you had triggered a silent alarm connecting to my room when you broke out of your cell? After all, you couldn't have thought I'd just leave you there unattended with weapons, did you?" Eric began a slow pacing circle around Zanishiria, amused that she would not speak but that she kept such a wary eye on him as he moved. They stepped in unison, whips still entangled, until Eric released his whip as Zanishiria tried another time to crack it away. The two whips sailed away from them, coming apart, and landed between them.

The two fighters stared at each other, calculating their next dance, before slowly shuffling closer to the two whips. Eric reached for the one flung closest to him, Zanishiria's, and slid it toward his person. A moment later, Zanishiria did the same, doing so almost casually, causing Eric to frown slightly at her lazy response; however, the lack of concern had him on edge, too, as the older Las'wa continued his careful prodding of her defenses as he walked around her, observing her stance. *She has been trained well for a young one but, even because of that, she cannot be too advanced yet; however, I must still be cautious if I am to finish her off. She was trained by Tyracor, and that just cannot do.... Master should never have taken on another apprentice at his age.* "So, Zanishiria," he struck again, boredly, knowing his attack would be easily thwarted. "Which weapon, besides the one we hold, would you prefer to cut the heart from a creeshts? Would it be the creeshts sword or the preshair short-sword, perhaps? Or maybe a naginata or the dao ax? Hm? Or are these just too boring to use since your whip outmatches them anyway? Would the Trayshan broadsword be a worthy choice, then?"

Eric soon tired of the stupid game of cat and mouse. The assassin girl was not answering him anyway. "Here's another question, miss talks-a-lot. If you had to kill the best assassin on Obseen, would it be in his bed or in a duel!" He suddenly leapt at the youth and put a loud emphasis on the word duel as he did.

Zanishiria brought up a preshair shortsword in a split-second counter to his whip's trust. A tiny glimmer lite her eyes as she watched Eric gasp in surprise. She had been told she had the fastest reflexes their shared master Tyracor had ever seen. Apparently, her skills were enough to take Eric off guard. Just as quickly, she unleashed her own whip's wrath as the other Las'wa tried vainly to fling his wrapped whip's tail off of her sword. The man had to sidestep the attack she unleashed and give up his ground. Finally, he made a last attempt by rolling towards Zanishiria and readied himself for a punch at her abdomen.

Knowing the move was too close for her to swing accurately, Zanishiria jumped back and let his whip slide off the blade. Eric immediately straightened his tall stature, satisfied to be freed from her, and the two dark-haired assassins faced one another, glowering.

"That is it, you little crip." Eric growled. His inability to get inside her defenses starting to irk him. "Master was never one to pass up on talent and I see he was not wrong again; however…" He shifted his weight to his stronger leg and readied himself for another attack. "You are not my equal and certainly not the "man killer's" either. Kye reysh'ka sora!" ["I will spill your blood [in this fight"]. He spat out vehemently.

"Va kye shaw merie'im lai sheti las là sora." ["And I will make sure you taste your own blood."] Zanishiria replied back. She recoiled her whip and replaced it on her belt. Her hands swept over her other weapons and she replaced the blade with a two-edged kaskara sword. The next moment, the young warrioress was launching herself at her nemesis with a silent fury in her eyes.

Eric was quick to attack her with his preshair whip. Zanishiria recognized his style as a five-looped eirisashem defensive attack and stepped to avoid it. [Attacks created for the preshair whip are given names using the number of movements used (eiri) and types of movements (circular = sashem).] The first loop whooshed to her left in what was to be a left-flanked attack then it arched behind her. She ducked and rolled to miss a head-laceration; her roll taking her to the left—away for the third loop sequence. As she came to her feet, she had to leap a full meter in the air to avoid another double-loop that whiplashed back to the right. Zanishiria then used her kaskara to block the final movement before it could splice though her stomach.

The block, however, brought the tail lashing backward and she had to spin away from the broken thrust of the deadly tail to keep from cutting herself.

When she finished Zanishiria found herself farther away from Eric Sorey. Unperturbed, the youth rushed the traitor again. Right as he readied his whip for another attack, Zanishiria leapt sideways and rolled away—a feint. She found her feet again just as Eric unleashed his whip and ducked under its slender tail. Just as she felt the air on her back, she tossed seven, sharp suriken at her enemy. Four of her weapons bit into the obsidian floor but two left big, welting cuts on his right thigh and a third slashed his hand. Eric hissed and nearly dropped his weapon.

Quick to react to the sudden opportunity, Zanishiria swept closer to her adversary to leave a long slash mark on his exposed back from his right shoulder to hip. A roar echoed through the room as a cry of pain escaped Eric's clenched lips. If he hadn't struck blindly out with his whip, Zanishiria would have attacked again, but, as her opponent started striking out with no care where it went, she knew better than to stay in striking distance. Quick as a dart, she jumped back out of range and watched her clan's traitor with wary anticipation.

When Eric finally tired of his charade, he stayed hunched where he was, panting heavily and taking no notice of the thick stream of scarlet blood that made its way down his hand and fingers in a sticky mess. Similar lines of blood formed down his torso and right leg to collect in an inky pool on the floor.

Zanishiria shuddered inwardly at the mess and thanked her lucky stars that she had yet to be cut by his whip. A preshair whip, if not properly cleaned and set can still hold the killing poisons in its scales. *That is why you must watch me carefully as I make your first one. If you don't and you are cut by the whip, then you will die a slow and painful death.* Those were the words of her master, and now Zanishiria understood them. Unnerved, Zanishiria realized what she had just thought. Suddenly frightened, she looked at the whip in Eric's hands: her whip. *My whip never had the chance to set. My training required us to rush through the tempering process so I could have it ready in time to come surface-side.* She locked eyes with Eric. *What have I done? Even the vilest of men should not have to die the kind of death a wound from preshair scale can inflict....but there is nothing to be done now...the poison had no cure. It will seep into the bloodstream unhindered to destroy his red and white blood cells one by one...he will bleed to death...*

Eric seemed to have the same comprehension, for a cruel hiss escaped his lips, then a hysterical laugh. Eric lifted his pained face to eye Zanishiria like a cornered preshair. "Bravo, seimora! You have really gone beyond the rules of our "code" to have brought with you such a tool of death. To kill an emperor, a weapon that will finish him even without a final blow....how cruel." He cooed and found his feet. "You may have ridden me of my life-blood, seimora, but I have yet to go down. What is not a better way for this to be my end than to take you with me?" His demeanor changed into the malicious face of Air'is Soreneay. "Now, it is my turn to be entertaining. I will show you how to play my game, seimora. It is one where I make all the rules." Another hiss rose from his throat and only enhanced the loud scrape from his preshair whip as he rose it to display it in front of him. Both hands on the black and scarlet scales, Air'is let his blood drip from his two-handed grasp. "You are in my playing square now, seimora."

Life had turned slowly for those, like myself, who are ignorant of its moving. I feel a day's eternity and forget to realize that death and my beginning are connected by too short of a chain. Yet, despite the many links I have added to mine that have staved off my inevitable demise; I find I am done trying for a life in these dank and unpleasant caverns we call the coursa.

I have seen the errors of my ways, my apprentice, now that everything is said and done. A man as old as I is not needed or heeded by the ones so full of youth. My shunning only proves I have been on this soreiy (world) for too many of its turnings.

And, too, I regret all those errors of mine that neglectance had wrought. Perhaps, if I had been even half of what my seivier had been I would not have shown you, my only apprentice, how to be impatient in your own ways. Maybe if I had the foresight I do now, Seimore Ze'is and Seimora Mei'cor's deaths could have been avoided...but then we would never have another whip master in training like Zanishiria—not that we will have her for long.

So, I have committed too many mistakes and many lives have paid for them. I am not a very good whip master as I should be; therefore, I will not interfere or correct this soreiy again.

I leave my position as a leader in the Legion and as a subject of the seimreal unfilled, for your wishes, my apprentice, are to not have such an inheritance. It is, perhaps, better this way. Someday, Master Quinn will fill that position as will our seimreal.

I also leave behind my preshair whip, for I have no need for it where I will wander.

I have left my journal for you, Tyracor, so you will have the secrets of all the whip maters before you. I have the hope that they [the words] will be as useful to you as they were to me, but take caution with them you must, for they hold some secrets from years past that can cause chaos to some, pain to others, and loss from too much hope for many.

Take care my young apprentice. I regret that I could not tell you how proud I am of who you have become, and I am also deeply sorry that I shared no comradery with you about your apprentice, but I have no more need for such a rift between us. Yet, it will be left as it is, except in my mind. All you will need to know about that is that you have only yourself to fight now.

Oshay, Tyracor, I leave everything to you with fiduciary.

---Shay'renor

Master Shay'renor put down his preshair fang utensil and glanced once more at his words. "Well, it's done now." He continued with a sigh. "May my work and the works of those before me be put to a good use by Tyracor, though savya preserve us, I hope that boy doesn't do anything foolish with them." Shay'renor grasped his thick, worn journal and brushed the front cover gently with his fingertips. "Every page except the last three hundred have been filled, Lor'enez." [Name of Shay'renor's seivier] He whispered the words softly and flipped through the obsidian stone pages carefully. Every word was as stark and clear as when they had first been written on the Xsorian-crafted stone-paper. The care in each line was well memorized by the old master, and he knew each hand that had written the Las'wa words. With slight hesitation, Shay'renor closed the journal and heaved it up to sit next to the well-used preshair whip on Tyracor's elevated bed platform. The old master brushed his fingers over his familiar weapon, uncaring of how it cut his skin, before he tore himself away. "Good-bye, my old friend. May you protect someone else on the 'morrow."

Shay'renor walked through the empty streets of the slumbering city Shairceeo là Coursa. The asrouc in the walls glowed a light blue that beamed up the walls, creating an illusion of otherworldliness and hidden power. The light cast itself in a way that let Shay'renor's older eyesight pick up the hundreds of symbols and other carvings that dotted the enormous walls and towers; each was carved perfectly to match the style of even the oldest of the symbols, ancient Las'wa, put to the walls hundreds of years before. "I believe I will miss the grandeur of this place." He commented sadly, but he continued on his way.

The old preshair whip master made his way through the towering buildings until he reached the outskirts of the city. There he turned to the southeast bridge on the banks of Shaisor until he finally merged with the eight bridge of the city— Eirhom. Shay'renor paused on the threshold hesitating for just a moment. A final glance back at the city was all he would allow himself before stepping onto the Eirhom.

The waves rapped gently against the old stone of the bridge but as always it never spayed high enough to jewel the passers-by. Again, Shay'renor paused, this time in the middle point of the bridge, so he could take in the last sight of the expansive lake as it moved in inky purplish-black ripples around and away into the large cavern. Not a single noise, except the calm lapping of Shaisor, blessed the master's ears, and, for just a moment, the old man wished for the plaintive cry or whisper of the words "oshay, seivier" ["Good-bye my master"] that would have been muttered on a different occasion. But no sound appeared, so Shay'renor took a deep sigh of sweet mineral-coated air and proceeded on his way.

The bright light of Shairceeo là Coursa faded away into the cave's darkness, and still the master walked unhindered for the asrouc awoke its shining ethereal color as he wandered. Shay'renor never glanced back once the city faded from view. He continued unerringly deeper into the ceero [darkness], far past the normal treading grounds, until he found a slippery but well-worn path into the saysora lá ceero, which he took. [Heart of the darkness or underground] The path he chose wasn't made by human feet, rather it was the making of a creature many feared to find but all gave deep-respect toward. Shay'renor knew this. He followed the enormous path as it carved its winding way through the hard obsidian stone. As he travelled deeper, he relaxed, glad to be in his element, and began to sing softly:

Kye neir'is lai vréi ey lá Cherso laindrai.
Va lo kye eravand? Slacoum vorz shaira ladrum.
Ais sorain là soreay va las lor va zane coursa.
Com kye'na shaih lá shaira ladrum, kye slai là Eirim là Ky'veir.

[I have followed your road to the Great City's lair.
And what do I find? a great jewel of power.
It glitters of silver and red from fire and black from darkness.

But, I didn't come from riches of power, I came for the Harem of the Wise]

The song faded away into the abyss until not even the well-trained ears of the whip master could hear his last word. Silence reigned over the underworld as Shay'renor continued his journey to the empty and cold core. It was only when he reached the first large cavern there that signs of life of the dangerous kind began to appear. The master had finally reached the realm of the Ky'veir.

Each cavern held pools of water that surrounded the ever-continuing pathway. The bottom pools gave off a mysterious purple, blue, red, and green light in irregular patterns that merged together to create a silvery color that was purer than any human could ever create. The silver beams then disappeared into the impenetrable blackness that hid even the jagged ceiling many meters overhead. Only a steady dripping from collected moisture could be heard.

Shay'renor walked carefully on the slick pathway and paused briefly at times to listen for sounds. Nothing happened, however, and every cavern was as quiet as the last. Finally, the old master came to a cavern filled with the hot mists of moisture that came from the main hot springs. This cavern seemed to breath in a way that the others hadn't. Pools of shimmering silver water were pierced through with scarlet lights at the bottom of the pools. The florick mosses around the hot spring were an irregular shade of goldish-black that warmed of a medicine more powerful than the common silver-colored mosses. The unusually color surprised Shay'renor enough that he bent closer to investigate.

"Yei aerrrssom éssssoummm kyyee?!" ["Who dares disturb me?!"]

The loudly hissed words of the older and less used Las'wa tongue startled Shay'renor. He straightened abruptly and glanced around the spacious cavern almost nervously. "Y'is kye, Shay'renor lấ prev'aron re Las'wân rēal." ["It is I Shay'renor the preshair whip master of the Las'wa clan."]

"Va pprevv'aaarrroonn! Lai nnevvienn lấ kky'vveirrr. Lai nnna'sssaihh nnevvierrrsss corrr!" ["A whip master! You search out the Ky'veir. They do not venture here anymore."]

Shay'renor started, his nerves on edge as he fully comprehended what the words meant. In a sudden, effortless lift an enormous preshair snake emerged from the steam. The snake was monstrous in a way the old master had never seen and it had to be at least three hundred years old, according to its size. Each of its knife-like scales were larger than a Trayshan shortsword and gleamed slightly at the edges to emphasis their deadly sharpness. The snake angled his head so only his enormous, right eye, which was a jeweled orb of amber and scarlet, could cast the reflection of the pitifully tiny human below. The preshair then opened its mouth to show a smile of sharp teeth and two-meter-long fangs.

"Kye'ssh là ky'emm. Lai nnna'sssaihh ssseimm'nna lắ kky'vveirrrss sssiennoumm." ["I am of the rogues. We do not serve the Ky'veir any longer."] And with a final hiss, the preshair struck out at the whip master Shay'renor.

A loud scream echoed through the ceero that night, and everywhere it went, it pierced into the hearts of every creature whose ears heard it.

Chapter Sixteen

    Master Shay'renor was just one of four preshair whip masters to disappear into the coursa. He was one-hundred-and-eight-years old and was the eighth whip master to the date of 4023 S.D.; however, as a preshair whip master, he was only the first. He had been born during the "First War" when the Las'wa people had migrated to the underworld. At his twelfth birthday, the master Lor'enez took him on as his apprentice and together they explored the caves of Obseen. During once such adventure, they came across a dead preshair—an unusual find—and created the first preshair whip. Lor'enez easily switched his own whip methods to accommodate Shay'renor's new weapon, and they soon created a training program that allowed for a preshair whip master to become the ultimate fighter. Their new methods were then tested on Lor'enez's second apprentice and later his third, though the master continued to use Shay'renor's continuing knowledge on the weapon.

    The training was soon expanded until the requirements to become a preshair whip master meant that a trainee must be able to handle a large assortment of other weapons before the deadly whip could be attempted. In turn, this program became the model for the thirteen preshans, selected to assassinate the emperor, as well as the only training method deemed trying enough to learn the preshair whip. Master Lor'enez continued further by taking his own group of students, called the Tiez [Thirteen], to attempt to create more whip wielders. Of these thirteen, only three finished their training, the rest dying from the program or from wounds inflicted by the deadly whips. This result alarmed Lor'enez. Thinking his ways flawed and unsuitable, he vowed to repent for having taken such talented students into too vigorous a training and ruining them. That day he discontinued being a seivier. Shay'renor, however, was unperturbed by the difficult training and felt Lor'enez had pointed him in the right direction. To prove his point, he wandered deep into the caverns of Obseen and vanquished a young preshair in a one-on-one fight. His victory, the first time in recorded history of a human killing a preshair, was the beginning of a new era for whip masters of the Las'wa—

becoming a ritual that continued for years. It became the way to mark the passage of a whip wielder into a prev'aron.

Rock outcroppings became easier to see with a human eye as the first sun began its cresting beyond the horizon, so Lap Torez switched his windshield back to its normal setting and relied on his acute eyesight to guide him across the plains of Nyhore. Ahead, the jagged and daunting heights of the Valeén cliffs surrounding the Taysor valley came into view. In a shorter time than it took the suns to rise, the Torez brothers reached the Valeén.

Lap guided their hover-car so that it would take them to the northeastern point of the Taysor Valley. Lap glanced aside to where his brother was sleeping. *"You kemf! Just keep on sleeping while your brother, who's never been here before, ferries you into Taysor."* [Irresponsible or unreliable person]

"Don't you ever call me kemf again!" Page interjected loudly and forcefully into his younger brother's thoughts. *"I have been keeping watch on you since we left home and do not need to correct you—as of yet."* His words left Lap's mind abruptly, leaving behind a slight ringing sensation.

Lap looked away toward the Valeén and tried to soothe his head. "There isn't a scratch on her." He spoke out loud to forget his pounding headache.

"I know." Page acknowledged gently. *"Now, watch for a pointed column and steer to its right. Take the second drainage to the left and follow it until you are at the base of the cliffs."*

"Then what?" Lap asked as he complied with the other's orders.

"Just keep going. I will tell you when we get that far."

The column, called Veyars Point, was easy to spot for it rose a good five meters above the other outcroppings, and the second drainage was also easy to locate; however, it was a daunting drainage with high cliff walls, sharp obstacles, and hundreds of tight, almost too narrow, turns. It took all of Lap's skills just to navigate the passage let alone at a speed such as he did it in, but he soon found he had made it through alive.

"You are the craziest driver I think I know." Page muttered, rankled by his brothers wild driving though outwardly he still looked to be sleep.

"Sorry, but you were the one to teach me, you know. You're not underneath being reckless either."

Page formed a smile in Lap's mind. *"I don't try to kill myself in the process. WATCH OUT!"* Lap swerved a sharp-edged outcropping then barely squeezed under a downed tarol tree. *"That's it, after today, you are never driving me anywhere again."* Partially frightened for his life and annoyed with his brother's reckless driving skills, Page thrust his thoughts into his brother's head and took control of the younger mind as he had not had to do for many years. For the remainder of the journey, Page drove through Lap's mind. Once they reached their destination, the elder Torez untangled his mind from his brother's and gently withdrew.

"I hate it when you do that! It's rude and inhuman."

Page had opened his eyes by then, but he looked away and closed them again in shame at his interference. If Lap hadn't been as observant as he was, he would have missed feeling his brother lock his feelings away.

"Oh, what's done is done, bro; let's just let it go."

Page gave a small nod and pointed for Lap to set the hover-car down in a rocky crevasse. The two brothers climbed out and Lap set up a camouflaging shield over the vehicle. Then they began the long trek up the cliffs. Page led the way with an easy certainty, but his chosen route was anything but pleasant. The numerous cliff faces they had to climb and even backtrack on made their progress slow and exhausting. Even the deft Lap had a hard time climbing and slipped on a difficult section only to be caught by his brother at the last second. By the time they had climbed up the Valeén, the second sun was beginning to appear.

Page led them to a small outcropping and allowed his brother a breather. He took out some bread and a leather canteen of mipa juice. *"Here."* He handed the food and drink to his brother. *"We still have a way to go, but I don't think we will make the top by sun-up. I was hoping to get there by the time the third sun rose so it would blind anyone to our passage."*

"We can hurry, can't we?" Lap took a gulp of juice and wiped his chin.

Page leaned his body out into open air and glanced above and below them before pulling himself back in and shaking his head. *"Not even hurrying could get us there in time.*

We will just have to hope no one's patrolling the area ahead; there's no telling who we could run into."

"How many clans are going to be here?"

Page shrugged. *"Most perhaps. This will be the last stand for the Renegades and the Guards. Whichever falls will lose this time. Every clan knows this, so many will be coming in since last night or even before. This clash between the two sides will cause the whole planet to shudder, I fear."*

"Let us go now, then! We need to reach father before the fighting starts." Lap stood up and put his uneaten food in his own bag. He glanced at his brother determinedly. *"I will lead because I climb faster. We will reach the top by the time the third sun rises."*

* * *

The Torez brothers finally crested the top just minutes after the third sun appeared. The obsidian stone of the Valeén was already beginning to warm to the touch and would soon be too hot for uncovered skin to touch. Lap had known this and had pushed their pace all the way to the top, but now that they were there, he felt the toll it had taken on his body. It took the rest of his strength just to crawl behind a cool and sheltering boulder before he collapsed. Page joined him momentarily looking slightly better than his younger brother.

"Well, we made it." Lap thought to save his breath. He panted and lay his head against the cool stone.

"Yes," Page agreed, *"I should never have doubted."* He paused for a few breathes. *"We can rest here for a little while. Our strength will still be needed to climb down the other side."*

Lap groaned at the mention. *"Even after a while, I don't think I will have the strength."*

"Yes, you will." Page dug through his bag and pulled out a leather pouch. *"Here, eat a strand of this."*

"What is it?"

"Zanishiria gave it to me. It's florick moss from the underworld." Page separated a single, silvery strand from the cluster of long florick mosses and rolled it into a ball before handing it to his brother. *"She said it held the qualities to heal and renew a body. It should work for overexertion as well."* He then popped a strand into his mouth and watched his brother follow suit.

"Hm, I guess it works." Lap said after a time. *"I'm not quite as sore as I was a few minutes ago. Anyway, it tastes good."* Page nodded in return and closed his eyes. *"So, how are you planning to catch up with father?"*

"I'm not completely sure because he wasn't really expecting me to follow him. We'll just have to be very cautious until we find out where he is."

"What sort of plan is that? You sound as if you haven't thought this through at all."

"I haven't." Page admitted. *"I was in too much a hurry form what I learned to think through everything."*

"Well, you might want to. It isn't wise to enter a war zone without having a plan." Lap reminded him.

A laugh escaped into Page's thoughts. *"Sorry."*

Lap's voice followed with his own amusement. *"I was just thinking... it's funny that I wanted to come. Now we both just up and left without a plan, didn't we?"*

"Yes." Page echoed Lap's laugh. *"But, I'm glad you did anyway. After all, it isn't wise for just one Torez brother to go shallaunting across the countryside by himself."*

"Oh, right." Lap joked. *"Double the trouble is so much better."* The two Xsorians lapsed into a comfortable silence. Their quiet alerted them that they were not alone anymore, for in the shadows of the nearby boulders, there were other eyes watching. Each moved closer to the two brothers until they were just meters away. Still, the brothers kept an act up of being unaware.

"Page."

"Yeah." They continued to pretend that they were resting.

"How many are around us?"

Page, who had the less noticeable mind touch, reached out with his mind. *"I count five here with twelve more by the edge of the cliff. I can't sense any more, but those I sense are Trayshans, I believe."*

"So, how long do we wait?" Lap asked as he used his mind link with one of the Trayshans to see who the others were.

Page was also looking at the assassins that surrounded them. *"There are only a small number of them, so we shouldn't have any problems making ourselves invisible to their minds."*

"That's no problem." Lap answered, but Page could feel that his brother wasn't really paying attention. So, the elder

brother sent a questioning feeling into his brother's mind. *"I heard you."* Lap replied, slightly miffed. *"But, I was just noticing that the Trayshans' tunics have their emblems of high office on them."* Page looked through the eyes of a Trayshan and very quickly found the emblem of two Trayshan katanas crossed together behind the Trayshan symbol [Zair'ek]. There was no mistake, it was the emblem of the Berzén and Berris of Thror in Traygor. *"And look,"* Lap exclaimed and pulled his brother's attention to two people in the shadows to their left and center. *"It's Tyre and Tearrì Sinhail!"*

"And that is their eldest son behind them. Okay, these assassins are on the Renegade's side, so we have no need for deception."

The Trayshans crept closer with their weapons drawn, but held back from attacking before their leaders gave their command. Tyre raised his hand but froze it there and waited for his wife's decision—she being closer to the two unrecognized assassin youths. Nearby, Tearrì was still studying the sleeping forms of the assassins. "Kembre'ek ē'i." She whispered and stilled her husband's hand.

Yet, before they could study the two assassin youths further, the brothers opened their emerald eyes to look directly at the two Trayshan leaders. "Tér'koum." Page greeted them in their language. The other Trayshans tensed and readied themselves to attack. "We are not enemies, Berzén, Berris. We are the sons of Tà sharay Khan Torez. We are on our way to meet him."

Tyre signaled his clansmen to drop their weapons, then he and Tearrì strode to the two Xsorians. "Our apologies young Torezes. We recognize neither friend nor foe anymore."

Page gave a slight bow with his head in respect. "Understandable, Berzén. We both realize there are many here that do not support the Renegade Army."

"Still," Tearrì spoke up, "There are many others that do. For two Xsorians as yourselves, crossing the war zone is made easier for your mind-reading abilities; for us it is as dangerous as facing a heard of Taréniks on the plains of Nyhore."

"Dangers there are still, Berris." Lap replied to her statement.

Tearrì looked away from Page to study Lap with a frown but then she eased the expression. "Indeed. And the two Xsorian Tà sharids walk in the midst of it. There has to be some reason?"

"There is." Page answered calling her attention back to him. "I have learned much of the emperor's plans that were too alarming to wait for the war to end. I must find my father as soon as possible and report to him."

"You have news that is great enough to be said during wartime?" Tyre questioned.

"Yes, I am afraid. The need is dire. Not only does it affect the fate of other peoples on other planets, it also explains the silence of the Las'wa."

At the mention of the powerful clan, Tyre's eyes flashed. "Then, it is eminent that we get the two of you to the Tà sharay swiftly and unharmed. Come! We will take you. With your telepathy, we should be able to circumvent many traps."

"Just like that?" Lap sounded surprised.

"I have learned that when a Torez says something it is best to heed the advice. You say your need is urgent, so we will give you that. [Zair'ek] move out!" And, just like that, without questioning the validity of Page's claim, he gathered his clansmen and the nineteen assassins, led by Tyre, stalked down the shadow-cast wall of the Valeén.

Another resounding crack split the silence of the room and seemed to chase the light of the coming dawn away to the darkness. Air'is let the whip end fly and dance around the room with little head for where it landed. He hissed out a terrible laugh each time his whip licked over his skin and cared little that more of his blood was spilled to the scarlet-puddled floor.

Across from the crazed Las'wa, Zanishiria stood deflecting any onslaught of the deadly weapon with a preshair fang-sword—a weak but only defense she had against the untempered whip. She refused to leave the area she already stood on, for she knew it would not help to dodge a weapon as unpredictable as the whip under the circumstances. She only had one chance to survive the encounter: by using her decreasing advantage to outlast the wild charade of the traitorous Las'wa man before her. There was no true strategy to Air'is's swings any more, and Zanishiria knew she had to wait for Air'is to lose enough blood for him to become dizzy or pass out.

As the minutes passed, Air'is lost a lot of blood but seemed not to weaken. The younger assassin began to suspect he had expected such an encounter with her and had eaten a large amount of florick mosses and savya (and perhaps even doped himself with more blood) before entering the fight. If that was the case, the plants and extra liters of blood would sustain his body for many hours yet.

Suddenly, the traitor's swings faltered and the young Las'wa knew she had a chance. With a strong leap, Zanishiria launched herself at the older Las'wa and came down to his right. She blocked his whip's next attack and rolled under its arching body. Her hand came free of her sword to hurl four suriken before she had to block the next curve of his whip. The preshair knives spliced through the muscles on the back of Air'is's right calf; however, instead of a painful cry and collapse to the hard floor, Air'is answered her injury with a laugh of pleasure at the pain he felt. "You may fear pain, seimora, but for me it is pure glory."

Zanishiria frowned at the statement. "You're getting delusional. No wonder you were kicked out of our clan."

Air'is smiled. "Oh? You think that was the reason? Truth is, I wasn't too different from you. I was to be trained as a whip master but that berk [idiot] Tyracor declared me not good enough and failed me. He ignored my training for his "prized" student Des'send—who died not three months later from the training. Shortly after that, I got in a spat with another man—you father—and for my insolence I was cast out of the city. However, my crime was not a big offense for such measures, so why, then, seimora, was I forced away?"

"You lie to keep your innocence." Zanishiria let a slight edge into her voice. "You didn't just fight my father, you also fought Cerrém'ariz, the head council member. For that you were exiled forever."

"But, it was not I who tried kill Cerrém'ariz but another of the val'eya-class so they could frame me."

That came as a direct insult to the Las'wa youth. "You lie to disarm me! I may have been young at that time but there are many witnesses against your statement. You argued with Cerrém'ariz in front of my father and the seimreal then used your recursed whip to try to end the high councilman's life. That is how it happened. You were cast from the coursa for such a crime."

Air'is paused to study the young girl before him and he saw in her a powerful will. For the first time, he recognized the hard look in her eyes that had been in her father's so many years ago. "Your father also spoke of integrity and honor, but—I must say—he was given more claim to it than you. But you, Zanishiria, you see me as no one has: as a true warrior. Why is it, seimora, that I see in you a leader as I have not seen in decades? Yet…you are now also considered an outcast…The seimreal loses much by renouncing you." He paused as he found himself rambling on with more detail than he had intended. "You…never before have I been honored to fight someone as truth-worthy as you. If I am to die today, then I am glad that I do from the hands of a person such as yourself. Now….come! You and I will finish this fight as it is meant to be: honorably."

"You have no honor, Soreneay, and I have renounced my own." Zanishiria said with a mix of anger and sadness. "But, fight we will." She raised both her weapons, two swords, a creeshts-sword and a preshair fang-shortsword, and locked them together. This time, she viewed Air'is as her equal. The sudden change in her perception stripped away all the boundaries she had created between them, stripping her to a level as barren and lonely as his own. "I will take you this time, Air'is Soreneay."

With an unspoken agreement, the two fighters shifted their weight, and the second round of their fight began. Air'is struck out at Zanishiria's shoulder with his taken-up creeshts-blade but he allowed her to perry his move so he could redirect the strike to her left hip instead. His next attempt was blocked and Zanishiria pushed him back with the spine of her sword. She then spun around to reposition herself to attack his right flank, but each move the one fighter made the other anticipated. They spun around the room, thrusting and parrying in a deadly dance to the death. Finally, Zanishiria sensed Air'is's fading and took the offensive to let go a succession of thrusts that pushed the elder man back and took a toll of his strength.

Air'is made his stand only a few meters from the back wall. His opponent paused and leapt away, sensing his sudden determination to not give another step. But she stayed away only a matter of seconds before she was back to tormenting the tired and bleeding assassin man. Air'is was barely able to block her last attack before she reversed her thrust and aimed for his exposed left hip, then shoulder, then sternum. Her final swing was too quick for Air'is to keep up with and left a biting wound in the man's chest. He hissed and backed into the wall. A breath later, and Air'is had dropped his shortsword for a kora-blade.

Zanishiria was there to strike again before he could raise the new sword; however, she barely made it out of the way as Air'is unsheathed the curved blade. The two swords collided and their clang echoed across the large room.

Zanishiria growled and pressed against the older man's blade. She would not let Air'is take back the step he had lost. Her grey eyes met his in defiance right at the moment that she gauged the direction of his force. In a display of unusual speed, she repositioned her sword alongside his's inside edge and slipped past his blade. Her own struck home against his lower ribcage. Caught unguarded, Air'is finally cried out in pain over the deep injury and crumpled into a fetal position on the ground.

Zanishiria loomed over her prey like a silent shadow as Air'is lay, hugging his arms around his wound. The sudden dramatic ending to their fight allowed them to become aware of footsteps nearing. "They will be here soon, seimora." He hissed in warning. "Why do you not end me now?"

Zanishiria kicked his kora away. "No. I have done enough; there is no reason for me to go through a killing stroke now."

Air'is Soreneay closed his eyes in a hidden shame. "I deserve that way to die."

"Not by my hands, you do not."

Air'is closed his purple eyes against his pain and hissed. "Then go before they reach here." He urged. "Here," He began to pull more preshair weapons from his belt. "Take these, they are of the finest quality and you will find a better use for them than me. Leave your faulty whip and take mine."

Zanishiria hesitated but the footsteps echoed nearer driving her to respond. "Very well." She took his weapons. "You will not have need of such a weapon, though."

"Quite the contrary." Air'is smiled hollowly. "I have been wanting to give the Royal guard a beating for a while now." He stood up clumsily and placed his back to the wall to balance himself. "Manscor is down the fifth hall to the left, twenty-seven doors down, third chamber—that is if he hadn't already left to a safer place."

Zanishiria's face was as hard as stone. If she had any remorse for the guards, she did not show it. She accepted Air'is Soreneay's words at face value only because she did not know her way around the emperor's quarters. Without anther exchange, she backed away from the Las'wa traitor and found the hallway the other had indicated. Never once did her eyes stray from Air'is's face. The preshair whip wielders bowed to each other before she slipped into the hall.

The young assassin entered the indicated hallway just as the Royal guards streamed into the training room from the main entrance. As she ran, she heard the surprised shouts of the guards as they were stopped by Air'is. If any noticed her, the Las'wa did not give them time to pursue. Onward she ran until she had gone to the chamber Air'is had instructed her toward. The door she came to was ornately designed in rich golden and silver metals, its umber wood gleaming under an amber tarnish. If this wasn't Manscor's room, then Zanishiria wouldn't know where else to turn; she certainly could not scower the whole palace in search of him. "Well...here it goes." She muttered and her strong fingers curled around the old-fashioned doorknob.

* * *

The commander of the Royal guard yelled for his men to pull back from the insidious Las'wa man but his words went unheeded. Five of his men rushed the scare-faced man only to be immediately sliced apart by the knife-like scales of his weapon. Angered, more took their place only to meet the same fate. Commander Farnyk could see very clearly that his guard would not be just defeated—they were being massacred.

Annoyed with the lack of discipline, Farnyk yanked the young soldiers closest to him by their tunics until they fell in a heap behind him. He had no idea how many of them he did that too, but finally, he had over half of the remaining command behind him and the rest being massacred before him. He turned away from those that were already lost to take command of those he could, hopefully, still save. He yelled until his soldiers regrouped and began to follow his commands.

There were about forty Royal guards in front of Air'is Soreneay. Over twenty-five lay dead at his feet. In his hand was Zanishiria's preshair whip, blood-stained with his and the guards' blood. Air'is smiled grotesquely at the thought and readied his stance for the next onslaught. His intent was to kill them all before his life-blood ran out. This will be amusing! He thought in glee just as the reorganized Royal guard rushed him. Air'is watched as the commander ordered one of his men to go for a laz-rifle, while the rest tried to distract him. The Las'wa smiled, he would finish off the commander and the other men long before the man ever returned.

The guards tried to overpower Manscor's traitorous assassin, but the preshair whip had an eerie, methodical slash that easily sliced through flesh and bone as if they were made of paper. Every time the guard pressed closer, more men were cut down, and the rest filled their void. Finally, there were only nine men felt standing before the clearly exhausted Air'is Soreneay.

"Why don't you attack me?!" Air'is hissed. "You have force pikes and guns, don't you?" His words seemed more like a taunt because the guards had, in fact, left their better weapons in the brig and only had force scepters and swords with them. Those weapons were inadequate to fight the longer preshair whip and the guards knew it.

With a fierce war-cry, Air'is Soreneay launched himself at the remaining Royal guards. His whip quickly raked them down and silenced their death cries. Then, in a flourish, he cracked the whip around himself and let it constrict around his torso and neck. "Coursa shym'oriz!" ["The darkness prevails!"] He cried out and pulled the whip around himself, feeling the hot biting of the scales tear into his flesh, bones, and innards.

When the young Royal guard returned, he found piles of corpses surrounded in puddles of rich, red blood. In the center lay Eric Sorey, whose name later was found out to mean, "forever a dangerous traitor". [Soreay = forever; Eric similar to Las'wa éris = traitor]

Chapter Seventeen

The Zair'ek are the Trayshan elite, and the group that serves under the Berris and Berzén of Traygor. To see the symbol of Zair'ek on the sleeves of a Trayshan is to show the highest status among the mountainous people of Traygor. They are the toughest, most enduring fighters in all of that territory and will, most assuredly, replace ten assassins in one fight.

It is never wise to have the Zair'ek opposing you: you will lose.

The dawn over Nyhore started with a greying shadow over the darkened plain. In a few hours, the first of the suns would rise over the Valeén to the east. Seven shapes lay bundled in damp cloaks among the warmth of the blue-green-and-purplish grasses of the Nyorian plains. All were sleeping as restfully as they could manage in the uncomfortable chill of their clothing.

Finally, old Hareoska shuffled, unable to sleep from the chill, and stretched his aging joints painfully. Each cracked sickly. "Oh, what I wouldn't give for more of that Lakean magic right about now." He grumbled and sat up cross-legged.

"You're not the only one." Dorsetti's voice came through muffled in his cloak. "My blasted arm feels like it's been beaten and splintered a hundred times over."

With Dorsetti's statement, Master Quinn leapt to his feet and hurried over to fuss about the man's shoulder. "Oh, hush up!" He ordered as he applied mica ointment over the injury. "You should be grateful that I have this along, you blout. Now hold still!" When Quinn was satisfied with Dorsetti, he helped Hareoska apply a thin coat of the silverish gel to his joints, then he recapped the pouch and hit it away before anyone of the others started begging for relief. "We will eat then continue on our way."

Sunashi rolled over unhappily. "Can't we have a little longer to recuperate?"

Roko clubbed the young master over the head. "No, you oaf, we cannot dally here long. We have no idea when the ships might be departing. We risked enough stopping to sleep."

"Fine." Sunashi growled, ribbing his head. "It's not like any of you find me worth listening to anyway."

"Not true!" Roko argued, "We don't listen when you act like an oaf is all." Sunashi immediately shut his mouth to keep back any more comments he might have.

The masters were quick to wake up and eat the meager rations they had brought with them. None spoke during that time but proceeded in mulling over their own thoughts on all they knew of the Nyorian spaceport. Their breakfasts were quickly consumed and the masters hurried on to their destination.

Security at the spaceport was sparse, for most of the soldiers were in Taysor, so the Legion Leaders were able to slip into the port unnoticed until they neared an area where the emperor's private starships were docked. Guards were stationed in pairs of seven on each corner of the dock. Everyone had a laz-riffle and a force pike. Between the two groups of guards, on the eastern side of the building, was the second of the three entrances into the main hanger—and it wasn't guarded.

"They've got that door encoded." Roko informed the others as he dropped his di-scope. "We wouldn't be able to get it open by the time they reach us."

"Oh, don't count on that." Yoshida argued. "All you need to do is give me two minutes and I will use the chip the Tà sharay gave me last symerei to blast through their security. It should be able to reprogram all the systems in the complex." [Symerei = Xsorian name for half-year]

Sunashi looked at the dark-haired man quizzically. "I thought you said you never tested it before?"

Yoshida shrugged indifferently. "It was from the Tà sharay—I'm not worried."

"It's decided then." Hareoska interrupted, finding the reasoning sound enough to not argue the point further. "Yoshida will open the door while we create a distraction. Dorsetti, you go with him to cover his back. Roko, Sūn', and Corsetti will take the south wall, Quinn and I will take the north. Try not to alert any of the other guards and keep scuffles to a minimum. Agreed?" The others nodded. "Very well. Yoshida, give us a minute-twenty to get into position them make your move... Okay, let's shoot!"

The masters slipped stealthily away from Yoshida and Dorsetti. They hurried along the buildings as quickly as possible, being aware of the other guards and their dwindling time limit. Though the distance was long, both groups managed to make their points before their time was up. Quinn and Hareoska hid themselves among some tarn brushes on a slight incline looking down of the northern side of the hanger bay. Opposite them, Roko, Sunashi, and Corsetti hunkered down in the shadows of another building.

As one, they all rushed out of their hiding places and, like shadows, stole to the base of the docking bay complex. Hareoska blew suraik darts from a dart gun at his targets and all seven of the guards fell down. Quinn helped the old master drag the bodies away from the sight of the security cameras before they headed back to Yoshida and Dorsetti's location.

The other three masters weren't as quick. Roko, Sunashi, and Corsetti had no darts, so they had to down the seven guards at close range. Sunashi, being faster and younger, reached the guards first, armed with a kastane sword in hand. Roko and Corsetti followed after in attack position Diambolé. [Two practitioners mirror each other in attacks, one left handed the other right; partner form.] Sunashi's first swing took a guard in the abdomen and another in the rib cage. The two guards' cries alerted their comrades of their fate. Sunashi rolled away backward between the two incoming masters' advance and came to his feet behind them to create a Tripèrdon. [Adding a third person, behind, in a triangular shape, third takes defensive guard over the other two that attack.] Roko's blade followed in the hole Sunashi left in his wake. He slashed up at a guard's torso while Corsetti's took the next man in a vertical thrust down his front. The third assassin then broke away to Roko's left to double-slice another man. Sunashi spun away from that attack to perry a soldier's shot at Roko before killing that man as well. The final soldier, freaked at the skilled assassins' attacks, tried to run away but Master Corsetti spotted the man and called to Roko. The smaller man sprinted toward his friend, leaping up as he neared, and jumped into Corsetti's locked hands. Corsetti used Roko's momentum to propel the other assassin nine meters in the air to land on the receding back of the guard. When Roko straightened, he turned around and nodded that they were finished. He sprung away from his quarry and headed towards the side of the hanger bay where the other Legion masters waited.

As the three masters joined their friends, Yoshida finished up his task. "All systems are unlocked." He announced and grabbed the chip form the computer drive. "Let's go."

Dorsetti pressed the door's switch and it glided open softly. The masters paused only long enough to get a quick lay of the inside before sprinting into the large building. The room they entered was a side bay off of the main hanger and was, surprisingly, unoccupied. Apparently, it was used for workers' rest breaks, for it boasted three couches, a computer system, and a long table holding a tray of pastries and carmoel tea. A large window across the room looked down into the enormous hanger below.

"Ooh, cozy." Sunashi cooed sarcastically and sauntered over to the food table. He picked up a pastry and nibbled on it. "This is so gourmet." He grimaced in disgust and replaced it on the tray. "Whomever is supposed to work here hasn't been for a while."

"You don't say detective." Dorsetti jested at his former apprentice and tip-toed closer to the window for a look.

Meanwhile, Yoshida crossed the room to the computer and sat down to study its contents. "He didn't log out either. All the files are uncoded including the scheduling. Kiys, this is easy!" Quinn glanced over Yoshida's shoulder at the schedule. "See," Yoshida pointed, "They've already sent four victory-class starships to Planet X. The rest are to be sent around dusk tonight, once Emperor Manscor gives the order." The dark-haired assassin's fingers flew across the control pad as he scanned page after page of information. Suddenly, he stopped with a low whistle. "You catch that?" He asked Quinn as he backed up to the previous page. Pausing, he searched for the words he had glimpsed and pointed. "They are shipping large quantities of traznic ore from Shatray and sydro-melted steel ore from the Smelter lands. You know how many ships they could build with that amount?"

Master Quinn nodded. "At least fifteen—more if they created smaller ships, and with hull plating made of traznic, they could withstand numerous blows from UEF lazer-cannons. Blast it! We should have seen this coming. Manscor will try to overtake the other governments if we—or better yet Zanishiria—doesn't stop him first."

A siren went off in the complex causing the masters to leap to their feet. "They found the bodies." Corsetti commented as he left his position near the door.

"Well, I'm up for some fun, anyone else?" Sunashi fingered his kastane's hilt.

"We must try to take over the remaining five ships." Hareoska included. The others nodded and, as one unit, they drew their weapons and signaled for Dorsetti to open the door into the hanger bay.

The rising of the three suns cast a mixed light of blue, white, and yellow that blinded anyone's eyes looking eastward, but this was an easy cover for those that traveled to the west. For the small tangent of Xsorians, the natural cover was welcome in the area of war.

Khan Torez led his men unerringly toward the barely visible cluster of tents across the enormous valley of Taysor. He stuck to the tarol forests and larger tarn bushes to hide from unwanted eyes. The Xsorian con'stól fanned out in a diamond behind their leader and exchanged point guards every few minutes with strict discipline. Slowly, they edged closer to the outskirts of the city Taysor.

The thunderous pound of waterfalls alerted the con'stól that they were nearing the city limits. Cautiously, four of the assassins split from the main contingent and crept ahead to warn against Royal guards. Khan Torez signaled his men to break right and left as he searched the surrounding area with his six senses. Satisfied the way was clear, Khan strode forward toward the Renegade camp. Four perimeter guards rushed forward as he neared with their weapons pointed at his person.

"Who goes?" One shouted demandingly as his fellows eyed the surrounding trees for Khan's companions—not that the con'stól would let themselves be seen.

Khan stared the man down until he flinched away from his gaze. "I am Khan Torez, the Tà sharay of Xsenume. I have come to speak with your leader, Royal Qusairo."

"How d'we know you're not an enemy?" Another asked, suspicious.

"You would dare challenge me for falsity?" A hint of warning was covered by Khan's amused smile. "Go, I bid you, seek your leader for conformation, but realize my well-trained, telepathically powered con'stól could attack you before you could have the words from your mouth. A long way we have traveled to get here to stand meekly under the guns of insolent questions. Go, but for your comrades, I bid be quick!"

A young man hustled away in fright for his leader's tent, and returned a short time later, followed by a red-faced Lord Aslén Doz. Aslén frowned at his men and waved their weapons away. "How dare you threaten the Tà sharay this way! All, away to your duties! These men are no enemy to us."

Khan Torez smiled and stepped up to Aslén to shake Qusairo's brother-in-law's hand." I thank you, Aslén, but we need to see Qusairo."

"Immediately is not possible." He waved the Xsorian into the camp quickly and entered his own tent for privacy. Khan followed him inside with a frown but resisted his urge to grab the information from the lord's mind. Inside the tent stood a small, square table that held a large map of Taysor. "Qusairo is not with my forces, you see." Aslén explained and pointed to a silver pawn at one point near Taysor." "We're here near Cascean Waterfall. Qusairo is five miles north at the mouth of Taysor Gulch, Major Calamas and his men have taken Sorian Bridge, and Captain Raynward is at the council house." These areas were marked by a red, yellow, and green pawns respectively.

Khan studied the map silently for a moment before asking, "And is Qusairo protected now that he is apart from the rest of his forces?"

"Yes," Aslén replied as he filled two glasses of mipa juice for themselves, "Shy'ree, his protector has not left his side from the beginning; however, I have been separated from Qusairo since last night, so my intel could be faulty, but Shy'ree is not one to leave Qusairo without a good reason."

Khan became slightly alarmed. "Who is this Shy'ree? I thought his protector was Lord Vanyn?"

"You do not have to fear Shy'ree." Lord Aslén soothed and set their cups beside the map. "Lord Vanyn was killed little over a month ago, during a battle at Hashiem. Shy'ree stepped into his place upon his death to protect Qusairo and had stayed with him since"

"But who is she?" Khan asked, still unsatisfied. He knew enough of Honoreds that could infiltrate the Renegades from previous years against the superiorly-trained assassins.

Lord Aslén eyed him, surprised at the persistency of Khan's conviction, and shrugged. "No one knows which clan she is from—as she did not give one—but she is well-respected by the Legion of Leaders and is highly spoken of by Dăveed Quinn. All I can tell you about her is that she is very skilled with wrist blades and katar, and she wears unusual armor of shiny black-and-red leather."

Black and red leather? Khan sat down in the offered chair and sipped his mipa drink. *That sounds similar to what Lapsair said Zanishiria was wearing when he first met her. Could it be made from creeshts or, perhaps, preshair skin?* "And, what does this Shy'ree look like?"

Aslén was looking over battle strategies and answered the Tà sharay in a preoccupied manor. "Dark hair and slate eyes, slim but muscular. She is one hell of a fighter. She taught her forces a sign language that makes it easier to change orders without talking in situations where that is valuable."

"No last name?" Khan coaxed.

"Nope, not that I know of. Like I said she came recommended by Dăveed Quinn; he seems to be close to her."

Sounds like she is Las'wa...like Zanishiria, she wouldn't give a sur-name or clan affiliation. And the description, too many Las'wa were known to be dark-featured... Khan Torez sat back in his chair and allowed a slow grin to light his face. "This war is going better than they had promised." He muttered.

"Pardon?" Lord Aslén looked up.

Khan shook his head and watched Aslén pour over his notes. Aslén was enveloped in his planning, barely even bothering to flip his long, chestnut hair from his face, as he shuffled through the piles upon piles of obsidian sheets around his desk and bed roll.

Finally, Khan stood and drained the rest of his glass. "I should be going with my men. It's best to start before more of the confrontations begin."

Aslén straightened and gave the Tà sharay a bow. "I'm awfully sorry I could not help you more, but are you sure you want to venture the valley at this time? We will be re-engaging soon, and you could slip away then."

"No." Khan shook his head, "We will go now before more time slips away from us. I will feel better when I see Qusairo face to face." He turned to leave but paused as he pushed the tent flap aside. "Oh, have you had any other dark-haired and unnamed assassins join your army of late?"

"Yes, now that you ask, we have. They all joined Qusairo's army over the last few months. All were amazing fighters, too. Say, do you know who they all are?"

Khan smiled secretly and started to leave. His answer could barely be heard over his shoulder. "They are our saving graces."

A blinding golden light blared into her eyes as the door opened. Instinctively, Zanishiria closed her eyes and raised a hand to shield her face. A moment passed until she could coax her eyes to open to the bright glare of the third sun. The room came into focus; the one she had entered was all inlaid in glass allowing the room to be swathed in gold as Obseen's third and final sun rose over the Valeén.

Unnerved by the distraction that had left her compromised, Zanishiria stalked through the empty ante-room to the next doorway, but hesitated in touching its metal handle. Slowly, she reached for it...the metal was hot under her hand and she had to force herself to gulp down a scream at the pain. She grit her teeth defiantly and turned the ornate doorknob. The door yawned wide to cast her into a world of darkness and frost. Through her gamma lenses, Zanishiria could make out the chilling laces of ice that wove across the cold obsidian walls. After the heat and glare of the glass room, the iced stone seemed odd and ominous; however, the darkness was more familiar to Zanishiria, who had been born to it, and it soothed her nerves some.

A third chamber lay beyond the ice room. What would be in that one, Zanishiria could not venture a guess, but after the two totally opposite rooms, she was prepared for almost anything. Setting her burned hand on the cold handle numbed her pain away. Feeling better, she wrapped her fingers around the handle for a few moments longer, took a deep breath, and pushed the old-styled door open.

* * *

Manscor glanced up expectantly as his west door yawned open. For the first time, he laid eyes of the young assassin-girl his "shadow" had captured. The fourteen-year-old stared back with eyes of grey stone, wary and hard. Manscor gave her a once-over assessment from his chair, taking in her snakeskin tunic still stained in blood and arsenal of weapons.... her belt of snakeskin leather seemed unusual but the emperor skimmed over it, not noticing its significance. Boredly, he turned away and picked up a black queen from the chess board on the table to his right. He slid the queen to a checkmate position across from the white and ruby-adorned king piece. "It is amazing how predictable this whole game is."

Zanishiria eyed the emperor cautiously and sidestepped along the wall with a preshair dagger in her hand. She quickly flitted her eyes across the large lounge room in assessment, taking in the five leather sofas, four tarol-wood coffee tables, a long refreshment table, and the chess table, before returning to the emperor. The "man killer" was alone.

"You will not attack me." He said confidently and pointed to the southern wall; the decorative tiles there shifted and a screen appeared and turned on. "Or risk your friend's life." The image of Master Teera holding a knife to a still unconscious Tarin's throat, materialized. Zanishiria even recognized the cell she had been in just an hour before. "Try anything and Tarin will die, unknowingly, by you."

"Terra would not kill her apprentice."

"Oh," Manscor eyed her venomously. "You think not? Just try her."

Zanishiria knew the bluff. "You cannot use that to stop me from fighting you. I declare my intentions of taking you on the square."

"Oh, and what odds are you offering me to make it worth my while?" Her dark grey eyes narrowed in response. "The Renegades have sent you for a simple solution to their problems, at least that is what I am told you are for....a fourteen-year-old girl to take down the emperor."

"I am not from the Renegades."

"No.... with the armor you wear and weapons you use, you are a Las'wa." Manscor's brandy eyes looked her over keenly. "Though the preshans were supposed to be vanquished...I see one was missed."

"Sabina missed one."

The emperor's eyes flashed at the knowledge that Zanishiria knew who had taken out the preshans. "Indeed...it seems she has."

"You will fight me." Zanishiria used the same knowing tone the emperor had used on her just minutes before. "My offer, that is seems you are so set on, is the conclusion of this war. The fighting will stop when one of us is dead."

"It seems like such a simple solution, doesn't it? A one-on-one duel to decide the fate of the planet, but what if you lose young assassin? There will always be another to take your place."

Zanishiria rose her head defiantly. "If you lose there will be no other."

"Youth makes you arrogant." Manscor commented and stood up to pour himself a drink from a glass quart. He ignored the defensive assassin as he gulped down a sweet liquor then waved to the chess boards. "I am winning in strength and numbers, you know. If I lock you away, my guards will easily vanquish the Renegades and the whole masquerade will disappear."

"There would always be another fight. Many on the planet will not bow to you...you will be fighting until the day you die."

"You really think so?" Manscor smirked. "All the strongest leaders will be killed after this battle. The Renegades are pulling out all their stops against me in this "last" battle. After they fall, the populous will bow to me, the strongest of the Assassins' Guild. That is how your system works."

"That you say that shows you understand us less than you think. You believe you have tracked every move, every battle, but the Renegades expected you to do everything you did up to this point; and that you were unaware of me, the last preshanen, shows you did not see their trump card. The numbers of your opposition have increased in the shadows. It is we who control the field, not you."

"You exaggerate your power." Manscor snarled.

"You only wish." Zanishiria stepped to the chess board, keeping it between her and the emperor, and surveyed the arrangement. "I am assuming white and red are the pawns of your forces and black the Renegades?"

Manscor swirled the contents of his glass arrogantly. "The field is laid out in perfect order."

"Your proportions are wrong. You have just lost another handful of guards and a bishop. " Zanishiria smirked and turned to the board, ignoring the ruler flippantly.

Manscor narrowed his eyes angrily and strode closer to the table. "Where, sighp? I shouldn't have."

"Another pawn was taken by a ruby-black bishop and the bishop by the black queen on the right side of the board, third line."

"I don't have a ruby-black bishop, baka!"

"Oh, temper, your high-ness." Zanishiria mocked. "You should make one of your bishops so. After all, your bishop did forsake you for his own kind."

A low growl escaped Manscor's lips. "Who? No, I know. Blast him! Eric was always a loose string. He never really gave me any allegiance."

"He only left you because he found in me a common ground. We are the same, he and I. Air'is will always be true to the oldest deference of the Assassin code: honor and respect of those who show the same."

"That man had no honor. He was just a pawn to be used."

Zanishiria's responding look said, *see my point?* "Then you would be a pawn, too, for the cycle works both ways. Air'is got what he wanted, and you followed along blindly. You two shared in a position of dominating power; either could have commanded the planet. In fact, he was your first choice for your replacement, if needed, was he not? Teera may be your favorite but she lacks the same influence as Air'is commanded."

"No one knew that."

"You think no one knew? The Renegades have files on your power base. They could see how you used Teera and Air'is as your right and left hands; both command your armies but it was Air'is that truly terrifies your people. Air'is was the better fighter but Teera had more ambition. In the Guild, skill is respected more than conniving and string-pulling. That was why you kept the two hands at separate functions. Teera would lose in a contest against Air'is."

"How dare you!" Emperor Manscor slammed a fist against the table, causing Zanishiria to leap farther away. "You assume too much for one so young."

"That you act out so shows I am close to the mark." The assassin-girl replied. "You do not like to be the one on the lower hand."

Manscor clamped his lips shut and turned away to the refreshment table again to keep from making a worse retort. Here, Zanishiria was winning with her words. He downed a drink and slammed the empty glass on the polished wood. Behind him, the assassin-girl watched him with wary eyes, keenly aware of his changes of mood. She waited for the emperor to finish and turn back to his elaborate crystal and gold-in-etched-silver chessboard to touch the black queen. "How do you see the board, then?"

Surprised at the request and turn of their conversation, Zanishiria kept one eye on the man across from her as she analyzed the chess board. Taking the black queen Manscor had indicated she should move, she took it and repositioned is diagonally to the white-and-ruby king. Emerald eyes watched her stoically as she shifted around other chess pieces to create a new field. The Las'wa backed away from the boards as the emperor leaned in to see what changes she had made.

"We are nearly equal?! How can that be?!"

"It is as I said: we knew more than you thought we did." Zanishiria's eyes flashed as she said the words.

"You are certainly from the Las'wa clan. They were very deviant and studied war-planners."

"Las'wa....I am clanless, "man killer", just as Air'is was."

"The preshans were Las'wa, which makes you one of them."

Zanishiria did not answer.

"You carry with you a weapon that can cut through human muscle and bone with great power, leaving them in ribbons. What is it?"

"You must fight me to find out."

Manscor's eyes narrowed in anger and calculation. "Very well, I will consider your request for a duel."

Zanishiria opened her mouth to get the emperor to confirm his participation, but just then a secret door opened on the eastern wall and Teera Sabina entered the room. The Suez master leveled a laz-gun at Zanishiria. She looked more than pleased to pull the trigger. "I see you did take Sorey's bait. May I deal with her, My Liege?"

Manscor knew what Sabina asked but he denied her. "You may take her away. Knock her out with a suraik dart, if you will."

Undeterred to be denied a killing blow, Teera grinned evilly. "Certainly, My Liege." She took out a dart gun from a pouch at her waist. "You don't know how long I have wanted to do this, Zan."

Zanishiria suspected. She hated the woman just as much as the Suez hated her. She launched herself at Teera, unwilling to go down without a fight. Zanishiria defiantly reached for the enemy master even as a dart managed to catch in her exposed neck. As the sauleen flowed into her system, Zanishiria's counterattacks against Teera became less fluid, less impressive. In less than a minute, the assassin-girl fell to the floor in a deep sleep.

"That was pleasant." Teera purred as she toed the unconscious youth at her feet. "Though killing her would have suited me better."

"We will not be killing her, yet." Manscor ordered as he took his seat that he had left upon the young assassin's arrival. "I have not been offered a decent duel in years….I may just take her up on the offer."

"You should not let this little crip make you so preoccupied with the Renegade army at your door."

"That is what I have you around for, Teera, my dear." Manscor replied. "I give you full reign of our forces as I have my way with this one. From the reports on the girl's fights, I think she will be a fun amusement for me."

Teera's eyes flashed at the opportunity. "Very well, My Liege."

Glowing in her victory, Teera knelt down and spoke to the youth as if she could still hear. "Tarin told me once he had feelings for you, you little bitch, but Manscor will make sure that he remembers where his true alliances lie. After all, I cannot allow my "devoted" apprentice to fall into the clutches of the likes of you. That is a promise I will meet with blood." Teera chuckled and slit her palm to prove her promise had merit. Zanishiria lay, unaware, as Teera's warm blood dripped down her face and hair.

Chapter Eighteen

The codes of a true assassin of Obseen are strict and honor-based. At first glance, they seem to be little things, but on a deeper inspection there are many levels to them that create a very complicated system of ethics. In this system are three main levels: honor, name, and clan. Depending on the clan or an assassin's own sense of integrity, however, even these three levels have many sublevels that most non-Obsarians don't understand.

Honor for every occasion is the most important code to uphold. Honor for self, honor for family, and honor for clan. A high regard for life is among this level, for most clans feel life is sacred. Along with this, is a sense of respect to any other person; however, it can easily be lost if someone has done wrongly or acted wrongly. In general, though, honor must be how each assassin sees it and how they uphold it during their life.

The names of every assassin carry special meanings. For some, a name represents their position in the clan—such as the Torez name of Xsenume has always been the clan leaders— or what weapons some assassin families specialize in—an example of this is the name Shriek from the Neitiege clan who use the terrifying sound a Stikes long-ranged-boomerang makes when thrown. Yet, the greatest use of name comes from each clan's language—such as what Seircor C'vail's name translates to: (roughly) "swift darkness" and "warrior of the dark". However, names can be taken away by a clan if the council feels the assassin in question had greatly dishonored their ancestral line. Air'is Soreneay ["lasting jewel" and "waters of eternity"] lost his name for slaying a council member. For it, he not only lost his name but was thrown out of the clan—the highest punishment available before death. Without a name and being clanless, Air'is could not join any clan or seek protection of the High Council; therefore, he renamed himself according to his new position. It is rumored he named himself "dangerous traitor forever" because he deeply regretted what he had done but knew he could never go home.

The third level of code, is the upholding of the clan and its honor and integrity. Being that there are seventy-five clans in all on Obseen but only seventeen High-clans, each clansmen had a duty to first represented their clan and then uphold the strength of the Assassins' Guild. Until Manscor ended the practice in 4019 SC, fighting tournaments were held for two weeks out of the year, in different cities across the globe, to show what each clan was capable of. Prestige and leadership roles could be won during such tournaments.

Golden rays streamed in through the open window to fall on the king's weathered face. His closed eyelids twitched at the warm sensation. Coming out of his morning meditation, King Lapsair glanced above the window in his tiny meditational chambers to the crest of his family's line hanging there. The bright gold star crowned with polished rubies and emeralds glittered softly above the beautiful streams of sunlight making it stand out like a star in the night. "Let the Novastone crest shine for years to come." He whispered in his regular conclusion to his morning silence, then he stood, feeling his older bones creak in protest, and limped back into his adjoining bedroom. He stopped in surprise as he entered his room then sighed, resigned, and went to sit at the base of his bed. "I reasoned you would be calling."

A sinister laugh followed his statement and an assassin stepped out of the shadows of his room. "You always pretend to have control, King Lapsair." Master Teera sneered and reached for a garn fruit nestled among the king's breakfast on table near the door. "I must say, the service in the Taysor Palace is as good as always."

Lapsair watched her impassively as she chewed on the tiny, green fruit. After some time, he stood up and reached for a mipa while he waited for Teera to continue her chattering until she came to the point of what had bought her to his quarters.

Teera wiped away a spray of garn juice from her lips and sighed contently. "Yes, food is always better at the palace."

Lapsair ignored the emperor's pawn as he slipped on his boots and rich-colored cape. Finally, he turned his attention back to the assassin-woman. "Spill it out."

She rose her eyebrows as if to say "you think I have something to say?" then the look was followed by an amused chuckle. "Impatient today. Why does it matter how long I take? I am not here to kill you."

"As I knew."

"Yes, you are a know-it-all." Teera's smile soured. "The Emperor Manscor has signed for your arrest." She held out the obsidian sheet that Lapsair didn't reach for. "I will be taking you to our glamorous cell blocks in the Royal wing."

Much to the Suez's disappointment, the king merely shrugged and told her to "lead the way". His response made her job so boring and worthless, and once it was done, she was itching to run her scepter through something. She retrieved her weapon and headed for the front lines, eager to find some action. After all, what could amuse her more than fresh blood spewing from the rebels?

The sharp morning air seemed to hang throughout the tense camp. The young prince stretched stiffly beside his companions and stifled a yawn. "It feels so oppressive out here today, even the mykets won't chirp in the dawn."

"They can feel our nervousness." Seircor gazed out over the still valley the Renegades had settled in. "There will be little of pleasant sounds today, not until the battle is over at least."

"No, not until many hours afterward," K'sho countered. "The animals have a great respect for the dead. The cries of mourning will sound well into the nightfall before nature picks up its lost melody."

Seircor glanced down at the younger assassin with a masked concern. "You speak from the experiences of the Battle of Syltha."

"Yes," K'sho whispered to himself at the painful memory. "My mother fought at Syltha but for naught. She was one of those captured."

Anmero watched as Seircor placed a comforting hand on the Sinya youth's shoulders. Again, he was struck at how human the assassins seemed now that he knew them. It was odd to see how much resolve and respect each had for one another at their age, how much more mature they were than the youths Anmero had grown up around. They have lived a harder life than most people knew in an entire lifetime. Turning away from the two assassins, Anmero walked to the small breakfast table for some fruit, more out of respect for the pained assassins than for need of being hungry. There, he was met by his mother, whom he had been reintroduced to the night before. The last time he had seen her was eight years before when he had been sent to M2, at the age of eleven. Anmero realized he had missed his mother more than he had thought.

Asilisa put her arms around her son in a warm embrace. "I hope you slept well considering the circumstances."

"Yes, mother, I did." Anmero returned the hug and pulled back out of her arms. His emerald eyes took note of the ever-deepening worry lines on her beautiful face. He knew there would be many more before the day was over. "I have decided to join the battle today alongside K'sho and Seircor."

Aslisa's visage grew very still, then she let out a defeated sigh. "I thought that you would come to me with such a statement; you are such like your father: stubborn and resolute. However, my son, you are not in practice for such fighting and have only wielded a sword for two weeks—."

"I was trained in fencing before, as you know, and the sword in not much different."

Aslisa's tight lips said what words she did not voice: that her son's skills were not up to par with the assassins he would encounter that day. She could see the firm set of his jaw and knew that her concerns fell on empty ears. "Still, I ask you to reconsider. The Honoreds of the emperor and the Royal guards have fought and trained all of their lives. Even the knowledge you have is lacking compared to that."

The prince recognized the argument from his father the night before; however, he had already made up his mind. In fact, it had been made up since the hour he had learned of the sacrifice Zanishiria was making with her life against the emperor. If she was willing to give so much for the people of Obseen, then the least he could do was play his own part. "No, mother," He shook his chestnut-haired head in emphasis, "I will not be deterred from this. This is father's legacy to help the assassins win their freedom from the Emperor and I feel it is my duty, as his son, to do the same. This is who I want to be seen as by the assassins of Obseen. I will not cower from this fight."

Lady Doz gave a small, sad smile and squeezed her son's shoulders. "That I can understand—and respect. You and your father are much the same, giving promises and keeping them. Just…. just don't let your vindications claim your life."

She receded then tot eh tent she shared with Qusairo, leaving Anmero to his thoughts and breakfast.

Seircor and K'sho joined him and the three young men ate their food in the quiet reflection of the morning. No one spoke of the coming battle.

Their peace would not last. A half hour creaked by and news came to the army on sprinting feet. An outrunner came yelling at the top of his lungs that Captain Raynward's troops were being attacked. The final battle had begun.

Anmero sprang to his feet in an instant and collected his weapons, following suit of the rest of the army. The tents were left standing like empty husks that would be taken down later by those who were not joining the fight. The three young men joined the ranks of Qusairo's army on the west side of the valley. Qusairo acknowledged his son's presence solemnly and directed the three companions to stay by his protector, Shy'ree's side.

Dăveed Quinn showed up a few minutes later like a stalking shadow. He and Shy'ree shared a brief moment huddled together, whispering to themselves, and shared a passing hand squeeze before Dăveed came to Qusairo and offered the leader two bows of greeting—one from the Baras clan that he represented and led and the second a normal bow of respect. After the quick greeting was over, he proceeded to tell the news he had come running bearing. "Major Calamas had been successful in advancing into Taysor. He was able to merge with Raynward in the appointed time; however, both forces have been hesitant to push forward, as the Royal guard has pulled back to the palace once again, and they suspect some kind of trap being laid. All the forces seem to be concentrated near the center of the city. Aslén asked all to await your orders for the advance."

Royal Qusairo gazed into the shadows of a tarol tree as if seeking answers from it. The price of the situation was high and costly, yet the forces had to take Taysor by nightfall if the ending strokes were to be met. The Renegades did not have the staying power to make more than another day against the capitol so all the forces had pushed to arrive and win by the rise of the two moons. Still, caution was imperative to keep from unnecessary losses, even if it showed the advance down. "Tell Sieck and Aslén to send ahead our "Stingers" in search of any laid traps. I would have them not lose men because of negligence. Raynward and Calamas may do the same if they have the man-power, or they can send in any volunteers."

"Sir." Dăveed Quinn repeated his bows and turned to leave, not before, however, leaving a parting word with Shy'ree. "Your "Stingers" send regards that you fair well. They will fight to their upmost to honor your clan and this army." He lowered his voice to whisper the last. "I myself offer my regards to you to stay safe too, sor'eya." ["Beautiful/ lovely", usually said to a lover]

Shy'ree chuckled and her slate eyes shimmering with a knowing look. "Don't let that flattery go too far into that head of yours, Quinn, you still have many trails to run today. Lai vaun'ya é saun." [(You) be cautious and safe."]

For those, like K'sho, who knew Dăveed Quinn, it was a marvel to see the man blush a bleat red. His quick sprint away was outright unnatural. K'sho eyed Shy'ree inquisitively before commenting to his friends. "It seems there is more to Qusairo's protectorate than we know."

"Of course, young Sinya." Qusairo grinned deviously, having overheard the comment. "Those two have certain…attractions that keep my job interesting, to say the least. It makes an old man feel young again at heart." The looks the three young men cast among themselves made the leader laugh. "As if none of you have had any flirtations yourself."

"Father, I am not sure that is appropriate for the time and place."

"What?" Royal Qusairo feigned innocence. "I was just talking about my leaders. Was there something there to upset you?"

Anmero sighed but relished the small breach in the tension that had built in the company. "No, father…never mind." If joking and thinking of more fun or mundane things could help with the feelings of impending doom, then it was best to let it be.

Qusairo sensed the mood of the three young men. He straightened back into his serious leader pose, knowing the time had come. "We should go now. The others will be moving their forces toward the palace. We should not be late to that meeting. Shy'ree," The assassin-woman straightened, "Sound the advance. The sooner we reach our convergence point, the sooner we can strengthen our front." The dark-haired woman rushed away to call out commands to the gathered army. All the fighters came to attention, weapons at ready. Royal Doz waited until the mass began to move before turning to his son and two attendants, who waited by his side. "There is no need to put such scars on your soul, my son." He said quietly. "It is not your wound to carry."

Anmero recognized his father's words as the man's last attempt to pull him from the fighting. "Sorry, father, but this is my burden to carry. This is now my home and I will fight to see it freed from the Emperor's grasp as much as the rest."

Father and son met matching eyes and countenances. The elder's face showed pain but he accepted his son's brave words. "Then stay close to Seircor and K'sho. I will see you at the end." He wrapped his arms around his son protectively before the other Doz could protest then stepped back to give the two assassin youths a serious look. "You will bring him back alive."

Seircor bowed deeply with K'sho only a step behind. "I will defend him with my life, seimore. Mé kye shéva, kye sacor moré'lái. Le valas ré'mear." ["Until my death [takes me], I will protect your son. This is promised in blood."] He finished by slitting his wrist superficially with a creeshts knife and let small drops of red bead on his skin. Qusairo finished the tradition by entwining his arm in the Las'wa's and locking their wrists against one another's. "Kye'enen." ["I accept."] The two broke, their pact made. Seircor motioned his two companions to follow him. "Together, we will not fall. Your lives count on us working together when the fighting gets thick."

K'sho countered softly. "All of our lives count of it." His words could not be denied.

As one the seven assassins rushed onto the overpass. The five security guards there stood stunned at the sight of them and were unable to raise their guns before Sunashi and Yoshida cut them down. The two younger masters kept their weapons pointed at the corpses until the others passed then they glanced back at the room they had left for signs of pursuit. Corsetti and Roko led the group calmly, their weapons at ready, as the security alarms continued to blare.

Guards streamed into the hanger below converging around the emperor's starships. Soon, there were fifty soldiers per ship, a fair number to pit against seven assassins. Quinn studied the enemy' numbers, unconcerned, while Hareoska muttered strategies beside him. Dorsetti, though in pain, tried to point out a weak point in one of the guards' groups, forgetting his arm in the excitement. Quinn barely managed to cover his hiss of pain before it alerted the guards to their post. Once he had, however, he whispered. "Yes, I saw. The fifth ship is surrounded by young cadets straight from the academy. We will attack there first. Roko, I will need you to make a little distraction first."

"I'd be happy to." Roko smiled mischievously and pulled out a pouch full of powders from his belt. "What'd you have in mind?"

Quinn shrugged. "A quick acting gas or an explosion. Something that will lower our odds quickly without endangering us. And, nothing too noticeable; I'd like to keep our odds low."

"Coming right up." Roko reassured him and selected a vial half full of yellow powder, the other half blue. "You might want to cover your noses, this stuff expands pretty far, and we wouldn't want any of us paralyzed, now would we?" The masters headed his warning and placed Ghannish-created masks over their mouths and noses. The small, film-like masks allowed clean air through and would filter out the deadly poison. "Here goes." Roko warned and threw the vial over the railing. A moment later, an explosion tore through the spacious room then dispersed.

Dorsetti muttered a "that's not noticeable?" as it ended; the others kept their comments to themselves.

Everything seemed unusually hushed. That was until the ringing in their ears quieted, and the cries of wounded soldiers filled the space. Curious, Sunashi peeped his head over the railing only to duck back again with a paled complexion. "What the hell did you use?"

Quinn cast an accusing glance at Roko and looked over the railing himself. Below, the greenish cloud was just settling, revealing the mess in the hanger. All two-hundred-and-fifty of the soldiers had been in the blast range; those closest to it had their exposed skin burned and their clothes were incinerated. A few still cried out in their agony, with a handful walked around blindly calling for help. The other soldiers had fallen to the floor unconscious or dead. Disturbed Quinn turned away from the ghastly sight "There was more than paralyzing powder in that dose."

Roko's eyes widened and he searched his pockets fervently. With a groan, he took out a vial full of yellow and green powder. "I used the nervesian with the iodecper instead of necepdine."

"Iodecper? That is a deleterious powder." Hareoska commented from behind Roko. "It's not good to lace the two rivals together, I thought you knew that."

His slight was taken gracefully, in not contritely, by Roko, who knew just how awful his mistake was. Almost inaudibly he whispered in Shynorean, "Meshek nés vuslean. Shec nu emleun." ["You served your master well. Go in peace."]

Hareoska laid a hand on the red-haired master's shoulder and squeezed. "We need to go, lad, our work is far from over." Roko nodded and brushed aside his anguish. Hareoska nodded encouragement and signaled the other masters. "To the ships."

The masters sallied across the final span of the overpass and down the steel steps to the silent bay below. By then, there were no soldiers twitching, just silent bodies. Yoshida and Sunashi glided near more of the bodies to check them out then raced to regroup with the others. Roko turned his aging eyes to them as they returned, his question peering out from above the thin face mask.

"They are just unconscious." Yoshida assured him. "Only a few suffered a worse fate." Roko's sigh was visible.

The last of the five lancer-class starships sat with its hatch halfway open like a partial yawn, welcoming the seven masters to enter. In suspicion, the masters spread out to survey the surrounding area. Roko, accompanied by Yoshida, carried a canister of anyon liquid to the hatch as the others searched around the ship for hiding soldiers. Yoshida easily broke the code to the hatch before the others returned, yet he waited for Roko to throw the canister inside and allow the smoke to disperse and settle. They all joined up again at the opened entrance.

"Corsetti, Yoshida, you first." Hareoska said.

"Oh, I see, you want us to check for ambushers while you stay safely out here." Corsetti joked as he and Yoshida jogged up the landing ramp. He sobered quickly as they got on task. The interior was dark, expect for a few emergency lights, and no shadows moved as they swept through the rooms, one by one. Finally, Corsetti popped his greying head back out. "The coast is clear; however, someone must have been here. There are some things left undone."

"Things?" Quinn asked, sharing a glance with Hareoska.

Corsetti shrugged. "A holding cell was open, a tray left out with crumbs on it, the warning lights are on, and the pilot's chair was warm."

"How is that considered "undone'?" Sunashi asked, referring to the chair.

Dorsetti frowned at him as if he found that unnecessary. He glanced up at Yoshida then for conformation. "The military wouldn't overlook those things."

"I do not think this was a military man's actions."

"Meaning?" Hareoska questioned. Yoshida only shrugged.

"Let's go in then." Quinn urged and headed up the ramp with the others following. The ship was just as the two masters had said: all dark and unused, except for the few mentioned details. The holding cell was small and even more dimly lit than the rest of the vessel. An old trace of human musk remained trapped there, proving someone had been in there, and there was a blood smell as well. The tray sat untouched, some food crumbs from days past scattered about in hard pieces. The chair Corsetti mentioned was no longer warm. Cautiously, the seven of them searched the cockpit, mess area, and others rooms again.

The small group of leaders regrouped in the mess area after their search. They still felt that something wasn't right but were finding their search unsuccessful. Tiredly, Sunashi sat down with a huff. "We must be paranoid."

"It's still too uncanny." Roko countered. "We cannot have misinterpreted the signs."

"It must be someone well-mastered in subterfuge." Quinn commented.

Just then something grabbed onto Sunashi's shoulder and held tight. He gasped and tried to break free from it only to realize he was not at the right angle to. The others rushed forward to help, weapons in hand. Dorsetti swung his wakizashi at the object but it struck the hard surface and bounced off. Uncertain, they backed off, much to Sunashi's surprise.

"We need to make sure it can't hurt you." Quinn told Sunashi to keep him from panicking. He and the others tried to see what bound Sunashi but the darkness was imbedding their eyesight. "Damn, we need lights. Yoshida."

"On it."

As the "Code Master" hurried away, Quinn told Sunashi what he knew. "We cannot cut it with a weapon. I suspect it is some kind of programming. Yoshida should be able to figure it out."

"Of course, you would know that, Quinn of the Baras." A voice, familiar and not unkind, sounded out into the room. It trembled slightly as if the person was weak, but the words spoken held their own power. "Drop all your weapons, Masters of the Legion, and I will not hurt you."

"I am so not doing that with a stranger unnamed." Roko spat back.

"Quinn?" The voice held the question.

Quinn felt he had heard the voice somewhere. With a nod he asked the others to lower their weapons. With slight hesitation, his order was carried out. The masters all stood, unarmed, waiting for the person to show himself or release Sunashi. "We have done what you asked." Quinn eyed the darkness to the man beyond.

"I said drop all of your weapons. You still have some on belts that I can make out."

Annoyed the masters cursed under their breaths, except Quinn and Hareoska who followed the instruction. After a little coaxing, Quinn was able to get all but Dorsetti to place their weapons before them on the carpet.

Dorsetti stubbornly protested. "That man had my apprentice and I am supposed to just put down my weapon and trust he won't kill us all once we are unarmed. Not on Sun's life."

Quinn opened his mouth to respond, but the stranger answered before him. "If you were in my place, Ranarro Dorsetti, you would do the same." The voice cracked like one that had not been used in a while. Its huskiness made it sound worse than when it had trembled.

Surprised to be named, Dorsetti let his hands empty his belt of extra daggers and darts. "You've said those words before." His brow wrinkled as he thought back. "I remember those words during the "Power Struggle" thirty-two years ago."

"Yes, as I recall I had met you and Quinn at Nyashio, before the end of the war. We had been on different sides then, but you took me in when I was injured in battle." As if the memory weakened him, his hand relaxed on the controller that held Sunashi to his chair. The young master rocketed away from the odd contraption.

"Alrik Kagar?" Quinn remember suddenly.

"Yes." The voice answered. "We meet again after all this time."

Voices. Men's voices, one old and one younger. Both sounded familiar. Slowly, her brain began to lift out of the fog, and she was able to recognize the speakers. The Emperor Manscor and Tarin Saerric. Zanishiria listened to the emperor discuss how politics should be run, asking questions of Tarin from time to time. The young man answered back hesitantly, it seemed, as if he was unsure is he would inadvertently insult the ruler. The subject itself lacked true heart and consisted mainly of Manscor's own ideas than any of the assassins' codes.

She allowed her eyelids to open, albeit slowly, so she could glance around the room before the other occupants noticed her consciousness. She should not have bothered; they weren't paying any attention to Zanishiria's still form anyway. The couch she had been laid upon was plush, with mahogany leather and inlaid massage and heat comforts. A maroon blanket had even been thrown over her with a care she had not expected; however, Zanishiria was suspicious of the comforts the emperor had afforded her.

The tense conversation died at the table, directing the assassin-girl's dark eyes toward it. Tarin sat in the closest chair, his back rigid and his hands in tight fists. His plate sat before him untouched showing his caution at being drugged again. His nervousness radiated off him plainly. Zanishiria could not see his face, but she guessed his features were hard as well. Across the redwood table, however, sat a perfectly relaxed Manscor. His long, near-black hair had been pulled back into a warrior's tail and bound in a Xsorian-made obsidian cord adorned with jewels of high value. The sharply pulled back hair emphasized his chiseled features, high cheek bones, and cream-colored skin. Even his rich-brown eyes seemed to gleam as they contrasted with the emperor's scarlet and black robes of command. [Though called "robes" they are a military-style uniform with draping sleeves.] At that moment, his piercing gaze was on Zanishiria.

"So, you have awakened and so soon." He frowned in consternation. "I thought the sauleen would hold you a few more hours."

Zanishiria narrowed her eyes. "Your concoctions do lack a dramatic flair. I've had stronger."

Manscor chuckled, more so because the sound unnerved his guests than from humor. "Sauleen is hardly one of my drugs of choice. It is as natural as they come... and seemingly not strong enough for a trained preshanen. However, you should feel no ill effects."

"It's hardly natural compared to real sleep." Zanishiria growled and pushed herself to an upright position. Manscor seemed too cheerful compared to his earlier attitude. It grated on Zanishiria's nerves. Yet, she could see a calculating look behind the mask the emperor wore. He seemed to be gauging her reactions, looking for any trace that the sauleen was still affecting her—which it was but not strongly enough for the assassin-girl to not push passed the effects. She made sure to not sway or slouch as she came upright, just to spit the man. "It is a little after twelve, almost the thirteenth hour. Noon is high upon us and you are here eating delicacies while a battle is just outside your gates."

"You really enjoy being an annoyance." Manscor replied pointedly. *How could she have known that? She has been asleep and the lighting here is not from any windows.* "In case you cannot tell, I am not worried about the little skirmish outside these walls; it had little to do with me."

"It has everything to do with you." Zanishiria spat out the words like they were venom. Tarin seemed to jerk at the harshness of her words, his first sign he had given to show he was not drugged. Zanishiria stood up and came to his side. He didn't respond to her touch, however, when she laid a hand on his shoulder. "You are such a monster."

"As you knew." Manscor replied.

Zanishiria ignored the suave answer. She turned to Tarin and whispered in Neitiegic, "Kous'own ori nous an'orlei?" ["Are you safe/unharmed?"]

"Sy." Tarin answered in return and raised his chin to give her a forced smile. "Cous'eth ī'enē." ["Yes, just a little shaken."]

"I am touched." Manscor interrupted sarcastically. "It is no surprise you understand Neitiegic, Zanishiria of the unnamed, but I also understand it. Remember, I own the Neitiege. Do not think you can get by with secrets by using other languages."

Zanishiria glared and spat out a retort, "Ē karshk'nek rezouc!" ["I know that, idiot!"]

"And Trayshan." Manscor laughed. "My you are the linguist, aren't you? Why don't you put those skills to good use and join us for lunch?" Zanishiria's glare deepened and she surveyed the food with distaste. "Come now, why would I poison my own food? If I wanted to have you two dead, I would have done so long ago. Besides, I prefer killing my victims myself. Poisons are just so…outdated."

Zanishiria's loathing flitted across her eyes as she slid into the seat next to her friend. With defiance written all over her face, she stabbed a piece of ketet meat from Shaytyar with Tarin's unused fork. Tarin watched her curiously as Zanishiria bit a hunk of the bird meat off and chewed it. Finally, she swallowed and set the fork down. A minute passed with Manscor grinning smugly an "I told you so" and Tarin waiting wide-eyed. Nothing happened as Manscor had said. That fact relieved Tarin, who had been worried of poisoning. He really had been hungry but hadn't had the courage to try the cuisine before him. Tarin took up his fork and began eating, now that Zanishiria had stifled his fears.

The tension seemed to ease in the room immediately. Zanishiria watched her handsome friend eat, noting how ravenous he was, and was sad to see him in such a state. She eyed the emperor with an accusing look that the man just blinked at. Finally, he gave her a reaction, one she did not expect: "Here," He threw Zanishiria a cloth, wetted on one end. He motioned to the dried blood on her cheek. "That is inappropriate for meal-time. Teera had a need for her own satisfaction but I care not to have the sight at my table." For once, Zanishiria was in agreeance, now that she was made aware of the smear on her cheek. She wrinkled her nose as she wiped the blood off. Satisfied, Manscor relaxed into his chair and waved to the array of food before them. The assassin-girl took his meaning as politely as she could and filled her plate. She would eat because food was vital to staying alive but her thoughts were already on what she needed to do later.

The lunch was delicious, Zanishiria could give the Emperor that. The ketet was seasoned in Imari spices that brought out its flavor of smoky gaminess and lay over a bed of greens. Little roles of mipa, garn, and barq cherries sweetened in honey and milk satisfied a sweet craving the assassin had not realized she had. It went well with the side dish of crème tarts and valliss. [A Royal pudding] Even the drinks seemed to be extra special with a touch of vanilla and meekroot added to the already flavorful punch. For the two assassins that lived in simplicity, the meal was quite decadent.

Manscor had finished eating long before and sat studying them, his look almost like a pleased parent allowing his children to enjoy the comforts away from war. He had always been around such indulgences, being a Royal, and he had almost forgotten that not everyone got to enjoy the bounty of Planet X. The two assassins across from him had certainly lived hard lives. Teera's apprentice looked weary, his system still recovering from the poisoning Eric had given him earlier. Beside him, Zanishiria showed the signs of war already taking its toll on her lovely features; she was careful to keep her face neutral and hard, though the eyes and mouth looked pinched some. Battle wounds from the previous fight with Senior Master Rainier almost looked healed-over, a miraculous healing from the Las'wa herbs she took but the healing could not hide the fact that the healing tissue was tightening from scarring. That the teenager had enough energy to put against the emperor in word and duel amused and awed Manscor at the same time. *She could well be a skilled adversary, if given the chance to grow up some,* he thought with reluctance. *Still, she is only fourteen by reports. What could she be capable of at this age? Someone thought her good enough to be assigned to challenge me...and she took on both Sye Rainier and Eric Sorey. She can compete at Master level, so perhaps she is a natural proficient, a prodigy.*

Sharp grey eyes rose to meet his as the emperor thought. Wariness was quick to rise then a glare as her dislike of his attention brought her defenses to bare. "Yours is a deadly silence." Zanishiria commented, much to both of her table-mates startlement. "I do not trust a man who eats his food with no concern that his one guest was sent to kill him."

Manscor wiped his mouth delicately before addressing her indirect challenge. "I do not order you to eat nor did I need to offer such to you, Zanishiria." He purred out her unusual name, finding the exotic syllables to his liking. "But, you need your strength for obvious reasons. I could have killed you the moment you came to my doorstep, but I find your proposal for a duel stimulating. I can't have my opponent dropping dead because of hunger and thirst when such is easy to provide. It would dampen my victory over you on the square."

"It wasn't a proposal. I will fight you one way or another."

Manscor chuckled at her interruption and spread his hands wide. "Nevertheless, it will happen now. If the clans want a duel then, by all means, we will give them one. But, why you? Why not someone older and more experienced?"

It was the question even Zanishiria had wondered. Why the Rebels' choice of the young preshans? Since she had had one full year aboveground, she had come to learn her capabilities were among the highest at the Guild. Preshans were superior fighters... Her pause had both Manscor and Tarin waiting on baited breath for an answer. Finally, she replied, her answer well-thought out. "Experience is merely something one gains with time. To base your assumption on my age alone cannot tell you what my capabilities are."

The emperor's eyebrows lifted in surprise at her unusually mature statement. Then, his face relaxed into a smile, followed by a hollow applause. "A sharp mind you have. Here the reports stated that you were only a common student, a little young for fourth-year but capable enough, but your words show you have years over your Obsarian-age."

"I have kept a low profile from you and your allies. Your reports will not be accurate."

"You think you are better than you have shown?" The emperor queried.

Her eyes flashing was proof enough that she knew she was. "I just beat your man, Eric Sorey. How good do you that that makes me?"

Manscor sobered at the underlying threat in her words. Eric was the only man, to date, that had bested the emperor in a duel—not that anyone knew, of course. Keen eyes narrowed as he took in the young Las'wa again. Indeed, there was much he and his allies did not know on the girl. Still, it would not do to admit such to his enemy, so he chuckled in amusement. "The Las'wa do love their deceptions. If you have indeed deceived us, then I think I am going to have fun with you."

The ruler stood, letting his chair scrape painfully across the obsidian and marble floor. He felt the assassin's eyes on him as he crossed the room to a covered wooden desk. With a ring-studded hand, Manscor lifted the red, silken cloth, revealing a wide array of weapons hidden there. Manscor proceeded in picking up a dagger and unsheathing it. "You weapons are different from those I have ever seen. Except years ago, in the Battle at Barashi."

He turned to the two trainees, making the dagger glint slightly. "It is a preshair dagger, isn't it val'eya? [Assassin] I have seen one other like it. The craftsmanship is exquisite." He sheathed the weapon and returned it to the stash. "These weapons are all yours. Quite a collection, I might add. Once I am gone, you are free to sharpen and clean them as you wish. I will give you both six hours to prepare yourself and sleep. We will fight as the first sun sets." The emperor strode to a doorway concealed in the wall and coded it to open. "Servants will come in to clear the table...I hope you have manners to not do anything untoward them." The comment brought a glare to the younger assassin's eyes. Manscor was amused by her quickness to anger. He started to turn away but then thought of one final thing. "Oh, and Tarin, you might want to make amends to your friend. Her life could end tonight."

Chapter Nineteen

(Master Quinn) "Not much was told of what Zanishiria and Tarin spoke about as they waited for what would later become known as the "Shéev'al la Manscor va Zanishiria". Rumors have said they confided to each other of their feelings, others that they discussed their lives, and still others said they did not speak at all. Certainly, Zanishiria and Tarin have never said what really went on, to date. It is my belief that the two friends spoke to the other as fighters would, trying to keep nerves down and gearing up for the fight of a lifetime. I also am under the belief that Zanishiria taught Tarin this song in Las'wa during those hours of imprisonment, for I have caught him singing it regularly when he thinks he is alone":

> Coursa, coursa, ey rel'yé, laus ky'noas va mé'yé le sevin lai'rei.
> Coursa, coursa sa va arnum ai cév lí ky'çor. Kye rï'ora là sevim; Kye rï'eta là rei'sein.

> Coursa, coursa rei sevym'lâ lá sorvï lí carsa'na. Mor kye'real lá dí'm srie sorvï kye carsa'na tai.
> Coursa, coursa sa va arnum ai cév lí ky'çor. Kye rï'ora là sevim; Kye rï'eta là rei'sein.

> Coursa, coursa ey par'yé, syn ky're noair'ein laus'eim là eta'vai, çu là nuair shay.
> Coursa, coursa ey rel'yé, laus ky'noas va mé'yé le roya lai'zàra, le sevim lai'rei.

> Coursa, coursa rai sevym'lâ lá sorï lí carsa'na. Mor real'yé là dí'm srie sorvï Kye carsa'na tai.
> Coursa, coursa ey par'yé, syn ky're noair'shay, laus'eim là eta'vai, çu là nuair shay.

[Darkness, darkness be my pillow, take my hand and let me sleep in the silence of your deep.
Darkness, darkness long and lonesome is the day that brings me here.
I have felt the edge of silence; I have known the depths of fear.

Darkness, darkness hide the yearnings from the things that cannot be.
Keep my mind from constant turning toward things I cannot see.
   Darkness, darkness Long and lonesome is the day that brings me
here. I have felt the edge of silence; I have known the depths of fear.
   Darkness, darkness be my blanket, cover me with the endless night;
   take away the pain of knowing, fill the emptiness of night.
   Darkness, darkness be my pillow, take my hand and let me sleep in
   the coolness of you shadow, in the silence of your deep.
   Darkness, darkness hide the yearnings for the things that cannot be.
Keep my mind from constant turning toward the things I cannot see.
   Darkness, darkness be my blanket, cover me in endless night; take
   away the pain of knowing, fill the emptiness of night.]

   The nearer they got, the harder it became. It was as if the entire territory of Shatray had been declared a war zone. Some of the fighting was done miles from the capitol Taysor and was between smaller clans, like the Quelesti and Thereq, and larger ones among the seventeen ruling clans. Just getting through the scuffles wore out the small party as they struggled to reach the city of Taysor. Presently, the Trayshan [Zair'ek] was engaging in an altercation between a group of Suez and Stikes clansmen.
   The two Xsorian brothers stood back-to-back as the resisting assassins attacked. Lap held his falchion broadsword in a defensive stance, ready to protect himself or his elder brother from a close attack. Behind him, Page was equipped with twenty round suriken and fifty hand blades, five of which were in hand. Twelve bleeding bodies of downed opponents littered the ground around then, most knocked out but many sporting cuts from Page's great aim. Nearby, the Berzén and Berris and their eldest son were also fighting close by each other; but, according to Trayshan customs using each other as cover was cowardly, so they fought one-on-one. Both ways proved successful against the enemies, as seen by the number of moaning bodies on the ground.
   "Five more!" Page warned his brother, as he readied his weapons. *"Suez using does, katar, and scepters."*
   "Gotcha." Lap tensed and rose his sword from its waiting position. *"Just tell me what you need."*
   Using their telepathic link made the brothers seem like godly fighters, scaring most of the enemies that engaged them. Those that dared to attack could barely hide the fear in their

eyes. The five assassins in front of Page showed the same reluctance. Still, they charged because they had to—or face the wrath of their leader Teera Sabina. Their nervous thoughts beat torturously against Page's mind.

"The outside right is attacking first." Page informed his younger brother then he let loose three knives and four suriken. Five hit their intended targets, taking one in the neck, the others in the side, and one in the groin. The last two whooshed dangerously close their intended targets and bit deeply into the trunks of tarol trees beyond. Page sunk to his knees in the next instant as Lap thrust his sword around to block a scepter aimed at his brother's head. Lap knocked the weapon away and thrust at the woman's shoulder, leaving a deep puncture wound. His attack allowed Page to roll behind him and ready himself for other attacks.

Shane Sinhail blocked another attacker nearby. The sixteen-year-old Trayshan perried the Thereq's sword thrust and used his katana's sheath to knock the man out. He turned immediately, always in motion, to stop another attack aimed at his neck. The two assassins struggled to push the other back, but only for a moment, before Shane ducked under a floundered down-left stroke and put his shoulder into the other man. He gutted his opponent as the man began to fall. Blood sprayed his face and tunic as the man drifted past, but the Trayshan merely wiped it away and charged the next enemy before him. As Shane engaged the next swordsman, another slipped behind him to double-team him. The first let go a sneer, giving his partner away to the Trayshan. As the two attacked, Shane blocked the first then used a wakizashi taken from his belt to run the second through before reperrying the first and stabbing him through the stomach. The two choked out shocked screams and sunk to lifeless piles at the youth's feet.

Shane looked away from the downed men as his father yelled his name. Turning, he threw his wakizashi into one assassin trying to surround his father. He sprinted over simultaneously to his throw and engaged another assassin as his father faced the other two fighters. Shane opened his man from right shoulder to left hip and paused to study the field. Behind him, Tyre Sinhail slashed one of the men's thighs, causing him to scream and clutch at his gushing wound. Unfazed, the Trayshan leader spun around and thrust downward, catching the second man in the skull. His spin brought him back around to dismember his first opponent. The Berzén froze in his final thrust as the two men fell to the ground. He assessed the situation, like his son, and relaxed to nod at Shane. "We're done here. The Torezes are just finishing."

Shane nodded mutely and went to collect his weapons. As he did so, he watched the brothers as they fought, silently approving their style. Lap acted as defensive against all attacks, while Page threw knives and suriken as opportunities presented themselves. Like one being, they attacked and perried as the three remaining assassins that circled around them. *"Right!"* Lap mind-shouted and perried downward as Page sliced the man's legs and took another man in the throat with a well-aimed throw. Lap thrust three times at the maimed enemy and knocked him out with his hilt. The last Suez rose his sword and charged; his last thought being that he was still doing this for Master Teera. Page and Lap straightened and shared pained glances. Both were still tormented by the dying words of the dying. In sadness, Lap told his brother, *"They all died believing they were right in this war."*

"Yes." Page fought back a tear of sympathy for them all, *"But, it is not right for us to be fighting each other in the first place. We are all assassins, all people from this planet, yet we let a Royal kefp't divide us so deliberately. This is what must be stopped."*

"But...the war has been going on for years."

Page looked away. *"It will end tonight, I feel. That was what Zanishiria told me; she will fight Manscor for good or ill. Either way, the war will end by one of their strokes."*

"Tonight." Lap's thought echoed in Page's head. The elder Xsorian could tell Lap was thinking about the young Las'wa cast out. He sent out a silent hope for her to be all right then switched his thoughts back to the present. *"Come, brother, the Trayshans wait."*

The Torez brothers joined the Trayshans in silence, exchanging a nod with the Berzén. The small, roughened group sprinted off then, blending in with the forest shadows. Ahead, far to the south, rose the crystal towers of Taysor Palace, gleaming like silver beacons. Unerringly, the Trayshan group headed for it in hoped of reaching the Ta sharay and his con'trore fighting in the city.

* * *

The fighting on the outskirts had started at daybreak; however, Qusairo's main group was still tensely waiting for enemy engagement. The streets the army marched down were deserted, making everyone nervous, but none of the Royal guards appeared. Disconcerted, Qusairo halted his army in the shadows of the buildings and called a runner forth. Then, more waiting began as they waited for more news.

Royal Qusairo called Anmero, Seircor, and K'sho to his side as he reviewed their data with his ever-present protectorate. Seircor listened attentively as the two leaders argued over their next action. Beside him, K'sho listened aptly, as well, but kept glancing suspiciously at the surrounding buildings. "Seircor," Qusairo asked the Las'wa youth, "You have been in contact with your council. Did they mention anything that seemed suspicious? They would know if we are heading for a disaster."

Seircor straightened and his countenance became stern. "They were worried enough to send nearly half of our clansmen to the surface. If that is not a cause to be cautious, I do not know what is." He directed his question to Shy'ree. "Lai rēsy seimreal, carsa'na lai? Carsa lai shi'emé sorï?" ["You are in contact with the council, are you not? What are your thoughts on the matter?"]

Shy'ree ignored Qusairo's irritated scowl as she replied. "Seimreal sayen'or sori. Hé, kye ein seimreal carsn'na lei nor'lais. Seimreal sé sayen'or Zanishiria say'na. Ké Zanishiria say'na, osho'na lai sheev'al Taysor sheen'an. Reyh'lai Obseen sayvan." ["The council worries about such matters, however, I feel, they wouldn't have sent us if it was too dangerous. The council also worries over if Zanishiria will fail. If she fails, nothing will keep us from attacking the Taysor palace. We promised Obseen victory."]

"Yais'lai nom'oro Zanishiria? Zanishiria seimora'en va sheev'al sayva'an nom'en." ["Why do you burden Zanishiria so? She was our seimora and will fight until death takes her."]

Shy'ree stared at Seircor as if he was an idiot. "Ey sayva lai sayva'men carsa'na nom'oro. Zanishiria ete'vaien eysie preshanen. Sé sheen'an seim'anol va sheen'an morchenz saynor alé." ["One life over the many is not a burden. Zanishiria knew that when she became preshan. But, winning is more important and it must happen at all costs."]

Seircor lips tightened in anger but he receded his convictions for Shy'ree's common sense. "Crey, lai rein. Kye moreay kye she'na." ["Okay, you are right. I am sorry for my misstep (overstepping)."]

Shy'ree nodded and made a motion in siihshe to show she accepted Seircor's apology. They returned their attention to Qusairo and Shy'ree told her leader her thoughts, minus all of the points of the conversation she and Seircor had just had. "We both feel that we are being led into a trap; however, our aim is the palace, so we must go there nonetheless. How you get there is your choice, seimore, I will do as good a job any which way you want me to do it."

Qusairo watched as his wild protectorate turned and walked away to speak with the returning runner. He sighed. "She speaks the truth, sadly." He gave Seircor a wan smile. "It is our goal to make the palace." He paused and redirected the conversation, "Seircor, what were you really talking about? I recognized Zanishiria's name."

Seircor seemed reluctant, but he finally replied to the Royal leader. "I am not all right with my closest friend being the main trump card of the Las'wa. However, Shy'ree reminded me that that was decided years ago, when the preshans were first created. That Zanishiria is the only one to make the surface is testament that it is her path in this war."

"But, it doesn't have to be!" K'sho argued joining the conversation in support of his friend, too. "There are more than enough Renegades to attack the emperor and his forces. She doesn't have to be the one to take the emperor down."

"It must be her." Seircor countered softly, his voice barely audible. The other youth quieted as he saw the anguish in the Las'wa's grey eyes. "It was the price Zanishiria asked for herself. It was what her dead parents, and, too, her dead brother, would have done if they were alive to take her place. The Coursay'soras are our clan's strongest protectors. They all chose this path." His words subdued all other complaints; both K'sho and Qusairo knew the burden and honor that that position in a clan was about.

"It still sucks." Anmero mumbled the words they all thought. Irritated, Anmero pulled his cloak closer around himself and joined his new friends and father as they leaned against the obsidian building. They all felt too much grief to speak more on the subject.

The runner and Shy'ree came back to the group. The man was still huffing some but he was able to speak clearly enough to his leader. "The guards are being pushed back to the square. Raynward had moved to counter their retreat. Major

Calamas had successfully joined Aslén. Captain Sieck is injured but continues his advance from the west. Also, sir, we have word of two separate clan regiments heading here to meet with you."

"Which clans?" Qusairo asked in wonderment, impressed to have more support.

The runner panted for more air before answering. "The con'stól from Xsenume led by Tá sharay Khan Torez should be here any moment. As for the other, we think they are Trayshan, but cannot confirm. They sent a runner ahead to ask you to wait."

"Very well." Qusairo waved the man away to rest. *Trayshans he says and the Xsorian tá sharay? We may yet win this war.*

Twenty-three of the stealthiest assassins around appeared out of the forest a moment later and headed to the army just inside the ring of out skirting buildings. They halted in a formed line and met Qusairo's troop's eyes calmly. Then, a tall man, with styled obsidian armor adorning his slender build, stepped out of line. He gazed with piercing, emerald eyes at the Royal leader from under his shocking white mane. Finally, he adverted his eyes to the ground and clasped his hands together in a Xsorian salute. "Royal Qusairo, I am honored to meet you face to face. My con'stól had travelled for our city to join in the final chapter of the Royals' War. I am the Tá sharay of Xsenume city."

Qusairo returned the salute the very same way, except with palms outward, not together, in Xsorian custom. "And, I am Royal Qusairo of the Renegade army. I am honored to have the con'stól in my army. A true blessing it is to have their Tá sharay grace us so. Your people's reputation precedes you. We are also awaiting another group. You and yours are welcomed to eat and rest while we wait." He paused to allow everyone to hear and repeat his words to the full army.

Tá sharay Khan Torez stood passively as the news was passed. "My con'stól will accept your offering of food but will remain on watch, Sire, as we are most appropriate for the post. By your leave." He asked permission despite not really needing to. Qusairo was impressed with the leader's manners and bearing.

He gave consent. "As you see best, Tá sharay."

* * *

Sounds of distant battles reached their ears, causing many to pace in frustration, but none of the fighting seemed to be nearing. The noonday suns, reaching their peak in the thirteenth hour, bathed the assassins and Royals in sweltering heat. The shade from tarol trees was their only comfort.

Prince Anmero and company stood near Royal Qusairo as the leader spoke with the Tá sharay. The prince couldn't hear everything the two leaders said but he caught some of their words: "Page…digging up…Manscor…Las'wa….in turmoil." He was frustrated that he wasn't included in the discussion but he knew better than to complain about it. Yet, hearing some words was driving him crazy, especially when he heard Zanishiria's name come up.

Khan Torez was struggling to block Anmero's loud thoughts out as he talked to Royal Qusairo. Annoyance wasn't a usual emotion for the Xsorian leader, but the prince was relentless without even knowing it. He was about ready to send the youth away when Qusairo waved his son over. To Khan's relief, Anmero's mind quieted.

"My son was with Zanishiria for over a week." Qusairo was saying as the Tá sharay collected his thoughts. "But you already knew that."

"Of course." Khan smiled as he remembered when Zanishiria had dragged the exhausted prince into Xsenume City.

"I'd also like you to meet K'sho Rease, Redair's son. He is a close friend of Zanishiria's, from the training center." The slim youth walked over and bowed his short-cropped, silver-haired head in respect. His unusual crimson-and-grey eyes met the Tá sharay's with a respectful directness. Khan returned his bow. "And Seircor C'vail."

Khan took one look at the tall, dark-haired youth and widened his eyes. "Sà, Las'wa seré resoum'lai mē'ekalé? ["So, the Lakeans walk around us undisguised?"] He asked, sounding surprised at the support. "Zanishiria could not tell me if that was the case or not."

"Crey, lai me'seré las asrouc lai'byne saçor." ["Yes, we walk unhindered in the light to give you our support."] Seircor responded and flashed a friendly smile. "Zanishiria told me a little of your discussion. She asked me to tell you "lai oroshay'na'." ["You ae not alone."]

The Tà sharay accepted the Lakean's words just as he had Zanishiria's. A look passed between the two assassins as they acknowledged each other's friendship with the in-question assassin-girl. The moment passed and the Xsorian leader turned back to Royal Qusairo. "Redair has spoken of his son's friendship with the Royal girl." He acknowledged K'sho again before finishing his thoughts. "It seems even he was not aware that she was of the Las'wa and not a Novastone. Had I not met Zanishiria the first month she appeared in Taysor, I would not have known myself. She did well in keeping a low profile."

"That was the intent." Shy'ree suddenly appeared by Qusairo's side. Her abrupt interruption took all of them by surprise, seemingly to her amusement. "We [the Las'wa] did not want the emperor to know of her or any of us surface-side; since he discovered our plan with the preshans last year and murdered them we could not have the same mistake happen with our only card."

The Tà sharay, knowing what her real intention behind her words was, quickly replied to the unsaid accusation. "You cannot blame your allies for that, val'eya. We would never betray the clan that has led us through this war."

Shy'ree's face darkened. "We could not find who betrayed us."

"Betrayal! You all abandoned us after that incident. You could have kept communication between any one of your allies but you did not." The Tà sharay let a hint of anger reflect in his tone. He, himself, was not too angry at the Las'wa but there were many clans that were—and had voiced their grievances to the Xsorian leader. To Khan, it seemed as if the emperor's plan to destroy the preshans had done its damage, if most allies were at each other's throats.

Shy'ree began to curse in Lakean. Fortunately, Seircor stepped in then to calm her and keep her from insulting the Tà sharay, who knew their language well. "Zanishiria had explained our reasons to you, Tà sharay. As for the other clans, we could not help not informing them. The risk would have been too great, but, perhaps, we can all make amends after this war is over. Our allies may be surprised to find just how involved we were this last year."

"Kye mureak, Seircor." ["I thank you."] Khan bowed his head respectfully. "That would be enough."

The conversation was cut short from its intent when the Tà sharay's con'trore strode over. The tall, slim-built man bowed to the leaders, tapping his thinly chiseled obsidian breastplate in respect. Khan waved his man to tell them what he came over to say. "Tà sharay, Royal Sire, the Trayshans have been spotted not a stone's throw away. The con'stól is tailing them in. It seems that the Berzén and Berris are among them."

"The Zair'ek? They have travelled from Thror through this war zone?" Qusairo's awe barely registered on his face.

"Yes." Khan replied. "The Berris expressed her intent to continue the leadership the Coursay'soras showed at Barashi. Still," He flashed a grin at her daring, "Tearrì had always been one to rush into any fight head-on. This was probably an enticing battle for her."

"I'm sure." The Renegade leader returned the grin, for he knew the inside joke well. "Kee'van, how long until they arrive here?"

"Ah," The con'trore turned to look back at the tarol forest. "Right about now, Sire." As if on cue, the small group of Trayshan warriors stepped out of the shadows. A moment later, the tailing con'stól emerged as well, like silent ghosts, to come and stand around their great leader. The rough-looking group of Trayshans did not seem surprised that they had been followed by the Xsorians, but, then again, they would never show that emotion publicly if they had been. In the very front, center stood the burly and roguishly handsome Tyre. He stood with a stern expression as his brown eyes surveyed the gathered army. As if in boredom, he turned to the tough-aired woman beside him and motioned her toward Qusairo and the Tà sharay. The Berris stepped up to the two leaders and executed a sharp Trayshan salute. Both leaders returned her greeting. The lovely woman's topanish eyes flashed as her head straightened then a partial smile lit her lips. "The Tà sharay of Xsenume was not one to miss us. This is good."

"You came for the Tà sharay?"

Tearrì gazed at Qusairo. "We came to fight; however, we have two assassins looking for Khan Torez." The Berris and Berzén turned aside to allow the two youths to pass.

Khan Torez's expression immediately darkened at the sight of his sons. Both Page and Lap felt his anger beat against their minds. Hesitating some, they walked up to their father but managed to make respectfully bow. *"You had better have a good reason for rushing here through this war zone, Page."* Khan growled at his eldest son. He blatantly ignored Lap, which only meant he would reprimand him at a later time. *"I told you to come after the fighting was over, yet you come just as the battle is young."*

Page took the reprimand with calm grace. *"And had I followed that order, we would never be rid of this war."*

Khan paused at his son's words. *"You wish a conference?"* To which a nod was given. *"This better be worth this time, Page."*

The others had seen the reunion as merely a silent assessment. Only the Xsorians could have heard the words exchanged between father and son—and only Lap had since the con'stól politely tuned out the two's mind-reading. Yet, as the Tà sharay shifted his still composure, they could mark his anger as easily as if he had spoken it. "Royal Qusairo, Berzén, Berris, it seems I must call an immediate council with you all. Page wishes for you all to hear his words."

Just like that, the order was received and the leaders gathered for immediate council in the alley of a near-by building, away from the army. Left behind were the group of young men: Lap sighing and being resigned at being left out; Anmero standing, bewildered at the suddenness; Seircor staying reserved until more information could sway his judgement; and an annoyed Shane took to cleaning his katana.

They all kept silent for some time after the leaders left, until the Xsorian youth finally broke the awkwardness. "I'm going to be tanned bad this time." Of course, the other four could only look at him baffled. Pushing aside his thoughts of what his father would do to him, Lap grinned at the young men around him. "Hi. I'm Lap Torez. And, who are all of you?"

Chapter Twenty

After the preshans were slaughtered, all traces of the Las'wa disappeared from the surface. Angered and confused, the allies of the Lakean clan began to assume the Las'wa had abandoned them to their fate—especially after how many loses the clan had suffered since the Battle of Barashi. So, to have so many "clanless" assassins matching descriptions of Las'wa surface during the end of the war was quite surprising. Even for the Tá sharay, who had had close ties with the deceased leaders Ze'is and Mei'cor Coursay'sora, the sudden presence of Las'wa in the Royals' War came as a shock. To not be abandoned after so much resentment left a lot of guilt on the consciousnesses of many clan leaders. However, this also gave the clans much hope…. there was still those who would fight until the end, for all costs. Such a promise helped give rise to the courage needed to finish what the Renegades had started.

Screams of pain echoed through the square accompanied by the clash or bang of weapons. All about were bloody corpses of Royal guards, Honoreds, and Renegades alike, but the armies still engaged despite the numbers piling up at their feet. More fell as the two forces drew together on all sides; however, none could tell which side received more losses.

Amid the throng of red-clothed Royal guards and black-tunicked Honoreds strode a very satisfied Master Teera Sabina. She laughed sinisterly as she ripped apart a clansman from Corez with her scepter and moved on without pause to intercept another Renegade. This man she clubbed though the head and let him drop lifeless before her as she turned to her servant. "Davin, find out where the Royal is. I want his heart on a plate."

Davin bowed. "Right away, Honored-One." He scrambled away through the mess, hacking at enemy assassins as he did.

Teera turned back to the task at hand with a predatory grin. "I wish I would get that reaction from everyone." She leapt at another man and easily took him down. The man's companions gave her a fearful look and backed away. To terrify them more, the Suez master licker her scepter's ruby head clean. The young fighters tripped over themselves in a panicked flight as Teera jeered.

Davin appeared next to her at that instant and kept his voice contained as he faced her wrath. "Honored-One." Teera turned to look down at him. "Commander Regis says Royal Qusairo's forces have yet to engage today."

"What!" Teera sobered with a glare. "He isn't at any of the battle sites? Qet'thz! He had to be here somewhere. That man leads the Renegades, after all."

"He could have pulled back to protect himself. We are overpowering the enemy."

"Hardly; he isn't that kind of man." Teera snarled and used her scepter to block an oncoming arrow. "Qusairo is a fool not a coward. He would never abandon his sorry army." Master Teera turned to make her way through the throng of Royal guards and Honoreds. "I want him found, Davin! If not at the square, then another part of the city. The war hangs on that man."

Davin paled at the task she had given him. Find Qusairo in this mess? He would need to enlist some of Terra's best Honoreds. "Yes, Master Sabina. Right away….if I don't die in this melee first."

Master Teera, of course, didn't care.

The princess scurried through the hallways, evading the Royal guards on her way. She finally paused outside as intricately carved redwood door and glanced around warily. Scarlett fished through her pockets until her hand came upon the silver pin there. Then, with practiced skill, she picked the ancient-designed lock. The door swung inwardly on well-oiled hinges, revealing a darkened room. Quietly, the princess snuck in and closed the door.

"Really you have no need to sneak around. It's not like I don't know you are there." A shape lifted of a couch near the back wall. It halted in an upright position and froze. "Why sneak in the first place; it doesn't suit you, my dear."

Princess Scarlett huffed out her shocked nerves. "You know you could give me a break, father. I'm not an assassin, after all. It is such a bad thing that I wanted to see how Master Teera treated you? She isn't exactly sympathetic, you know."

"Nice of you to remember that, but I am quite all right." The king stood, albeit slowly, as if he was pained. "Though you chose to come at such a dangerous time. What if someone saw you?"

"They didn't father." Scarlett strode over to King Lapsair and took a hand in hers. "The assassins and guards are too busy retaliating to notice one lone shadow in the dark. That made it rather easy to slip in here."

King Lapsair sighed and embraced his daughter. "Still, you can't be too careful. After all, you and Zanishiria do get mixed up now and then."

"I've heard Zanishiria is already a "guest" in Manscor's chambers. They are set to fight at dusk."

The aging king paused, his body becoming still as glass. He seemed to remember to breathe after his lovely daughter hugged him. "'Tis a shame one as young as her had to be drug into this. It's sad really; we could have prevented such a thing."

"You have worried about her long enough, father. She is a very capable assassin, after all. Now, you need to think about yourself." Scarlett ran a hand over her father's arm. "Master Teera didn't hurt you, did she? Any bruises, cuts, broken bones?"

Lapsair gently pushed her way to arm's length. "I am fine, my dear. Teera was in a rather good mood today. Bruises on my wrists are all I received," And one broken rib, "Now, tell me all that is happening. I must know."

Scarlett looked away. "The Renegades have been fighting all morning. They managed to push the guards back to Terrís Square, soon they will be pushed into the walls of Taysor Palace. Also, Master Quinn has sent word that he and six others have secured the emperor's hanger bay at Nyashio. He reported that nearly twelve zets of traznic and at least as much of sydro-smelted steel was on board—more than enough to make military warships on Planet X." [One zet equals about 90 tons]

Lapsair's eyes narrowed slightly in thought. The, speaking more to himself, he said, "That was what the Coursay'soras' warning was about. "The emperor's wrath was not in great riches but basic, hard matter. His quest is to see the stars" or so Ze'is said to me once. He was referring to metal ships."

"So they knew all along?" Scarlett broke into his thoughts.

"Yes." King Lapsair strode to the small table by the couch and turned on a lamp to shuffle though a pile of clothing articles until his hand touched a hard object. He pulled a thin, Xsorian-obsidian tablet from a coat pocket and sat down on the couch. Scarlett joined him a moment later with curiosity in her eyes. "Ze'is gave this to me at Minith, in case he died—that had been two months before the fight at Barashi. It contains secrets they uncovered throughout the two years of the Royals' War they led."

"But it's all written in riddles." Scarlett noted in slight despair. "How do we know what their words are supposed to mean?"

"That," Lapsair leaned back with a sigh, "Is what I have been trying to discern for six years. It seems no one is really sure."

"Great." Scarlett groaned and leaned back against the couch in an attempt to reach better light from the shaded windows near her. "You don't want to open the shades?"

Lapsair chuckled at her discontented grumbling. "Oh, come now! It's as bright as if there were twenty candles in here."

"You mean two." The princess responded while preoccupied with the first riddles. "Hey, have you read this one: upon a rock, stands a mountain tall. Never will it baulk or roll aside, but strong it will stand against those who will topple its river companions wise."

An exasperated sigh followed. "Yes. And that one that says: the doors were closed long ago and can only be opened by those who know its key; that line is followed by: to see our words, seek one who knows our fathers. Those two lines start the whole letter off. It just befuddles me how Ze'is thought I'd be able to understand his gibberish."

The princess giggled. "He was always like that, father. Would you have expected anything less from him?"

"No." The Royal king smiled guiltily. "But, I think he could have used less Las'wa word-games with me concerning something like this is so important."

Scarlett nodded in silent agreement and continued reading the Lakean passage. Finally, she slumped down deeper into the plush cushions with a defeated sigh. "This is all Ligésh to me. Are you sure this wasn't meant for someone else, someone Las'wa?" [Ligésh: one of the names given to O'washia's Hy'gual language the natives speak (mix of Korean).]

"Hm." Lapsair filled up a glass with garn wine, as he always did before getting into a long discussion or meeting. "Well, that could be, but then why give it to me and not his heirs? No, it had to be for me…somehow. Well, let's get to it, shall we? We have a few hours yet to figure this gibberish out." He sat down heavily beside his daughter. "Read from the top. Keep going, even if it sounds absurd."

"Okay." Scarlett took a deep breath and plunged in. "The doors were closed long ago and can only be opened by those who know its key; to see our words, seek one who know our fathers. Cling tight to the solid stone, for it well never falter, and trust it later to never break the promise it gave to its river companion. Months from now, will come a score to ravage from the jewel those who have the key. Beware! Its tides will come in Symdia-enon. [1st quarter, Xsorian calendar] Leading the score will be a venomous desert se*f*a [Viper/snake] that will strike down those of the winds. However, upon a rock, stands a mountain tall; never will it bulk or roll aside, but strong it will stand against those who will topple its river companions wise. The wisest of mankind will suffer the fall, for they are the ones of all-knowing. Yet, seek the wisdom still to find the key of the forefathers on their breasts. The lights will be extinguished for a time, for night falls on even the strongest. The world will turn to the Eirhom-rei [Eighth year, Las'wa count] before the shadow will become dawn. Shéva [death] will come in droves until that time. The river storm will fall down in Siehom-rei [Second year, Las'wa count] and won't recover its roar until the time of the windstorm, yet, keep the battle cry wholly until the keys can be released. The score will push back the winds from the stony gates and mass a legion of molten matter. The score's wrath is not in great riches but basic, hard matter. His quest is to see the stars. Yet, it is not the score's time to take the jewel, so take it back, the winds and mountains and stones will do. By the hand of the wise, the score will be cut down, and the jewel will shine again."

The words stopped at the edge of the page, yet there seemed to be a piece missing—or unwritten. Scarlett studied the interesting message in deep thought then sat back. The last words she had spoken continued to flow about in its song of hope, causing the princess to forget the rest of the passage.

"He took the poetic license of the Lakean clan to heart." King Lapsair suddenly spoke out in slight mockery of his friend.

Scarlett eyed his oddly and carefully set the obsidian sheet on the coffee table beside her. "It's a simplistic message. The riddles are only to protect those involved in their secrets."

"Oh?" Lapsair sat up with interest. "So, you understand it?"

"A little." They leaned over the slat together as she explained. "The Lakeans always used objects to represent clans and ideas. In here, there are many—the stones, water, wind, a jewel. Some Lakean words are used as well. Eirhom-rei and Siehom-rei are the years eight and two. Shéva was their word for death and score comes from their phrase shíc'moré, to kill a man. The word symdia-enon is the Xsorian time-count for their first quarter of the year." Scarlett's voice faded as she continued to scower over the document.

After a long pause, King Lapsair sat back and chuckled despairingly. "So, even you are confused. The languages in there are easy to notice, but their significance is not, and all the symbols spread throughout the piece just cause me a headache. Really, if anyone understood this, I'd give them anything as payment." On second thought, he corrected himself, "Well, maybe almost anything."

Giving up, the princess straightened to face her father. "I don't even think you're supposed to understand this message. You weren't as close to Ze'is as some, you know. Perhaps, he sent this to you only for safe keeping. Someone else was the intended recipient."

"Doubtful." But the king looked as if he was lying to himself. "Besides, who could read it? It's all gibberish."

"To us." Scarlett argued gently. "Would that old martial-arts teacher still be around?"

"Who? Shathahel?" Lapsair guessed. "Maybe, but he's quite reclusive. I would doubt if he had a wish to speak about Ze'is—never did after his death."

"It's worth a try." Scarlett pressed. She and her father stared at each other, thinking, until the king nodded in reluctant agreeance. "Very well, then, I'm off to see Shathahel." She picked up the Lakean manuscript and hit it in a hidden pocket. In one quick motion, she donned her cloak once again and headed for the door.

"Be safe." Her father called behind her.

Scarlett looked back as she shut the door. "Be strong, father."

Kee'van entered the side alleyway in front of the procession of leaders and made sure the area was clear of any intruders. The leaders entered once he gave the okay and fell into place to start the conference. Qusairo took the west wall with the Berris and Berzén opposite of him. Khan Torez took up Qusairo's right and Shy'ree took her place next to Qusairo. Page finished the circle next to his father. No other high-ranked officers or assassins were allowed into their conversation.

Qusairo opened his hands wide, to include them all formally, and was the first to speak. "Before we begin, Page Torez, I would like to say that time grows short. My men should already be at the battlefield. What you have to say, young Torez, had better be quick."

The seventeen-yea-old Xsorian responded with dignity, straightening to his full height of five-foot-ten. "What news I bring is vital to the survival of your army." His words were meant to shock his elders. "And, that concerning the Las'wa. I did not come in haste to see your armies suffer." The leaders accepted Page's words solemnly, some even grimly. They nodded for him to continue. "Tà sharay, Berris, Berzén, Royal," He spoke to them all formally, "I was asked to hack into the emperor's files the falling evening. In doing so, I uncovered some information of dire importance. It would seem that the emperor has had some dealings with the Las'wa lavre'l. [To turn against/ reference to traitor(s)] Among these, he had taken prisoner some of those in the Legion of Leaders captured at Téresh. This act from the one called Teera Sabina, the emperor's "right hand". Another man may have also been at work, a man I am not familiar with. His name is Eric Sorey, also spelled Air'is Soreneay.... helped with plans for the emperor to take down the Legion of Leaders."

"Air'is was a traitor from our clan. We cast him from our clan ages ago." Shy'ree offered the information with a dark glare. "He had been close to Ze'is Coursay'sora until he was caste out. No doubt, he gave the emperor vital information on our clan and its workings."

Berris Tearrì interjected her own thoughts. "This is not good news you bear, and more I am sure you have. This fact on Air'is is ill indeed—I myself knew the man in his youth. However, if he had indeed positioned himself with the emperor, then why haven't we seen more betrayals? He knew much of the Lakean Resistance and its inner workings." He words were directed at Page, showing she felt him the most knowledgeable and giving him full respect.

"In my opinion, and not fact," Page replied, "I think him still loyal to Ze'is Coursay'sora. At least his actions and reports thus far show no signs of deception toward the Las'wa, only incomplete truths. He was a silent partner in the emperor's plans, though a very influential piece when needed. It seems he was used to hunt down those Legion Leaders in Thereq. He also seems to be a "handler" for one code-named the "Shadower" an assassin hidden from all but does the dirty deeds for Teera Sabina and the emperor—alongside Air'is. For the secrecy surrounding him, he held a very high position of power with Manscor."

"The news of this lavre'l is not great but does not affect the outcome of this war today, my son. What else do you have for us?"

Page paused, closing his eyes as if to read a data file hidden behind his eyelids—which none would have put past the best hacker on Obseen. He opened them a moment later, revealing somber eyes. "I uncovered files of traznic and sydro-smelted steel. Apparently, the emperor has been collecting small quantities of these metals for eight years; however, only recently has he begun to ship over twenty-five zets of these metals off world."

"That's more than enough to sustain a small fleet of starships!" Tyre growled out from his place next to his wife. "It must have been stolen from us, no doubt, for we were not aware of any traznic being sold to the Royal guard."

"It could have been black-marketed." Qusairo pointed out. "There are a few assassins capable of getting Trayshan traznic for a high price."

Page nodded in agreement. "That is so, but I feel your attention should be taken away from that for now. The metals are being shipped to a docking station near Planet X. The project's name was the "Hammerhead". I don't know what it is about, but there were hints to a large ship of some sort being built there."

"What kind of ship?" Royal Qusairo asked, alarmed.

"I am not sure…the files were quite vague on all the major points but I am guessing at an enormous war vessel. There are over one thousand men stationed at project "Hammerhead", over half are security."

Khan's slanted his eyes as he came across a suspicious thought. "So, it's true, then, the rumors about the emperor. He is preparing to head spaceward after his duel with Zanishiria and the fight with the Renegades."

"It would seem so father."

"Then my men must see to stopping him for sure." Qusairo interjected. "Manscor must not be allowed to take this war off planet!"

"Agreed." The leaders echoed the Royal. Page felt that they were about to leave the tent, much to his dismay." "No!" He suddenly said, hoping to stop them. The leaders looked at him expectantly.

"No, we must allow the emperor to leave?" Qusairo spoke for the others, trying to find the cause for the youth's sudden outburst.

"No….that's not why I said that." Page almost looked embarrassed. Being a mind-reader sometimes had him five moves ahead of everyone because he could tell what they were going to do next. "I have one more thing to say: The Royal guards intend to lay a trap around the palace, just like at Barashi."

Those words had all the leaders frozen, all other thoughts overridden. All but Qusairo had been at Barashi. They knew the death-toll and the loss of the greatest of their leaders too well. Now that the Renegades had more than a handful of great leaders in Shaytyar, it was important that the past was not repeated. "A trap." Tearrì echoed Page's words. "Barashi was not just a trap, it was a massacre." Silence followed he words as the past horrors hung in the air. "What do you know, Tà sharid?"

Page had lowered his eyes when the leaders had paled at the mention of Barashi. The images the past battle had brought up were very vivid and horrible. He could barely lift his emerald eyes to meet the Berris's. "They are planning to attack just as they did back then: most likely they will cut a large force off from the rest and surround them. Then, they would use the guns and bombs like they did back then—a UEF ploy more than that of assassins and guards. With that kind of firepower, they may not use their guards, so there may be a short pause when they pull their men back, unless they have sent them in on a suicide mission. I could see Teera Sabina doing so just to keep her men from knowing their sacrifice. The guards have yet to deploy all their forces yet, either. Still twelve hundred guards and three hundred Honoreds are in reserve....at least by my count last night."

Qusairo took the news with a blank face. After all, they all knew that a trap had been in question. Knowing it was a certainty changed nothing; it just showed that the emperor had known they would reach the Palace and had planned for it. Hanging a lure so close but out of reach had been one of the emperor's favorite tactics. "This isn't good, young Torez, but thank you for verifying our worst fears. Now, can we get to it?"

Page nodded solemnly. "Yes. I hope I have given you enough to help."

Khan grasped his son's shoulder and gave a small, proud smile. "Yes, Page. You have been helpful. Thank you, my son."

Chapter Twenty-One

In the history of the five Obsarian wars, the Battle of Barashi is considered the bloodiest. In it, eight hundred assassins were felled in some of the worst ways. Only a tenth of the Resistance made it out alive.

Through all rhymes and reasons, Barashi should never have taken place. It had not even been the leaders' of the Resistance's idea to make a stand at the isolated city. It was only when the army's route to Xsenume City was cut off that they had to flee as quickly as possible toward Traygor. The Resistance never made it to Imari's border, for half of the Royal Guard was waiting in ambush at the small city of Barashi for them to pass by.

The Lakean Resistance took a stand at Bariant Square when they realized they were closed in on all sides. It is said that a third of their fighters were felled there as they scrambled to find sheltered vantage points against gunfire reigning down from the rooftops. The remaining fighters were able to hold off the guards for seven days, against odds of eight to one. Assassins loyal to the Lakean Resistance hurried to help their ambushed comrades; however, it wasn't a second Resistance army that appeared the eighth day of the fighting, it was the rest of the Royal guards from Taysor....

Ze'is and Mei'cor Coursay'sora, main leaders of the Resistance, had ordered a group of their fighters to secure the secret passageway to the caves from the beginning of the fight and had begun evacuating any assassins they could manage to do without. Seeing the new army appear, they knew that the Resistance was doomed. Ordering all remaining fighters to the caves, Ze'is, Mei'cor and a small handful of their best fighters covered the retreat. Their final standoff allowed the remaining army to get away from the battle. All sixty-nine of the remaining assassins did not survive that last night at Barashi.

"What do you mean, "we meet again after all this time?" I don't even know you sheeq." [Char word means stranger] Sunashi spat as he backed away from the shadowy figure. Unconsciously, he rubbed his sore shoulder where, just moments before, it had been held in a sharp, iron clasp of machinery.

"I was not referring to you, zeni [trainee], I was speaking to my aquaintants."

"Enough Alrik, Sunashi is no longer a trainee!" Dorsetti ordered the man hidden there. "And we are barely acquainted ourselves. It would be best if you would show your face."

The shadowy figure did not move from his hiding place.

Quinn sighed and motioned for the others to step away. "I feel that time have been hard on you, Shadon. Why do we find you here, in a Royal starliner?" [Shadon: nickname Quinn gave Alrik Kagar]

"If permitted, Quinn," Alrik Kagar's voice answered with a quiver, "May I have some repast while I share my tale?"

"Of course." Master Quinn motioned for the mess hall's long booth. "The others will take chairs away from us. Food is minimal but I can provide what I have." The others masters stepped away to tables on the other side of the mess hall and took their seats. In quiet agreement, they allowed Quinn to take the lead with this overly-cautious assassin-man. "Now, will you come join me, Shadon?"

In response, the shadow moved from the darkened corner. Sunashi's gasp spoke for all of the masters' shock. Alrik Kagar looked like a shadow of the former man he had been. His current age was fifty-two but he looked more like he was in his late seventies. Recent ordeals had aged him drastically. His body was in poor condition; it was shriveled and pale like a ghost. An interrupted scar traced from his right nostril to right ear and disappeared down his neck. It was obviously a more recent wound, as it still looked raw and puckered. Blood, most likely from the face injury, had dried thickly on his shirt and pants and was marred with mud stains on the left side of his body, as if he has fallen in a puddle on that side. It wasn't until Alrik accepted Master Quinn's hand, though, that any of them noticed how gaunt the Therequian really was. Gently, Master Quinn helped the stiff, fragile man into the cushioned booth and laid his warm cloak around the man's shoulders. Then, he placed some food, with his last supply of florick moss he had gotten from King Lapsair, on the table.

"May I ask what happened, Shadon?"

Alrik Kagar paused in between bites and seemed to freeze in place. To Quinn, he seemed like a scared liauq [lizard] quivering in the Bialthian grasslands. Yet, when the assassin turned to face him, Quinn saw anger, not fear, in the man's face. "Do you remember the pits of Syltha? The place where that one Royal-assassin Secrant captain skinned that Sinya woman alive right infront of us when we were captive there?"

"Yes." Quinn swallowed what little moisture remained in his mouth. "The rest of the tale is not much better, and that woman was only bringing us water." The older master muttered to himself.

"I met that captain two months ago in Takato." Quinn's head came up in surprise and anger. "Yes, he was still alive, Quinn. Even better, he was working for Manscor's interrogation sector."

"Is that why you look like that?" Dorsetti asked from his perch across the room.

Alrik Kagar turned to include the rest of his audience. "No, Master Dorsetti, I have Eric Sorey to thank for this." He caressed his scar gingerly. "No, the Secrant captain died under my blade for the horrific crimes he has committed. It was just that the Honoreds caught me before I could escape to Xsenume."

"So, this Eric Sorey is the new torturer?" Hareoska probed.

"Well, not really." Kagar let out an eerie chuckle. "They say he is the emperor's "shadow. He struck me as Lakean, though, the way he came into the room and all. Treated me like he was one, the way he tortured me through honest combat like Lakeans ae known to do as punishment. He was one hell of a fighter."

"The Lakeans do not side with the "man killer"." Yoshida pointed out. "It seems unlikely that this man was Lakean."

"I had thought so too, but he was definitely dark-featured and his eyes reflected like they contained gamma lenses. You would have known just be looking at him."

"This war is messed up." Roko muttered angrily. "The whole damned thing. And now the Lakeans reappear, but not in the force they promised."

"Then you do not know much about this war." Alrik Kagar countered, his statement bringing the master's words to a halt. "I have been all over the planet these past few years and there is much I have seen of this war that surprises me. There are more Lakeans surface-side than we have been led to believe... Like this Eric Sorey character. When he found me, I had an obsidian tablet given to me by Rel'aun Ser'vela—yes, that great Lakean seivarel—who wished me to run it to King Lapsair. [Seivarel is a general/or similar to post in Las'wa society] Eric must have known what it said, even with it written in Lakean for he made sure to smash it to oblivion before turning it over to the Secrant community. It was strange, really, to be beaten up but have all of my secret information protected like that."

"That man seems like he loved to double-play if you ask me." Corsetti stood up as he always did when thinking and began to pace the length of the booth. "But, all of this only steers us away from our original question." He stopped and set accusing eyes on the Therequian. "Only a person who wishes to hide the truth plays around a foul-berry bush."

Alrik Kagar shrugged the accusation off. "My other tale is far less entertaining. After I was tortured by Eric, I was thrown in here and have been here since. It really isn't a bad cell, though, as far as cells go."

"Why didn't you leave?" Roko wondered out loud. "This is a ship, after all."

"And go where?" Kagar ran a hand through his long, greying hair, wiping the dark stands away from his scar. "For miles around there are Royal guards. I would have been lucky to make is as far as a mile out of Nyashio. And, what would the point be? At least here I can wander around a Royal starship without being bothered. Oh, and I couldn't leave anyway. Eric rigged the doors to not open from the inside and the guards don't come visiting. You could say I have been left to rot in this Royal cell."

Quinn winced at the thought. The man he had known would have hated this imprisonment. The only way Alrik Kagar would speak this way was if he really thought this was his end. He sure looked that way. "It's a good thing we stopped by then."

"Yeah." Alrik gave his the ghost of a smile. "You had a grand entrance too, but how did you get past the codes?"

Quinn bobbed his head toward Yoshida. "Thanks to Khan Torez."

"Of course, the "Code Master"." He chuckled. "It figures." Kagar bowed in respect of Yoshida's skills. "So,

Judeao, my friend, what are you going to do now? It seems odd for you to show up here so geared up for a fight."

"Well..." Quinn started but Sunashi interrupted with a devious grin. "We steal a few warships as payment for all our troubles and go wreak havoc on a certain space station above the planet."

Quinn shrugged helplessly. "What he said."

"Sounds fun." Kagar agreed. "So, let's get cracking." The man rose stiffly as he stuffed the rest of his meager meal in his mouth. "I'll even give you a tour of my fancy new home-away-from-home as a bonus."

The door to the private dining room swung open and two Royal guards came through fully armored and wary. Zanishiria eyed them boredly and continued organizing her weapons on her person. "You can wait outside...I will be there in a few minutes." The guards hesitated but finally, reluctantly, left again.

"They obey you?" Tarin wondered in surprise.

Zanishiria gave him a "yeah right" look and continued with her task. "They just follow Manscor's orders, which are to say, he probably told them to not bother me if I say." The young assassin-girl picked up her final weapon, the preshair whip Air'is had given her and wrapped it around her waist in a quick-release way. She turned to face her friend fully then and studied him. "Will you be okay? I mean...you weren't really supposed to be involved. I feel as if I haven't done right by you, having you here. I—."

Tarin cut off her words. "I have never heard you ramble before." Zanishiria averted her eyes, covering up whatever emotions were in her eyes. "Are you almost blushing?! No way!" Tarin subdued his joy, knowing it came more from nerves than actual feeling, and gave the younger assassin a more serious answer. "No, Zan, I pulled myself into this. You are not to blame. In fact, it is not I you should be asking. The real question is: are you all right?"

"Yes." Zanishiria replied immediately, trying to act tough, but then her grey eyes took in Tarin's concerned gaze and she let her bluff fall away. "And no.... I mean, yes because I have been trained and chosen to do this and no because I am not sure if I am ready for what is ahead. I have already done too much, killed too many…." Her thoughts were on Sye Rainier.

Tarin stepped closer and reached out a hand to take hers, knowing what Zanishiria referred to. "Your master chose her own path, Zan. How were you to know that she would try to stop you at all costs or that your skills were above hers?" The beautiful Las'wa wanted to tell Tarin that she had known her skills were above Sye's, her real master; Tyracor; had made sure of that, but it seemed irrelevant to say such about the Senior Master of the Guild. Tyracor would certainly look down on her for having gotten the woman killed—and so she regretted the action. Keeping such words to herself, Zanishiria gazed up into the handsome face of her Neitiege friend and nodded. It seemed to make him happy that she agreed.

"You are braver than I." Tarin continued, in a whisper. He pulled her in for a desperate hug and clung to Zanishiria as if he could make the world stop turning. When he finally pulled back, his eyes were moist with tears he would not let fall. "I am here, Zan because I want to be here. Let me stay…" Without waiting for an answer, Tarin bent over and kissed Zanishiria lightly on the forehead, startling her at his sudden impulse. Zanishiria stilled and kept herself from pulling back; she could allow Tarin that one time to express his feelings.

A lone tear escaped from the younger assassin's slate eyes and trailed down her cheek. The sign, rare and vulnerable, struck a chord in Tarin. He suddenly realized that underneath the assassin-girl's calm exterior, she was, quite possibly, terrified. Tarin offered an encouraging smile and indicated the door. "There must be a reason you were chosen to fight the emperor. It is time I find out what it was your clan saw in you."

Zanishiria nodded, again stoic, and let Tarin pull her to her feet.

The Royal guards straightened nervously as Zanishiria and Tarin walked out into the hallway. The leader, his rank symbolized by the mark of Roses, cleared his throat and pointed to the right wing. "Follow me, young assassin. Our lordship awaits you in his private dueling room." The man proceeded forward, the others falling along the sides and rear around the two youths. Zanishiria gave Tarin one last, determined glance and stepped forward, closer to her destiny.

* * *

Through the blood-orange-stained glass lay the powerful capitol city Taysor. The streets, that looked so quiet and serene through the window's view, would soon be filled with the war cries from the two opposing armies. "This city will be mine soon. Very soon." Emperor Manscor murmured and turned away to study the dueling room he had had prepared for the fight.

Red curtains, made of royal satin, had been pulled back to revel the eight, ceiling-high windows that allowed in as much of the pane's rosy-orange color. The color washed the cold black-obsidian floor and white-marble of the walls in its hues, giving the room a livelier tone. The intricate gold in the wall sconces and the training square's border were set alight as well, near-blindingly. The room seemed awash in hundreds of red and golden hues, bright and defiant.

In the center, the fighting square had been cleared of all weapons' display stands, leaving only the Emperor's most favored weapons hanging on the three walls; his backups for the coming fight. The emptied space gave the two combatants a full fighting square of two hundred-by-eighty meters—one of the largest on Obseen. Manscor nodded in satisfaction and pride at his dueling room. All was set.

The large, double doors opened at that moment and a small entourage of Royal guards escorted Zanishiria and Tarin Saerric in. "Your Majesty, the traitor and Master Teera's apprentice, as requested." The leader called out from the line.

Manscor waved his guards away. "Shut the doors. Stay out of the room until I call." He waited for the obtrusive guards to exit the room before walking over to his two "guests", stopping a safe distance from them. "I hope that your coming here means you have prepared yourself as best you can." Zanishiria stood tall, nodding at the implied question. "I would hate for you to not have all you need during our fight." The wording had the assassin-girl's expression falling flat. Manscor smirked at her reaction and walked around the two youths to the wall behind them.

His hands, now naked without his rings, curled around the hilt of his favorite kaskara sword. "I have kept you waiting long enough, young Las'wa. After all, one year would be enough to make anyone's blood boil." Manscor turned back to find Zanishiria already in a defensive guard, holding a creeshts sword between them. Tarin looked from his friend to the emperor with tight features, as if not sure if he, too, wanted a weapon in hand or just to be away from their vicinity. "Young Saerric, I reserved a place for you by the center pillar. I thought having your back to the windows would give you the best view of our fight." Tarin nodded mutely and strode away to the indicated spot, relaxing to be further away.

"Now then, Zanishiria, let is see what a young assassin like you can do."

The assassin-girl backed away so she was at the center of the room. She collected herself and fell into a forward stance, sword-tip pointed the emperor's way. Manscor nodded his approval of her form and took up a sideways pose, with his sword pointing at Zanishiria's heart.

The world seemed to still.

Manscor was the first to attack, coming at his smaller opponent in a quick burst of speed. Zanishiria easily spun and blocked the thrust aimed at her shoulder and followed his slash around to her opposite side and down to her hip. There, she reversed her blade at the last second and pushed Manscor away. Taking up the sudden gap between them, she launched forward in a long lunge; however, just as fluidly, she changed her movement into a spin at the last breaths-width and caught the emperor in the back with a three-stroke cut. Impressed, Manscor barely managed to block the moves, and his last perry was too slow. He came away with slashed clothing. "You are good." He commented as they split and circled each other. "You have learned several different sword styles, I can see—impressive—and your technique is sound…but what if we spice this up a bit?" In response, Manscor took a suriken from his belt and threw it at the wall, where it bit firmly and held. A moment passed and the ground began to tremble. In moments, the floor was transformed into an uneven landscape. "How is your footwork?" Manscor challenged.

Zanishiria had already moved to a more suitable fighting area near the windows. "You should really be wondering about yours."

"Oh, aren't you the smart-ass? Amusing." Manscor laughed at her haughtiness and strode toward the assassin-girl with full confidence in his abilities; this was his training square, after all, he knew its features inside and out.

As he neared, Manscor's footfalls became faster, until he was speeding at the Las'wa. With weapon raised, Zanishiria met him head-on with a thrust that took her under the reach of his arm, where she loosed a cut at his exposed ribcage. Her thrust took her on past the emperor. Zanishiria slid to a stop and spun around quickly to cross swords with the next attack. A preshair dagger slipped into her hand from a hidden place in her sleeve and she sliced at Manscor's right knuckles as their swords were locked. Blood came quickly to the shallow wounds.

The two fighters broke, danced a space to the right, and came together again in a downward thrust. They continued into a perry to the right then left, with Manscor aiming for the girl's hip. Zanishiria followed the emperor's motions as if they were in a choreographed dance, easily blocking each of his attacks. Spinning out of her next perry, she aimed for the emperor's right shoulder, blocking a second thrust to her left thigh with the preshair dagger. Once she was able to move the dictator's sword back around to center, she deflecting his next sword thrust at her inner knee. The speed of her perries were strikingly quick. Even Tarin, their observer by the window, could hardly follow the blocks. Zanishiria was in top form, seeming to match the great Emperor Manscor at his best.

Frustrated, the emperor broke away to reroute a thrust at Zanishiria's abdomen and sent the girl backwards with a series of thrusts and perries. His plan was to catch the assassin against a fake boulder setup twelve paces behind them but Zanishiria's good memory warned her of the intent. With five paces remaining, the young Las'wa threw eight chitz at the Emperor. Manscor raised his swords to knock the deadly Trayshan weapons aside and returned his attention back to his opponent only to find her running away from him, toward a large pillar. Smirking to have her back exposed so poorly, Manscor sped after her. *She is trapped. No one turns their backs to another unless they are at wits end. She must be realizing she isn't as good as she thought to fight me.*

Just as the Las'wa youth neared the pillar, she hopped slightly to click her heels together; then her next jump launched her person at the pillar's round face. Zanishiria crouched in midair, so her feet were the first to touch the smooth surface, and her boot clamps latched onto the hard stone. Like an otherworldly spider, she scrambled up the pillar until she was four meters above the emperor's head. From there, she released her hand blades from the stone and kicked away from the pillar to somersault over her enemy. Zanishiria landed eight paces behind Manscor with her sword at ready. She raced at his unprotected back.

The emperor was almost impaled on Zanishiria's weapon—and would have had he not had the sense to roll away at the last second. Manscor came out of his roll against the hard, eastern wall and reached for two laz-axes hanging next to him. With one in each hand, he heeled his dropped sword away and powered up the new weapons. "You are quite impressive," Manscor said with a dry smile. "The basics are always easy to learn but how are your abilities with multiple weapons, hm?" Zanishiria was unperturbed by the man's constant jeering—he was only testing her for weaknesses anyhow. She followed suit by replacing her creeshts sword with two wakizashi blades and shifted her weight to accommodate a different fighting style. Her movement told Manscor all he needed to know: Zanishiria's skills with other weapons were as good as all her other points. "I haven't had this much fun since I killed Ze'is Coursay'sora at Bariant Square. You fight like that rebel."

The ruler's remark didn't stir Zanishiria in the way Manscor had predicted. "You tell me of a man I was too young to know. This fight is not for him; it is for all of the clans you oppress, and not the father I have no recollection of."

* * *

"A father did you say?" Tarin heard Manscor ask his friend. The Sinya wondered if he, too, had heard Zanishiria right. Had Zanishiria just said Ze'is, leader of the Lakean Resistance and assumed ruler of the Lakean clan, was her father?

Zanishiria' voice floated to Tarin faintly over the scraping of her two shortswords as she crossed them together. "I am Ze'is's only daughter."

Chapter Twenty-Two

Though Zanishiria had taken an oath to give up all ties to the Las'wa and to her family, there was one card the assassin had that would throw the emperor for a loop: her ties to Ze'is and Mei'cor Coursay'sora. Her parents had been the worst thorns in Manscor's side. Even after their deaths at the Battle of Barashi, their names were the war chants the Renegades took up against the Royal. That Zanishiria was their last poisonous dart, their legacy left against the emperor, was the one power the young Las'wa had against Manscor; it was, also, the one reason that gave the fourteen-year-old her courage; she was the last of the line of Coursay'sora's. It would be revenge that would keep her from caving against the emperor. She would not stop until her parents' and brother's deaths were answered for.

--Master Quinn

"Is this news true?" Aslén questioned the runner worriedly.

"Yes, Royal Doz." The youth replied. "I was told this by Leader Qusairo himself." Again, the wiry, dark-featured runner repeated his message, "The Royal Palace is a trap. Our forces must be united before we reach the perimeter or we will be destroyed."

Aslén sat down at his war table to think. "Did Qusairo give you any details, young——."

"It's Coryu, Royal Doz, and yes, he and Protector Shy'ree send you more news." Aslén motioned for the young man to go on. "Page Torez, son of the Tà sharay, found the plans for destroying the Renegade army. The emperor wishes to perform a massacre like the one at Barashi. Be aware!" Coryu finished with a strong warning tone and bowed his head in respect. Right before he left the tent, Aslén called him to wait. "Yes, Royal?"

"What did this Shy'ree say? She tends to add more than Qusairo."

Coryu paused then turned around to address the leader. "She says, Royal Doz, know our people have been loyal even through the times it seemed we were not there. This is the moment we have waited for. Our time has come to take our leaders' places in carrying the battle home.'"

Aslén listened intently, his face in a slight frown. As Coryu finished, he waved the runner to a chair. "You, of course, know what she means." A nod answered the Royal. "Then can you enlighten me? You are like her, similar features and such. Tell me please, are you the Lakean force promised us?"

Coryu responded by pulling aside a lock of his black hair from his right temple. There, cut into his light skin, was a scar in the symbol of the Las'wa [people of the night]. After a moment's pause, the young man let his hair fall back into place. "We are not of the original preshan group promised you...they were killed on ascent last year. Only two of them survived. One came back to us injured to tell us the news, the other has been acting on the preshanen's own and is not under our orders."

"Zanishiria." Aslén muttered to himself.

The Lakean looked startled that Aslén knew. "How are you privy to her name?" He ordered sharply. "Which contact gave you it?"

Aslén was taken aback by the venom in the youth's voice. "If you are thinking I have any intentions of traitorous actions, I do not. It was Tà sharay Torez; he was thinking Zanishiria had connections with the Las'wa. It was just a thought, but now that I think of it, she did appear about one year ago out of nowhere on the day the preshans were supposed to."

The fire in Coryu's eyes seemed to soften. "The secret is safe with him, though I am not sure what I should do with you."

Alsén's pulse sped up at the implied threat. He racked his mind quickly for an answer, then remembered the ritual both the Lakeans and Trayshans used to seal promises. Slightly panicked, he looked around for something to draw blood. If Coryu found his actions strange, he didn't say, but he did seem to know what the Royal was looking for. In a flash of his wrist, a creeshts knife appeared in front of Aslén—hilt first. The Royal leader took the weapon with care and slit his left wrist, wincing, and extended the bleeding skin toward the Lakean. Coryu stared at him a long moment; Aslén dared not breath.

"Kye'eith, I accept." And the sinewy wrist of the young assassin stirred the blood into the Royal's arm. Then, like a predator striking its prey, Coryu launched from his chair toward the door. It was only one single pause at the entrance, where he said, "I will spread word of caution to the others," before the Lakean youth was out of sight.

Aslén watched him leave, in awe of the pure deftness of the young man's walk as it carried him quickly from the camp. Once Coryu had blended in with the tarol tees, the leader turned away to ponder what to do about the trap awaiting his forces. Yet, a part of him was still thinking of the young Lakean man. Something about him had both reassured and froze Alsén's soul. For only a moment, he let himself dwell on the feeling, then, with one wish to Coryu to be safe, he pushed the runner from his mind.

Sneaking through the darker streets of Taysor, Scarlett managed to make it to the old master's tiny hovel without being seen by the fighting armies. Shathahel's little apartment was dark, but the door was unlatched, so Scarlett knew the old recluse was home. Without a knock, she slipped inside and found herself in the dining and kitchen area. The only other room in the apartment was covered from her view by a long, tattered drape.

"Um, Shathahel?" Scarlett called out uncertainly. "I, um, need to speak with you. King Lapsair sent me." For a moment it seemed the old man was not there, like many who had left to avoid the fighting, but finally the drape was pushed aside by a worn, wooden cane. A wise-looking old man followed the intricate cane through the doorway and tapped his way to where Scarlett stood.

"King Lapsair sent you, you say?" He muttered quietly and reached out to feel Scarlett's face. "Zanishiria? I thought you had other business today, child."

Scarlett smiled at the man's mistake. "It is not Zanishiria, master, it is Scarlett Novastone, King Lapsair's daughter."

"Scarlett? Well I'll be." Shathahel frowned. "You two look more alike each day, yet no way are you sisters. You know, you really should change something or you will keep old geezers like me from telling you apart."

"I do wear earrings, master." Scarlett reminded him gently.

"Ah, that doesn't help me!" Shathahel proclaimed. "I ain't going out of my way to feel your ears now, no way! Get bangs or something."

"Yes, master." Scarlett answered trying not to let the joking smirk on her face carry into her voice. "But, not right now. My father wishes to consult you on a message given to him."

"Why'd he not say? The lad could'a got an answer lickity-split."

"Ah...my father is being held under house-arrest by order of Master Teera Sabina and the Emperor. Long story." Scarlett jumped ahead to the message, "Could you, please, help us, Master Shathahel? It's a message from the Lakean clan."

"Oh from them, is it?" The blind master got a thoughtful look on his face. "So, they sent it to Lapsair. Good choice."

Scarlett could barely breathe in relief. "So you know about it then?"

A grunt was her answer. "Come, sit down young one. I will help where I can, but, be warned, I know little more than you. Ever since those Lakean preshans were killed, the Las'wa have been silent. No doubt, they worry about who to trust."

Scarlett sat on the cushion indicated to her, the only other piece of furniture in the room besides the other pillow-cushion. She slipped the thin obsidian sheet from her inside coat pocket and set it infront of the other pillow. Shathahel paused, his head cocked as he heard the stone document thud on the floor, then, as if he could see it, he picked it up unerringly.

Moments passed silently as his fingers felt the contours of the words on the page. He muttered occasionally under his breath as he read but didn't ask Scarlett for anything. Finally, he set the sheet on his lap. "If only Coryu was here right now. That stupid lad has run off again."

"Coryu, master?"

"Huh?" Shathahel stopped his mutterings. "Oh Coryu? No one special, young lass, just my guest. Showed up four months ago. Had the feel of a Las'wa about him, but no bother, he is not important." He picked up the obsidian sheet again. "Could you read this aloud, little lady?"

"Hai, master." Scarlett picked it up and reread what she had said to her father. When she finished, she glanced up at Shathahel expectantly. "It confuses me, master."

Shathahel chuckled, "The message isn't for you."

"I know that, master, but who is it for?"

Without answering, Shathahel stood up and tapped his way back to the other room. He paused at the door to motion the princess to follow then disappeared behind the drape.

"You must stay here, my son. It is too dangerous for someone untrained such as you—especially now that we know we are heading into a trap."

The prince straightened in indignity but kept his emotions under control. "I know how to fight, father. You are not the only one here who wishes to help the assassins win back Obseen; I, too, can help these people, or why else did you make me come here?"

"I had you come home, Anmero." Qusairo had to check his frustration at his son's stubbornness—he had inherited it from him, after all. Why, after two days, did Anmero have to bring up the subject of why he was brought back from M2? "I wanted to see that you were safe with my two eyes. Rumors had spread that Manscor had found where you were hiding."

"A bluff you were sure the emperor would pull." Anmero set his jaw. "We are in the middle of a war zone. M2 was a much safer bet."

Royal Qusairo rubbed his eyes in annoyance and plopped down in a chair by their map table. "For the hundredth time, Anmero, I say no! You are a Royal, a prince. I cannot have my whole Doz family on the field. If I and your uncle do not survive, I need you to take up our holdings. I cannot have you out there!"

"You would rather I have your legacy than make my own way. The assassins look down on easily-given prestige. I want to go by their rules. I am here and I will fight."

Qusairo stood up and began to pace again. He was getting anxious. His army was all ready to move and here he was still dickering with his nineteen-year-old son. "I have no way to protect you in the fight. The enemy we face has years of experience on you. I will not allow you to go out there to die!"

"He would not be safe anywhere, Royal Qusairo, if we lose today." The two Dozes turned to Seircor as the Las'wa entered the tent. The group of young assassins had grown to five (counting Seircor). They filed in after the Las'wa and saluted the leader. Seircor straightened and continued. "You know as well as I that as soon as your son stepped on this planet, he was no longer safe. Even if you keep him back, there will be someone after his life. In truth, Anmero is safer fighting alongside us," he indicated the five of them, "than staying back with Asilisa and the others."

Qusairo frowned and turned away, knowing he would be outnumbered if all the youths chose to stand on Anmero's side. Why, he wondered, had so many young assassins been ensnared in this war, and not the others? Was it the Lakeans that had started the trend or was it that if one came the others stepped forward too? It didn't matter, of course. Qusairo knew it would not help the situation he found himself facing. They were here, with a strong leader, and needed an answer.

"There are five of us to protect your son." Page Torez added as extra support. "and, we aren't your average assassins either."

Qusairo was going to snap back that that didn't comfort him much but refrained from the remark. Calming himself, he turned back to Anmero and studied his son as if it would be the last time. "Keep my son safe," the Royal whispered, "Don't let me regret this decision."

Chapter Twenty-Three

In 3987 S.D., during the Dark Revolution, young Senior Master Judeao Quinn created a band of masters and high-positioned clansmen. These many leaders—the number is unknown—agreed on the secret council as a means to impact the war and bring it to an end. Through the next decade, the leaders' council grew to include many clans around Obseen, thus establishing the Legion of Leaders as a full-network force.

Even though the Legion was filled with prestigious assassins, none of the leaders announced themselves publically—as per their agreement—which kept these Legionnaire members in positions that helped gather key information in the Royals' War. Only those most-trusted were aware of the Legion; all others heard only rumors. Such secrecy has allowed the Legion to spread information in a way not influenced by the Assassins' Guild (currently controlled by Emperor Manscor).

Very little stays hidden from the Legion of Leaders, and the Legion lives to serve all of Obseen with the best of intentions.

"There is the place we were to meet Captain Sieck." Captain Raynward told his unit's leaders. The third division of the Renegade army had taken shelter two blocks away from the assassins' council-house. The seventeen-sided house loomed to their northwest like a silent beacon shining a brazened ebony in the blaze of the noonday suns.

"Shouldn't the captain already be here?" One of his leaders asked.

Captain Raynward shrugged as if it did not matter, though in truth Sieck's men were twenty minutes late. "The Tepaun Bridge was not the easiest entrance to the main city. They could have been detained by the extra fighting." As if the captain's words were a signal, a runner came up to the group of leaders.

Dăveed Quinn bowed to Raynward. "Captain, a flag is being waved near the council-house. It seems to be the red crest of stars of Captain Sieck's unit."

"Seems to be?" Raynward asked catching the young man's remark. Assassins rarely misused their words.

"Yes, sir." Dăveed nodded the way Master Quinn would have. "But, I have my suspicions. The flag is the same, as is the location, yet I still feel bothered. Where is their out-crier? Call it a hunch."

"Captain," One of his men called, "I see nothing wrong with the situation. If Captain Sieck is here, we must rejoin him quickly and head to Taysor Place. We have already lost time as it is."

"Then we rejoin." Captain Raynward agreed, albeit reluctantly. He gave Dăveed Quinn a look. "But cautiously. Keep all units battle-ready and alert. I want action if anything is out of place."

* * *

Hidden behind the large council-house was a huddled force of three hundred Royal guards. Nearby, in four of the abandoned buildings, skulked a mass of eighty more men; these were Honored-One Master Teera's personal Honoreds force.

"They come, Master." An awe-lusted youth whispered as he scuttled to the black-armored leader. "They don't suspect."

Master Teera nodded arrogantly. "They fear the lateness of this joining, but even caution can't save them. They are as good as dead." She lifted her scepter to her lips to taste the dead captain's blood drying on its azure and metal ridge. "They will have as swift an end as that Captain Sieck had." She turned away from the youth still standing there to motion her men to their ambush sites. In only a matter of seconds, the council-house's perimeter looked empty. Teera smiled vilely and retreated into the council-house's high-arched entrance. Soon, half of Royal Qusairo's Renegade army would not be coming to the leaders' rescue. Manscor would be very pleased.

* * *

Captain Raynward's troops approached the council-house slowly. Twelve scouts, assassin all, trod a thousand paces ahead of the group. Fifteen others covered the sides and rear of the small army, keeping keen eyes on the deserted buildings and streets along the way.

"See?" Raynward's confident man said, "There is no enemy army here. The captain made it fine and is waiting in the council-house."

"Well, then go open the bloody doors." Another snarled, still worried at the silence. He gave the brash leader a push at the entranceway then rose his weapon again in readiness. The army eyed the surrounding area again, keeping a nervous eye at the buildings while some watched their arrogant leader stride to the enormous, glass-thin obsidian double-doors.

Dăveed Quinn, still wound tighter than a coil, crouched next to Captain Raynward, his emerald eyes riveted to the cool stone of the entranceway. Suddenly, he caught the slight flicker behind them as the confident; Renegade leader reached up to open the door. "Don't open it!" He yelled out just a moment before the sapphire-adorned scepter smashed through the thin stone into the man's face.

The tattered drapes closed behind her in a slight billowing of dust. Scarlett covered her mouth as she coughed and glanced furtively around the darkened room. "Master Shathahel? I can't see let alone follow you."

"Pardon, child, pardon." The blind master apologized somewhere in the gloom. "I forget that others need their eyes to see." Rummaging sounds followed as the old man searched for a light. "That stupid thing should be here somewhere. Ouch! Where'd that spike come from? Oh, look, I found my good old quill. Hm, don't know what that is…ah, here it is: a good piece of asrouc." Unerringly, the blind master threw the stone at Scarlett's feet, already glowing. "Okay, missy, come and I will show you what you wish to know and some you probably don't."

Scarlett paused at his words before stepping up beside the master. She glanced to the tabletop that the man was clearing and noticed another obsidian sheet, like the one she carried. "Master, is that—?"

"Yes." Shathahel interrupted harshly. He frowned at the heat in his voice and tried again. "Yes, young Novastone, and no. It is from the Lakeans and is the second half of your riddled note, but it is not your answers." He stabbed the cleared place by the slab with an old, bony finger. "Yours can be set here. Read the two: yours and mine."

Scarlett read through her father's passage. Near it end, she skipped over to Master Shathahel's sheet and continued, "...yet, it is not the score's time to take the jewel, so take it back, the winds and the mountains and the stones will do. By the hand of the wise, the score will be cut down, and the jewel will shine again. However, the score's power reaches far and many sa*f*(a) take his hand. They will hunger for his buried power long after his fires have gone. The "key" is the wind's only hope to restore the jewel's fragile core. It must be found before all it too late...The score may become vanquished through the wind's efforts, but the desert serpents will grow in comfortable holes until their time has come to bring the score's shèvana [destruction] to the jewel. The wise must find their key, for they, too, do not know whose breast it hangs on! The Harem know but, alas, the wise have lost knowledge of them. Shèvana would be on us all!" Scarlett shot her eyes up to Master Shathahel in surprise. "Master, this cannot be the other passage. Destruction on us all by killing Manscor? Surely, Ze'is wasn't meaning that!"

Shathahel's face dropped in sadness. "His words are for his Lakean people and the clans. It is said he had the gift of foresight. Twelve years ago, he predicted the outcome of this war. Twelve years ago! The threat of Manscor was just beginning then, yet he saw when each crucial event would happen: his death, who Manscor would choose as successor, who would fight against the Emperor, and when Manscor's reign would end—and by whose hand! He knew it all Scarlett. All! Except," the old master stepped to a dark-paned window by his work table and stood as if he would see through it, "He didn't understand the "key" or what it was. You see, there was a time when the Lakeans were linked with something called the "Harem of the Wise" but that is gone now, lost. And, with the loss, so was the knowledge of the "key'." Shathahel turned his face to Scarlett. "Ze'is felt it was very important, more so than taking down Manscor. Without it, he thought the world, as we know it, would end."

* * *

Blood sprayed across the emperor's face as one of his laz-axes slashed Zanishiria's thrusting arm. The young assassin elbowed him in the nose, breaking it in recompense for her injury, before the two broke apart from their close quarters. Manscor's hand clutched his pouring nose to stop the blood from entering his mouth and clog his breathing. He paused to catch his breath, keeping his sights on the Lakean youth, and prepared himself. Without hesitation, he reset his bent nose.

Across the square, Zanishiria was giving the emperor the same watchful look as she smeared her acquired wound with ointment and bound her forearm. She came back to a defensive stance as Manscor wiped the blood from his hand.

"If you keep this up, young siph, my men will be clearing your tattered corpse from the floor." Zanishiria glared and gulped for air. She could see the same strain on the emperor's face and knew he was just being egotistical.

"Looking around I would say you're a lying saught. There is more of your blood than mine." She stood up boldly and wiped her weapons clean.

Manscor could not help clucking at her defiance. "You're very brash—I like that. It has made these past hours amusing, but surely you are feeling the throb in your arms and back by now. Why not just give up, Zanishiria," Manscor hissed her name out, "And save yourself the pain I have yet to administer?"

"I am not the one that is shaking with fatigue, man killer. I have been known to last four days. Can you?"

The two combatants had been fighting for over two hours; the obsidian floor was beginning to become blood-adorned from their administrations. Manscor's weapons, of which he had already traded three sets of, were strewn about the floor. Among them, were Zanishiria's own: a sword, wakizashis, chitz, and some throwing blades. The young Las'wa's current weapons-of-choice were two preshair knives, double-sided cutting edges, which had bitten deep into Manscor's limbs. Of course, the emperor had just proven he could return the favor for all the injuries he had received.

Refreshed from the small reprieve the wounded man had given her, Zanishiria stuffed a wad of sayva and florick moss in her mouth and swallowed them quickly. The instant energy and healing powers tingled through her body, readying it for another long dance with death. If the emperor noticed his opponent's usage of the Obsarian plants, he paid it no mind. The many years ago, when he had faced-off with Ze'is, the Lakean had done the same thing—and still lost. Zanishiria would be no different than her father. Bringing his humming laz-axes to bear, he vowed he would see Zanishiria undone. In response, Zanishiria rose to a full upright stance and swung her weapons about to loosen up her wrists. The two combatants charged each other by silent agreement.

At the final moment, Zanishiria leaped away and, through a flurry of movements, brought her left blade at the emperor's ribs. She spun as the weapon was blocked, ducked a laz-ax parry, and struck upward from her crouch on the floor. Her blade nearly took Manscor in the lower jaw, but he bowed backward from the attack. At the next breath, Zanishiria whirled and hooked the emperor's knee with her foot. The man fell to the floor and rolled away to come back at the assassin unshaken. Manscor swung his right arm at Zanishiria's raven-haired head while, at the next opening, thrusting at her abdomen with his other laz-ax. His right arm followed its swing around to block Zanishiria's downward thrust and both his weapons closed toward her exposed neck. In avoidance, Zanishiria summersaulted backward, making sure to stun him with a blow to his chin. Once the assassin-girl landed back on her feet, she rushed the recovering emperor.

Manscor's nose had begun to bleed again from the concussion of her kick but he ignored the sticky flow as he blocked the oncoming attack. The next moves became entangled as the two fighters spun across the fighting square. They leapt over obstacles with little head to them; even the steady rise of a small, false-hill did not slow their dance. Then, suddenly, Zanishiria broke with a curse. She hurled herself away to regroup—only to slam into the nearby wall. She sunk to the floor, slightly stunned.

Manscor paused, satisfied, from his overlooking perch on the hill. He had managed to sink a laz-ax through the small tear in her snake-skin armor, where the Senior Master Sye Rainier had been able to land a wound on the girl's thigh. From the looks of the blood dripping down her leg, he had cut her old injury open deeper and wider. "All that is left," he crowed as he jeered down at her, "Is to let you bleed yourself out." The emperor jumped from the hill and slowly advanced toward his prey.

* * *

"Attack! We are under attack!" Someone yelled out as the lone leader fell to the ground, his face a mess of blood. Movement occurred on all sides as Captain Raynward's and Master Teera's forces were spurred into action. Weapons clashed against weapons and cries of battle matched cries of pain. There was little order to the melee; defend yourself or be killed. All of Raynward's men knew it, and their merciless attackers showed their own desperation. The air was thick with the feeling.

"Quinn!" Captain Raynward shouted to the young assassin-man beside him. Between desperate flurries of defensive moves, he managed to clip out a command to Dăveed. "Quinn, you must try to reach Royal Qusairo. Tell him his northern flank has been compromised. Also, warm him of this danger. You must make it to Qusairo!"

Dăveed hid the doubt he had of making it to the Royal alive. The captain knew, too, how futile the battle was, yet Dăveed had come to respect the aging man. He would try to survive, if only to honor Raynward. "I will get through, Captain."

It didn't seem Raynward heard, but Dăveed knew the man was already counting everything on him. As quick as a cat, Dăveed was making his way to the outer edge of the fighting, his two tiger claws hacking furiously to clear a path. The wave of fighters seemed to open miraculously, enough so to let him through. Without a second thought or backward glance, Dăveed took the opportunity to sprint toward the tarol trees.

* * *

Mater Teera surveyed the fight from her spot near the council-house doors. She smirked as more of the Renegade army fell, ignoring the count of her own fighters—more of hers were Royal guards than Honored assassins anyway. She was none too pleased to see a lone fighter making his way swiftly from the field, however. "A runner." She hissed. In truth, it may be good for Qusairo to learn of his force's demise, but Teera was angry that her men could be so negligent as to let some filth go. "After him!" She brazened out to her nearby Honored associates. "I want that man dead."

Tath Enor and Xemin Cour'noum, two of Terra's best fighters, leapt to the task. Their Honored One only watched them long enough to see them leave the fray.

Satisfied, Teera averted her sharp eyes to the task at hand. Just like Captain Sieck, this Raynward would not live many more minutes. Master Teera sneered at the thought, for it had been she that had taken care of the other man. She had seen the fear on the captain's face. Emperor Manscor would be pleased to hear about both men's cowardness.

A victory crow sounded out calling Teera from her reverie. Her forces had ended the fight quickly. None were left alive but one—all the rest [the bodies] were butchered messes. As promised, her minions had left the captain alive, though doing so had cost some their lives. Jeering, Teera strode arrogantly through her forces to the bloodied Captain Raynward. The old man lifted his peppered brown-and-grey head defiantly as the emperor's most cherished stepped near. "Your men made such nice training partners, captain." Teera gloated as she met the man's gaze. The other blinked, a show of his pain he tried to keep hidden from her. Master Teera enjoyed even that small torture. "Captain Sieck's men were just as easy to kill." A gleeful, mocking laugh escaped her lips. "You should have witnessed the man's face as I slowly tore him apart." She leaned down to whisper the last part in Raynward's ear. "His screams were so sorrowful, I could have cried, except…" And she straightened back up, "He is not the type of man I like… though, I did make sure not to maim that lovely face of his." All of the emperor's force broke out laughing as if the words were a great joke.

Captain Raynward's face paled in disgust, erasing the final colorings of rage he had saved.

Teera snickered at the ashen-looking man, knowing she was taking away what resolve he had left. *Royals, so pitiful. They break so easily when barraged by foul words. Assassins, at least, can hold until the real beating begin.* "Shall I kill you like I did your friend, Renegade? Or would you like a different sentence?" The captain gulped back a retort, knowing the assassin-woman was trying to bait him. He knew his fate was sealed. Now his only thoughts were on the young assassin he had sent to warn Qusairo.

"No preference?" Teera asked mockingly. "Well then, since you are not into playing with me, I will have to make do with my own amusements." Just as she had expected, the man's face turned white but he uttered no words. *He really is boring me.* The emperor's favorite knelt down to the other's eye level and reached out for his hand. The Renegade man's eyes widened in fear and he paused his breath. *Yes, you should be scared of me.* "You know, I should be companionate for your circumstances and let you go crying back to your pathetic leader but," her touch turned menacing as she twisted Raynward's thumb until it snapped sickeningly. The man could not hold the scream as the pain overwhelmed his senses. "I really am not that lenient." She proceeded to snap his long fingers like sticks. The man's screams heightened as his misery continued. Satisfied with her work on the Renegades' left hand, Teera turned to the other hand, yet untouched, and continued her torture. Once done, she placed her bloodied hands on either side of Raynward's face, holding his bobbing head still. "Enjoying yourself? I thought so. Being a traitor to our emperor grants you all kinds of pleasures, you know." A laugh, better heard from a large cat, tore for her throat as she released the Renegade captain and stood up. "Davin!"

Teera's dark-haired assistant pushed through the emperor's soldiers to his master's side. "Yes, Honored-One?" He replied softly.

"My scepter, if you would."

The man lifted the assassin's heavy sydro-smelted steel and sapphire weapon with care. His sharp, chiseled features remained neutral, though behind his blue eyes, the young assassin-man knew the pain that awaited the Renegade soldier.

Teera did not seem to notice the sympathy her assistant felt, for she took the scepter quickly and turned back to her task. "Once we are done with you, filth, I am heading to the main square where I will kill your precious leader. The Renegades will fail to regain Obseen today, and you won't be there to witness it!" With a mighty backswing, Teera clouted Raynward across the face, the sharpened sapphires biting long wounds across the aging face. Without pause, Teera Sabina swung the other way, hitting her captive hard enough to send him sprawling. She continued her assault with one steady stroke after another until Captain Raynward was a bloody heap on the council-house's flagstones. With a final, downward, thrust, the Honored-One landed the finishing blow to the back of the man's head. "Davin." Teera called gain as she turned away from her work.

"Take this "thing" to the Renegade camp and give them this message: after today they will receive the same fate."

Chapter Twenty-Four

S.D 4013:

"I was the last to enter the caves that horrible day at Barashi. I alone witnessed the bloody, yet valiant deaths of our great leaders. Even when the pain was evident on their faces, the Coursay'soras continued to fight—fight for all of us they wished to go on with life. Their bravery is what keeps me going when all seems lost. It was their last gift—no their second-to-last-gift—to me. And, I keep it forever as a reminder of the life we are fighting for: one without a dictator. Their other gift is found in their children. If bravery is hereditary, then our leaders have endowed it in their two children—the girl especially. What this means for the future of the Las'wa clan and Obseen I do not know, but the Coursay'soras paved the path that I now follow.

"May theirs be the right one." –Tyracor

The forest was the best refuge the young man could ever have had against his two pursuers. It was the place he knew well, for his father had forced him to train within the tarol trees until he knew their pathways and secrets by heart. Perhaps, it had been only the master's drive to teach such, but the son had a feeling it had been his father's foresight that really had decided the fact. After all, Dăveed Quinn had never seen his father make a choice without a good reason—and today was a very good reason.

The Baras had chosen an old, weather-gouged trunk to hide in—after he had realized he was being pursued. The old tree concealed him well from the sharp eyes of Master Teera's Honoreds and, along with the rustling of the tarol grove's leaves, had proven to be a safe haven. No matter, Dăveed knew he could not stay invisible forever. Royal Qusairo needed his message too badly and Master Teera's cronies were good trackers; they would catch his trail soon if he stayed too long.

A branch snapped nearby causing Dăveed to turn toward the sound. It was too amateur, that sound, and Quinn felt himself caught in the trap. He had waited too long. Warily, he shifted his tiger claws to a defensive position and paused. The forest's gentle melody floated along, unhindered by the gruesome bloodbaths that rained throughout its massive interior. But, there was a chordance out of rhythm…

Instinctively, he blocked the cast kusarigama before it struck a fatal blow to his head. [Kusarigama is a Japanese weapon; sickle with long chain and ball at end of chain] He twisted away as the iron ball bounced off his weapons and rolled away from his hiding place. The kusarigama's round end fell again close to his head, splintering a dead tree trunk. Dăveed jumped aside and blocked the next swing of the ball—only to see it covered the attack of the second assassin's saif. [Saif is an Arab sword with hook at end] The sydro-smelted steel tiger claws captured the sword in its hook, giving Dăveed time to see his attackers.

Tath Enor's intense blue eyes burned though the entangled blades. One, partially hidden under the lone silver lock of hair, seemed to be impenetrable; the other was held wide in shock under the bangs of the man's chestnut hair. "It's Dăveed Quinn!"

"Aye." Xemin Cour'noum's baritone voice replied. Dăveed spied the willowy youth standing on a strong tarol branch beyond Tath's left shoulder. The man, like his partner, wore a deep crimson and black tunic that contrasted starkly with his white hair. Xemin held his kusarigama's ball-and-chain in his left hand while his right lazily swung its sickle end. "Aye, it's Quinn. Ready to play in the real leagues, Center boy?"

Dăveed eyed one man then the other. He knew both well enough; they had been a part of his class at the training center, however, they had left the Center months ago to join Teera's Honoreds. They were no longer bound to the codes and honors of the Center and Teera certainly didn't care that they have any. Their only mission would be his death. "Indeed, Xemin, I will do what I must to get my message through—and that means that I go through you!" He broke the hold his tiger claws had of Tath's saif and used the other to thrust at the man's abdomen. The Honored leapt away to give Xemin, his backup, room to cast his scythe at Dăveed's head.

Dăveed ducked to avoid the thrown weapon and spun to knock it away on its return course. Perturbed his partner's feint didn't word, Xemin jumped down from his perch and launched himself at the Baras. Through intricate counter swings of his ball, the willowy Honored forced Quinn into retreat—toward waiting Tath. His quick sneer alerted Dăveed to the plan just as he reached within striking distance of the sword; he rolled to the right just as Xemin released his kusarigama's ball-end. The weapon whistled past Dăveed's right shoulder and sent Tath diving away.

"For partners, you two really like hitting each other." Dăveed commented as he faced an angry Xemin and flustered Tath. He rose his tiger claws in preparation for the assault he was sure his words would insight.

"Yeah, what would you know of it, Quinn?" Xemin replied in response to the criticism. "Your father pampered you with easy sessions of one-on-one."

"Against the whole class you mean." Dăveed corrected and broke the distance between them. Xemin thrust out with his scythe as Dăveed cut at his thigh, then arm, and neck. The kusarigama wrapped around one claw, the chain becoming stuck in its grooves, and Dăveed pulled taunt against the other man's grip, making that end of the weapon useless—unless Xemin had the sense to pull him off balance. Forcefully, Dăveed drove his tiger claw into the trunk of a close by tree. The blades stuck firmly, leaving Xemin handicapped and barely able to fight Quinn as he attacked.

As Dăveed neared, his left hand wandered to his belt, where a dagger his father had given him was hidden. The Baras curled his fingers around the weapon's cool handle and unsheathed it with slight reluctance. Even as he dodged Xemin's kusarigama's ball-end, Dăveed was remembering his father's words about the hand blade he was about to use, "Dăveed, my son, I am giving you this dagger for times when nothing else can help, but, I warn you, this is not a weapon to be used lightly..." Dăveed realized he had never tested the dagger before and wondered what was so different about it that it caused his father to bid him to be cautious. *Guess I get to find out.*

Xemin noted his opponent's lapse of attention and readied himself for a direct hit at Dăveed's head. With a final swing, he released the kusarigama's ball-and-chain and waited for his enemy to fall dead at his feet. Honored One would be proud. The other man rose his left hand in an instinctive display of protection; the ball whizzed right by...and kept flying off into the dense underbrush of Taysor's tarol grove.

Dăveed, in a slight squat, and shocked Xemin across from him stared at Quinn's raised hand and the dagger it held.

Suddenly, the son understood what Mater Quinn had warned him about: the dagger—not even made of metal but an organic substance—could slice through steel like it was a piece of mipa fruit! He could only imagine what it would do to a person.

Xemin Cour'noum seemed to have similar thoughts, for he shook his head in fear and backed away from the Baras clansman. He hid, dishonorably, behind Tath Enor, who had kept himself out of the way, and said cowardly, "He's yours now, partner. I will be right behind you."

Tath held firm against his partner's shove. He, too, knew the significance of the dagger's actions, but was not prepared to cower in front of an enemy—especially when Dăveed was someone he knew. It would be just plain dishonorable. "It seems we have a dilemma, Dăveed Quinn."

"Yes." Dăveed answered just as calmly. "Unfortunately, you and your fine friend are still in my way."

"Yes, it would seem." Tath glared at his white-haired partner as he scuttled around a safe distance from both fighters. Xemin shrugged hopelessly but showed he had armed himself— with Tath's spare kissaki. [Short sword] "And, what should we do about that, hm?" The question was intended to say: what would two enemies decide to do when faced with such a decision?

"There are options." The reply came simply. That raised an eyebrow. "But, there is one I would prefer over the others."

Tath Enor, against Xemin's objections, cocked his head inquiringly. "I will listen, prompt me."

And, so, Dăveed Quinn began on his proposition that he hoped would keep the capitol from being bathed in more blood than had already adorned its obsidian surfaces.

"Does it burn?" Manscor inquired vilely as he approached Zanishiria. The young assassin sat, clutching her dripping thigh tightly, her weapons forgotten by her side. She did not answer. The emperor walked only close enough to be out of her striking distance and stopped, bringing his laz-ax blades together so that they crackled threateningly. "My, my. For a moment, you had all the vehemence of a se$f$(a), the next you are lying here helpless—all from your pride-begotten weaponship! Is this all they taught you in your stank, snake-ridden underground? The Lakeans have fallen far if they send a fighter such as you, and as young too. You are not worth my time."

Zanishiria stilled, not even allowing her sharp tongue to defend her clan. She could see the emperor had wanted the other reaction and was pleased she had not courted it; however, it did prompt the man to step closer. Too close for her comfort. But, Zanishiria's training would not let her die so easily. It, and instinct, screamed at her to live. Live! Without a real thought to what she did, Zanishiria reached above her head, her hands coming to rest on the cool, wooden body of a mid-ranged weapon. She pulled it off the wall the instant her fingers found the handle and thrust the weighted end at the approaching emperor.

Manscor barely had time to register the halbert thrust at him. He felt it bite into his side, tearing his flesh, among other things, as he scrambled away from the weapon. Surprise and shock kept the pain at bay until he was a safe distance away from the Las'wa girl. Then, he crumbled to his knees on the floor to inspect his side. He knew immediately that at least his liver if not also the right kidney had been grazed in the thrust. *Stop the bleeding!* He thought and was on his feet running to his emergency cabinet inlaid in the wall by the fighting room's entrance. The mica shots in there would save him by stopping the bleeding and speed healing time.

Zanishiria paid little heed to the emperor. She was too shocked at her actions. How had she known that the halbert was above her? She knew she had located all of the objects in the room when she had first entered but that had been hours ago. "If I had been wrong…I would be dead right now." The pained hiss from Emperor Manscor brought Zanishiria out of her state. The only fact she needed to know that moment was that she had remembered and was still alive. She would like to stay that way! Reaching down quickly she retrieved her preshair knives and spun toward the emperor—her thigh forgotten.

By the door, the ruler was sticking himself with a mica shot, feeling the instant relief it brought. Internally, Manscor could feel his blood clotting by his organs and let go a sigh of relief—if he didn't get hit near his liver again, he should survive the injury. Suddenly the ruler's warning system went off in his head and he turned to see the assassin-girl striding toward him. He barely dodged the swing at his neck and picked up a weapon before he was engaged again.

Zanishiria pushed him back twenty feet, using furious movements to keep him hustling backwards. Just as the emperor was beginning to recover his senses, he brought a laz-ax to block a downward thrust only to have his opponent changed her weapon's angle and sliced cleanly through the axe's metal handle. She dispatched the partner weapon just as effectively and had the Royal scrambling away in well-founded fear.

Zanishiria tore after him, merciless in her attacks, as Manscor scurried across the altered floor, collecting a weapon to defend himself. The emperor kept running until he could find his chance to collect himself. He could see in the Las'wa's grey eyes that she was more than determined to kill the man in front of her—she was not fighting for anyone but herself by that point—and that was deadlier than a young woman with a mission of revenge.

Manscor had seen the look before in one other: Air'is Soreneay. Their faces were suddenly very strikingly the same.

The emperor finally realized he could not run anymore. The strain on his body more than his pursuer's and it was costing him precious minutes he needed to finish the fight and find emergency medicines to heal himself. Taking a strong hand on his picked-up hand blades, he turned around.

A short distance away, Zanishiria stopped her pursuit and rose her weapons defensively. "Done running, man killer?" Her voice was riddled with an icy hardness.

The ruler responded by lunging at his adversary, slashing to the right, left, diagonally, and across with his blades. His foe blocked each deftly and rolled under the last thrust to nick the emperor's chest with her right knife. She forfeited a deeper cut to continue her motion into a crouch, where she bit deeply with her other knife into the man's inner calf muscle. An agile summersault rolled her away from range. She came to her feet. The two engaged again in a clash of scales and steel. Blades fully occupied, Zanishiria opted for a kick at her opponent's groin then thrust her left knife at the man's shoulder as Manscor instinctively curled against her foot's impact. Angered and pained, Manscor back-handed her as Zanishiria's thrust touched its target—only the energy of his retaliation kept his shoulder from a worse wound.

Zanishiria was knocked off balance. She quickly recovered but felt one of the emperor's blades catch her on the ribs, the lazer of the blades going through her snake-skin but being more an annoyance than hindrance to her next attacks. The Las'wa forced the ruler back many paces, keeping him ever dancing as she took out her pain on her people's oppressor.

No longer were her physical wounds on her mind. And, even though her thigh and ribs were still bleeding, her movements did not faltered. Everything within Zanishiria was crying out to put an end to all the hell she had been through to get to this point, this day against Manscor: the loss of her parents then her brother, friends long-left, her seivier away from her for a year, her clan having denied her name to protect themselves, and the stupid war that had given her all of the other losses in the first place.

Now, Zanishiria's struggle would end one way or another.

* * *

She's a wraith, Tarin thought, finding no other word to describe his friend before him. The Neitiege had known Zanishiria for almost a year-and-a-half but never once had she looks so deadly like she did at that moment. The Lakean's face had lost its youthfulness, looking now twenty-some-years-old. She radiated a power so intense, her whole being seemed involved in the fight. The way Zanishiria handled her weapons, precise and biting, made it seem as if she was in a duel against a lethal creature not the emperor.

"Has she been hiding so much of herself from me?" Tarin whispered, afraid to know the answer. He knew no one at the Center taught students to fight so vivaciously and even masters outside of the Center did not strive for such deadly accuracy. "Oh, shēēv ["shit"], we have all been so blind! Zanishiria has always been a killer, a true assassin in all that that word entails… Her age kept everyone from seeing it—even me. She really is agent of the Renegade Army or—no—she is the Lakean Resistance's last endowment. Had there ever been a Zanishiria Novastone, the girl I called friend?" Doubt began to swirl about Tarin's heart. "Master Teera….maybe you were right to not trust her. I know not this young woman before me!" Unheeded by Tarin, tears fell down his skin, caused by the thoughts that plagued his mind. More than the Emperor's reign could be lost that day.

Chapter Twenty-Five

Tarin Saerric is one of the most honorable assassins I know. Though still young, he is so exacting in his ethics and integrity...When he came to me after the war's end, he had so much confusion over the fight with Manscor and Zanishiria—and confusion easily leads to hate. Never had I imagined that the youth would be subjugated to watching the deciding battle, nor that he would have such a mental "breakdown" after seeing it. Oh, if I had somehow had the foresight to keep such innocence preserved, how I would have done better for the young Neitiege man! Instead, I sent him to the wolves—so to speak—by giving him ideas of grandeur about his "friend" who was supposed to be the savior of the Renegade army. How I regret now my decision to put such trust into the boy; foolish of me, to think that friendship alone would stave the evils of war.

--Master Quinn

"The Royal guards have been pushed back into the city!" A Renegade assassin yelled out to the Royal. The man had pushed his way back through the ranks of Obsarians to reach their leader's ear. Shy'ree C'vanil nodded to the fighter and sent him away with orders to keep pushing toward Taysor Palace, at the center of the city. The man left enthusiastically, glad that such progress had been made. Shy'ree, however, looked apprehensive. "Leader, this strike has been too easy. I feel we are going at this too recklessly."

Qusairo nodded, having similar thoughts. "I should have kept that youth, Page Torez, by my side." But, no, he had sent all the young men to the eastern flank where they could protect his son amongst the strongest section of his army.

"He said, "like at Barashi'."" Shy'ree reminded him. "Barashi was fought within the city. Our trap lies there."

The two stood rooted in place, studying the obsidian buildings that lined the street. Qusairo frowned grimly as he remembered the layout of the city. Taysor's streets funneled into a main square right in front of the southern and eastern wings of

the Palace. The square stretched around the emperor's Royal
building at the north and west, too, but it was the area the Royal
guards were being pushed back into that worried the Royal. "The
emperor will get to see us massacred from his suit as his men
take us in the square."

"Leader, we must pull back our people."

"They would know we expect something if we do. I
cannot split my forces either because his would surround us in
groups then." Royal Qusairo paced restlessly as he thought
through his plans. "What I need is Captain Raynward and
Captain Sieck's forces! Major Calamas and Aslén have already
reached their advance from the west and east. Have the runners
said anything?"

"All but their two, sir." Shy'ree averted her eyes on
some thought. "Van Kennet and Dăveed Quinn. Both should be
making their way back here." The woman refused to tell her
leader her worries on their absence. "Leader, I have a
suggestion."

Qusairo paused his pacing. "Yes, Shy'ree, what is it?"

"Let my clansmen search the city. We will hunt out
those traps for you."

"I—." Qusairo was at a loss of words. "It is a good offer
but I would not feel right sending your people in alone. You
have already sacrificed so much and lost so much."

"And it is still our choice to go, Royal Qusairo."
Shy'ree's tone was full of conviction. "This is how we serve. Let
us."

The Las'wa waited, poised, as her leader continued his
pacing in silence. The army was already advancing into the
second block of buildings but at least the leaders were advancing
slowly. They had been warned to have some caution; though
Shy'ree feared it would not be enough. Finally, Royal Qusairo
turned to her. "Your people have the choice. In the name of your
revered leaders, Ze'is and Mei'cor, I allow any Lakeans that
wish to go in, shall. However, I would like most to stay with the
force."

The raven-haired woman suppressed a relieved smile.
"Thank you, sir. This is a good course of action." She turned
away before the Renegade leader could change his mind and
called out is Lakean, "Las'wa, Qusairo rey'moré sei van'àl.
Shairhom sho. Leimor corray shay'nor Qusairo. Slai traisa!"
["Qusairo orders a scouting party. Thirteen go ahead. The rest stay to protect

Qusairo. Find the trap!"] Immediately, thirteen assassins broke away from the army and lined up in front of Shy'ree. Others—all with dark hair, light skin, and darker eyes ranging in shades of brown to greys—came to surround Royal Qusairo. The leader had not realized so many Lakeans had joined his army until they were before him.

Shy'ree C'vanil eyed the thirteen volunteers, her silvery eyes flashing as she noted which ones had come forward. She paused in front of a tall, clean-shaven man. "Say'orin Ts'nor, "Orin", a cousin of one of the Las'wa seimreal, I ask you to lead five others to the palace square. See if you can find another force hiding there." The man rose a fist to his heart and bowed his head before leaving with a selected group of assassin clansmen. Shy'ree turned away to the remaining volunteers. Most were of the regular val'eya class but were still good fighters; however, it was the young runner, hidden at the end of the line, that caught her attention. "Tai'eya!" She called out and nodded approval at the young man's quick response. Shy'ree studied him as he came to stand before her. "You are Cour'eysan Evalaus, student of Tas'na Seivier." Coryu nodded confirmation. "I reassign you from your runner's post. Take these others around our eastern flank and search for Captain Raynward and Captain Sieck's forces. Report anything peculiar." Coryu bowed his head sharply and signed his group to leave. The five Las'wa sprinted away to their mission, Coryu in the lead. "We will find what trap the "man killer" has laid, Royal Qusairo." Shy'ree announce to her leader. "Just buy us some time."

"I can do that." Qusairo replied. *It's the least I can do to repay their help.* The Royal yelled out a command that was passed throughout his army. He prayed it was enough.

The five lancer-class starships reflected Sarius's light, blinding the eyes of the pilots when they dared to check their companion's positions. It lasted for half an hour—the time it took for the Royal starships to be stealthily piloted out of Nyhore, over Xsenume, and out into space. The great sun was setting at the capitol, Taysor, and the eight masters had taken advantage of its departing glare, though it hurt their eyes to do so.

Now in space, the glare of Sarius and its two reflecting suns dissipated leaving the asters in the cold dark. Without the painful distraction, the beauty of outer space was allowed to take hold of its visitors' attention. The planet below looked to be shades of browns, purples, greens, and blacks. Beyond, however, the Abyss Solar System sparkled in its own radiance.

"I haven't been up here in over fifty years." Hareoska whispered, his awe carrying through the comms from the fourth ship. "It looks so familiar, so unchanged, like a long-lost friend."

"You always were the sentimental one." Roko teased form the cockpit of ship two.

Corsetti, sitting beside him, reprimanded him with a look and a slight grin. "No worse than you were the first time we flew, Roko."

"At my age," Hareoska replied to them both, "You learn to be very sentimental."

"Oh, I can't wait."

Sunashi's laugh broke over the comm at Roko's sarcasm. "When he gets your age, Master Hareoska, he will be a cranky old wizard! The trainees will have a hay-day with him."

"Stars know you certainly were." Dorsetti muttered at his apprentice's words. He chuckled at a former memory and slapped Sunashi on the back with his good hand. He was relieved that his apprentice had picked up the knack for flying when he was young; Dorsetti's arm was beginning to throb from overuse. The master commed over to ship one, piloted by Quinn and Alrik. "So, what's the plan when we reach the space station?"

Master Quinn relinquished the controls to Alrik Kagar as he focused his attention on the task at hand. "That would be a nice thing to know… I haven't been to High Port for over five years, and I don't think any of you have either?" Even Alrik shook his head, no. "Therefore," Quinn continued, "I can't say what the Royals have done to it. We will need to find guard uniforms in these ships to slip past security. Other than that, we will have to wait for Yoshida to hack through more codes." Quinn glanced over to the fifth ship, which the "Code Master" had commandeered.

"No problem." Yoshida replied to the unspoken request. His jade eyes flashed in pleasure. "I am having the most fun tackling the Royal's codes. They are a challenge but not like anything Khan Torez put me against. It probably will only take five more minutes to get us high-clearance passes to the space station."

Putting the five starships on autopilot, the assassins scrounged the holds for uniforms. By the time the small warships reached High Port's boundary sensors, all eight men had transformed themselves into "proper" Royal guards. Acting obediently, Master Quinn slowed his posse to a drifting speed and waited for the space station's controller to call.

"Reverent, we have been waiting for you." A warm, youthful face appeared over the five ship's comms.

Master Quinn responded in kind. "We too, controller. The situation on the planet had gotten quite heated. I am glad to be out of there."

The controller laughed, having not noticed the slightly haggard, and completely unsoldierly-like appearances of the starship crew. "We can certainly accommodate you with some quiet, sir. After His Excellency deals with those rogues we will be called to Rhône. [Capitol of Planet X] I hear whatever warship the emperor has planned is almost complete. You might even get to see it."

A warship? Master Quinn smiled cheerfully at the controller, but inside he was frowning. From the information Yoshida had stumbled across, the emperor could have built a whole Royal battalion—not one ship. It must be enormous! "I would be delighted to see the craft, but right now a nice cup of coffee will do. Which bay would you like my men and I in, control?"

"Sending that now." The man replied and transmitted some coordinates. "See you down here in a few minutes, Reverent. General Kett would like to brief you and the crew in the lounge. It will be down the hall, second door on your left."

"Thank you, control. Out." Master Quinn cut off contact to the space station and continued his instructions to his comrades. "He was a confident lad! Seems this will be easier than we thought. Yoshida, wait for us to take the lounge then hack into a computer. See if you can lock their systems. We will meet you in the control room."

"Right." Yoshida answered, business-like.

Unable to contain himself, Sunashi fingered his kastane sword and grinned, "This will be fun." Indeed, it was; the bay the masters were assigned was empty of personnel. The Legion men smiled mischievously at each other and headed out the bay's door. High Port was as good as theirs.

Chapter Twenty-Six

S.D. 4013:

I felt so horrible, awful, torn into pieces—no words can really describe what it was I felt—to leave my seimorar [leaders], my closest friends, behind. Now, looking at the Coursay'soras' daughter, I feel even worse. The council wants revenge for their leaders; they have even enlisted Art'or Coursay'sora in a special preshan unit. The boy will be taught to kill the man responsible for his father's death. And his sister, this girl, not quite four-years-old has been forgotten in these chaotic times. There is only one thing I know to give her, and that is the knowledge to keep herself alive. Yet, I am anything but Ze'is's daughter's savior. What I know, the training I put her through, could perhaps kill her in the end. What kind of gift is that? Ze'is would be furious with me for putting Zanishiria through it. Creeshts-áet! It's the only way I know, though. The seimreal won't let a preshair whip master raise a child unless I am training her. But I do not trust Zanishiria to anyone else…

Ze'is Seimore, I am so sorry!

--Tyracor

"Hold the line!" Aslén Doz shouted over the din of battle. The Royal commander's eastern flank was holding but, after fighting for a week and—currently—three hours straight that day, he could see his line straining. Luckily, the Trayshan assassins had posted themselves amongst his men. The tough, mountain people were fresh and able to take up twice the slack of the others.

The Royal guard had been tightly concentrated on this block of the city, which had kept Alsén's forces more than busy. The Royal had wondered about the strong defense but had been too preoccupied to ponder his situation; he had left that to Berzén Tyre who apparently was well-coached in army tactics. So far, the Trayshan leader's strategies had proved effective against the emperor's pawns. But, Royal Aslén wondered how long even that could last.

In a sudden, unexpected wave, the Royal guards retreated from their hard-won position. The scarlet-clad soldiers disappeared down the block, heading for the main square. The Renegade army, having learned caution form their commander, held back, waiting for Aslén and Tyre to direct them.

The two Trayshan leaders hurried to Royal Alsén's side. The Berris looked fiery but wary, her warrior leader's temperament calling for caution. "This relief bodes ill for us; I feel the Royal guards are trying to bait us."

Aslén nodded agreement and faced the emptied street. He felt the questions in his fighters' eyes and knew his next decision must be reached soon. "Page Torez!" He called out. The Xsorian youth moved away from his band. The other young men, including Alsén's nephew, came closer—but not close enough to intrude. "Page, can you link with the Tá sharay?"

"Yes, Royal." Page answered though he looked slightly unconfident, a rare expression on his face. *I haven't tried form this distance yet but I will try.*

"I will help." Lap shared with his brother and stepped close enough to provide his support. *"They need not know."*

Page nodded to his brother's words. "What do you wish me to say to my father?"

"Ask him if the Royal guard has pulled back on his front." Tyre instructed.

Page bobbed his white-haired head and closed his eyes to concentrate. He reached his mind out in the general direction of Khan Torez and called out, *"Father! I need to speak to you."* A strong answer came back but Page was unable to grasp it with his power. Lap, who was better gifted with distance telepathy, caught his brother's hand and helped his mind stop floundering so much. The instant touch linked father and sons quickly. With the three-way mind bridge, the elder sibling's words came through clearly to the Tá sharay.

"Page, what is it for you to call me during battle?" Khan sent a feeling of fondness with his words so his son would not think him angry.

"I apologize for the intrusion. Royal Qusairo and the Berris and Berzén wish to know if the Royal guards have pulled back on the other two fronts." He pictured the guards retreat in his mind's eye.

"They have here, yes. Major Calamas is nervous about the situation." Page sent back that Aslén felt the same way. *"Let*

me see if Royal Qusairo is ready to confront the trap you have told us is set for us. I will reach for his thoughts..." The Tá sharay broke off his link, leaving Page floating in a mist-like silence. Behind him, Page could faintly hear Lap relating what had just occurred between the two Torezes. With Lap controlling the mind-focus, Page could not hear the others' responses but could tell by his link with his brother that they were anxious to have heard Khan's response. Page wanted to say something out loud to help calm those around them, but his father linked back with him, casting Page's mind back into the distance. *"Royal Qusairo's thoughts show the Royal guards have all pulled back to the main square. The square..."* The Tá sharay's voice melted off as he turned his senses to another thought. Page groped after his father's familiar mind-imprint. Finally, the Xsorian leader seemed to notice his son's insistent call and reopened the link. *"Sorry, Page. I just got lost on a thought. Tell Royal Aslén and Trayshans that I fear the trap is upon us. This situation is following all the precursors to the Barashi incident. They will lure us to the square, surround us, and pick us off in small groups. Be careful, sai'aun!"* [A Xsorian endearment meaning: "one close to my heart"] And, just like that, Khan Torez pushed his son's mind-link away.

Page came back to himself already spurting out what his father had told him. He was unaware of what he said but could see his words seemed to make an impact on the three leaders standing before him. By the time he finished imparting the Tá sharay's words, Page was fully back to himself. "And so it would seem Royal Qusairo will advance his forces to the Palace but with great caution. Some Las'wa have been sent forth to find traps laid before them." Lap eyed Page curiously, for he knew their father had not said all that, but Page had felt his words were correct. His intuition had grasped that last remark as he had faded away from his father's mind-touch.

"So, Qusairo believes we should not show any signs that we are ono their plans. He hinted as much to me earlier." Royal Aslén spoke his thoughts out loud. "I think we should be just as cautious if we proceed forward...or we can hold back here and move in if the main army is surrounded."

"I suggest a different tactic, Royal Aslén, Berris, Berzén." The group turned to find five Lakeans running up to them. The leader came up to bow to the three leaders. Aslén remembered the youth as Coryu the runner he had met the day before. "We have just come from the council house where the two captains were supposed to meet up." Aslén nodded to show he knew to what Coryu referred to but he could not help frowning at the words. Had something happened? The Las'wa's next words confirmed his feeling. "Captain Raynward's men have been butchered. I found the Honored One's flag at the site. Teera Sabina's forces have been taking us down one by one. Your force is her closest target. We," Coryu paused to indicate all of the Lakeans, "Believe she is planning to attack your right-rear flank."

"Captain Raynward and Sieck's forces have all been killed?!" Royal Aslén was stunned. Almost half of the Renegades' forces had been with the two commanders. "This is ill for us indeed. The guards now out-weigh us three-to-one!" All around the Renegade fighters dropped their heads in mourning and despair. Many voiced their fears of being unable to win with the sudden losses. More than one assassin was cussing at the horrible news. The three leaders looked grave. They motioned to Coryu and his Las'wa to join them in a mini conference as the rest of the army shifted about in consternation.

As the leaders deferred, Prince Anmero observed the people around him, feeling their sudden hopelessness that had come over them at the recent news. Only the Trayshans and Las'wa seemed to project any sense of retaliation. "Can you all really think this war is done just because of this loss?" Anmero heard himself question out loud before he could sensor his thought. Those assassins and Royals closest to him rose their heads in shock at his words. His companions turned their eyes on him to warn him to keep quiet but he could not help himself. The reaction the fighters had given made him bolder to speak out again. "You have all fought for, what, eleven years now?" K'sho nodded at the question. "There have been many setbacks and many losses in this war—yet this is the end or so you have all told me. We need to fight until is truly is the end. It is so close! Surely, this army can hold out for that."

"What the hell would you know about how to fight this war?" Someone yelled at him angered by the prince's words.

"I don't." Anmero answered truthfully. "You are right on that. How could I know what it is like to fight against this tyrant and his armies? I have long been gone from this world into a hiding of my father's choosing. But, I do know what it is like to live in fear and to suffer alone and struggle to hold onto hope." Anmero met K'sho and Seircor's gazes, finding himself filling with conviction. He could see his two new friends were listening to his words with rapt interest—indeed, even the leaders had pulled out of their huddle to hear him. His uncle's eyes were especially keen on him. Emboldened, Anmero stepped up beside his uncle so all the soldiers could hear and see him. Even if it was with anger or resentment, Anmero thought the emotions were better than feelings of despair. "Not even this morning, I heard all of your convictions, your dreams, of a world above the hold of an emperor. Would you throw all this aside because the losses are becoming so great? I know of those of you who won't ever give in. Despite odds being against you, I know that you people of Obseen are stronger than that! As long as there are those of you who will still fight there is always the chance that this time, this day, will lead you to your victory. The Royals' War is not about me, in fact it may not even be about you [this army]. It is about what this world can be, what it should be! Is that not enough reason to finish this battle?" His deep, piercing green eyes met his uncle's.

Aslén could not help smiling. His nephew was born to lead. Fondly, he set his hand on Anmero's shoulder, taking up the stand the young man had set. "Yes, Anmero is right. He may not know how we have felt these past years, but we do. The enemy has ever fought dishonorably but I say damn them for it! I will not let them continue to rule Obseen this way. So, if Teera Sabina wishes to fight us then I say let's take her head-on! Who wants to do the same?" An angry shout grew to include the whole army. Everyone was more than fired up to take on the infamous Honored One of the Emperor's. Following the lead and instruction of the five Las'wa, they all began to stream into the northeastward streets. Aslén gave his nephew's shoulder a squeeze and followed his army forward.

Hanging back, Anmero rejoined his small group. To his surprise, it was the aloof and dangerous-looking Shane Sinhail that greeted him first. "You know, you are not at all what I expected, Royal. To have bolstered up this army so quickly…commendable. I will be honored to fight by your side today."

Anmero bowed, knowing full well the honor he had been bestowed. "I thank you, Sinhail, but the honor is all mine." Shane flashed Anmero a small smile and strode ahead to speak with his parents.

K'sho Rease filled the Trayshan's vacancy. "That was wise of you." He bobbed his head Shane's direction. "Making allies with the Trayshans will be fortuitous for your future here. You will go far if you continue to make such connections."

"As if I was trying." Anmero joked. K'sho chuckled. However, Anmero took the Sinya assassin's words to heart. He was going to live here as long as he was able. Making some new friends and allies now would only help his future prospects—not that he had thought to influence them any.

"Anmero," K'sho brought him out of his ponderings. Anmero raised his eyebrows in an unvoiced "yes?'. "Thanks for helping to bolster the army's resolve. We all needed that."

Blood clung in dried streaks down their bodies, a testament to the deadliness of their duel. The metallic taste and smell of the vital liquid had not been able to clear from the room and was mixed with the smell of sweat and the taste of tenacity coming from both fighters. The hour was getting late. The light of the full moons shining through the large windows showing the time that had passed. The moons lite up the desperate scene, lighting the emperor's grimacing features and making Zanishiria's pale, bloodied skin look nearly apparition-like. The comparison between the two assassins was a creepy foreboding to one of the fighter's doom.

"Your body is failing you." Zanishiria stated emotionlessly. She panted slightly; her hair, wet with her sweat, sticking to her face and neck. Most of the blood on her torn Las'wa clothing was not her own, with exception of the crusty lines on her left thigh and right forearm—her only serious injuries.

Manscor looked far worse. His left side injury was still trickling in spurts, draining him of his life's blood. Neither the ruler nor Zanishiria seemed to notice their pain much but it was clear that fighting for nearly four hours was wasting what life forces they had left. Manscor's ignorance of his pain and his plight had him snapping back a reply to Zanishiria's half-hearted goading. "Like you give a shit over Your Emperor's body."

Zanishiria's face was blank. "I care not except to know I am in better shape than you." Her words were hollow of any victory. She suspected—now that she had crossed weapons with the ruler—that Emperor Manscor had not been in a serious battle since he had taken on her parents all those years ago. His arrogance and pride had kept him from staying in the kind of shape and skill he needed to beat her. If she played her tactics right—and could keep herself from giving away any killing shots—she felt bones-deep that she had the duel. "I especially care not for the man calling himself "emperor". You are master of fewer than you think, man killer." Zanishiria flickered her preshair knives clean and sheathed them casually—almost to the point of being mocking. "If a girl of fourteen can mark the emperor this much with less damage to herself than it makes one wonder how you expect to stay Emperor over the Assassins' Guild. You are weaker than me."

Manscor opened his mouth ready to match the Lakean's audacity with his own, but he closed it knowing it was foolish to contest; after all, he was the one standing there in the moonlight of the two moons, Saula and Nianne, bleeding to death. To act unwisely in front of the two youths would be more than demoralizing—it could spell the end of his reign if either of their words got out. And, against Zanishiria, any show of weakness was deadly. The assassin-girl was already too keen of the knowledge that his options were ticking down to zero with the drops of his blood down his left side. No, the emperor was not foolish enough to contest the assassin-girl's words. Yet, the reprieve Zanishiria was giving her opponent by talking and not fighting him was welcoming—damn the thought! "You are a very smug wench for someone who has yet to win this bout. Would you like a glass of wine and some tarts to go with that attitude?"

Zanishiria didn't even scoff. "Master said you liked to talk a lot when you were losing. Looks like he was correct about that."

Manscor scowled at the insult. "You talk a bit yourself, you arrogant se*f*(a)." His features looked cruel and desperate in the glow of the moons, the blood and sweat there competing against his chiseled features. "You know, you are much like your father—pompous and smug. Of course, that only lasted until his last, tormented breath. Hm." He smiled vilely, relishing in the old memory. "Yes, and he died because he was too busy worrying over everyone else's safety and not his own. Foolish martyr."

Zanishiria was not baited. "Ze'is Coursay'sora was a very honorable man and leader—more than you could ever be. Yet, I myself barely knew him. Your using his memory against me is useless, as it was you who took him from me before he could have that kind of hold on me. It is foolish to try to give me harm with such memories and words." With slow, precise motions, the assassin-girl pulled two razor-sharp shée fans from their places below her shoulder blades. The metal fans gleamed dangerously in the silver light, flashing their sharpened edges with a proposition of death. "I see you have been buying time to catch your breath, wise but not wise enough. I hope you are going to exchange those hand blades you picked up for a more entertaining weapon. I would hate to have to chase you around with those wimpy things."

Manscor would have agreed if Zanishiria was not an enemy to him; however, he knew that the small self-defense blades in his hands were no match for the large, fighting fans the girl now held. How could someone have such a diverse assortment of weapons on her person? She had, so far, used three kinds of swords (a shortsword and knife too), many suriken, chitz, hand and foot blades, two Royal laz-axes [courtesy of him dropping them], preshair gauntlets, and now the shée fans. What else could she be hiding in her preshair-snakeskin armor?

The emperor knew the question was important—indeed his life depended on the knowledge. He had not been as prepared as he had thought given that he had had some time to observe her for weapons. Thinking quickly, the emperor turned to the closest wall, not wanting to waste the time the assassin was giving him to gather a weapon. He selected a nodachi [Japanese long sword] from the weapons display and whirled to face Zanishiria, who was viewing his weapon-choice blandly.

"You are drawn mostly to swords." Zanishiria observed. She raised her shée fans. "You rely on them too much." Quicker than a flash, she closed the distance between them. With a sudden flick of the wrist, she launched a fan at the emperor's face, a move not wise when all weapons should be held as long as possible before releasing. The emperor moved out of its way—only to find it coursing back into the assassin's hand and a chitz speeding on its old line. *She used it as a distraction!* The sharp Trayshan weapon struck him on the face, shattering his right cheekbone, below his eye. A quick stroke of his hand saved him from a worse fate, yet Manscor had no time afterward to think as the Las'wa continued her attack, both fans swirling in her hands.

Manscor blundered through his perries, not bothering to find his own attacks, and tried to ignore the new wound to his face. Zanishiria forced the emperor over a sharp rise in the floor and down a fake boulder-strewn ledge. She was skilled in using the floor to her advantage. It was obvious that she was used to uneven footing for she flitted over the rocky surface like it was water. The random rocks were also weapons, ones she used quite well to keep the emperor always in retreat. She used her shée fans to create new projectiles as she passed by the numerous boulders. Many of these were flown at the ruler's face and feet.

The tired ruler tripped over a stone and tumbled off the ledge. He rolled away when he hit the floor, despite that Zanishiria had not followed him on his fall. The emperor picked up a discarded bowcaster and spun to face the Lakean above him. He loosed a dart before the assassin-girl could register what he had in his hands. His first cast struck Zanishiria in the right shoulder, underneath her collar bone and just inside the line of her shoulder joint. The second shot was skillfully deflected by a shée fan.

Manscor dropped the emptied bowcaster to take a better hold of his nodachi. He rushed back up the small hill to attack the maimed assassin. Though pain distorted the girl's features as he approached, she still brought up her arms in defiance to block Manscor's attack. The motion seemed futile. Manscor gleered down at her. "This will finish it."

"No, it won't." Zanishiria replied and perried his attack, even as her right shoulder protested with the arrow embedded in its capsule. The young Las'wa pushed through the feeling and refused to yield; it would mean her certain death.

Zanishiria began a string of counters to the emperor's sword-style. Seeing an opening, she released her left fan, flinging it into the emperor's sternum. The weapon hit the end of its near-invisible connection cord, the small wire taking out some of the force to its intended target; however, the blow still had enough oomph to knock the wind from Manscor's lungs, as well as, leave a deep gash in his clothing.

The ruler gasped and backed away from his opponent.

"That move was commendable." Zanishiria told the emperor, referring to the bowcaster, "However, one move alone cannot win this duel." Without so much as a flinch, she wrapped her fingers around the dart shaft still in her chest and pulled it out. Blood pooled from the wound instantly. "This dart is not long enough to puncture my lungs—had it been I would be how you are now." She tossed the dart aside. "I am ready to go again, man killer."

The emperor's returned look showed he did not match Zanishiria's enthusiasm.

Chapter Twenty-Seven

Before the wars and the start of the assassin clans and clan systems, the Royals controlled much of what the planet's inhabitants could—and could not—do. What little power the skilled killers has was set only to how they built their homes and how they survived on the deadly planet. Yet, time passed and the Royals slowly relinquished their firm hold on Obseen as they themselves began to feel "looked down upon" by the New Earth's government.

Angry and resentful at the UEF's views toward them, the Royals of Planet X gave the assassins permission to create their own government and free rein to establish Obseen in what ways they saw fit. Beautiful cities were constructed during this time and the intricate class-system made of respect, honor, and skill became the heart of what held the assassins together. The seventy-two clans became established and Obseen began to grow into its own power.

—And the Royals, they became known not as guardians against the assassins but as partners. Trade agreements between Planet X and Obseen benefitted both peoples and strengthened their abilities to work separate of the UEF. Obseen was the powerhouse of warriors, hackers, and skilled artisans and Planet X was the industrial and starship center of the Abyss Solar System. By the Royals' War, most of the UEF control of the two planets was just a thread of its previous chain and it would take a lot for the UEF to re-establish any dominance over the two nations. However, if Prince Xi (Manscor) did win the claim to his throne, would the partnership of Planet X and Obseen dissolve? And, would it set the stage for the UEF to make an excuse to overthrown both governments? Soon…. time will tell.

High Port station was quiet, it being minimally staffed with the war raging on below. With its bare-bones staff was also a feeling of informality; only the general, Jim Kett, remained composed and in uniform. He preferred that, though, because his young soldiers would have been anything but easy to manage if they had had to respect all edicates while being "imprisoned" in the relatively small space station.

Currently, all stationed guardsmen were in the lounge, excluding the two on-duty controllers. Most were engrossed in an intense game of Rûm eh Dér [Royals' card game]; however, some, like Cadet Jenny Ankins, were busy studying from one Royal Guards' handbook or another—the girl never seemed to take a break! General Kett shook his head in amusement at his soldier's typical hobbies. *I am pretty predictable myself,* he thought as he returned his eyes from the screen to his reports, none of which held anything important. Sighing, the general picked up the next folder—for he coveted obsidian thin-sheets over computer hard drives—and began to survey its contents. Boredly, he muttered, "Couldn't the Emperor give me something more worthwhile to do than wait? Or he could have sent us to Rhône ahead of schedule. What could that hurt?" He glanced out the window to look at Obseen and caught his reflection on the pane. "But, I guess that's too much to ask of a grey-haired, aging, and loyal fellow like myself. Though it'd be nice for something more interesting to do—not just for me but for these young upstarts." *Oh well, guess I need to get over myself.* He turned away from the dark-studded view of Obseen, though the planet held more interest than his reports, and forced himself to view a list of new recruits' test scores.

* * *

"Security is pretty fax around here." Sunashi commented as he and the others padded down the hallway. "You'd swear this wasn't a time of war."

"It isn't." Master Dorsetti countered. "Up here they don't have to worry about getting caught up in crossfire and politics. Their only concern is to wait for orders."

"Now that sounds boring even for the likes of an old master like me."

"Ah, you're not that old, Hareoska." Sunashi joked. "We youngsters still have to rush to keep up with you, so you got some years left."

Master Hareoska merely grunted and motioned for Dorsetti and Sunashi to pause. He hunkered his old fighter's body against the steel wall and glanced cautiously around and into the lookout window in the door they had stopped at. He peeked inside. "This looks like the lounge we were to meet at. Tell the others to come up from their searches. There are seven inside. I think there are more around—probable at the control room—but we would need to check with Yoshida."

"This really is easy." Sunashi said again as Dorsetti commed the others.

"Very." Was Hareoska's reply. The two masters waited while Dorsetti finished his relay. He nodded to them that their job was done.

* * *

"Damn this is a boring job!" Cadet Pete Marshel complained and took a noisy slurp of his mipa drink.

His partner, Cain Duquet, yawned and removed his feet from the control board. "Yeah, just waiting to direct the Emperor's starships every few days does get rather repetitious."

Pete's brown eyes got a mischievous glint and he looked at the viewing screens before turning back to his command partner. "But, it's free hour in the commons—meaning we can play a bit of Obsarian dice while watching out for the next command scheduled in an hour."

"Ah...I'm not sure that's allowed." Cain replied glancing at the monitors. "General Kett would have us on lunch parole for months if we are caught."

"So," Pete grinned devilishly, "We don't get caught. Come on, you can make the first cast."

Cadet Duquet still looked apprehensive but allowed his partner to cajole him into a few heated rounds. They were in the mist of their fourth go-round when Cain caught movement, out of the corner of his eye, from the hallway monitor. "Hey, dude, wait. I think someone's outside the door."

Pete glanced at the monitor then at the clock. "Nah, you're just seeing things. There is still twenty minutes left before change."

"No, I am sure I saw something." Cain put his cubes down and stood up to change the monitors to view more of the hallway. "Hey, look, the cam outside our door is stilled."

"What? But it was just checked and overhauled two days ago." Pete left their gaming pieces as he came over to study the cameras. "Huh, well, maybe a circuit still isn't right." He shrugged. "We can call Daren to fix it at the end of our watch.

No need to call him on his break." He started to turn back to their dice game.

Suddenly, the coded command room's door opened with a whoosh. The two cadets turned in surprise, which soon turned to shock, as a lone man charged through. Pete opened his mouth to protest the intrusion, but the assassin knocked him unconscious before he muttered a single word. Cain, being a little quicker, had tried to reach the alarm, yet only managed to brush his fingers against the console before he, too, was knocked out cold. Their attacker gently moved them out of the way, being kind enough to make sure they were in comfortable positions, before taking a seat at the control board. A quick glance and a moment of reprogramming and the "Code Master" had High Port station exactly the way he pleased. "'Kay, boys, Yoshida here, you are clear for the takeover."

Dăveed still stood defensively, his dagger in sight as a warning. Across from him, the lanky Tath Enor eyed the weapon warily and eased his saif to a neutral position near his thigh. Dăveed bobbed his head relieved that the other fighter was willing to talk reasonably; however, Tath's partner had not shown the same desire forcing Dăveed to keep his threatening blade at ready. "I am relieved that you are willing to negotiate, Enor."

"I don't do this because of you or that weapon."

Quinn was not perturbed by the other's dark tone. "I would not think to accuse you of such. Sympathy I mean."

Tath shook his head. "No, definitely not because of sympathy." His eyes changed then letting Dăveed see the young man's fatigue. "This war has gone on a long time. I have fought for the emperor for almost three years. My family has been involved for its entirety. I..." He trailed off, afraid to speak his mind while his partner was there. Obviously, the two men did not trust each other with their weaknesses.

"We are all tired of fighting against ourselves, our clansmen, our friends." It seemed Tath agreed, for wetness filed the man's intense blue eyes—tears unable to be shed. Dăveed almost wished to walk over and lay a consoling hand of the Téresh assassin's shoulder. Almost—but for the steely presence of Xemin Cour'noum.

"Ah, you are both such damned sentimentalists." The white-haired assassin growled though he scooted away nervously when Dăveed shifted his dagger about. "Wars are necessary, especially when defects like you Renegades are running about protesting our emperor. At least I know how to be loyal."

"And I know how to be just." Dăveed challenged, his countenance looking much like his father's. "We are not a people to be ruled by one man. We rule by councils and high councils, which keeps power from one individual. It is dangerous that we assassins have sunk so low as to allow one man to dictate to us—a Royal no less! And we call ourselves assassins and allow this? No, loyal I will never be so long as a ruthless, self-absorbed prince sits on a claimed throne. This is Obseen, not Planet X. For stability, we do not have royalty!"

Xemin flapped his lips unable to respond, he was so affronted. Tath, however, seemed to compose himself with Quinn's words. The willowy youth dropped to his knees contritely and offered Quinn his saif. "You understand our people better than those I serve..." Xemin protested behind his partner but Enor plowed on. "I...I listen not to negotiate with you Dăveed Quinn but to offer you your freedom for our capture. Your cause is a just one; mine...mine is only one of death. I have held you from your task for too long and beg you to forgive my rudeness. I ask for my life in your hands. As for Xemin, I ask you pardon of him only what he requests."

To see another assassin bow to him vexed Dăveed—even if he could sympathize with the other. "Enor, Tath, do not ever stoop to such levels! We are assassins you and I. Keep your dignity and stand. You want my advice, get up and look at me honestly. As for Xemin," Dăveed glared at the cowering Honored, "I will deal with him if I must. As for you, I accept that you wish to let me go and would welcome you to come with me. I go to save my people from slaughter. My people will accept you, better than the fate you are promised by Teera Sabina if you return to her. I accept you as honorable and I accept you as released of any debt to me. Go where you wish." Silence followed; the young men were too shocked that they had slipped into high-level ceremonial edicate to debate further. Finally, though, Dăveed forced himself to move, remembering his mission with acute anxiety. The two Honoreds had taken too much precious time from him. He turned, sheathing his father's dagger, and started to sprint away.

Xemin moved to intercept but Tath called him off. The white-haired youth hesitated then halted, sullenly, letting Dăveed sprint away. "We should have killed him! He—he deserved that."

Tath Enor said nothing and just continued to watch Dăveed Quinn's retreating back. *No, that man does not deserve death. He is very respectable. I must thank him if I ever meet him again. That he deserves.*

Chapter Twenty-Eight

The Royals had only a few holds left on Obseen (after the treaty granted the assassins back their planet). Taysor was still their strong-hold on the Assassins' Guild, made especially known by the large Taysor Palace at the capitol's center; the enormous landmark was still home to over three hundred Royals. However, most other planet-ports were given back to the clans. Above world, though, the Royals' kept their space-stations active. High Port was one such station still under Royal control. During the emperor's reign, it was his main port of trade and transport and a gateway to his then-controlled Planet X. Any and all ships to and from Taysor were directed through High Port.

The emperor tripped again, nearly cutting himself with his own weapon, as he tried to perry Zanishiria's shée fans. His opponent stepped out of his nodachi's range and threw one of her fans again, half-heartedly, as she allowed him to find his footing. "You little se$f$(a), why not just hit me?"

Zanishiria caught her shée fan and twirled it intricately around her fingers. "Perhaps, making you thoroughly embarrassed is good for you, stars know you have treated others through mockery."

"Oh, you are a bloody luminary now! Trying to instill manners in me, an emperor. No wonder you were sent here; your people probably wished I would kill you just to get rid of your praundering."

The Las'wa almost rolled her eyes. "You would need more than me to make your comportment bearable, Royal crit...and if you swing any slower I could go get a mipa juice and be back to watch you start the next one."

"You insolent...!" Manscor raged and increased his attack. His swings became wilder as his speed quickened, yet he was still unable to mark the Lakean girl. Zanishiria backed over an incline, deftly avoiding its craggy surface. She beat back the nodachi's blade only enough to keep herself from harm and it was obvious that she was toying with the emperor. Luckily—for Emperor Manscor—only Tarin Saerric was around to see his ineptitude. The emperor was, after all, regarded as one of the best assassins on Obseen. If he was not, doubt would be cast on him by his followers. Doubt, Manscor was assured, Tarin would never tell to anyone—but Zanishiria was a different case. The Lakean youth doubted if she lived through the fight.

The assassin-girl's brows were knit thoughtfully—not in concentration but in analysis—as she deflected the emperor's drunken-like swings. "Insolent I may be, "she suddenly said, her voice quiet, "But, I can see you are not up to fighting. You will die at this pace and not even by my hand. It is your body that fails you, not your skill. Just surrender to the Renegades and spare your life."

"I will not, sighp! I am emperor. It is you who should surrender if you so wish."

Zanishiria jumped away across a small crevasse. "I was sent to kill Prince Xi, the false Emperor of Obseen, not a swaggering fool. It is dishonorable for me to take advantage of a man so incompetent."

"Incompetent! Fuck you.... this fight is a fight to the death. Any death is death sweetheart, no matter how it comes, though you seem not to have the stomach for it. The Las'wa were stupid to send such a sentimental whelp!" The emperor leapt toward Zanishiria in his anger but his foot slipped on the crevasse's slick edge. Flailing, the emperor fell backwards—and down to the hard, obsidian floor below.

Zanishiria watched his fall and stood, waiting, for the man to get up. Manscor didn't move. Cautiously, the young assassin slipped to his side. *He's knocked out.... from blood loss or his head? She wondered. Both most likely.*

Tarin, who had begun to zone out as the fight had reached five hours, was slow to his feet. Uncertainty was etched on his face as he approached the stalled fighters. Once he realized it was the emperor lying cold on the floor, he rushed over. "Don't touch him!" He ordered Zanishiria vehemently.

Zanishiria backed away from Tarin and Manscor. "I am not like him." She reminded the Neitiege icily. "I would not kill a man lying unconscious on the floor."

"He would show you no such mercy." Tarin replied, just as cold. His meaning being that Zanishiria was a fool not to do the same.

"Then that is the difference between you and me." Tarin's countenance quickly turned sour at her words, but Zanishiria was not done speaking her mind. "He was compromised the instant I struck his right side. The man killer should die. Yet—I refuse to fight in any way that is dishonorable to the clans and the Guild. That morality is lacking in this war and it has for over ten years. You may call my actions foolish or worthless but I know there was a time when such respects were highly valued among the assassins. It was this man, this time that such dignities have been lost to us. I refuse to follow his example." Zanishiria felt her fatigue draining any real anger she had toward her friend. Five hours without reprieve was taxing on any fighter but she would confront any threat Tarin could potentially offer if he dared—only to stay alive.

"He would not show you the same mercy." Tarin repeated, more meekly this time.

"And it does not matter to me; I am not Manscor." She started to turn away.

"What now then? The clans won't accept the war over until the emperor is dead. Are you leaving this duel and does this mean Obseen's fate is in the hands of the armies outside?"

Zanishiria paused and turned to look at the handsome young Stikes. A small, almost-smile went flitting across the corners of her mouth drawing the tired look away. "This duel is comical—the emperor knows it as much as I do. The truth is that I expect only the armies to have any influence in this war. My fight is pitiful at best but I came for the deaths of my family, anyway, and not for the victory of the Renegades." Tarin looked taken aback. Zanishiria was not wanting to end the war? She was on a revenge killing? It did not seem like the same assassin-girl he had sat with for hours preparing for this fight. "So, what do I do now that my enemy is unconscious? I wait and sleep and try and heal as much as I am able until we can finish what we have started. It is all I want to do—and that is absurd.... that I want a revenge killing more than the freedom of this planet." She shrugged. "I am as selfish as that Royal. Are we really any different, he and I? We both would rather fight a ridiculous duel than worry about those people dying outside these walls."

"But what if Manscor dies in his sleep, would the war not be over?"

"And you would court such a thought?" Zanishiria muttered, shocked that Tarin even proposed such a notion. "No,

Tarin...he will not die because you will not let him. That you will do because of who your master is and what clan you are from. For your associations, I will not let you end him."

Tarin's eyes looked shaken for a long moment then they turned pained. "You would think me so cruel? Is it because of Master Teera that you think I could be like her? Do you know me not at all?"

The Las'wa mirrored his look. "No, Tarin I have never thought of you as cruel but practical, yes, you can be. As for Teera Sabina—you cannot deny that she has that kind of influence, even over you." Tarin ducked his head and Zanishiria knew she had not said the right words to deny his brutishness. "I know you are no physician but you were always capable of learning poultices and binding. You can use some of this," She tossed one of her medicine bags, "Florick moss and savya work wonders especially when used with mica. You can stop his internal bleeding and let his liver heal. Use anything else you can find in the medical chest by the door. I trust you can do that."

Tarin Saerric did not reply right away. He picked up the bag she had thrown at him and stared down at it in his hands, lost and forlorn. Finally, he said, "I had never thought you so selfish or so blasé...you had always been the one to speak up first to the concerns of others. So, this is the true heart of Zanishiria." He looked up at her with blue eyes hard as stone and as cold as ice. It stilled the Las'wa's soul. "Thank you for finally making yourself so clear to me. The fool here is me to think that you were the best of us..." He turned his back to her and began his check of the emperor's vitals.

Zanishiria almost reached out to touch her friend's shoulder but a warning in her heart told her not to. The whisperings of the end of their friendship beat against her thoughts but she stilled it; to have such a grief on her mind when she still needed to be clear for fighting would do her no good. Feeling suddenly exhausted, she trudged over to the large bay windows and sat down laying her shée fans in easy reach by her side. In another motion, she took out another packet of savya and florick mosses and started the long, tedious task of cleaning her wounds and bandaging those she could.

She finished her first-aid to her person a half-hour later and scrounged her pouches for food disks packed with the healing herbs of her people. Her hunger sated, she forced herself to her feet to collect her scattered weapons. She avoided the two figures across the room, finding Tarin was ignoring her too as he labored over the wounded body of the ruler. Then, finding nothing else to do, Zanishiria chose the safest corner in the large fighting room and curled up into it. "I will be ready for you, man killer." She whispered as she let her grey eyes close into a forced light-sleep. Beyond the sounds of Tarin's labors and the musky smells of blood and sweat, Zanishiria began to drift into a dream of her past...

"You know, Zan, if you didn't let Tarin and K'sho convince you to take nightly excursions and lose your sleep, you wouldn't be so exhausted during training sessions and get maimed this badly."

"Yes, master." Zanishiria replied to Sye Rainier as her cinnamon-haired instructor helped her patch up a nasty cut on the back of her right shoulder.

Sye laughed sweetly at her student's abashed look. "I swear, no matter how angry I am at you, you always give me that same, apologetic look. Sometimes, it's like you only do such to console me into believing you won't do it again—just to sneak off and do it all over."

Zanishiria deepened her false guiltlessness. "Never that, master. I do mean it when I tell you."

"See, there you go again!" Sye teased and finished adjusting the bandage. "Okay, that should do it." The Nalcian woman nodded, satisfied, and collected the bloody linens. Just as she finished, Tarin and K'sho popped their heads into the room to collect their friend. "Now, boys, you really need to be less demanding on Zan. This was the twelfth wound she has acquired this week! When she goes home, the Royals are going to think we are trying to butcher her."

Tarin chuckled, his blue eyes shining, but he quickly gave a serious face. K'sho gave their contrite answer: "Yes, Senior Master. We will try to keep ourselves from the more dangerous activities, and we won't stay out so long at night anymore." So, Zanishiria's friends had heard the last of their conversation.

Sye sighed and waved the trio out of her room. "I don't really trust the innocence of your words, Rease. Just promise me you will be a little less reckless and I might be able to sleep at night."

Zanishiria made sure she was the last one out, trailing so she could bow respectfully at her teacher. "Please, be less curt with them, master, for it is I who coerces them into our mischief."

"Of that I know well." Sye Rainier replied, "But, they encourage you, too."

The young assassin-Royal averted her eyes, almost blushing. "Yes, I suppose so, master."

Sye chuckled and shooed her apprentice out the door. "You just need to be less vivacious then. Now go, I have meetings to attend."

Released, the spirited girl sprinted down the stone hallway, finding her two friends waiting for her on the bridge leading to the gardens. Fifteen-year-old Tarin Saerric was leaning casually against the engraved stonework, knowing full well that his tall, sculpted frame was very attractive. K'sho stood next to him, Tarin's smaller shadow, his arms supporting himself as he leaned over the bridge's trusses to watch the delicate fish swimming by. Seeing Zanishiria near, K'sho straightened and grinned broadly at the black-haired assassin-girl. "You didn't tell her your injury was from pestering rooks, did you?" [Rooks are bird-like predators that nest in the Vallés]

Zanishiria shook her head and joined her silver-haired friend in watching the colorful Royal fish play in the water. "She would lose it if I said that."

"Yeah, she would. So," K'sho turned around to look at both of his friends equally. "What do we want to do now? There's still time before dinner and evening session."

Tarin's eyes glimmered mischievously. "We could go find the Charlocks.....I heard they were going to practice on the forest endurance course. We could go beat them at their game." [Charlocks are one of the teams at the training center (name of)]

Zanishiria shook her head. "Sorry, but one adventure was enough for me today. If I get another injury so soon after this one, master will keep me in solitary for a week."

"Oh, that's right." Tarin's enthusiasm dimmed. He studied the assassin-girl, finding her words out-of-character. Usually, she could last longer than either he or K'sho on endurance courses—and she loved showing off. Finally, really looking at her, he realized she was trying to hide the slight shaking of her arm from the pain of her wound. At most times, she could hide her pain to the point that not even he could tell, but Tarin was learning to read her subtle signs and she must be hurting enough that even she could not help herself. "In that case, we could stay here at the gardens? I need a nap anyway...or I guess I could actually prepare for the assignment Master Hareoska gave us.... It was due today, right?"

"You haven't done it yet?" K'sho said, alarmed.

"When does he ever?" Zanishiria teased. "He procrastinates to even sleep so why does it surprise you to find he forgot another assignment?" Tarin rolled his eyes and attempted to grab her for her taunting. She allowed him to get a hold around her waist, but only for one second, before slipping free and tossing him to the ground. "But, staying in the gardens sounds good."

K'sho grinned at his two friend's usual antics. "Okay, then, the gardens it is. You lead the way?"

"Sure." Zanishiria released Tarin's arm and backed away, unpinning him from the lock she thrown him into. "The North Fountain?"

"Sounds fine." Tarin agreed and cracked his abused arm.

The trio sprinted off, Zanishiria leading, flanked by her two friends. They sped through the maze of floriculture, never missing a turn. Minutes later, they reached the gigantic, northern fountain, its plume sprouting twelve meters in the air to drop into the enormous, square base below. Zanishiria halted near its spray, barely winded, and breathed in the misty air. K'sho collapsed to the fountain's marble base, talking in mouthfuls of the cool air. Tarin joined him and reached over to splash his face with water, clearing it of sweat. Zanishiria finally joined them a minute later.

They sat there, silent and comfortable in each other's company, while the spray came down in full force. After a while, K'sho started a discussion with Tarin on stealth tactics—the assignment Hareoska have given them. Even though Tarin knew most of what K'sho spoke of, he welcomed the extra information knowing his friend was a genius when it came to battle-tactics and espionage. Any creativity was always thought highly of by Master Hareoska. When K'sho was satisfied Tarin would not fail the class, he stretched and mentioned needing to do an errand for his master. He excused himself.

Zanishiria waved K'sho away, her eyes trailing him as he rushed away. "Maybe we should head back to?"

"Why?" Tarin asked. "There is still plenty of time to kill before evening, and isn't the sound of the fountain soothing/"

Zanishiria eyed Tarin carefully, her deep grey eyes seeming to know more than she let on. "If I didn't know better, I would say you were trying to woo me."

Tarin cleared his throat, taken off his balance at her directness. "Ah, no, of course not. I just don't want you to feel like you need to rush away just because K'sho has to go do work. You do need to rest once in a while."

"As do you." Zanishiria replied pointedly. Tarin grinned at the rebuke and protested no further. "K'sho leaves us alone a lot more these days…"

Tarin looked away to the waterfall. "I haven't noticed."

"Oh yes you have. I know that you both like me—and K'sho has voiced his feelings to me in the past. I told him I would never come between the friendship you both have by choosing either of you. K'sho…took that to mean I didn't not feel for him as he does me—and that I have a fondness for you. He would never compete with you even in this."

Tarin shifted, suddenly uncomfortable with Zanishiria's directness. "He believes there is something going on between us."

"Is there?" Be honest was what Zanishiria would have finished with but she knew she was already pushing Tarin.

Tarin could feel the fine line he walked, one he knew his beautiful, wild friend would not let him cross. "In truth," he started, "I do think of you as more than just a friend—but we are too young for such as people would suggest. And there is K'sho….he knows how I feel and I he. You are right to make a stand to not come between us."

Zanishiria let the silence build between them until the world seemed still. Then, she continued, "I see you both as very dear to me. And, I cannot put one before the other. Soon, these times will change, for I have heard the tides of war have shifted our way. The armies draw near and this Center will be torn into two. We should not stand separated for this very reason."

"This is the first time you have spoken of the war so openly. Why now?"

Zanishiria dodged the question by issuing one of her own. "K'sho has been your closest friend, so surely you know which side he is drawn to?"

Tarin stilled, his eyes narrowed. This talk was close to defecting language. Yet, Zanishiria had a point with her question. Tarin nodded warily. "He never says out loud but I have my suspicions."

"Indeed. I ask you then, Tarin, do not make your closest friend an enemy just because of his choice—ever. There has been enough pain in this war already."

"I won't."

"I know you would never mean to." Zanishiria interrupted any other words Tarin might have. She hesitated before reaching across the distance between them and took hold of Tarin's hand. "I merely warn you, for both your sakes." The intensity of her words made Tarin pause. "Tí kamoenein." ["I cherish you." Neitiege]

Tarin inhaled sharply and stared into her grey eyes. "Zan…" It was the closest she had ever come to admitting any feelings. And, yet, Tarin knew it was as far as she would ever go. He closed his eyes as if to shield himself from reality. For just a moment, he would savor the words she had given him. Time became filled with the sounds of the fountain behind them. Finally, he reluctantly opened his eyes again. His look was almost pleading. "I know what you want to ask of me—and the price of it. I can handle still being friends with K'sho even if he does go to the other side….but you…." The Novastones would also be with the Renegades, he came to the sudden realization. Of course Zanishiria would have known about K'sho's loyalties because hers were the same. He gulped and said, his voice strangled, "Zan… please don't go where I cannot follow."

Don't go where I cannot follow…

"Tarin…" Zanishiria murmured, physically reaching out as the dream faded. Her hand knocked against something hard and she startled awake. "Oh…. the wall." Her memories returned of where she was and the protests of her battered body filled her thoughts with the next breath.

The assassin-girl could not believe she had fallen asleep so deeply; certainly, her pain should have kept her awake, it throbbed badly enough. She cursed at herself for letting herself drift so and quickly leapt to her feet, weapon in hand. Yet, despite her lack of awareness, it seemed the Lakean was the only one active within the transformed fighting room; Tarin Saerric had found sleep as well, and was laying within close guard of the still unconscious Emperor Manscor. His steady breathing showed he had not heard Zanishiria's distressed voice and the emperor certainly hadn't. Slowly, Zanishiria relaxed her guard, it being a useless waste of energy, and took to prowling the vicinity instead.

The twin moons cast a bluish light over the city. Their brightness lured the young assassin to the large windows. The view outside was eerily calm, none of the soldiers present seemed to move. "It's nearly four in the morning, I reckon. The armies must have called a truce for the night, though most should be starting preparations again. I wonder….are the Renegades all right?" Her soft voice drifted away as shapes, darker than the surrounding buildings, caught her attention. Her gamma lenses in her eyes readjusted making her able to see the crests on the figures' uniforms. "Royal Guards…and by the numbers of them, it must be most of the force. But—." *But, why have all of the Guard come to the main square? The man killer or Teera must be ordering some kind of ambush around here…* "Qusairo, surely you were aware of this? I do hope you are." She pleaded with herself, "I wish you to know. Please, take care." *For all of our people's sakes.*

Chapter Twenty-Nine

"Assassins are known as having higher tolerances to pain and an acute aversion to using medications, or so our sources quoted; however, these "super-humans" are not invincible, though they do display beyond normal hardiness. On recent study, I have found many of Obseen's habitants to be superb herbalists, enlisting their knowledge to seek out plants of remarkable healing properties—those even greater than mica plants from Sentinal 1. [Note: mica's healing powers are widely known and have been used to cure cancers, cardiovascular diseases, and autoimmune disorders.] But, these killers, of which I point out rarely seem to get sick, have found both poisonous and healing plants on their prison planet that contain properties higher in quality than any I have ever seen. As I write, they are healing a youth of a debilitating wound, another of the "Stone Blindness" virus that has attacked half their world. Supposedly, these herbs can heal injuries and illnesses worse than these, with little to no telltale sign that the injury even existed. Incredible! It is rare to find such disciplined and knowledgeable a people. Could their arts of healing help our people?"

--unfiled report by UEF Dr. Daniel King

Five shadows snuck through the silent city. They paused frequently to reassess their surroundings, yet it seemed they did not stop at all. Steadily and stealthily the small group was able to infiltrate the enemy's outer lines. One by one, the shadows picked off the guards and made their way to the main force.

[Thirty are eliminated.] One signed to their leader, the young Cour'eysan Evalaus. All easily saw the small hand signals through their creeshts gamma lenses and signed agreement. Coryu motioned he understood then signed, [Be careful. See how many we can take out before the hour. Do not stay past the time.] The other four signaled acknowledgment and moved out.

Minutes passed by with agonizing slowness. Each member of Coryu's small force wondered if their next targets would sound the alarm but none did. That did not console the

Las'wa, however, who were suspicious of the quiet. Being that deep into the Royal Guards' forces was unsettling. Coryu checked his time by the moon's shadow. It was almost four—his party should head back. But, the young Tai'eya hesitated as his sharp, ice-grey eyes caught sight of Honored-One Teera Sabina's tent across the Terrís. "The man killer's wench." He hissed in loathing. "Today, you will die by my hand." Yet, he was not naïve enough to go kill the vile assassin in her tent; however, he vowed to keep his promise as he slipped away. "Today."

Coryu's second-in-command came up beside him as he crept back into the shadows. Her gaze followed his to Teera's tent. [The man killer's morta. We will make sure to look for her today.] [Morta is Las'wa slang for "whore"]

[No!] Coryu signaled back. Tyen looked at him oddly and asked for an explanation. [It is my kill, for what she did to our brother a year ago and for our parents at Barashi.]

Tyen studied Coryu's countenance, her own beautiful face etched in worry. [I miss them too, moré [brother], but not for revenge will I kill the morta but because I can keep Sabina for taking more lives. That is what our sey'ben (family) would want.]

Coryu had never been close to his older sister, he himself the youngest of the three siblings and the only one to choose to live as a Tai'eya, alone from his family and clan (except, of course, with his master who he trained under for sixteen of his twenty years). Looking at his sister now, he realized how little he really knew of her—not like their brother Mekai'eko, who he had visited freely since age ten; Tai'eya and preshans were the elite in Shairceeo là Coursa and able to meet as often as they wanted. [I still want Sabina as my own.] He signaled sharply and whirled away from Tyen before she could answer. [We head back now. Each Las'wa for yourselves, find different routes back to the Renegades. Success is ours!]

Con'trore Kee'van was on watch on the Renegade's north-western ranks, tired from battle but dutiful enough to stand watch for his Tà sharay. It was the fourth hour in the morning, nearly time for the rest of the army to wake up and prepare—and almost time for himself to be relieved for a quick nap. Yet, Kee'van sensed the morning was not normal, and it was not just because the day brought them to their first battle at Terrís. No, strange things were afoot, vile traps being set, different commands of the armies (both Renegade ad Guard) being overrun, and interesting visitors were wandering about. Kee'van was not sure which he would want to run into; they all sounded bad.

A sound came to his left and Kee'van turned, expecting to see his relief coming, but the man who wandered out of the shadows was not a Xsorian con'stól. Kee'van was ready to take his shaysword in hand when he mind-heard the tired young man say, *"Qusairo; this man must help me get to Qusairo."*

"Who are you?" Kee'van asked but the exhausted man didn't answer, nor did he form anymore words in his exhausted mind—except *"Made it, so tired..."*

"I am tired too, friend." The con'trore answered and received a blank look. "You seek Royal Qusairo?"

The man nodded, his movements sluggish. "I have...an urgent message...for Qu-sairo." Kee'van made out the words through the man's panting. "Is he...in this...camp?"

Kee'van took pity on the runner and went over to lend his shoulder to the other—who was clearly ready to fall off his trembling feet." I could take you to him, but you do not seem to be in any condition to walk further into camp. I could mind-link with the Tà sharay and have him come with Qusairo?"

The young man looked horrified. "No! The Tà sharay need not be messenger for me....I can go to them." He pulled himself loose of the Xsorian as if to prove it. "I ran this far. I know going a little farther won't kill me." *"It's beyond rude to ask leaders to come to the call of a mere runner."*

Kee'van chuckled at the though. "They would not mind helping one of their own." The con'trore received a blank look in return. "Come, I will take you to Royal Qusairo."

The runner was true to his word. He stuck closely to Kee'van as they wound through the buildings, pushing their pace ever so slightly. Kee'van couldn't help admire the young man's stamina. He could sense the pain the other man was suffering and pushing through. Because of the man's determination, Kee'van made sure to reach the command tent by the shortest means possible.

As they entered the tent, Royal Qusairo and Tà sharay Torez were already there, looking expectantly at the runner, and ready to hear his message—most likely they had been warned ahead of time by Kee'van of his coming. As soon as they saw who the Xsorian con'trore had brought, they were quick to provide the man a seat and refreshment.

"Royal, Tà sharay, I need not these things." The tired man protested, but neither would have it.

"Nonsense! We won't have you dying at our feet. Accept a drink and food and our deepest respects, Dăveed Quinn." Royal Qusairo signaled Kee'van to join them. "And you, con'trore, I know you need a rest, too." Kee'van sat beside his leader, looking just as ready to refuse as the Baras man he had brought. He seemed curious to know that the runner was Master Judeo Quinn's son. The two leaders allowed their guest a few swallows of micapa and a chance to eat one mincé cake before bombarding him with questions. [Micapa is mipa fruit juice mixed with honey and revitalizing herbs] "Young Quinn, what news have you? I have been worried, as no communication has reached me about either of my two captains, and your absence was most concerning."

Dăveed Quinn gave the Royal a sorrowful, exhausted look. "I ran all the way from the council house as fast as I could—even having to fight some of Teera's Honoreds. I barely escaped the battle there, thanks to brave Captain Raynward."

Qusairo's green eyes looked pained. "What happened?" he asked quietly.

"We met at the council-house at the appointed hour but found no trace of a flag anywhere. Knowing our forces might be hiding inside to keep hidden from the Guards, our front man headed for the entrance to call them out. The first man to reach the doors was struck down instantly by the Honored One herself. From here, all hell broke loose as her men surrounded us from all sides. I am the only one who escaped, by plea of Captain Raynward to get this message through to you. I doubt Teera Sabina left anyone alive."

"No, she was never one for that mercy." Kee'van muttered regretfully.

Dăveed was too tired to respond to the remark. "I got stopped by two Honoreds about ten minutes after I escaped the battle; I knew they would have chased me all the way here and knew playing maun'cendo was wasting time so I faced them before I got too tired." [Maun'cendo is a game assassin children play to practice sneaking around]

Khan Torez asked, not unkindly, "And, how is it that you are here now?"

"The leader of the pair let me go." The three listeners looked shocked that an Honored would do something like that. "He and I came to an understanding…." Dăveed barely explained and only to erase the doubt he saw in the others' eyes. "He was tired of this bloody war too…"

"Indeed…aren't we all?" The Tà sharay relived the scene through Quinn's memories. "It seems many are tired of this war—as they should be. Maybe, more will follow this young man's example." He nodded to Royal Qusairo that what Dăveed had said was the truth. The Renegade leader took the Tà sharay on his word and mind-thought that it was time to let Dăveed Quinn rest from his ordeal. "You two rest now. I have wired this place with pressure alarms. They will go off if anyone comes within one hundred meters of this camp. Join the fighting when you are recuperated and not before." The Xsorian leader gave his man and the Baras a stern look to make sure they would do as he said. "We need both of you at your best today." In afterthought he added, "You did well, Quinn, to make it here to warn us." He bowed in high-respect. Royal Qusairo also bid them to rest and the two leaders left the tired men alone in the command tent.

Kee'van was ready to turn to Quinn and tell the young runner he would wake him in two hours, but the drained assassin was deeply asleep, his hand still clasping a cake. The con'trore smiled kindly at the scene and, just as gently as he would with his own son, removed the piece of food from the calloused fingers of the Baras and covered the man in a light blanket. "Be well, Dăveed Quinn." He whispered and huddled into his chair. He closed his eyes and found his own sleep.

"You should wake, young lady." The old assassin master said, gently shaking the princess from her sleep. "It would be much easier for you to return to Lapsair if you left before the armies wake."

Scarlett murmured and forced her tired eyes open and pushed herself to a sitting position. "It must be four in the morning."

The blind master cocked his head, listening, and smiled cheerfully. "More like four o'nine to be exact, with twelve—no fifteen—seconds give or take."

The dark-haired princess shot the old man a withering glance, knowing he would not see it. "Very well. So, you think I should leave by the south-western streets of town? Father is being held nearby the training center. Or, maybe the fighting will be too heavy there? Going directly west could be better."

"The later." Shathahel replied, busying himself with a loaf miet and butter. "The fighting will be based around the Palace." [Miet is a grain from New Earth, usually made into bread or cereal]

"All right, the west it is." Scarlett came up to the round table the master was eating at and began buttering her own breakfast. "Thank you, Master Shathahel, you have been a great help to my father and I."

The old man shuffled embarrassed and turned his face away to hide his happiness. "It was nothing I shouldn't do for you. Ze'is Coursay'sora would expect nothing less." He turned to flash a small smile then turned away, heading back to his room. "Be safe on your way. Be watchful of the guards. May I have assisted you well."

"Master." Scarlett whispered after the old man and bowed gratefully at the retreating form. Then, putting together a light lunch of bread and jam, the princess collected her cloak and left Shathahel's dim apartment, starting her cautious path back to her father.

The obsidian city was cast in a rusty-gold light, but it was a silent beauty. The dark, ornate city seemed to be holding its breath, waiting for the final clash of Royal guards and Renegades. The silence was too eerie for Scarlett to be relaxed about—she not being an assassin or trained to handle the uneasy trek through the capitol.

Half-an-hour passed with agonizing slowness. Scarlett felt the need to be cautious, especially as she neared the training center. She slowed her pace further. There was no guarantee all of the assassin in Taysor were concentrated around Taysor Palace, in fact, the princess highly doubted all had left the training center when the fighting had started the day before. She only hoped there were those loyal to the Renegades around. She being King Lapsair's only daughter and well known around the capitol made her a target. "Please be so." She murmured and held the cold lazer-rifle barrel to her pounding chest. Senak'y

Lake came into view passed the growth of the tarol trees that marked the edge of the city. The indigo waters seemed so calm, like smooth glass, and Scarlett paused to view it.

A mistake.

"Weapons down, Royal bitch." A gruff assassin ordered, bringing a halbert force-pike to Scarlett's back. Scarlett froze in panic, her fingers stuck to her weapon. "Kap, take her weapon." The assassin instructed one of his companions as a group of six trainees came up to surround Scarlett. Obediently, the smallest and wiriest of the youths came forward to pry the Royal weapon from Scarlett's sweaty hands. Once the princess was freed of her weapon, the group's leader came to Scarlett's front, revealing his roughened, dirt-covered face. The princess instantly recognized the middle-aged man for Suez—and most likely an Honored. The man obviously recognized the Novastone woman. "Well now, this is a tasty surprise. What foul errand had your poor daddy sent you on at this hour? But, surely, you know the great Lapsair is on house-arrests, so you must be going to free him?"

"He can easily free himself from your slimy hands whenever he wants."

The leader chuckled at Scarlett's defiance. "I hear your cousin, Zanishiria, has a rude tongue as well—but, of course, she will be dead soon if not already; which, by the way, is where your father will be once this war is over. Dead like all the Renegades." The man licked his lips in delight. "The boys and I are already celebrating. D'you wish to join us little missy?" The look in his eyes warned Scarlett the man had been drugging himself high off of Shinning spice from the Tomb (Sentinal 2). If he was stark mad, she was worried about the others. A fearful look around revealed all but two with clouded eyes. Scarlett gulped and started a slow retreat—not that she really had one.

The two youngest youths were quick to stop her, easily taking hold of her in their trained grasp. Scarlett lost all hope of escaping in one piece and submitted to the estranged group. She prayed that the experience would not be too traumatic and stole the last of her strength to protect herself for any offenses the young men and delusional Honored would do to her—and, silently, she thanked the stars that she had left the Lakean tablets in Shathahel's care.

Chapter Thirty

"...As a final aside to my document on the assassins' use of herbals, I add that these people find using drugs for pleasure as a sign of weakness; the act of taking any—most notably Shinning—is frowned upon. Shinning is a drug seem on Sentinal 2, and is a hallucinogen as well as a mood-altering substance. Though such a drug is hard to obtain on Obseen, there are still quantities of it found among the youth, especially those in contact with the Royals' (mainly in Taysor). The use of Shinning seems strikingly more potent to these people than others I've studied..."

--unfiled report by UEF Dr. Daniel King

"Kill them all!" Honored One Teera Sabina raged as she threw back her tent's flap. The unfortunate messenger, who had reported the loss of her entire front line, was slowly dying on the tent floor where the leader had left him. "The Las'wa have surfaced and struck while you lazy bastards were sleeping! If it wasn't for needing you today, I'd have you all killed for this lackluster security." The last remark Teera reserved for herself and Davin, who had come to her side. Her quiet assistant flickered his gaze in her direction but showed no other sign. His master's words were aimed at the incapable guards and not his person.

The unfortunate souls Tera's words were aimed at coward in fearful reverence, all coming to hustled formation so as not to anger their leader further. "Here we are right outside our Emperor's Palace walls and you inbeciles let the vilest of our enemies sneak around in our mist and slit over eighty men's throats! None of you would have lived if I had hear that our Emperor was lying dead right now." She had sent a runner to check on the ruler's duel. Tarin had only sent word back that Manscor was still alive and had not been targeted by the Las'wa. "But, since he is not dead, you must all show penitence by fighting twice as hard—to make up for the dead men you must now replace. I want those shek'fa dead before noon!"

* * *

"They come!" Someone yelled from the front line. All around, Renegades fingered their weapons but stayed within the shelter of the buildings. The small force had been in waiting since Coryu Evalaus's group of Lakeans had returned, their weapons gleaming dully from their duty. "They will be moving soon." Coryu had informed Royal Aslén calmly and had turned away to prepare his weapons.

Now, the twenty-two-year-old Las'wa was standing close to Price Anmero's group, his intense grey eyes studying Page for any sign that the Xsorian had to give on the enemy's position. "They will be more than elated to find Qusairo here. We would be wise to keep a close watch for that, or on his moré."

Page tuned his attention to the older assassin, though he still kept some feeling out for the Honored One's forces. "We stay by Anmero, Tai'eya. Royal Qusairo has asked this of us. You have no duty but what you decide."

Coryu flicked his eyes over Anmero, as if assessing the lean, chestnut-haired Royal. He thought little of Anmero Doz, if seemed, by the way his eyes turned away, unimpressed, but he shrugged just the same. "I will stay only so long. I have a different agenda than ending the emperor's reign—nice as that would be."

"Revenge holds little victory for those lost." Page replied, his gaze looking outward to the street once again. "You would be far more rewarded for letting it go than pursuing it."

Coryu scowled at the Xsorian. "It is rude to pry, Torez."

Lap laughed at the rebuke, having heard a snappy thought from his brother in his head. "Your thoughts are so clear we could read them whether we wanted to or not." Coryu soured. "Relax, Cour'eysan, we know your actions are valid, but, still, you would be wise to calm that fury. We would welcome you with us if you so choose."

"Revenge is for the weak-at-heart."

The small group turned to find Shane Sinhail approaching. K'sho and Seircor were by his side, all having returned from a quick meeting with Qusairo. "If the youth wants to work for such vulgar means, let him." Coryu's face really darkened then, having no tolerance for the arrogant Trayshan beynor. [Beynor is the title for heir of Traygor] He was about to spit back a response when Shane continued, "But, in these times, we are all less than honorable." He stepped his full, iron-muscled height beside the smaller Las'wa man and looked down at Cour'eysan until the Lakean backed away, then he brushed past him to survey the streets. "In these times, I would accept even your help—though I would much prefer your smarter clansman, Seircor."

"Enough already!" K'sho commanded, stepping between Coryu and the others. "Qusairo warned of a three-pronged attack form Teera Sabina's forces. I suggest we drop this dispute for better aims."

"Precisely my thought!" Lap chimed in.

Page nodded. "The Royal guards are nearly to the front lines. It will start momentarily..." His eyes looked around the small group, though they seemed to be focused elsewhere. "The small group that Zanishiria requested defend Prince Anmero has grown larger—though I suspect you will need less saving, prince, than we believe. You were taught by Seircor and Zanishiria after all." The prince bowed his head to the Xsorian. "I have no fear in regards to what we must do. We will get through this coming fight."

"My respects, Torez. I am honored to be by your side today."

"A'iy." Page looked away, hearing voices only his brother and he could hear. "The first have engaged. We will be met in two-saun's time. [Saun is similar to minutes] I suggest we partner up?" The others moved without question, following Page's order. Lap stepped up beside his brother and unsheathed his falchion in same rhythm as Page readied a round of shuriken. Seircor and K'sho moved closer to one another, flanking Anmero. To either side, Shane Sinhail and Coryu Evalaus headed to the fore, their swords gleaming in the dawn light. The sounds of shouting and weapons clashing reached their ears and a breath passed, then the fighting appeared. "See you at the end." Page stated calmly, "We fight for Obseen today!"

"You grimy-spitting, double-crossing, sons-of-bitches!"

"Who-oa!" Sunashi joked at the insults from the foul-mouthed cadet. "We've got some live ones today, don't we, Marco, Daren?"

"Sunashi," Dorsetti gave his apprentice a withering look. "Stop pestering the "grainies'."

Sunashi grinned. "But, the fun in it!"

"It's only fun until you're the one at weapon's point." Corsetti whispered as he passed behind the younger man's back. "Just keep a close watch on 'em."

The seven masters had rounded up all of the personnel aboard High Point Station and tied them up on the comfortable chairs within the lounge. Sunashi, Corsetti, Roko, Alrik, and Dorsetti all stood at strategic points around their captors, their weapons casual but far from being put away. In the southern corner, Master Quinn and Hareoska were "having a friendly chat" with the general, and it seemed the grey-haired leader was being forthcoming on his end.

"What are you going to do with this station?"

Sunashi spun around to answer the cadet's question. He was not really surprised that the woman was the one to ask; she had proved to be more smart-assed than some of her companions. "Anything we want to, honey." The young assassin-master grinned and bent down to her eye level. "The usual most likely: take the valuables, kill the crew, and blow the station up. You know, the fun stuff."

Alrik Kagar rolled his eyes from his position behind the woman. "You make us sound like petty pirates, Sun." Yeah," Roko piped in just to pass the time, "You could have said we were here for the adventure of it or something. Or idiocy…we old men certainly are for that."

"Nah, the whole pilfering and burning is more entertaining." Sunashi argued, "Wouldn't you agree it's more exciting, Ms. Ankins?"

Cadet Jenny Ankins frowned deeply and tried to match Sunashi's stare for stare. She quickly averted her gaze when Sunashi rose to the challenge.

"I'd be terrified of you if I was her." Yoshida's gentle baritone voice broke the silence of the room. The entire group turned to see the Code Master pushing the two still slightly stunned cadets into the lounge. "I picked up some strays. They were happy to be relieved of their watch duties."

"Yoshi! What took you so long? The party's already well under way."

"Yeah, with cookies and chips and draughts I am sure." The Code Master answered drily and thrust the two cadets into Sunashi's care. "You rewrite the whole station next time and I will sit on my ass."

"I was hardly on my ass."

Yoshida ignored the younger man and continued on into the room, walking over to join Hareoska and Quinn. "The station is all ours. I've checked all the data logs too. Quite the cache. Oh, and I know the destination for these ships. Did you know the Royals have an off-world docking bay?"

"That's news to me." Hareoska replied and set a demanding eye on General Kett.

The weathered Royal stared calmly back. "Built under order of the Emperor himself. It is under the highest security. Only three people, outside the facility, know what is being built there."

"And you're not one of them." Master Quinn filled in. The old veteran did not even need to shake his head; his eyes said it all—he was curious too, but left in the dark.

"That sounds intriguing." Sunashi volunteered a comment.

"Indeed." Alrik answered, casting an annoyed look at Sunashi before returning his gaze to the cadets. "There would be a fascinating find at that port—if the quantity of traznic and sydro-smelted steel is any indication. Manscor must be building himself a Royal fleet."

Yoshida quickly stepped into the conversation "A fleet I am not sure about, but a formidable ship, I could wager on. If we are all agreed, let's pilot one—or all—of the emperor's ships to Rhône. I can do some digging on the way. Maybe, I will uncover some of the data on Manscor's station."

"That works for us." Dorsetti spoke for himself, Corsetti, and Roko. Alrik and Sunashi nodded their own agreement.

"What will you do with my men?" General Kett asked, bringing the assassins' attention back to the immediate dilemma. "You certainly will treat us fairly?" He looked at Master Quinn, recognizing the man as the group's designated leader.

"You will be released, of course. Mind you leave us to do our business in peace. We have no need of prisoners. Yoshida will lock the door with an automatic timer. You will be trapped in here until we are safely on our way."

Jim Kett gave the assassin master a false smile. "That is the best I could have hoped for."

"Stand her there." The doped leader ordered his two youngest followers. Scarlett's captors obeyed quickly, forcefully pulling the princess to the indicated spot in their shadowed grotto. The Honored man grinned wickedly as he crouched down by a food stash the group had left in the middle of the rubble-strewn room. In slow, mocking pleasure he opened the bag of Shinning and savored some of the silver powder. Instantly, the man's eyes burned with the spice. The Honored's group joined in on the leader's hissing laugh but all waited to see what would happen next. Scarlett did not like the evil glint in the man's calculating, drug-induced eyes. "Let's give her some, boys. What do ya say?" The group howled their delight. "After all, she should enjoy our victory party. Being a Royal and all, I'm sure she is happy to serve her Emperor's men."

Kap, the smallest of the youths, bound forward, eager to please, with his own bag of Shinning. He held out a good pinch of the addictive spice to Scarlett's face and started to advance it to her lips. The princess reared back, struggling desperately to avoid the substance. She had heard of its ways of making a user seek "pleasurable" activities, usually at the cost of one's life if used enough and in high enough doses. Her two captors braced her easily enough and the stronger of the two forced her head still. Then Kap, using hands that were deceptive to his strength, pried her delicate lips apart and shoved the spice into her mouth. He slammed her jaw tight so quickly that Scarlett tasted blood in her mouth mixing with the silver powder. The instant flare of spice took the pain away and flushed the princess's body. A strong urge for desire rose up, filling her thoughts for all sorts of comforts: foods, air, heat, and, of course, the primal, carnal desires of the flesh. The need to attempt her most crazy of dreams, to fill the thrills she had longed for, and an ache to hold the nearest person to her washed over Scarlett's mind in hungry waves; she found herself lost. The feeling began to knaw at her.

Finding their captive no longer wanting to flee, the men holding Scarlett released her and stepped back. Their leader straightened from his crouch and stepped around their stash to come before the shaking princess. "I am sure we will enjoy this nicely, Royal. Bring out the other gals, boys! Let's have us a grand old time!"

Scarlett was too far gone to notice the other women and two young boys the group drug into the room and induced with Shinning. All of them became lost in the shaking desires that consumed them. Yet, somewhere in the depths of the princess's mind, she thought she came over the thought: *Stars, help me!*

* * *

It was so disgusting. He could not believe his eyes. "This is a bloody war, not a game! Is this really what the surface has become? Squabbling dogs and mindless fools! And Shinning? I can think of no words vile enough! It's disgraceful!"

"Are you just going to watch, seivier?"

"No, Shathahel, I will not. Thank you for bringing my attention to this abhorrence."

Shathahel turned his lifeless eyes on the Las'wa master. "I would join you in their retribution but I know you will make short work of them. I do beg hope that the girl and the others will be all right."

The seivier had already left the blind master's side. He ghosted through the run-down building to the right of the drugged party and crossed around the large span to the threshold between the two buildings. The sounds of the men taking the women made the master's blood boil, and he tightened the grip of his weapon. He forced himself to pause and try to calm himself despite the fury that coursed through him at the horrible offense of the intoxicated men on their victims. Mind focused, the seivier swung around, releasing the tail of his slender weapon and charged into the room. The Honored's group was too drugged up on spice to realize the danger entering their premises. Had the seivier felt any pity of them, he would have at least prolonged his killing of them until they had noticed him, but he was too disgusted to be so kind. In a matter of lashes, all of the Honored's men had been torn from their victims' bodies and ripped apart by the sharp scales of the preshair weapon. Drugged moans and panting filled the room as the fleeting echo of the preshair whip disappeared.

"I sense you were angry at them." Shathahel's voice drifted into the small area. "And here you were the one to teach against such feelings. Not that I can blame you…"

The seivier sucked in his breath and left the bleeding body of the final man. "Will they be all right?" His worry cut through his heat-misted mind.

"Yes." Shathahel answered as he huddled over one of the victims. "This serum should make quick work of the hold of the spice on their minds. Unfortunately, I can do nothing against the horror they will recall."

"It is enough for now." The Las'wa came to kneel beside the old master as the man finished giving the serum to Scarlett. "She looks so like my Zan." He muttered as he gently picked up the princess and hugged her to his chest.

"Indeed." Shathahel agreed. "Stay with her as she comes to. I am afraid she may react violently as the effects wear off."

Violent seemed to be an understatement. Scarlett started screaming and trying to claw at her flesh as she thrashed about in the Lakean master's arms. He clung to her tightly, fighting back his tears as much as he fought against the anguish Scarlett displayed. The entire episode lasted ten agonizing minutes. Finally, Scarlett let go one last tear-filled whimper and stilled in the seivier's arms. The other victims' screams stilled as well, and, in unison, the group of them sank to the floor exhausted and traumatized.

The Lakean looked down at the princess in his arms, shaking back the feeling that it could have been Zanishiria drug-induced and victimized. "I am so sorry." He croaked out, tears in his eyes.

Scarlett opened her dark brown eyes to stare up at the seivier "I—I remember you…" She murmured through bloodied lips. "Thank you…. for stopping…." The thought of what had been done to her froze the final words in her mouth.

"It is okay, young Novastone. You are safe now."

Scarlett's haunted eyes told that everything would not be okay but she trusted the Lakean master enough to close her eyes into an exhausted sleep.

"I have a place to harbor these people and assassins enough to handle moving and protecting them. You should go." Shathahel laid a hand on the seivier's shoulder as the other master gently lowered Scarlett to the stone floor and covered her with his master's cloak.

"You will go free Lapsair?"

"I have full confidence that King Lapsair can leave his imprisonment whenever he chooses. But, for you, I will check on him."

"Thank you, Shathahel."

The blind master waved away the compliment. "I have no need to hear gratitude while this war rages on around me. Go, Tyracor!" He slammed a finger squarely on the Lakean's broad chest. "Zanishiria may not fare well, I fear. The hours have passed too long to give me any hope of her success. If her fight reaches into the evening, I'm afraid she will die."

Chapter Thirty-One

"We feared as Prince Xi took more and more power for himself in Obseen's councils. Yet, it has not been uncommon for a Royal or two to make deep allegiances with the assassins, so we decided to dismiss the matter—thinking it would settle itself in its own time. All of us on Planet X turned our attentions elsewhere, to trade with the UEF, Al Tor, and the Sentinals. Even Rhône, the capitol and the prince's birth place, turned a blind eye to Xi's actions as he chose a life of a Royal-assassin.

"Too late, we realized the prince had loftier goals than training with assassins and entertaining their leaders. The murder of King Xi—later linked to his son—created an enormous uproar in our Royal ranks, for suddenly our head of sovereignty was replaced by his young, unproven son. Unproven, we found, only in title. Prince Xi may have lacked experience of years but his ambition to "rule over our neighboring prisoners" was cast starkly into the light. Faster than we had thought possible, the prince had pulled around himself very powerful supporters, Royal and assassin alike. There was no way to counter his quick succession.

"In the span of six weeks, Prince Xi had ultimate control of Obseen and the use of the most dangerous assassins in the system. He told the Royal families here on Planet X we were not his aim to control, but we found no way to counter his hold on either planet. Resistance proved to be a silent, untimely death.

"It seemed there would be no overturning newly acclaimed Emperor Manscor; however, there were assassins who would not stand for Prince Xi's final assertion of power (they never seemed the types to be pushed around so easily anyhow). The war started soon after that…

"Eleven years later and we are all still at war with Emperor Manscor. We, the Royals, find it hard to participate to our full desires against this maliciousness, but we support the Renegades as much as we can. Though I fear we cannot take this war much longer. The assassins have claimed they can destroy the emperor this time. I pray that they do. None of us—Royal or assassin—can afford to fight Emperor Manscor forever."

--Royal Lomont Laquen

"You should have killed me when you had the chance."

Zanishiria eyed the bedraggled emperor coolly from her chosen perch on a false mound exactly twelve paces from her enemy's resting place. "And become as callous as you? I think not, man killer. Mercy may seem a foolish choice but at least I live with a clear conscious." The Lakean youth fingered her most precious weapon's leather hilt absentmindedly, unaware that her face had turned grim as she thought of what opportunity she had lost by taking the higher road. "Besides, I have not had the chance to fight you decently since you took woozy with fatigue and blood loss. You weren't worth a fight over Obseen in your delirious state."

The emperor shifted himself to a stiff, bent-over position against the wall, taking note of Tarin for the first time, as the young Neitiege glided to his side with medicine and drink. Manscor noticed that Tarin scowled at Zanishiria's remarked and kept a hand near his katana. *Have the two friends had a falling out? Excellent!* "You are an arrogant bitch, you know that?" He replied to the girl's comments and took a sip of the strong, medicinal tea. "Kindness in war is a false act. You could have ended your people's suffering by slitting my throat as I lay unconscious."

"As if I did not think of that." Zanishiria hissed.

The emperor watched her dark, stone-like grey eyes slide to Tarin. *So, she had stayed her hand because of him?* Hm, Tarin Saerric seemed more useful than he had deemed. But, first, he had to deal with this smart-mouthed kid the Renegades had sent him. Ze'is Coursay'sora's daughter would learn why it didn't pay to follow her father's ideals. "You will not live passed this last mistake, Las'wa. Killing me when you were given the chance should have been your only priority."

A strange look ghosted over the fourteen-year-old's beautiful face and, surprisingly, was followed by a small, considerate nod. "Indeed, Manscor, you could be right, but…I never intended to live through killing you—only to take you with me. You are the only one with everything to lose."

Her words made Manscor go cold. *So, she could be the deadliest assassin he had ever had to fight?!* Most lived for an ideal or themselves or another person. She had only lived to kill him. He had not thought that possible in Zanishiria Novastone. She seemed too arrogant, too stalwart to the Renegade's cause to dismiss everything so easily. However, the girl had lost all the family she had ever known and—possibly from Eric's words— lost her clan as well. *In that way, are all the losses why she feels she could let it all go fighting me? Yet...what about the young man?* Did Zanishiria have any hold on this world because of him or was that, too, now lost with the change to their friendship?

Sobered, Emperor Manscor stood up slowly, realizing (miraculously!) that his wounds had closed over in a healing quicker than he had ever seen before. Pushing the odd thought away, he shoved the porcelain cup back into Tarin's hands and limped away to the closed doors of the fighting room. He felt Zanishiria's intense eyes stay on him the entire length of the floor. "Tarin!" He barked out. The tall, blond-haired youth hurried to his call and bowed. "How long have I been out and what is the time?"

"It is twelve-passed-one, Majesty, ah, fourteenth hour, standard day. You have been unconscious since two-fifty, second hour this morning. Your Royal guard have been engaged with the Renegades since dawn. They are pushed back to the square." Tarin sounded odd with his precise, military-like correspondence; nevertheless, the accuracy was very informative.

Soon now, my Honoreds will crush the Renegades. Let them think they have won. Zanishiria had already turned the tides against them by keeping me alive. They will soon learn. "Good. You have served me well, Tarin, for healing me of my injuries and guarding me. You will be justly rewarded when this war is over. Now, though, I must finish my "appointment" with Zanishiria."

"Let me fight in your place, Majesty." Tarin begged, bowing his taller height to below the emperor's in respect.

"I cannot allow that, as you well know. Our fight had already been claimed. Just continue your duty as my witness. That is enough." The emperor turned away from the Neitiege and thumbed his bloodied fingers against a panel on the wall. The ground began to shake. In less than a minute, the entire fighting square had restored itself to its original marbled surface. Satisfied, Manscor faced Zanishiria, who had leapt away from her perch as it had shifted and disappeared. She stood in ready position, meeting his stare with her own. "Today will be your last, se$f$(a)."

"You know, man killer," Zanishiria echoed tonelessly, "That line has gotten a little old these past hours. Especially since it was me, not you, watching the other person sleep from hitting his head." She almost said "it's embarrassing" but refrained from the sarcastic remark. Deeply, she knew she was tired of the wise-crack banter she and the emperor exchanged. And, had she known their duel would take so long—yes, partly due to her stubbornness for fairness and honor—she was not sure she would have pursued it so badly; though, she was glad to be fighting one man instead of using her preshair whip to slaughter hundreds of assassins and guards loyal to Manscor.

Manscor just stood studying the young assassin, allowing the time to pass by in quiet. Tarin shuffled behind the emperor, feeling the rising tension between the two fighters. Finding the sound distracting, the emperor lifted his right hand to wave the young man to his side. Still keeping his eyes on the Lakean, he said, "Tarin, return to your watch. Keep an eye on the sun. I fear this bout could continue into the evening. If this duel is not decided by then, I give you leave to end this fight." Tarin's blue eyes widened in surprise. He would have to decide whom to kill: the emperor or Zanishiria, if the time came? Manscor would not be trusting him with the task unless he believed Tarin was capable of killing his friend. Without a word, the young Stikes bowed and padded away. Manscor returned his attention to Zanishiria, forgetting Tarin completely. He didn't really trust that Tarin would be able to make the "killing blow" to his so-called friend. In fact, he intended to end the battle before that point. If possible.

A flourish of the emperor's wrist dropped a hidden Royal dagger into his right hand. He hid the movement by using his hand to wave Zanishiria back out to the center of the enormous training room "Sèp?" ["Again?" Suez]

"Crey." ["Yes."] Zanishiria stepped warily in the indicated direction, keeping a cautious eye on the Royal-assassin.

The emperor walked close to a discarded weapon as they neared the center and crouched down to grasp the hilt of his favorite kaskara. "I see you retrieved your weapons while I was out. A pity you did not have the sense to collect mine for yourself as well." *Not that I mind.* Zanishiria deferred to not say anything, her eyes looking dull. The emperor could have crowed in victory had it not been that just minutes before Zanishiria had smarted off. "If you are tired, Novastone, I could end this for you right now. Just think of all the pain you'd be spared."

Zanishiria rose her hands in a defensive fighting stance, her palms open and facing each other. She did not reach for a weapon, though it was obvious she was not unskilled in hand-to-hand combat. "You know I refuse. Stop blathering and fight me."

The ruler grinned at the girl's growl and shifted his kaskara in response. "Very well." He rocked back a moment, setting his sword for a forward strike, and strode into Zanishiria's range. His pace showed caution but his young opponent refused to be baited in.

Manscor closed suddenly, hissing viciously as he changed the angle of his blade. Zanishiria lifted her left arm to block, using her preshair snakeskin wrist-guards as a shield. Her arm continued in a circle, directing his thrust away as she brought up her other hand in a quick strike to his neck. Manscor saw the move and brought up his hidden dagger to block. The Las'wa barely registered the weapon before her open-handed knife-punch collided with the metal. Seeing the blade out of the corner of her eye, however, had her reflexively rolling her hand around it to avoid losing the limb, but the dagger still bit deeply into her palm. She hissed and let loose with an automatic knee to Manscor's groin and reversed her injured hand to grasp the emperor's wrist, twisting it hard enough to make him drop his knife. The move was quick enough that she managed to block Manscor's next kaskara attack without missing a beat.

The emperor found Zanishiria too close for a good sword thrust; however, having a double-bladed weapon allowed him different angles than a regular sword. The Lakean knew it too. Manscor used the swing Zanishiria had forced him to make to forcefully bring the blade back at the youth's face. He expected her block, using the momentum to arc his blade around her wrist guard to her now-exposed abdomen. Unexpectedly, though, Zanishiria fell onto her back, having realized her defensive crossed-hands push had left her open; she used the energy of her upward thrust to leave herself off-balance. She rolled away as soon as her back brushed the floor. As the assassin-girl found her feet again, she released the hand blades in her wrist guards and flashed them threateningly at the emperor before jumping back toward him.

The kaskara and preshair scales clashed off each other, the sound reverberating off the stone walls of the room. They continued to scrape endlessly as Zanishiria kept up a steady, forward-arching advance against the double-bladed sword. Manscor found himself forced backward many paces as the Las'wa stuck to him and never once left him an opening. By the time she finally receded the attack, the emperor had been pushed back ten meters.

Manscor paused, slightly out of breath, and let the girl retreat. A quick inspection of his sword showed the leader why she had jumped away: one whole side of his kaskara had been hacked away by the preshair weapons, leaving it completely trashed and blunted. Only the other side was useful—but not by a lot. "Ingenious weapon but completely useless use of your energy." Manscor turned to his opponent and began to say more, however, Zanishiria was suddenly upon him again, her arms already striking with unbelievably quick attack patterns. The Royal-assassin found himself too busy defending himself to worry about the damage the young assassin was inflicting on his kaskara.

Once the intense barrage stopped, Manscor knew his sword was dead. Compared to the sharp preshair scales, it was just a piece of scrap metal. Unnerved, the emperor dove onto the closest weapon to himself, trading the kaskara for a halbert. Zanishiria looked at him boredly, her eyes almost rolling and she set herself up for a longer-ranged duel. "Delaying the inevitable. This is becoming a joke."

"The only joke will be when I kill you in the end."

"Humor me then and kill me already!"

Chapter Thirty-Two

It is very rare to let duels go over five hours; indeed, those that do are usually in the cost of both fighters lives. Even rarer still are individual fighters who let a duel lapse longer than thirty minutes before fighting again or declaring victory. For Zanishiria to have let the knocked-out emperor sleep three hours, then, was unprecedented in Guild history—of course none of the Guild became aware of this fact until nearly four years later, when the truth came out to Master Quinn. Had the young assassin not stayed her hand, the Royals' War would have ended much sooner, as it was more lives were lost...

Yet, in the face of war, to have shown such integrity in a time of war also gave rise to a new standard of warfare, one that honored and respected life over all else. To have set such a standard when Emperor Manscor had shown none for nearly twelve years was a new and triumphant cry for what Obseen was wishing to usher into a new year. Yet, the cost of such fairness came at a high price...

They really did not want to die. At least, not this way. Yet, it seemed the Royal guards kept coming, wave on wave, never ceasing. When one battalion was held off and hacked down, another seemed to appear out of nowhere, coming at the individual Renegade groups from new directions. Somehow, someway, the Royal guard had surrounded the different parties and were choking them off. It seemed the battle had turned for the Renegades—for the worst.

"Stay closer to the prince!" Seircor ordered his small compadre as the number of guards increased. "By any costs, Prince Anmero must stay alive."

The Torez brothers paced the small perimeter the group of young men held, their shocking white hair falling untidily around their sweat-dropped faces. Both breathed hard, yet continued their well-kept vigil against the pressing forces. Their use of telepathy had quickly earned the respect of their fellow fighters—both working overtime to alert their companions to any dangers, as well as keeping their minds at the on-going task of defending themselves.

Shane Sinhail and Coryu Evalaus had quickly learned to comply to the orders of the Xsorian brothers and to Seircor as well, taking up the rear defense against the enemy attack. With the Royal guards always changing the direction of their assault, none of the young men had had a break from the action, and both Shane and Coryu were as sweaty and overworked as the Torezes. Only their pride and dislike of each other kept them from showing how exhausted they really were.

Flanking Anmero, taking points right and left, were the two more scholarly-type assassins, Seircor and K'sho. They stayed closer to the prince, not for the fact that Anmero was less skilled in combat, but more because of the oaths of protection they had given toward the chestnut-haired prince. Seircor defended Anmero because of his promise to Zanishiria; K'sho because he found he deeply respected the young Royal.

Suddenly, Coryu barked out an excited cry, his exhaustion vanishing from his face. "The emperor's morta! She comes."

The group of youths turned their attention to where Coryu looked. Indeed, Teera Sabina was striding though the bloody mess on the street a block away from them. Her Royal guards immediately cleared the path she wove through leaving a small space for their leader and her Honoreds. The emperor's prized assassins making short work of the Renegades that turned to face them.

"This is not good." K'sho muttered, whipping sweat from his brow. "We may not be a match for that."

"Agreed." Page answered through his teeth as he slashed out at another wave of guards. Lap was beside him in an instant to help keep back the new flood of enemies. The two Xsorians increased their efforts, giving their companions time to think through on what was coming for them. Page found a short reprieve and yelled back to Seircor, "Quick! Find an opening to take the prince away from here! Teera will target him."

"Away?" Coryu growled as he pushed passed the brothers, his creeshts sword hacking away at the enemy throng. "They can, for the prince of course, but I want Sabina. She will be dead by nightfall."

Page started to protest the Lakean's lust for revenge but Seircor voiced out to leave Coryu to his own path. "Yes, we will cover your retreat. Pull Anmero back before Teera sees him."

"Too late." Shane pronounced, stepping up closer to the others. "Prepare yourselves. We will have to fight the Honoreds."

* * *

"We see him, Honored One." One of Teera's assassins hissed, a pleased smile of his Suez face as he hacked down another Renegade.

"Hm." Teera grinned maliciously and swung her sapphire scepter across the face of an enemy. The man fell down beside her, his bloodied, broken face blank in death. "If I can't have Qusairo, his son will do nicely. And, the bastard is only protected by six youths! This will be easy." The ten Honoreds with Teera sneered and stalked forward like a pack of hunting vulgs. *[From Edis'daln, wild dog-like creatures]*

It was passing noon and the two assassins got up, finding they could not force their tired bodies to sleep over-long while their comrades fought. To their surprise, Asilisa Doz was sitting composed by a small table laden down with food and refreshment. The kind, Royal woman had them come, waving them to seats beside her. Dǎveed and Kee'van were too respectful—and too hungry—to tell her "no".

"I understand you both wish to be back out helping your people, yet my husband wished you to rest and eat first."

"We understand, Royal Doz, and thank you for this repast."

Asilisa smiled at Kee'van and smoothly reached for the teapot to fill his drained cup before the Xsorian could do it himself. "I am happy to assist you." She paused to also fill Dǎveed's cup. A few minutes passed in peaceful silence, then a bodyguard dipped his head into the tent and motioned to Asilisa. She excused herself, getting up gracefully to receive her man's news. Dǎveed and Kee'van shared a glance but continued to eat. Asilisa returned shortly after they finished, her delicate, red lips persed tightly.

The Tà sharay's con'trore waited until she was seated stiffly before asking what was wrong. The look he received for the Royal woman looked pained. "Are Qusairo and the Tà sharay all right?"

'They are fine." She answered tersely and shook her head as if to rid it of an unsavory scene. Kee'van refrained from reaching out with his mind to see what she knew. "My men caught an Honored; the man has claimed he was bringing m a message from Teera Sabina." Asilisa choked and had to compose herself. The two men glanced at each other wondering what she was leaving out. "It's Raynward. He's—." She couldn't finish. "Go see for yourselves."

Something felt wrong. Dăveed and Kee'van were quick to investigate, their sudden feeling of foreboding prompting them to action. The guard assassin that had alerted Asilisa to the issue did not look surprised to find the two men asking to meet the Honored; though, his face looked just as strained as his Royal master's.

The Honored had been placed in the hind-most tent, far from Asilisa. His sharp, striking countenance mirrored his enemy's, the sad look carrying into his deep-blue eyes. Dăveed and Kee'van were taken back at his expression—to say the least.

"What message do you carry from Teera Sabina?" Kee'van asked, stepping into a role of leadership.

The dark-haired man looked cautiously at the con'trore. "Con'trore Kee'van, Dăveed Quinn," The man began shocking them with a courteous bow. "I am Davin, personal assistant to Honored One Master Teera. She sent me here with malicious intentions—ones I wish not to reproduce."

Kee'van's eyes narrowed "All right, go on."

Davin paused, his attention switching to a large object, covered over by a cloth, across the room. The two assassins followed his gaze. "Teera wishes to spit in your faces." He stated, his words suddenly bold, then his voice changed to sadness. "But, I'm afraid all her actions do are create anger and grief. Your man suffered long under her hand."

"Our man?" Kee'van asked. He was too cautious to look under the cloth himself, knowing that there would be a body underneath. His light-green eyes watched balefully as Dăveed Quinn hesitantly walked over to the covered corpse and pulled back the cloth. The assassin's body froze at the sight. Then, it began to shake. "That was too cruel." He whispered.

Kee'van heard Dăveed's anguished voice in his head as the young man cried out the person's name. "Raynward." He repeated woodenly. He could feel from the reflection of Dăveed's mind just how badly the man had been tortured before death. He became intoxicated in the overwhelming anguish and anger of Dăveed's emotions; the feelings surging up in him from the sharing were barely containable. He wanted to rip Davin to pieces. Davin seemed to know what the sudden glint in the Xsorian's eyes was about for he opened his arms wide, palms open and inviting. He did not speak out loud but voiced his thoughts to the other assassin. "Go ahead. If it would help you. I have suffered enough having to watch Teera kill her victims so maliciously. Death would be welcome. It's the least I deserve after not stopping her from her atrocities."

"My anger isn't for you." Kee'van managed to say through a tight jaw. "We are grateful that we can at least give Raynward a proper burial."

Dăveed was quick to his feet, his father's preshair dagger in his hand. For a moment, Davin was sure his life was forfeit, but Quinn just stalked on by him and out of the tent. Clearly, the young Baras had a different target in mind.

Con'trore Kee'van watched the younger assassin leave, having the image of a hackles-raised bloodhound in mind at Quinn's angry retreat. He turned back to Davin, his emotions calmer now that he wasn't being influenced by his companion's feelings. "I regret the circumstances that we had to meet Davin. I am sure our paths will cross again. I do not believe any harm will come to you if you be respectful."

"Thank you." Davin bowed as the Xsorian turned away.

Kee'van left the tent and Honored behind, hurrying back to Asilisa's tent. The Royal was still there, sitting stiffly by their lunch, her eyes following Dăveed as he was shoving weapons into their sheaths on his person. She was too disturbed by the grizzly sight of Raynward's body to stop the seething assassin.

"There is no conceivable way for you to reach Master Teera in time to assort your revenge. She will either be conquered by them or our side will have been slaughtered."

Quinn glared at the Xsorian and continued preparing himself for combat. "I don't care just as long as I take a whole bunch of her crips with me. They are as much to blame for the massacre as she is. I will reach Teera if I can, but I will definitely take down some of her pawns."

Kee'van sighed, relieved that Asilisa could not hear any of Dǎveed's words. "Fine, you do that, Quinn. I, however, have only the desire to protect the Tà sharay. I have been too long from his side as it is."

Dǎveed stopped his furious preparations as if he finally remembered himself. "Royal Qusairo." He murmured and cast his eyes to the leader's wife still in the room. Quinn turned to her and dropped to his knees in front of her. "I apologize, my lady. I will go to Royal Qusairo and defend him from more of Teera's wrath."

Finally, Asilisa Doz let go a tiny, grateful smile. "My thanks, young Quinn." She reached out with a hand to clasp the assassin's thoughtfully. "Be well, and, please," her voice came out softly. "Protect my husband without extracting revenge. There is enough bloodshed as it is."

Dǎveed bowed his head to hide the shame in his eyes. He had been thinking of revenge, but for the sweet, honest lady before him, he would try not to. "Lady. I will do my best for your husband."

"I know you will."

"Surround them." Teera ordered her Honoreds. They hurried to fan out across the street, covering any retreat Prince Anmero's group would have had. All of the assassins lifted their weapons, flashing them threateningly.

A dark-haired youth stepped forward to challenge Teera's group. The Honored-One could have laughed; he was a Lakean, she had no doubt. "You're mine." Coryu growled at Teera.

Sabina rolled her eyes and rose her scepter. Her twenty warriors tensed and waited to be released. "Kill them all, but leave me this one. He seems to want personal attention."

The Honoreds crowed and launched at the seven youths.

* * *

Anmero gulped, though his throat was too dry to push any moisture down, and thumbed the creeshts sword Seircor has given him. The tall Lakean laid a comforting hand on his arm before repositioning himself between the prince and the Honoreds.

"We will protect you." K'sho promised from Anmero's other side. The Sinya readied his two kodachis. "Brace…here they come."

Page and Lap stepped into the Honoreds' path to give the others time to prepare. "Brother, let only the less trained Honoreds through."

"Agreed."

The Honoreds attacked from both directions, but much to their shock, the two Xsorians kept them from Anmero Doz quite effectively. The two white-haired brothers seemed to be everywhere at once, weaving through the enemy assassins as if in a choreographed dance. Only two Honoreds were allowed through their perimeter.

"Our turn." K'sho muttered and stepped forward to engage the Suez assassin before him. Seircor did the same, though he kept a closer distance to Anmero, just in case. The two Honoreds were dispatched with unexpected ease, as were the next two the Torez brothers allowed to pass. The last six Honoreds were not to be as easily baited, however. Seeing that the assassins they fought were skilled, the others were cautious to take on the Xsorians. These were the top of Teera's elite. They harried the Torezes until two passed by, not bidden by Page or Lap. As these clashed with the other two fighters, the four of the group (Lap, Page, Seircor, and K'sho) realized they could possibly be outmatched. These Honoreds were quite experienced. In slight apprehension, the prince's protectors knew that they had to outlast the Honoreds, not necessarily outfight them. The losers would be the ones that dropped their guard first.

* * *

Teera sneered at Coryu and baited the Lakean away from the others. "What a joy this is! I love murdering your kind." She continued when an angry flash sparked across Coryu's grey eyes. "Like all those pathetic crips I hunted down last year." She chuckled. "Those nine ran like scared little curs flushed out of their holes. They made such easy targets…and that wretched girl certainly didn't try to live when we captured her. She died screaming."

The last sentences elicited a curse from the Las'wa. "Lai bi'ek trai morta!" He hissed and leveled his creeshts sword at Teera.

The Honored One just grinned her predatory smile and let the Lakean advance toward her.

Chapter Thirty-Three

In the third year of Manscor's reign, a group of Royals and assassins came to the emperor and pledged their undying loyalty. Among them was an ambitious Suez woman, Teera Sabina. The emperor grew to love this woman over all of his subjects, finding her cutthroat approach useful against the opposing factions, and her passion for him kept her well within his grasp.

The Suez, Koresheans, Shynor, and Haukmen high-clans were quick to join the emperor's regime because of Teera Sabina's influence. Not only was Master Teera well-known to these clans, she was backed by the most powerful leaders of Obseen—at least at the time. There was little doubt that they, as well as many lower clans, would benefit from following such an influential assassin leader.

The sudden support to Master Teera and Manscor left the emperor no lack of highly trained assassins. At once, the group of Honoreds was created from those assassins Master Teera deemed skilled enough to serve directly under herself and the ruler. Sabina was assured her mighty leader would have no more fear of enemy assassins coming to disrupt his reign, as long as she had the support of the high-clans...

The hours had stretched on into a never-ending haze of fighting and bloodshed. It seemed as if there was no end to the push of Royal guards into the square, and Royal Qusairo's main force found itself somehow cut off from Major Calamas's smaller army. The only comfort to the Renegade's exhausted army was that the Tà sharay's con'stól and some of Shy'ree's Lakean warriors were still fighting hard beside them.

"This is taking too long." Qusairo panted to Khan Torez and ducked at a shuriken thrown his way "The sun is near to setting and we are no closer to the emperor. My men cannot last another day of this."

The Tà sharay batted aside more of the sharp knives thrown at the Royal and shouted an order to his con'stól. He, too, was getting tired but knew his men were in much better shape than his Royal friend's. Unfortunately, he also knew thirty con'stól members and twelve Las'wa could not hold back the flow of Royal guards, should more of Qusairo's men fall. "Your men will fight as long as they need, Royal Qusairo. Even now, though exhaustion fills them, they fight with all they have. I feel their conviction. As long as you stand tall, they will continue to fight."

Qusairo cursed beside the white-haired Xsorian and buckled down to a knee, his hand on a new wound at his neck. Khan was quick to cover his fellow comrade, calling the Royal's protector from the front line of their held circle. Shy'ree was immediately beside her leader, a salve from her clan already in hand. Khan Torez blocked more projectiles before stepping back closer to Qusairo. "My friend?"

The Royal waved Shy'ree's fussing hands off and tried to stand, saying, "I am fine, go back to fighting."

The Tà sharay knew better. He could feel how badly wounded the other man was. He also felt the Royal start to collapse and grabbed Qusairo's arm to keep him from falling. "Shy'ree!" He ordered the Las'wa woman to take hold of her leader. "We are but thirty paces from the Royal entrance of Taysor Palace. It is risky, but the ground there makes for a better stand than this completely open ground. My con'stól will force our way through. Your people will help the army push through to the space we create. I want to feel Taysor Palace's walls at our backs."

Khan was already issuing orders to his men and the army, not waiting to see how the Lakeans were handling the sudden pressure on them. His Xsorians worked quickly to push the Royal guards away. What holes they left behind them were filled in by the Renegade army. "Keep pushing! Fifteen paces to go!" The Tà sharay and his telepathic assassin warriors seemed to be everywhere at once, blocking weapons with an extraordinary grace and fury. The enemy guards had no choice but to give the ground the Renegades wanted.

* * *

"Over here. We should be able to reach the rooftops without the guards seeing us." Dăveed Quinn motioned Kee'van to one of the taller buildings around the Royal palace. He and the con'trore had sprinted all the way from Asilisa's encampment to the deserted southern section of Taysor. Once they had entered the city limits, they had slowed their pace to a cautious trot. Dǎveed, being more familiar with the city, had led the way toward the Taysor Palace; however, he had only been able to get them within three blocks of the enormous building before the large number of guards had forced them to find cover. "We should be able to cross the roofs until the square. I would like to think our people have gotten that far."

Kee'van searched ahead with his mind and replied with assurance. "They are to the very walls of the palace, but seem to be barely holding their position. I sense they fare poorly."

Davie felt his gut turn to ice. "I hope you're wrong." He whispered and rushed up the building's stairs. The rooftops were empty, all of them stretching out in identical, obsidian blacktops to the square.

"We can jump from roof to roof." Kee'van continued, pulling our two grappling guns and handed one to the Baras. "In case the spans too big, we can glide across."

Dǎveed nodded. They both sprinted toward the next roof and jumped.

* * *

"Major, sir." An assassin ran up to Major Calamas and bowed quickly. "We have spotted Royal Qusairo and his men across the square. They look to be in distress."

"Distress?" Major Calamas bashed his way to a safer area, dragging his messenger with him. "Numbers man, positions! Please, tell me our leader is okay." Before the man could answer Berris Tearrì and her husband came pushing through the mass of fighters. They, too, had come from the front lines. "Berris, Berzén, word on Royal Qusairo?"

"Sa." Tearrì nodded, her eyes flashing a fiery blue. "He and the Tà sharay have pushed themselves to the palace walls. A good place for a last stand, but their men falter. Qusairo does not seem well. With us separated, it had strained his men too much."

"We can force our way to him." Tyre interrupted. "It is only two hundred paces to the edge of the square, four hundred after that. The Trayshans can hack our way through, your men following."

Tearrì continued, "The loss of men of Qusairo's front would require such tenacity from us; however, there will be many casualties on our side."

"Few enough for us to save Royal Qusairo?"

Tyre nodded grimly. "If nothing else we will be a great distraction. Maybe those bastards will leave off Qusairo enough for them to recover some ground."

The three leaders looked amongst themselves as if seeing if one of themselves had a different opinion. None spoke. "Okay then," Major Calamas sighed in acceptance, "After you."

* * *

"Keep down and come slowly." Kee'van cautioned Dăveed as he waved the younger man forward. "There seems to be some watcher in the buildings to our right."

Dăveed nodded and crawled forward to the Xsorian's side. "We can see the whole square from here. Look, Qusairo's by the main Royal entrance. Damn, their group seems to be half-sized!"

"They are holding, though." Kee'van assured Quinn. "Quiet for a minute and I will try to reach the Tà sharay." The con'trore was already extending his mind to his leader, trying to carefully touch the Xsorian's mind without distracting him. But, the Tà sharay was too preoccupied trying to protect Qusairo to pay heed to a mind-touch. "There is no way to contact him without forcing myself into his mind—and I won't do that with the fighting."

"But are the others okay?" Dăveed was worried to see a slight swoon in his leader's stand, and the diminishing numbers of Renegade fighters alarmed him.

"They are faring." Kee'van avoided the question. "Let me see if there is a way for us to reach the Tà sharay."

"No" The Baras reached for Kee'van's hand to stop him. "We won't be able to get through that mass." He paused to think. "You mentioned a "watcher"? A sniper, you think?"

Kee'van was already searching, having caught Quinn's question before it was out of his mouth. "Hm…perhaps, though it's rare for the Royal guards to have snipers—yet…" He narrowed his light green eyes as his mind touched the other person's mind. "He is an Honored. He had a Royal, long-range rifle. There are others…" Kee'van paused again to search for the other presences. "Yes, three others. They are set up to shoot at our men in ten minutes."

"Ten." The implications hit the two assassins. "Tell me where. We can take them out before they fire."

"If we reach them in time." The con'trore pointed out where the four Honoreds were hidden. "You take the two to the left."

"Agreed." Neither mentioned to the other to hurry. They knew too well the direness of the situation if the Honoreds fired.

Dăveed hurried to the rooftop of his first target and clamped a cord to the stone. In seconds, he rolled over the side and repelled down to the nearest window. A quick, powerful swing smashed his lithe runner's body through the glass, and Dăveed recoiled the line as he jumped into the shards on the floor. "He better not have heard that through the noise below." Quinn muttered and crept through the hallway to the closest staircase. Two levels and five doorways down, Dăveed could hear the bored movement of the Honored as he waited for his instructed time to shoot. The man had not noticed Dăveed's presence, as of yet.

Dăveed tried to open the heavy, obsidian door slowly but the building was an older one and the floor had been ignored too long; there was no helping the scrapping of the stone on stone. Quinn silently cursed and readied his preshair dagger. The Honored had to have heard that.

Suddenly, the door was torn from Dăveed' grasp as the alerted assassin hurried to dispatch the intruder. The young Haukman that stood in front of Quinn, leveled his kusari at the Baras. The two enemies knew each other.

"Shigge Autaro."

The other man was not happy to see him. "Dăveed Quinn."

Chapter Thirty-Four

Master Teera is the most ruthless and exceptional pawn of Emperor Manscor's. At twenty, she caught the Royals' eye and became his link to the Assassins' Guild in Taysor... Having just finished her training at the center and procuring a position on the council as a Suez representative, she was the first to influence Prince Xi on his trail to becoming the most powerful man on Obseen. Needless to say, she was also quite power hungry herself and highly influential for creating the ripe environment for the Royal-assassin to take control of the Guild... Some, her loyal followers, would go so far as to say Teera Sabina is the one who created Manscor and his twelve-year reign...

"I will enjoy killing you, Lakean. Your kind has always been a thorn in our planet's side. My emperor was right not to let any of you join him."

"The only plague on this planet is you, morta."

Master Teera roared an amused laugh and swung her scepter around, as if testing its weight in her hands. "Your kind is always so defiant. It makes my victory that much more delicious."

Cour'eysan rolled his grey eyes and darted in with his sword, taking three testing strikes at the woman's defenses. Once he felt confident of his opponent's skills, he slipped out of her range again and circled her, a look as wild and as calculating as a creeshts' spiders on his face. Teera whirled on him and closed the distance, swiping her heavy weapon across her front guard. Coryu leapt cleanly away only to re-enter her space with an upward slash of his blade. He slipped to the right, Teera following, and thrust across and downward to block Teera's oncoming blow. His perry took him away from her again. He spun back to do a sweeping cross with his blade at Teera's ribs. She immediately blocked and thrust into his sternum, the sharp tip of her sapphire scepter glancing his breastbone. Coryu instinctively leapt out of her reach.

Teera lifted the sapphire tip to her face to smell Coryu's blood there. In haughty amusement, she licked the stones clean. "Delicious. Your blood is rich in anger and hate."

"Shév morta." ["Sick/disgusting"] Coryu muttered and came at a side attack to the Honored One. He kept a steady push to the next thrusts so that Teera had to keep leaping away from his sword. Coryu continued his advance by targeting her shoulders, neck, thighs, and back, always changing angles and positions around his enemy.

Teera seemed more amused than deterred by the Lakean's furious attacks. "Keep that up, se$f$(a), and you will get yourself killed by your own exhaustion."

Coryu ignored the comment, throwing seven darts. Most were easily deflected, but Teera was too slow tracking two of them. The sharp little blades bit deep into the Suez's thigh and right side. A hiss rose from the woman's lips; she was no longer amused by their game. Master Teera cursed and lunged at Coryu, placing herself well into his creeshts sword's range. The two enemies locked into a deadly dance of perries and thrusts. As they danced, Teera managed to push Coryu against the adjacent building but the Lakean youth kicked out, his heel connecting with his opponent's jaw and causing Teera's ear to ring. It stunned the master enough for Coryu to slip away from the stone wall and attack her from the right.

A bloody slash-mark bled down Teera's back. The Honored One roared and shouldered Coryu hard enough to knock him to the street. "For that you die a slow and painful death!" She brought the sapphire scepter down on Coryu's exposed skull.

Dazed, Coryu was unable to roll away from the next swipe of the Honored One's weapon. Blood started to pool underneath the Las'wa's head. His mind clouded with pain but he had the sense to raise his sword and slash blindly to fend her off. He wasn't sure what he hit but Teera screamed in her own pain and paused her attack. Coryu, however, was too occupied by the steady trickle of blood covering his temple and right eye to notice what he had done to his opponent. *It's so warm. So, this is what dying feels like in battle. I…came here to do something. What? I can't…remember. It's so warm…*

Someone cried over his fading body. "No! Cour'eysan, no!" But, Coryu was already drifting too far way to comprehend the words.

* * *

"Damn it!" Lap Torez hissed out as a lucky slash marked his cheek. The Honored that had blessed him with it grinned and jumped out of the Xsorian's range.

"Hang in there, brother." Page's calming voice commanded and two well-placed shuriken struck his brother's offender in the shoulder and neck, in payment for Lap's injury. The Honored's face contorted in pain and he spun away, grabbing at his throat.

"I will." Lap assured his older brother and stepped forward to block another Honored's sword thrust. "We outmatch this last fighter. Perhaps, you should help the others? I can take this one alone."

Page hesitated but could not really argue with his brother's logic. Besides, the other Honoreds were still pestering their friends too effectively. "Okay I will help Seircor. Yell if you have trouble." Page started to turn away to where their Lakean leader was engaged with the leader of Teera's Honoreds group.

Suddenly, Shane yelled out a warning.

Page snapped his head around to see one of the two Honoreds the Trayshan had been engaged with slip around the other fighter, who had effectively blocked Shane from countering the attack. "Anmero!" Page yelled in warning, instinctively throwing three shuriken at the enemy. He watched, as if in slow motion, as the weapons struck the assassin as he ran toward the prince, but, Page realized his throws had not deterred the man as he had hoped. The Tà sharid raced toward the prince knowing with a sinking feeling that he would not reach Anmero in time.

* * *

Shane Sinhail hissed at the sting of the wound the Honored before him gave him in his shoulder. He struck out blindly despite the pain and got the man to jump back and give him a few moments' relief. Blood trickled down his wounded arm, but the Trayshan was not aware of the damage inflicted to his person. He was pissed. His enemy had skillfully blocked him from stopping the other Honored. Shane had thought the two would stay with him until he was taken care of. He had been wrong.

They wanted Anmero Doz, the prince Shane stood behind trying to protect. There was no other target. Shane could have been a piece of rotting meat for all they cared; he was only an annoying obstacle. He realized it now—after the poignant fact.

"He dies." The Honored before Shane grinned. "And you will die with him for poor swordsmanship. It is a good reward for people with your insolence. Our emperor will be pleased."

"Not if you're dead." The Trayshan beynor growled and arced his traznic katana around the other's weapon. Shane dealt the arrogant man a glancing blow to his temple, watching as his sword spliced cleanly through his opponent's skull. He turned away before the body fell to the ground, his intense blue eyes already tracking the other Honored who had evaded him. He was already preparing to throw a dagger at the man's back before he had him fully in his azure sight.

Dăveed was quick to rush Shigge Autaro before the Haukman had time to register the preshair dagger in his hand. Shigge had always been slower at defensive exercises and Quinn was hoping to take advantage of his opponent's known weakness before the other could create an effective block. Shigge was true to form; Dăveed was upon him before the other raised his hands.

"I'm sorry." Dăveed murmured as he punched the younger man in the sternum and knocked the wind out of him. "I refuse to kill you." He continued saying to the stunned man. "But, I need you out of my army's hair until this fight is over." It was the closest he could come to apologizing to the Honored. Quickly, he bashed the hilt of his dagger against the man's temple and carefully laid the unconscious Haukman on the cold, stone floor.

Dăveed could physically feel the time counting down ten minutes. He wished to rush to his other target but caution persuaded him to take the time to pull apart the Royal rifle and thrown it across the room in pieces before he turned away. *In case he does wake*...Quinn reasoned and sprinted back the way he had come. He had six minutes left to reach the other

Honored—and a quarter of the way around the Terrís to get there.

* * *

"Qusairo!" Khan Torez urged the faltering leader to move behind him. "Qusairo I need you to keep conscious. Your army depends on it." The Tà sharay knew his words were in vain. The Royal's mind was slipping too easily from one tangled thought to another. It was hard to tell if the other leader even registered the Xsorian leader's voice. "Shy'ree, hold him up! I will keep the enemy weapons off of you. Try to get some sense back into him!"

"Kye mēk!" [I'm trying.] Shy'ree replied sharply as she pulled her leader behind the white-haired assassin. Without any gentleness, she threw Qusairo against the palace wall and rammed her body against his to keep it upright. Meanwhile, her hands were working furiously to administer what medicines she had left. There was not enough to stop her leader's bleeding and keep him conscious, but she made do as she could. "Lai'na è'ein. Shévé!" [We do not have time. He is dying!]

"Tai cam'ein. Shoar mēk'lai!" [We will make time. Keep trying!]

Shy'ree cursed and returned her attention to her fading leader. Khan Torez returned his attention to the fight at hand. The Renegade Army was in desperation, but he knew they could hang on longer. Somehow, Khan just knew that if they held on a little more, help would come. It was coming. The Tà sharay could feel the intensity from Major Calamas's forces some small distance away. They were aware of their leader's predicament. "Attack harder!" He ordered. The men around Khan Torez yelled the order and stepped up their intensity. Every one of the Renegades and Xsorian con'stól seemed to rally to the Tà sharay's confident command. *We will make it!*

* * *

"Renegades, listen up!" Tyre Sinhail commanded, his brazen voice carrying over the army to reach the volunteer fighters' ears. "You have all heard by now that Royal Qusairo is in need and that he and his men have taken ground at the Palace walls. We will go to him." The men were too on edge to cheer at their valiance. "It is over six hundred paces to where they are surrounded. Follow closely behind us. The Zair'ek is going to push you through to Qusairo." His final words brought the tired group to rally a call. Satisfied enough, Tyre turned to his wife and bowed his head. "After you, Berris. Your people will follow you wherever you lead."

Tearri's wild eyes blazed a fierce amber. Confidently, she turned and strode through her band of Trayshan warriors, aptly pulling her two ivory, metal-plated shortswords form their scabbards over her shoulder blades. "Come!"

A Trayshan war-chant resounded behind the Berris and Berzén as they marched toward the on-coming Royal guards. The looks on the guard's faces gave the smaller group courage; the brawn of the threatening Trayshan force was more than enough to instill fear in the enemy. The assassin-warriors were within the Royal guard in moments, hacking their way steadily through the ranks of scarlet-clad officers. Major Calamas's force followed closely, taking courage from their unwavering companions. Soon, the entire force was well into the thick of the guard. Only half the distance remained between Major Calamas's army and Qusairo's dwindling forces.

The two enemies were panting again—and bleeding all over the marbled floor. Zanishiria still looked the stronger, her young, athletic body shinning with sweat and blood. Opposing her, the emperor could feel a slight shake from fatigue in his limbs. He shook back the question of "why?" from his mind and repositioned himself in front of the Lakean. The Las'wa watched him coolly but made no move to counter the emperor's new stance.

Two hours had passed. The emperor was not happy about the fact. In one hour, the first of Obseen's three suns would begin setting. Even now, the slight cast of its yellow rays were lighting the large windows. It was getting too close to the time Manscor had given to Tarin to intercede in their fight. How could a girl last so long? All of the emperor's other opponents had fallen within hours of commencement.

"The Renegade Army is at your walls." Zanishiria stated suddenly.

Manscor started. The Lakean had said nothing at all since the beginning of their recent round, two hours prior. Her voice sounded low and wavered slightly in its tone. The words were correct, however. The sounds of battle were below the fighting room. Manscor forced back a wave of panic; there was still time for his Royal guards to push back the enemy hoard. "Are you implying that I will be overrun? I think you are sadly mistaken. If you were to look, you would know my forces still own the square."

Zanishiria lifted her chin, a spark of daring coming to her dulled eyes. "If you look."

The ruler was not going to take the false invitation in her words. "Tarin, report!" He commanded, eying Zanishiria warily—she could take advantage of any lack of attention he displayed.

Tarin's expression told the story before he spoke. "There is a fairly small Renegade force below us, Majesty. I would say about one hundred fighters at most. However," the words Manscor was hoping Tarin would not say, "There is a strong force of enemy fighters pushing across the square. About five hundred strong. The banner of Zair'ek is leading them." The emperor could have cursed. How did the Trayshan Berzén and Berris get passed his border guards? They could wreck enough havoc on their own.

"You will be overrun." Zanishiria almost smirked. Almost. "I could just keep you until they can have their way with you. Aiy? Yet...I would rather like to finish this. I have only been with you for thirteen hours, after all. It seems a waste to just give you up after all this time."

"As if toying with someone that long is even decent." Manscor grumbled.

Zanishiria cocked her head as if she had not heard the barely audible complaint though Manscor was certain she had. "Admitting such shows you believe you are already dead."

"After thirteen hours," the emperor exclaimed, "how can you still sound like an egotistical, philosophical wench? You're unbelievable!"

"After fifteen hours, how can you still be alive?" The look on the Las'wa girl's face was dark and carried just a hint of the exhaustion she refused to show. *How can I still be alive? I am so tired I could fall to sleep standing here. If he won't die soon, I am going to do something stupid—just as long as he dies with me. I would be okay with that. Maybe, I should die…I can't take much more of this.*

Manscor saw it: Zanishiria's attention was wavering. *She's good at acting but I am fairly certain she is close to the end of her abilities. I have rested, unlike her. If I play these next few minutes right, I could kill her.* Resolutely, Manscor breathed into his lower abdomen and centered himself. *This is an enemy I will not lose to. I will kill her!* Without outwardly showing it, the emperor readied himself for one final, resolved attack against the young assassin. Then, with as much force and speed as he could muster, he launched himself at Zanishiria.

Chapter Thirty-Five

A cold, premonition-airy draft scoured through the lighted city walls of Shairceeo lá Coursa. It wafted angrily into the halls and batted at the doors. Victoriously, it rammed itself passed Master Tyracor's ajar door and raced its feathery fingers over the book Shay'renor had left his apprentice. The pages turned and fluttered, finally stopping at the past passage the old master had written:

"Life had a light side and a dark; our world of relativity is composed of both. The tragedy of our lives are when we are dying inside—overwhelmed by our darkness—while still living without. Until we are truly committed to life, there is a chance for us to continue to draw back, to fall short of the edge that can save us. This one elementary truth is an ignorance that kills our light countless of times. Yet, there is hope still....For, one made of death may not reach the dawn save by the path of night. In this darkest hour of our souls, we can find who we are meant to be..."

Only minutes remained.

Dăveed Quinn could feel every second thunk away in his head. There were still five buildings to cross and he should have already begun entering the building the last sniper was in. "I may not make it..." He despaired but continued his run across the roof top. "I will make it!"

Quinn wished he knew how Kee'van faired, but the con'stól was Xsorian, the man better equipped for finding hidden enemies than he was. "He will be quicker than me. He may even be done." Dăveed collected that small hope and used it to push his tired body to its limits.

In what seemed too long a time, the young Baras reached the final building. He began his rappel only to realize the windows of the building had been shuttered, their thin sheet of stone locking him out. There was no time to look for another way. The time was too short and this building's face was much too expose; someone might have seen him running and could be sighting him in even now.

"The dagger!" Dăveed remembered suddenly as he hung beside the barring window. "Father said it could cut through anything." Quickly, he took the preshair dagger in his hand and angled the weapon calculatingly against the shutter's seem. "Please work!' He lifted his hand and drove the Lakean weapon home into the stone as hard as he could. It slid through the obsidian as easily as if it had been cream. Dăveed was in too much a hurry to be awed but he did thank the magnificent weapon as he sliced the stone apart. The severed shutters fell to the ground far below.

"Okay, then, now for the sniper." He muttered as he stepped safely onto the obsidian sill and into the room. "There may be time…"

* * *

The day had been long and boring for the Suez youth Tak'eth Sorēin had been tasked to sniping for his superior marksmanship skills, but he had not realized volunteering for the job would mean he had to endure long, lonely hours, while his blood boiled for the fight below him. Sorēin had a perfect view of the Terrís. He had seen it all—the formation of the Royal guard in the morning, the bloody start of the battle, the separating of the Renegades Army, and now the pack of enemies advancing on the smaller, nearly-defeated group.

"I should really make their efforts in vain." He muttered and checked his clock. "Two minutes. By then, the whole balance could change." With an unsure feeling—no one double-crossed the Honored One—he radioed the other snipers; however, only static met his attempts. "Taking "no comm silence" too literally." He complained and dropped his radio unceremoniously. ""One minute." He paused, still hesitant then shrugged. "They'll never care once this war is over. I'm going to take the shot."

Unerringly, he leveled his rifle, paused, and fired.

* * *

Dăveed heard the gunshot right as he stepped out of the room he had repelled into. "Damn it!" He rushed back to the window to look. There as too many fighters in the square to notice much, yet—yet!—the Tà sharay and his small con'stól looked more agitated than before. *They must have been shot at.*

Another shot went off. This one aimed at the advancing Trayshan group. An assassin went down.

Quinn cursed again and spun toward the door. *The Honored man must be stopped!* It was five doors down to where the snipper had been assigned. Dăveed made it there faster than he had ever run before. Tak'eth Sorēin was too caught up in his shooting to react to Dăveed's sudden bombardment. The Suez was out cold before he knew what had hit him.

But, for Dăveed, he knew he would always remember he had been too late.

"Qusairo!" Shy'ree sudden cry sounded strangled. The Tà sharay spun to the scene to see the burly Royal man collapse in the Lakean woman's arms. Khan already knew what had happened. "Sniper!" He shouted, his voice unnerving the fighters. No one liked snipers; they could shoot anywhere. Khan backed up to where Shy'ree huddled, to protect her from any weapons that may be shot her way. Another shot sang out, causing Khan to tense, but he felt the lazer had been aimed elsewhere—to one of Major Calamas's men.

The Trayshans were close. The Tà sharay could see them through the crowd. The shooting had not deterred them. It had to be the only good news of the battle. In silent relief, Khan waved the Trayshan leaders through his front lines, an enormous Renegade re-enforcement following.

Tearrì Sinhail came to Khan Torez bloodstained but victorious. "You looked to be in need."

"Ai'y. Qusairo," Khan started but Tearrì was already passed him, her eyes full of concern. The Tà sharay turned away to continue his guard.

Tyre Sinhail had been close enough to ear shot to hear the news. His brows were knit in worry but he didn't let the fact stop his vigil against the Royal guards. The tall, intimidating assassin-warrior yelled out to the rejoined Renegade army, ordering them to reorder themselves and attack their enemies. His presence was enough. The army regained its conviction and began to press back the Royal guards.

Khan Torez let the other leader take over, allowing himself to feel the fatigue and pains that he had kept at bay. *We may yet win this battle today.* But, sadness filled him then. *There are many casualties.* His mind drifted back to Shy'ree and the Berris, feeling their loss as strongly as his own. *We have lost too many good leaders to this war. I truly wish their lives are not in vain.*

But, even though the Tà sharay was standing in a calm vortex, the Royals' War raged on about him.

Prince Anmero felt his heart freeze as he turned to see the Honored assassin that raced toward him. The red-haired man had an evil glint in his eyes and a low snarl issuing from his mouth. The young prince had only seen a look like that once—when he had been cornered by a starved creatures back on M2. To see it in this man, this enemy, made his blood run cold.

"Anmero!"

Anmero watched as three shuriken were thrown wildly from Page's hand; that the Xsorian looked taken off-guard made the young Doz feel even more vulnerable. He fumbled to raise his creeshts sword, but the weapon seemed to move through a sticky mass. There would not be enough time to block the enemy's sais.

Someone jumped in front of the Royal prince just as the Honored's left hand came down. Anmero felt the spray of the other man's blood as the silver weapon pierced deeply into his clavicle. Anmero's rescuer struck out with his own pair of kodachis, slitting the Honored's throat just as he himself took the blow intended for the prince.

K'sho sighed in relief as the Honored choked and fell down beside him. "You are safe, Prince Anmero?"

The prince was too stunned to stammer more than a "yes".

"Then live a good life. Lead our people into a new world."

Anmero reached out and caught the fading youth's back, hugging him to his chest. "K'sho…!"

"St-stay a-live." The Sinya implored the prince, barely able to get a breath into his punctured lung. Blood flowed freely down his shoulder from his wound and onto the Royal's arms.

K'sho's lips moved, as if he wanted to say more but his voice failed him. His eyes began to cloud over and he relaxed into Anmero's arms. The Royal youth fell to the ground with K'sho's body still clung tightly to himself.

"Rraa! Die!" Shane Sinhail roared over Anmero. The prince glanced up to see the Trayshan block the thrust of another Honored—the one K'sho had left to protect him. In anger, the Trayshan left no room for doubt that he was going to kill the Honored man. In less time than Anmero had to breath, Shane had hacked the enemy to pieces. The beynor kept his back to Anmero, ready to take on any other attackers, but his voice reached the prince, "It's not over yet, Prince Doz. But…. I give you one minute to collect yourself, then we need you up with sword in hand."

* * *

Seircor heard the commotion behind him but the leader of Teera Sabina's Honoreds group was keeping him too busy to wonder what damage had been rendered to their group. The Honored he fought was a Neitiege, not as handsome as Tarin Saerric but certainly well-trained. Seircor had hoped the distraction behind him would be enough, but he had quickly found his opponent was as well-versed in swordsmanship as any other Neitiege and not easily swayed by outside influences.

"Your man dies." The Honored sneered at Seircor but the victorious smile was soon replaced with a frown as he witnessed something Seircor couldn't see. "Well damn." He commented and put his full attention back to their fight.

Seircor left the man's attacks become more urgent. "You lose men." He told the other through breaths. "You cannot have Anmero."

"Apparently." The Honored gritted his teeth in anger. He opened his mouth to comment more, but a sudden, well-placed throwing knife caught him in the shoulder. A hurt roar replaced whatever words he had. Seircor took the distraction Page had given him to turn his blade flat and knocked the man out as hard as he could. Relieved to have ended his fight quickly, he lowered his sword just enough to look about. "My area is clear!" He called out.

"We are all done," Page informed him, coming up beside the Lakean and laying an exhausted hand on Seircor's shoulder,

"The Royal guards are retreating from these areas. We have won this field."

Seircor nodded and sheathed his sword. He started to turn away to the others but Page stopped him with a touch. "K'sho…did not fare well, I fear. He…he died saving Anmero's life." Seircor's eyes widened and a strong urge to rush to the fallen youth overcame him. Page held him still, though, and Seircor feared to hear more. "Who else?" He whispered. Page looked about ready to choke on his own words. "Over half our army is gone. Coryu…. Coryu has lost to Teera I feel, and…" Page paused and looked away, "And I sense from my father that Royal Qusairo has fallen."

The Lakean sucked in a haggard breath. "Sei'aut." ["So many."] He whispered. "And Manscor?" He could barely hope.

The Xsorian's green eyes told the story before he spoke. "He lives….as does Zanishiria."

Chapter Thirty-Six

K'sho Rease was born to the clan Sinya and to parents that had a seat on the Assassins' Guild for over twenty years. He took up studies on the histories of Obseen and on multiple weapons; indeed, most that knew him thought he was a walking encyclopedia on any such subjects. At age fourteen, he was accepted to the Taysor's training center, under the tutelage of Master Lerrorn Unitaki. There, he became friends with the Center's "protégé" Tarin Saerric. Upon K'sho's fifteenth birthday, his mother was outed for treason against the emperor she and her husband had served faithfully for twelve years. The sudden shock made a blow to the very loyal Sinya, who began to question the man his family had served—albeit silently. When rumor spread of Zanishiria Novastone's involvement with the Renegades, K'sho finally got enough courage to admit to his closest friend about his misgivings over their ruler and the truth about his mother (though it was never validated, K'sho's mother was one of hundreds of assassins killed by the emperor).Thus, set the course for K'sho Rease to be with Prince Anmero Doz and the other youths fighting alongside the emperor...His sacrifice was in honor of his mother and those who fought the oppression of Manscor.

"Leave him alone, morta! You've done enough."

Honored One Teera Sabina glared at the assassin that stood between her and her prey; yet, the final wound Cour'eysan Evalaus had dealt her burned badly enough that the master knew it would impair her if she attacked her enemy's defender. She backed off slightly, feeling (irritatingly) like a cowering dog. She held her injured arm with her good one. The weight of her scepter made her injury burn worse, but Teera was not stupid enough to holster it while she stood amidst a bloody battle. And, the young woman before her had the markings of the Las'wa about her. Teera knew she could not take the chance that this fighter was less skilled than her other opponent.

"Your men are finished here." The woman continued, holding herself threateningly. "Go back to your Royal mok'érai. [Insult like "royal bastard"] I'm sure he will be dying soon. His reign has ended."

Teera hissed, a corner of her lip curling up in contempt. "You insolent Las'wa! So arrogant and self-righteous. That boy is dead; there is nothin you can do, and as far as this war goes, it is far from finished. Your army at the square is being slaughtered at this very moment and that inexperienced crip you sent to kill My Lord will also be dying—if she has not fallen already. Manscor is the strongest fighter on all of Obseen. He will not fall to a young bitch like her."

"Famous last words for a morta who is not there with her lover. Zanishiria is no beginner. She has killed preshairs, our whole clan witnessed it. Manscor will be no different from those deadly snakes."

Teera had heard enough. This fool was no different than any other Renegade bitch. They all thought the same. Growling, she stalked away, taking her scepter in her good hand to protect herself. Not that it was really necessary; with the Royal guard on the run, the Renegades had finished their attacks in that area— though some were still on edge—and were being stupidly compassionate, allowing the enemies that remained to retreat unhindered.

Tyen Evalaus waited until Teera Sabina's retreating form disappeared in the crowd before turning to her wounded brother. The older sibling was still breathing, but barely, and Tyen was very concerned to see just how much blood pooled around her brother's head. It was starting to coagulate in a sticky mass underneath her brother's bloodied cheek. She pressed her forehead to his and wet as her hands searched her pouches for savya and florick mosses. "Shey'aun, Coryu, na'i kye rē." She cried, "Kye shay ben'na lai, shey'aun! Kye mora sey'moré; Or'na!" ["Please, Coryu, do not leave me. I have no one left, please! I love you, brother. Don't go!"] As quickly as she could manage, Tyen began to administer what medicinal attention she could to her fading sibling.

And, desperately, she wished for him to be all right.

* * *

Only instinct commanded her now, and it saved her life. Zanishiria had been too exhausted to register the emperor's swift attack, but her reflexes alerted her to the threat just mere moments before his halbert struck; they moved her enough that only her right side was pierced. Zanishiria turned away to keep the glancing blow from killing her and quickly grasped her own, most precious weapon to counter Manscor's move. Faster than a flash, her preshair whip uncoiled and swung around the wooden shaft of the halbert. A single flick of the wrist constricted it quickly and its indestructible scales broke the fighting weapon in two.

Manscor leapt away as the terrifying crack of the preshair weapon made him aware of its deadly body. He got well clear, remembering the ghastly wounds found around Sye Rainier's neck, two days prior. He had no intention of meeting the same fate.

Not bothering with the emperor's retreat, Zanishiria was preoccupied with the injury she had sustained. Her punctured side screamed in agony, her torn gut making her very aware of the severity of the wound. The cold metal seemed to burn where it was imbedded. The pain was so overwhelming that Zanishiria was unaware she was gasping profanities under her faltering breath. Pull it out! Her mind screamed at her and the Las'wa ripped the metal halbert's head from her side. The wave of pain that followed made her dizzy but she forced her body to retain its balance in the world—just in time to dodge the Emperor Manscor's next attack.

The Royal-assassin had scooped up a nodachi again from the scattered weapons in the enormous training room. It was a Trayshan custom, made of traznic steel and Manscor hoped the great warrior-sword was worth the high price he had paid for it; his life depended on the quality of the nodachi to withstand the preshair weapon. Having seen Zanishiria wavering, the emperor had thought he saw his chance to take out the Lakean's head. However, the young assassin countered him by using the halbert's head to cover her as she backed away toward a wall. Her aim was off, more the throw was from reflex than skill, and Manscor found he could easily counter the bloodied weapon-head. Yet, the short time it took him to deal with the projectile allowed the young fighter to regain herself enough to fight back.

Manscor's attention returned to her only to realize the girl had used her deadly whip to pick up another weapon—this one a dagger—to slingshot his way. "Cute." The ruler growled sarcastically. "You think throwing objects at me will keep me at bay? Fairly pathetic trick—even for you." Timing the next aimed weapon's trajectory, the emperor was able to grab the dao's handle and fling it back the way it had come.

The dao flew straight at Zanishiria's heart. The assassin-girl's eyes flashed. "Cōr'a!" She yelled and flicked her whip out in an intricate dance of scales. [Exclamation; closest translation= "take this!"] The room cracked, the sound of scales and steel reverberating across the great expanse. A moment passed and the whip stilled. Hundreds of dao shards fell to the floor with a dribbling clatter. "You're next." Zanishiria whispered, her eyes shadowed in the dusky light of the first setting sun. The words were barely audible but felt more sincere than the banter the two adversaries had tossed to each other all fifteen hours.

Manscor shivered. The young fighter across from him straightened to her full five-foot-four frame and squared her muscled shoulders carefully, being attentive to her injury. Blood dribbled down her side in scarlet rivulets, and slicked her hands in the vital liquid, yet they held her preshair whip steadily. She glinted her eyes, her gaunt, pale cheeks becoming hollower, like a death-mask. Then, she took one then another calculating step toward the emperor. Manscor shivered again as she prowled toward him.

"You thought you had me." The Lakean continued, calm and deadly-low in her voice. "You did…but you missed. We both have lost opportunities to kill the other. But not much longer. Neither of us can last the setting of the suns. We are both wounded too severely; both suffering from blood loss, pain, and lack of needed energy." She paused to raise her whip mesmerizingly and slowed her advance. "It could not be more perfect."

* * *

Tarin had felt blood spatter onto his face when Zanishiria had ripped the halbert from her side. He wiped it away absently, his mind barely registering the smears of red on his fingers. His body, however, did. The Neitiege was momentarily lost to the fight as his stomach rolled at the thought of the sharp steel being torn from Zanishiria's person; the sight of the girl he had come to know and not know, pulling the steel from her gorged side sickened him.

Both fighters had been pierced now, multiple times, but Tarin could not block out the image of the Lakean's blood as it spattered out with Zanishiria's throw. *This has to stop! This isn't a fight, this is torture. They just keep ripping pieces out of each other.* Tarin cast his eyes to the suns. It was close to the time of the first sun's setting, but not close enough. *I can't take much more of this.* The Neitiege's stomach rolled again and Tarin could not control it; there was too much stink of blood and sweat in the air

—And yet the gruesome scene continued before his eyes.

* * *

The whip hissed out in a left arc then began an intricate, deadly weave through the air in front of Zanishiria. The girl danced with it, becoming as lithe and as light as the snakeskin weapon. She floated closer to the emperor.

This was the finale; the emperor could feel the conclusion in her whip's singing cadence. The sound was like rain, like the hiss of the sun upon the black Vallés at noontime, like the terrible sounds of the predatory snakes sliding around the Underworld. It was Obseen, untamed and otherworldly—and, it reminded the emperor that he was not. "I was never meant to win the battle against this girl…" Prince Xi whispered and started to lower his nodachi.

The wrath-like form beyond the flashing whip stilled her advance, but not her weapon. "Neither was I, your lordship." From somewhere far beyond her exhaustion, one single tear formed in her eyes and slipped down her gaunt cheeks. "It is the elements and the creatures of this world who decide what this planet is. No one person can change the course of its fate. Obseen is wild, untamed, and dangerous. Who are we to think we can rule it?"

"I ruled for nearly twelve years. I held the power of an entire guild of assassins. I would have ruled entire planets with your people in my sway."

"It was not our price to pay to you, Manscor." The Lakean had closed her expression once more. Its hardened form looked like chiseled stone. "You chose the path of the assassin—yet you took it too far. You know our codes, our laws. Now, finish it according to them! Let us be done once and for all. We all tire of fighting."

Emperor Manscor could have scoffed at the absurdity that the young assassin-girl was spouting, but, no, he too felt tired of the battles, of always having to be better than the next assassin to come along and challenge his authority. He was not as battle-hungry as his lover and the Guild would expect of him; aging through war had hardened him surely but it had also worn him thin. The incredible thing was that it was the young assassin-girl before him who echoed-back what was in his heart. He suddenly felt as if he was living in the hands of fate; a fate that had him now in its cross-hairs. "Fine…. we will finish it then." The emperor raised his sword again and stepped into the tangled pattern of Zanishiria's whip.

Chapter Thirty-Seven

"There is something about her that I admire. For a student, Zanishiria Coursay'sora is the brightest and most capable one I have ever met and had the privilege to train. Her will, a strength that her hard life has given her, and her convictions, following what her parents laid down long before her, are beyond my understanding. There is also an uncanny talent she has—which I have only seen in her father—that makes her such a warrior that can adapt to any fighting style and read any opponent in a very short study of observing their opening moves. I do not think I will ever see another assassin has the power and natural aptitude that she does.

"Even at her young age, I am convinced she will make this planet shake. Zanishiria does not yet know the destiny she has in store for her, but I hope that if I nurture her talent carefully, she will surpass all of the expectations put upon her. The clan and, yes, even my seivier and myself, have much invested in this young Coursay'sora—and I think she is even greater than we all hoped for. I say this because today I just witnessed this young assassin take down the most vile of creatures, a preshair that attacked the outskirts of our city, all on her own. Even me, her own master, could not keep up with her.

"In a week, she will leave with the preshan group we promised to the Renegades; her fight against the preshair made it certain that she will be among them. I am reluctant to let her go so soon, but Zanishiria is as ready as I can make her. Really, I think I fear that she may be greater than me and that I have nothing left to teach her... It is her reward to go with her brother to finish what her parents started all those years ago. The line of Coursay'soras is very strong and extraordinary."

--Seivier Tyracor

Manscor had known he had no chance to get in range with the preshair whip defining Zanishiria's defenses. He had taken the only direct way available to him—he lunged straight in. The nodachi flashed passed Zanishiria's vision. A breath later, she felt it pierce her left shoulder; its broad body cutting deeply into the joint there. Zanishiria let her eyes drop closed, fatigue overtaking her. *It is done. I can die now knowing I did all I was capable of doing.*

Emperor Manscor had hoped he could plunge his sword into the enemy assassin before the whip stopped him; however, he felt the sharp scales grab his forearms, torso, and thighs in its greedy grasp. It stole from him the force of his intended blow. Pain flooded into his thoughts, obscuring any other details in its intensity. The nodachi slipped from the Royal-assassin's hands.

Zanishiria waited for...something, but, she could still feel where the metal of the nodachi had stuck her shoulder. The weight of the emperor's body, sagging to the ground, pulled the preshair whip taunt in her hands. The pain, too, she should not be aware of if she was finally beyond saving. *Just let me die.* She sighed and slumped to her knees.

Then, the distant sounds of battle drifted to Zanishiria's consciousness. The Royal guards and Renegades still fought, though the reason for the war was gone. Someone must tell them. "St-stop..." She heard footfalls but the haze of her body refused to allow her mind to focus enough to know what was going on. The preshair whip moved. Zanishiria opened her eyelids with effort.

* * *

Time had seemed to freeze when the two opponents attacked one another. Just as quickly as the emperor sprung at the Lakean, he had been stopped. The preshair whip gleamed premonition-like around the leader's body. The nodachi in the ruler's hand came down on Zanishiria's shoulder. Then all seemed still.

Tarin hesitated as the two adversaries stayed motionless. He was uncertain what to believe: who dies, who wins, is it over? Yet, movement found him as soon as the emperor slumped over, wrapped in the deadly arms of the Lakean whip. The Neitiege wanted to deny it, but the emperor must be dead.

Then Zanishiria muttered something. Tarin started. The young assassin, the one he had called "friend", was still alive—if barely. So, too, was the emperor? Tarin wanted to know. He hurried over the Emperor Manscor's side, passed Zanishiria, who dripped blood to the hard floor. Tarin kept his eyes from her, unwilling to see how mutilated her beautiful features were. If the Royal-assassin's wounds were tale enough, Zanishiria's would be in no better condition.

"Your Majesty." Tarin whispered anxiously and touched the leader's curled body tentively. There was no answer. Tarin's hope vanished, yet, he still reached out to check the emperor's pulse. It was there, faintly! "Your Majesty, please hold on. I will try to help you." Very gently, Tarin began to untangle the sharp scales from Manscor's body, ignoring the rude bites they inflicted on his skin. Long moments passed but Tarin got the ruler separated from the weapon. Yet, it only caused the leader to bleed worse. "Zhik!' [Curse kind of like "shit!"] The Neitiege hissed and stood up, ready to run to the medical supplies by the door and to call for a physician.

Zanishiria shifted and pulled herself straight enough to look at her friend. Tarin froze in her distant, deep-grey stare. "They need to know the war is over." Her words slurred slightly. "Tell them."

"No!" Tarin answered her angrily. "Not as long as he still breathes. The emperor still rules."

A wan look passed over the Lakean's eyes. "More die. He dies. There is no need for these deaths. They need to know…"

"Then you tell them! I have no time. I still have a chance to save the emperor." Saying that, Tarin spun away, leaving Zanishiria standing, exhausted and drifting in and out of the darkness in her vision.

"Fine, Tarin… I see this is the way of things." Zanishiria slowly took hold of the nodachi in her shoulder and yanked it out. The shock reverberated through her system but it gave her enough clarity to regain her balance in the world. "I can go. I will…They need to know…" Slowly, she half-limped, half-dragged herself to the door.

* * *

The two guards still posted at the entrance started as the large, ornate doors of the training hall yawned open. They jumped to attention and turned to see who stumbled through. By the looks on their faces, they had not expected to see Zanishiria Novastone come out alive.

"Emperor Manscor is finished." She stated. They looked at her in shock. "Tell the armies to stop fighting." The Royal guards just continued to stare. Zanishiria sighed. *I guess I do look a sight; I feel like a sight.*

"But they would kill us once we said such." The one, older guard stammered. "We can't go. We served the emperor." He and the other started to back away in fright.

"No, wait…!" Zanishiria reached out to them desperately. "I doubt…" *they would…* She racked her tired brain as quickly as she could manage, hoping for a coherent response. "Take me to the entrance, I will inform the armies."

The two men seemed to hesitate, but the older guard finally softened to the youth's plea; he may have had children of his own for the look his features softened to be was more sympathetic. He stepped to Zanishiria's side. "You are very brave, assassin. More than I could ever be. I can take you to the entranceway."

"I am grateful for the assistance." The Lakean managed to say before collapsing into the man's arms. "Let me…rest until we get there."

The two guards shot concerned glances at each other but they worked carefully to lift Zanishiria's bloodied body into the stronger guard's arms. "The emperor?" The younger one asked over the girl's head. The older guard shook his head and motioned the man away. "Let's worry more about the angry fighters outside before one dying man. It's their code." He was looking at Zanishiria when he said the last. "I would rather save hundreds than have many killed to save one man." The younger guard couldn't say anything.

They finally reached the Royal entranceway. The ornate doors were still unbreached but the brazen trill of the fighting permeated through the thick wood and stones. The terrible sound woke the drifting assassin, unbidden, in the younger guards' arms. "Let me down." The man paused, unsure now that the battle was so close. "You can go warn your people to leave. I will give you ten minutes to do so. The Renegades will not harm any who lay down their weapons." Her carrier finally released her. "Thank you." Zanishiria bowed as well as she could and turned away from the guards. "Go." She commanded quietly and heard them take off down the hall.

Finally alone, Zanishiria leaned her head against the large doors, feeling the cold, smoothed wood against her forehead. She let the sounds outside fill her and give her strength as she counted the minutes in her head. She would be true to her word to the two guards who had helped her. Once the time was gone, she pushed all thoughts aside and straightened. Her hands splayed against the hard wood. *Soon, I can rest. Soon…*She chanted to herself and heaved against the entranceway doors.

* * *

The enormous Royal Entranceway doors groaned open. The Tà sharay's tired group of fighters, now complete with Major Calamas's Renegade army and the Trayshans, all sucked in their breaths, afraid of what might come out beyond the shadows of the awning.

All of the fighting slowed then ceased as the two armies peered toward the Palace in wonder. What was going to happen? Were more guards going to arrive? Was it something else?

A tired, blood-adorned figure hobbled, slow and pained, out onto the long stairwell landing, her precious weapon still curled in her hands. Her dark hair, wild and sweat-drenched, hid her face in shadows, but it could not hide the ghastly wounds that marked her arms, torso, and thighs. Her appearance seemed to tell the crowd the truth.

Still, Zanishiria mesmerizingly raised her head, coming to a tight but fully upright stature. Her eyes shinned otherworldly. "End your fighting!" She called out, mustering the strength to shout the words. "You have no more reason to fight." The armies looked on uncertain. Zanishiria paused to sweep her eyes out over their haunted, war-tired faces, seeming to meet and sympathize with all their pains and despairs in turn. She breathed deeply at last, as she looked into the Tà sharay's familiar, hope-filled green eyes. His stare gave her the power to muster the final declaration. "The emperor is dead! Manscor is dead!" As soon as her words were out of her mouth, Zanishiria felt all of her strength leave her. She had finally come to the end of her mission; she had done what her clan and the Renegades had asked of her. Now that is was over, she only wanted to fall into that comforting oblivion. She began to let go.

"Zan!" Tyracor yelled out as he pushed through the stunned crowd to the stairwell. He raced up it as fast as his aging body could manage and caught his apprentice as she fell to the cold stones. Zanishiria smiled wanly, not really seeing her master, and closed her eyes with a serene smile. "I no longer need to…"

Chapter Thirty-Eight

"Time passes us by way too fast. Joys and tears blur through the aging until they seem just mirror images of each other; neither one taking any true hold on our lives. We pass on into foreverness and find the world never unchanging.

"Our tears will pass with the passage of time, and proceed into happiness, for so goes the cycles. But, for now, our grief is real, our wounds fresh—yet we heal. In time, our lives will mend themselves. Yes, time. Even as these moments, these days are full of suffering. That is the way it must be during this ending of a war. So, for this time, we will bear the cost of surviving and bury the brothers and sisters that fell alongside us. As for tomorrow, I pray strongly that those that have survived can find a way to live beyond war, beyond discordance, beyond grief, in a land free of any one ruler. May it be..."

--King Lapsair S.D. 4023

Eight Days Later...

King Lapsair knocked on his daughter's door for what seemed the thousandth time that week. As usual, the princess did not call her father in; the king went in anyway. Scarlett lay, as she had since Shathahel first brought her home, in a fetal position on top of her bed. She kept her rigid back to the door, continuing her endless stare through the colored glass of her window. Their dark brown (near-black) orbs never left the picture of a beautiful, mountain hillock of wildflowers and lakes.

King Lapsair suppressed a sigh and came to his daughter's bedside. "Scarlett, honey," he began and sunk to the bed beside her. The princess cringed as he rose his hand to touch her, but other than that movement, she did nothing. The aging king bit his lip. Ever since blind Shathahel had brought the sixteen-year-old with the news of what had befallen her, her father had been trying to comfort his child and keep her from her fears. Yet, it seemed his presence only caused more fear. The princess had not eaten again, he saw. The gentle soup the cook had prepared had cooled long before. It seemed that maybe a tiny bit of the water was gone, however, though the Royal wasn't sure if that was just his eyes deceiving him—to keep himself hopeful.

"Scarlett," King Lapsair said again, "It's been over a week since that…you do not have to fear those men anymore. They are all dead. Please, baby, come back to me." His daughter just continued to stare. This time, the Royal man did sigh "Okay, you can stay that way if you choose." Lapsair gritted his teeth and took the assassin's stance in the situation. "But, you should know you are not the only one with wounds to show. Others need my help just as much as you. If you won't take it then I must take myself elsewhere. I won't be back to check on you for a long while." He hated himself for the words but he had run out of all his other options that he knew. "If there is still a part of the Scarlett I know and love, then grant me this one thing: you always cared for Zanishiria. She is in bad shape, still in a coma, since her fight eight days ago. You two always could understand each other. Could you go to her? She may wake with you near. Please, Sc—." Tears overwhelmed the king and he could not finish his daughter's name. He turned away before they slid down his cheeks.

* * *

An hour passed. Then without any outward sign, Scarlett pushed herself into a sitting position. She swung her legs off of the bed and reached for the cloak she always left by her bedside. The princess pulled it around her shoulders weakly and fastened it. She stood—and swayed in dizziness from her dehydration and lack of calories. It was then that her brain seemed to comprehend what the mound and tower had been in her vision: food and drink. She reached shakily and grabbed up the water glass in both her hands and drank of it greedily. The soup, too, was quick to her mouth but its calming aroma eased her pace and she managed to eat it slow enough to not startle her neglected stomach.

Then, turning way to the door, she found her way out of her room on unsteady feet. She found her stride and hurried through the familiar halls, her mind so used to their marbled finery that she did not really notice any of it. All of her thoughts were on one thing: her father had said Zanishiria was alive, unconscious still, but alive! And she needed her! Scarlett felt an overwhelming need to be close to her adoptive assassin-cousin.

* * *

King Lapsair turned away from the Berris and Berzén when he caught sight of Scarlett wandering past his eye. The two Trayshans quieted their conversation and let the king stare. Once Scarlett was passed them and down the hall, King Lapsair returned his attention to the two leaders. He was smiling through his tears. "You were right, Berris, Zanishiria was the perfect excuse to get my daughter out of her stupor. Thank you so very much for that suggestion."

Tearrì Sinhail was mirroring his smile. "I am just relieved that your child, too, is alive. She, as well as everyone else, will learn to bear the wounds of this war."

"I hope you are right, Berris."

Tearrì bowed to the Royal. "As do we all, King Lapsair." She and her husband began to take their leave. "We will see you at the council, Royal. Your presence there will be greatly needed."

The room was quiet, cast in shadows, and completely lonely—the perfect atmosphere for the young assassin. Alone, that was what he was; alone with his nightmares.

Tarin Saerric sat, trying to meditate, in his room, letting the hours pass by. Images filled his mind. Images of friendship now lost, pain, terror, blood—and death. He let each one pass through him, looking through each one without any more emotion. They had been gone over so much now that he felt nothing about the images as they came.

A week before, Tarin had been frantically trying to patch up the fading emperor. He had nearly finished when his master had rushed to her lover's side and ordered him away. Manscor had died two hours later, and Teera had flown away, off world, with no word to her apprentice. Tarin had locked himself in his room, accepting only enough food to not go hungry and meditated the days away.

The council was to meet in two days. A messenger of King Lapsair's had carried an invite for Tarin—he was expected to be there. Two days, and Tarin had all that time to sort through all he knew so he could present it to the Assassins' Guild.

The past does not matter now as much as the future. I will tell them all the truth as I know it...

All of the funeral pyres had been lit, all of the bodies of the Renegade and Royal guard armies had been burned and their ashes returned to the ground. The respected leaders, or the bodies of loved ones, were commemorated by the light of the two full moons, three nights after the end of the Royals' War.

Royal Qusairo had been one of the bodies burned. K'sho Rease was another. Anmero Doz had seen to their burials personally. Afterward, he had asked around and found out the most appropriate place to bury K'sho's ashes—beneath the rare willow tree in the training center's Northern Gardens. A finely carved marble stone was placed over the spot to commemorate the brave assassin-youth. As for Anmero's father's ashes, the entire Doz family had released them in their own way; Anmero had his cast to a western wind, Asilisa vowed to take her husband's back home to Planet X, and Aslén had carried his to the great waterfall in Taysor Gulch and let the waters float them away.

The great ruler and the kind Sinya would not be easily forgotten.

* * *

Anmero was just leaving Zanishiria's room, having been ordered to refresh himself and rest by the ever-vigilant Master Tyracor. The young Royal was too in awe of the Lakean girl's master to dispute the order, and, besides, he could admit staying awake watching Zanishiria's unconscious form for thirteen hours had exhausted him.

His tight muscles angrily protesting, the prince made his way down the two flights of stairs to the ground level. He knew he should go straight to sleep but the walk, all the way to his temporary room on the other side of the Center, did not seem too appealing. Instead, he turned aside to another wing of rooms, where the large handful of Lakean assassins had been given residence. He hurried past the dark-featured clansmen roaming the halls respectfully, being given bows in return to his now-familiar presence, and hurried to Tyen Evalaus's quarters. The Lakean woman looked up as Anmero knocked and entered, a curt nod welcoming the Royal in, yet her eyes were quick to turn away again, to the sleeping pallet and her brother.

"How is he?" The prince asked quietly.

Tyen wiped down her brother's sweaty face gently before answering. "He still wavers from this world and the other. The doctors have done all they could. The trauma to his brain had subsided, however. They believe he will live."

"That is good news." Anmero replied and came to sit beside Tyen. He sighed with fatigue and leaned against the wall.

The older woman looked at him with worry. "You were with her again? Any change?"

"The same."

Tyen nodded as if she had expected the answer. "She is not as willing to hang onto life as my brother. Coryu is trying, he's so stubborn, of that I know. But Zanishiria…. She had little to hold her here I am afraid. It is not her wounds that keep her in her coma, it is her mind." Anmero knit his eyebrows at the words, slightly angered that Tyen thought so of the girl he found so amazing; however, he was too exhausted to hang onto such trivial emotions. He sighed and let the feeling fade. Tyen seemed to realize how rude her statement had been for she turned away from her brother to place a hand sweetly against the prince's cheek. "Kye mureak, [I am sorry] Anmero, that was careless of me. I know how much you hope in Zanishiria's recovery. I should not dash your wishes so cruelly."

Anmero tried to smile in reassurance but Tyen could see the hurt in his eyes. "You only try to speak realistically. There is no fault in that. But, I will still believe that Zan will make it through."

"Then perhaps she will. Believing is very powerful medicine, after all." Tyen smiled sadly and lifted her hand away. She waved to the empty pallet across the room. "Sleep, prince, you look in need. I will wake you if the need arises." Anmero nodded tiredly and crawled to the soft bed. He was asleep in moments. Tyen watched the sleeping prince for a long time, her eyes softening in a new-found fondness for the prince. Quietly, she whispered, "I hope you are right about Zanishiria, prince. I really do."

* * *

There was a knock at the door. Seircor started and pushed himself away from the unconscious form of this friend, hesitate to release her cool, clammy hand. The Lakean looked to Tyracor but the master was asleep—a rare occurrence. Resigned, Seircor rose and passed the sleeping master carefully to float to the door.

A bedraggled figure greeted the young man. "Za—." No, this is, "Scarlett?" Seircor sputtered, surprised at how similar the princess looked to his friend. She nodded, wordlessly, and stepped around the assassin. Seircor closed the door and followed her back to Zanishiria's side.

Scarlett took in Zanishiria's fight-marked form in shock and reached out, gingerly, to trace one of the raw wounds. A tear formed in her eyes and she quickly dropped to her knees beside the assassin-girl. "Oh, Zan…" Tyracor stirred at his chair by the window and Seircor hurried to caution the master to silence. The two Las'wa exchanged hopeful glances and tried to still themselves and breathed in hope.

Scarlett took Zanishiria's hand in hers, worried at the chilliness in it. She bent over to rest her forehead against the Lakean's and felt the fire that raged there. Too, the princess noted the slight yellow cast of the assassin's usually light-colored skin. Jaundice? Did Zanishiria's liver fail her? "And you are so pale." She breathed, "You much have lost a lot of blood in your fight. You have suffered so." More tears escaped her eyes to drop onto her pseudo-cousin's face—she could not hold them back anymore. Scarlett cried and cried and cried, shedding tears she had locked deep inside herself for the eight agonizing days. She cried for Zanishiria and for herself and when she thought she was at her end, another sob choked her and she let loose again.

Finally, Scarlett still.

Silence filled the room and time passed.

Seircor leaned against the windowsill and felt his hope fading away into the black stone as the minutes ticked by. It seemed like that a lot these days, hopes fading away into the dark earth of the planet. Victory, it seemed, had come at a hollow price. There were too many deaths and too many injuries to believe in a better tomorrow.

And…it was his best friend that lay, half-dead in the world. Seircor had known there was a great chance Zanishiria would die in the Royals' War. The Lakean council, having learned that only Zanishiria had made it to the surface one year prior, had already written her off. They had never expected her to beat the Emperor Manscor let alone to still be breathing afterward. Even now, they thought she would die. He had not let himself believe that, however. Zanishiria was still alive after eight days past the longest battle he had ever heard witness of. Nearly sixteen hours of dueling without eating and very little sleep? Praic had to believe, then, that that meant she was still hanging on to some part of this world. Yet, as the days passed and Zanishiria stayed beyond consciousness, Seircor left a little more of his hope leaving him.

Today would break him.

Scarlett Novastone slumped over, having exhausted herself of tears. Zanishiria's flushed cheek burned the side of her face but she could not move away from it—she would not. "Don't you give up too, Zan, there are still some here who need you..."

"Not...give...up." An inaudible voice, husky and dry, like sandpaper, breathed by her ear. The princess twitched, wondering if she had only imagined the small voice. But, a finger jerked involuntarily under her hands. Scarlett squeezed Zanishiria's hand and thought the fingers felt a little stronger. She sat up and scanned the Las'wa's face anxiously.

Seircor noticed Scarlett's reaction and sat bolt upright; Tyracor mirroring him in intensity. Had something changed? They dared not to breathe. Seircor brought himself to his friend's side again. He noticed it first, having known Zanishiria her whole life and knowing her features better than anyone, there was a change. "Zan?" He took the assassin's left hand in his. "Shey'aun, kye tai'enen lai real'aun tă. Shey'aun, na'da ranē. Kye sor'enai lai. Ben'a...En'selan ky'me. ["Please, I saw you flicker your attention here just now. Please, do [action] it [repeat, continue] again. I am very much in need of you. My dear friend...Come back to me."]

"Pr—aic." The word escaped Zanishiria's barely parted lips.

All three of them heard that time. Tyracor rose from his chair and joined the others. "Tai'eya, kye real'yé mora lai." He touched his large hand to her cheek gently. "Kye reish'em ky'sayva laun, al'ana." ["Apprentice, I thought I had lost you."..."I have never been so scared in my life, beautiful girl."]

"Sei—." Zanishiria's mouth was too parched for her to say anything more.

Tyracor soothed her with his touch. "Ssh, mé'yé, Tai'eya. Shay lai valen sayva'en." ["Quiet/rest, apprentice. Save your strength for living."] The tall, elder master motioned to the water pitcher at Seircor's left. With warning, he tipped it ever so carefully and let only a few droops fall into Zanishiria's mouth. Her dry throat was quick to take in the moisture. Slowly, Tyracor administered a half a cups' amount to his apprentice, then he set the pitcher aside. "Lai taun'en?" ["Do you feel better?"]

Zanishiria slowly opened her grey eyes, straining them in the light of the late morning suns. It took her a few moments to readjust to the living world, but finally she was able to focus on her master above her. "Taun'en...esh." She answered haltingly. ["Been...better"]

Tyracor chuckled in relief and crouched down beside Zanishiria's other two bedside partners. "You have been unconscious eight days. A high fever, accompanied with jaundice and horrible sweating, left us fearing you would not make it passed the first days—but you kept hanging on. I am so glad you are alive."

Memories surfaced in Zanishiria's mind. Images of her fight, the vivid bloodstains, having plagued her even in the coma. She had feared their exaggerated portrayal, though the silent, unwelcome beyond had been more terrifying still. Yet, she also remembered the exhausted faces of the armies and the desperation in her master's voice as he had rushed to catch her. Questions formed in her eyes.

Master Tyracor recognized the look in his apprentice's grey eyes. His elated face tightened and his voice changed slightly. "A lot has changed since you were last awake." Zanishiria's eyes froze with the words of warning.

Chapter Thirty-Nine

"The pain of losing my closest friend was almost too much to bear. Still raw from losing my sister a year ago, the wound was reopened when I sat all those hours next to Zanishiria's bedside, hoping that she would open those intense eyes of hers again. It was almost worse for me to see Scarlett Novastone, that Royal who looks uncannily like the seimora; my breath was knocked clean out of me upon the sight of her...

"When Zanishiria did respond...I was so scared to even hope, thinking I had been hearing things, but when both Seivier Tyracor and Scarlett heard as well I was beyond elated...Having nearly lost Zanishiria, I realize how much her friendship means to me. There will never be another Zanishiria Coursay'sora.

---Seircor C'vail

They had returned to Obseen empty-handed. Whatever large spaceship the emperor had been building had not been on Rhône. The seven masters and assassin had stayed at the instructed docking bay on Planet X and scoured the city for all vital Intel on the code name "Hammerhead", but they had been unable to discover any trace of the "ship". More interesting, not one of the Royals knew where to look; the masters were not pleased and certainly baffled.

Master Quinn and Master Yoshida left their group at the training center and headed over to the Taysor Palace to meet with King Lapsair. There, too, were the Trayshan leaders, Aslén Doz, Major Calamas, and the Tà sharay in a quick, debriefing meeting before the council of the Assassins' Guild would keep them from talking amongst themselves.

A young man of seventeen-years met the two masters at the entranceway. He bowed formally, his shocking, long white hair falling over one shoulder to hide part of his face. He straightened and gave a friendly grin, the trials of the war in his countenance, and motioned for Quinn and Yoshida to follow him. A few moments later, the trio paused outside of some large wooden doors and the Xsorian escort paused, his hands splayed on the frame. He closed his eyes. A breath passed. "They are glad to hear you made your way here quickly. All are anxious to hear what news you carry from Planet X." Master Quinn kept back his response that they had, in fact, learned nothing. The telepathic youth turned his head to stare in concern but did not comment. Instead, he pushed aside the large doors and led the masters into the large council room beyond.

The small council had taken residence in one of the king's library, having pulled three long tabled together to form a rough triangular seating area. The two Royals and the major sat at the northern-most position, having allowed the Trayshans and Tà sharay and his con'trore to have the table to their right. The other one was empty, three seats waiting to be taken.

King Lapsair stood up as the masters and Xsorian entered. "Master Quinn, Yoshida. I am so relieved to see you have returned to Obseen safely. When I heard the bunch of you had stolen a Royal carrier and headed to Rhône I could not help but worry, yet, I understand your reasons for going, now, thanks to Page Torez."

Master Quinn glanced at their Xsorian escort in surprise. Firstly, for not knowing the Tà sharid on sight and, secondly, that he knew why they had gone. "Our reasons for going?"

"Ai'y." Page Torez bowed slightly. "Two days prior to the time you hijacked the Emperor's starships, I was running an assignment for my father." Assignment meaning hacking job, Quinn knew, for the Torez family were known as the greatest hackers on Obseen. Page continued, "I was deep in the emperor's database when I stumbled upon a file code named the "Hammerhead", a secret project of Manscor's nearly completed after half a cycle. Nearly six-hundred-and-thirty tons of traznic and sydro-smelted steel have been sent off to Rhône. The project was to be completed within the next month."

The two Legion masters exchanged disgruntled looks. "You say it should be complete?" Yoshida reiterated. The youth nodded. Yoshida persed his lips. "That is not good." They turned their attention to include the rest of the council to explain. "We searched Rhône for a whole week. There was no evidence of a "Hammerhead" anywhere on-planet or on the docking bays above. The emperor's project is not to be found."

"Where did it go then?" Quinn asked, looking between Page and Khan Torez.

The two Xsorians shared their own looks of discontent. Neither had an answer for the masters.

"There may be more." Aslén Doz broke in, directing the small council's attention to himself. "Master Teera Sabina travelled off world within the very hour of Manscor's death. She returned this morning looking rather smug with herself, not that that is anything new. Her destination was unknown, but Teera was definitely in on the emperor's project. Keeping an eye on her would be wise."

"That is agreed." The Berzén nodded. "They cannot hide a ship of that size forever. The Royals' Armada—headed by your nephew Raymond Novastone and the Doz family—would be the best choice of keeping an eye out for it off-world."

"We are very willing to do that." Aslén replied. "But the Assassins' Guild should be on alert as well."

The Berris motioned for silence. She stood slowly. "We are in agreeance here on all fronts, yet, Obseen had just gone through an enormous upheaval in Guild power. The clans are gathering for the first Guild meeting we have had in nearly twelve years. I can be the first to say a large, fire-powered starship is a high priority but I see our people in need of grounding and reconstruction before we can begin to focus on other dilemmas. Granted, my people, as I am sure all of yours, will put these issues as top priorities; however, my service is first to my clan and the Assassins' Guild. We must see what comes out of this clans' meeting before deciding where to put our focus further."

"Agreed." The Tà sharay answered for them all. "And speaking of the Guild meeting, there is one more problem King Lapsair and I wish to discuss with all of you." The Xsorian motioned to the Royal leader and took the thin, obsidian tablet handed to him. "This letter can directly from the Las'wa seimreal. It concerns Zanishiria." Silence came to the room.

Master Quinn felt a ball of ice in his gut. "Tell us."

Khan Torez looked as ill as the master felt. "The Lakean council wishes that this verdict be placed in the Guild meeting: Zanishiria Indigo Novastone is not recognized as one of our own. As such, no Las'wa can vouch for any actions that the hereby named assassin-Royal had committed. If it is deemed necessary by your high council, decide what punishment is required for the herby actions for the above named: killing of the Senior Master of the Guild, fighting an unclaimed duel in our council's name, and returning to Taysor's Assassins' Guild headquarters when a signed notice of her announced "defect of the Guild" of the Taysor training center has been posted in Taysor. She is entreated by the rules of "defect" according to Guild law. Sighed, Las'wa Ket'suwei [head of council date 4023]."

"That is outrageous!" Master Quinn interjected strongly. "This spells that Zanishiria is not one of the Las'wa! Her own people betray her when all she had done is followed their wishes!"

"Indeed." King Lapsair spoke sadly. "They want her judged as a Royal, as a Novastone. Tomorrow Zanishiria will be judged according to this very statement and by the will of the training center's council, led by Master Teera. With Sabina involved, the Guild will stop just short of killing Zan."

Major Calamas could not believe what he heard. "I thought that Zanishiria was an agent of ours, doing our biding? How can the council rule such?"

"The Las'wa seimreal are using Zanishiria as a scape-goat to keep their hands clean of any involvement. That was the reason behind the preshans and their oaths."

"Still, they are throwing her to the wolves. Master Teera will want her dead."

"And we won't let that happen." Yoshida reassured. "The Legion will keep that from happening. As for the rest…it is said she did kill Sye Rainier. They will try her for that, and her record of going off-world, even as a Royal-family decree, will be looked at."

"They are grasping at straws." Tyre muttered. "Why should she hang when she did exactly as we wished of her? It doesn't seem right."

"Yes, and to have her "trialed" without her present and able to reject their claims? That has never happened before." Tearri continued.

Page Torez was the one who answered that remark. "Actually, the Guild has the right to judge her now. There is word Zanishiria just awoke. They will expect her there tomorrow—whether or not she is truly in any condition to do so."

* * *

The morning had changed to late afternoon shadows. Her three caretakers had fallen to exhausted naps in different positions around the room, but, for Zanishiria, rest was the farthest thought in her mind. Scarlett's soft breathing beside her was regularly interrupted by inaudible, terrified moans—the kind of which Zanishiria recognized for some kind of nightmare, as she had had similar before. The sounds reminded her of the bloody events she had just gone through and were getting hard to stand. Very carefully, she extracted herself from Scarlett's arms and slowly pushed herself to a sitting position.

Zanishiria suppressed a hiss at the pains elicited from her wounded body; she glanced around immediately to see if her friend and master had stirred. Neither seemed aware of her movements despite her small sounds, so Zanishiria worked on standing. The room spun around as her recovering body came fully erect. She felt the blood drain from her face and reached out to the moving wall to steady herself. *I will not faint!* She willed herself and struggled to get a hold of the world. *You moved for me before, when you easily could have died. I have given you eight days to recover, now you work for me!* She berated her battered body. Her words seemed to have an effect, for her mind stopped spinning and tuned down the general scream of her injuries. Zanishiria almost sighed in relief. Almost. She looked again to see if Seircor or Master Tyracor had noticed. *Paranoid over your own friends. Creeshts-áet! Get a grip. Just go slowly and leave the room. You have little time before they stop you and a long way to go to reach your destination.* Willfully, Zanishiria made it across the room to the doorway. She glanced back once more as she keyed the automatic door to whoosh open then she limped out. *Let them sleep awhile yet. They deserve it.*

* * *

Many long, agonizing minutes later, Zanishiria finally reached the main level of the training center. She had counted the minutes nervously, wondering when Seircor or Tyracor would come to carry her back. Deeply, she hoped they would give her more time...The way to the North gardens was quiet, not one person moved around during the evening hours; most would, more than likely, be eating at that hour. It stayed that way as she continued into the garden.

Zanishiria breathed in relief and relaxed in the delightful smells of the exotic plants. The gardens had always helped calm her in troubled times and the thunder of the enormous fountain, in full flow that afternoon, soothed her troubled soul. The injured Lakean stopped to feel its spray on her palms but she only let the waters hold her for so long. The old willow tree's softly blowing tendrils called Zanishiria away—and the polished stone underneath it was what had really called her so far away. *Praic said K'sho's ashes were buried here.* The thought rocked her core. *I know how they say he died, saving Anmero...it was so like him to throw himself in front of another. But still—* "K'sho...there is so much I never told you...I...I loved you...." The young assassin sank to the grassy earth beside the memorial. Tears pearled out of her slate eyes to wash the carved ruins on the obsidian marker. Time slowed and stood still as Zanishiria relieved the memories of the friend she has cherished through that past year.

Footsteps neared from the Lakean's left. They paused. The mourning assassin barely reacted, but the uncomfortable feeling of the other person's anger pulled Zanishiria's attention to him. Tarin stood rigidly underneath the shade of a tarol tree. His sharp, blue eyes glaring at Zanishiria, full of emotions she would rather see on a stranger. The two friends were frozen in place.

* * *

"Zanishiria!"

Tarin and the Lakean flinched. Startled, they turned to find Seircor, Prince Anmero, and Page and Lap Torez running toward them, looking worried. The Neitiege squared his shoulders threateningly and confronted the other youths. Seeing the stance, they stopped just short of the grass, nearly five meters from Tarin Saerric. Seircor's hand was to his sword's hilt and Page's to his shuriken, just in case.

The handsome, blond-haired youth gave them a sour look. "You all desecrate K'sho's grave by coming her. Come any closer and I will—."

"Do what? Attack me? I can take you, you know." Seircor interrupted, his voice low and angry.

"T-tarin? Praic? What is wrong?" Zanishiria sensed there was something that had happened since she had been in her coma. Certainly, Tarin had learned to fear her but to include the others in his anger? She was confused.

Tarin's glare was redirected back to his original target. "Friends do not allow friends to get killed in front of them." Zanishiria barely contained the flinch she had at Tarin's words, but her friend did not seem to notice as he turned his eyes back to Seircor and the others. "You people.... you disgust me. Your words…I trusted you with my friend. He was to be all right, but he is not all right. He is dead!"

"We tried to protect each other as well as we could in that fight. K'sho just didn't want me to die. I owe him my life." Anmero said.

"You owe more than that, Prince." He snarled the word. "He died when it should have been you. I won't forgive that, ever!"

Seircor ground his teeth but kept himself and Anmero from saying something further to provoke the Neitiege. The Las'wa kept part of his eye on the Torez brothers in case they signaled that Tarin would do something they were able to "sense" first; the rest of his focus stayed on the angry youth before him. His silence only seemed to justify Tarin's accusation for him, for he deepened his glare, his face hard. The Neitiege assassin moved, as if to take hold of the dagger on his belt. Anmero backed away nervously at the action, coming behind Seircor in case the Lakean had to use his creeshts sword. The Torez brothers tensed, hands ready at their own weapons.

"Tarin." Zanishiria began to rise, hoping her plea would hold her friend from attacking. The handsome sixteen-year-old started, as if he had forgotten she was still there. His stony countenance turned to her once more. The chill in Tarin's gaze sent a warning knot to tightening in Zanishiria's stomach. A soft voice in her head cautioned her that she did not have a weapon if he came at her and she was not in any shape to take him in a fight.

"Com'ek ēl sai, vexor kesh mal tyi'amee." ["As for a liar like you, you are no longer my friend."]

Zanishiria's heart constricted painfully. She knew the possibility had existed that moment after the fight when Tarin had run to the emperor and not herself but it still hurt hearing it out loud. She opened her mouth to reply but found no sound would come out. Tarin turned away with a disgusted look on his face and stormed off in a tense huff, curse words under his breath.

It took many long, agonizing breaths before Zanishiria could suck in an adequate amount of air. By then, Seircor had come over to his life-long friend and reached out to her shoulder with a comforting hand. "Slai'aun. Les'aum taun'en shé." ["Come away. It's all right [safe] now."] However, Zanishiria knew that was not true. She felt tears slip down her cheeks unbidden, no longer able to be held back in her weakened state. Zanishiria let them flow silently. The others came closer to be a comforting presence. Page boldly came to his knees beside the assassin-girl and wrapped his arms around her tightly. Linked by touch he said the words they all thought. *"We are here now, Zan. What you just saw…I deeply apologize for. We kept it from you….but that was our mistake. Now you see what Tarin has become since your fight. I am so sorry… However, one friend lost does not mean you are alone. I know your actions have hurt Tarin but that does not shadow the fact that your doing so has saved many lives. There are many grateful for your courage and strength."* His mind flashed her a memory of many who he had seen come to the capitol thankful to be freed of the emperor's reign. *"And there are some who are waiting for you right now to tell you what they feel…. will you go speak with them? We can take you now…. or give you some time, if you need?"*

Zanishiria shook her head weakly against Page's shoulder. With their link, she could not hide her feelings of loss that echoed across her body stronger than her physical wounds. She heard the Xsorian murmur at the intense feelings but he was able to absorb them without being consumed by them. He knew her answer before she spoke it aloud, "Just give me a moment, then we can go back…"

The small group of young men nodded in understanding and backed away to give her some space. They let her touch the memorial stone of K'sho's one last minute before Seircor came near and asked to pick her up. Knowing she was too weak to protest, Zanishiria nodded and let her friend lift her up in his strong harms. Then, the prince, Las'wa, and Torez brothers made their way back to the training center.

Chapter Forty

The Assassins' Guild holds its training center's students and masters to high standards, as they are representing the entire planet; only the best are accepted to its prestigious program. During the reign of Manscor, a new "term" was added to this high code-of-conduct: defect. The meaning of defect, or defective, was to include those assassins that refused to follow the standards and expectations of the ruler (one of which was to be loyal to him and not join the Renegade forces). It be coined a "defect" was to mean that that assassin had gone against the code in ways that dishonored their clan, master, or the Center. For those individuals who opposed the Emperor, it was a way for him to put a "warrant" on their heads that he could act against. Few were given the title, for it was not used lightly, but those that did had to pay steep prices to regain their honor—or die.

A small group had gathered in the lounge below Zanishiria's quarters. They all seemed anxious with the assassin-girl's absence. The relief on the many faces that greeted her and her small escort was very transparent. Seircor stepped through them, the crowd parting for his ease, to place Zanishiria on a chair. As she settled her battered body into the deep cushions, her visitors began to fill around her, though many kept a respectful distance. Zanishiria's small band dispersed to comfortable couches and chairs—as did many who had gathered—to give space around the Lakean for individuals to come up to her.

Master Tyracor was the first to approach his apprentice, his face trying, unsuccessfully, to hide the worry from his eyes at her disappearance. Zanishiria sensed the change in her master and the others, all being very formal all of a sudden. She felt the need to bow to her master in great respect. "Sho!" ["No/don't"] Tyracor berated and was quick to give his own bow. "Kye'e lâ reyh'or, tai'eya." ["I am the one honored, my apprentice."] He extended his hand and held hers in his strong grasp. He squeezed, feeling how weak hers was in return.

He changed to the common tongue so others could know what they said. "Today is about you, my apprentice. We," He indicated to the gathered with his free hand, "Are here for you, because of you. Let us show you now our gratitude." He reached under his robes to take out a weapon very familiar to the assassin. It was the preshair whip of her master's, passed down from Shay'renor and his master Lor'enez before him. Its passing symbolized the master felt the apprentice would be the one to carry on the traditions of the preshair seiviers. "Kye ver lai'eyan. Kye rey'shon ai, val'eya." ["I want you to have this. You deserve it [assassin]"; by using this title he is saying she has moved beyond being just an apprentice; she would be considered full-fledged assassin].

Zanishiria's eyes widened in shock. She could only stare for a long time at the weapon in her master's hands. Then, tentatively, she reached out and took hold of the dangerous weapon, feeling how worn but still very capable the old whip was. "Kye reyh'or, seivier." ["I am honored, master."] The reverence in her expression told Tyracor she understood just how important the gesture had been. Her master smiled fondly and stepped away.

The Tà sharay and his two sons were immediately there to fill the space Tyracor left. The Xsorian leader smiled warmly and gave a deep bow before reaching out toward her face. He paused, waiting for her acceptance of his unspoken request. Zanishiria seemed to understand for she shifted forward, being slow against the pain her body protested with, and let the leader take her face in his hands. The Tà sharay then leaned forward to put their foreheads together, being as intimate with her as if Zanishiria was his child. *"At last, we meet again, Zanishiria. I, like all of us here, were deeply worried you would not pull through. I am very glad to see you so well. You had many losing hope these past few days—though they would not admit such."*

"Tà sharay..." Zanishiria acknowledged, deep respect in her tone. *"I am grateful you came with your con'stól. Many lives were saved because of your people's skills."*

"The same is true for you, you know. If you had not ended your fight when you did, many would not be here." The leader's words brought turmoil to Zanishiria's thoughts; mostly about the fact that she could have ended it earlier, when the emperor had been knocked out cold. The Tà sharay soothed

away her concerns. *"Do not degrade what good you have done. You kept integrity when so many would have just waved it away. This planet needs that kind of commitment. The pains you suffered, longer than I believe many would have taken, were all for this planet's good. Do not despair by thinking you should have done differently. All these people here are grateful for the sacrifice you gave. I have never been more awed by anyone than I have been by you. Your parents would have been very proud."*

Zanishiria wanted to tell Khan Torez she felt she was below such praises but the wise man broke their link before he could get into the argument. His eyes twinkled as he bowed and stepped aside, motioning Page and Lap to follow, though they both lingered long enough to express their own gratitude.

The Xsorians were followed by the Doz family, who also expressed their thanks for Zanishiria's service. Asilisa, though marked in grief, still managed to give a lovely smile and even hugged the injured assassins—who was quite unused to the affection. Zanishiria willed herself to let the woman express herself as she needed, sensing the grieving Royal was just that kind of person: a "hugger". Asilisa's smile in thanks reassured the Lakean she had done the right thing. As for Aslén Doz, he extended a hand to clasp Zanishiria's. "Thank you, Novastone, for getting my nephew to us safely. I am indebted to you for taking the trip to M2 with your cousin and for ferrying his across Obseen without getting caught. You risked much for our family." Zanishiria bowed to the Royal and then to Anmero, who only came up long enough to give his thanks and promise to talk more later before slipping away to let others have their turn. Many other followed, most Zanishiria knew only by name or reputation. Royals and assassins alike came forward to bow to her in respect and offer their appreciations. Zanishiria felt overwhelmed; however, there was a final dwindling of the line of well-wishers until only the Trayshan Zair'ek remained.

The two hard-featured assassin-warriors and their son had hung back until the very end; though in all respects they should have been among the first. Neither leader looked vexed by the order, however. Tearrì Sinhail strode forward commandingly, yet swept Zanishiria up in a surprisingly mother-like embrace. The Las'wa did not know what to do at the unusual decorum. The Berris said it for her, "Saur esh ekē vemek. Sek'vie rezshour sauv es lé en'iē. Kē shek'mos saur vek. Sauk ven shour." [Trayshan: "Your bravery is greatly valued. All here respect you for what you have done. I knew you parents well. They would be very proud."]

Zanishiria was surprised that Tearrì knew that she had been taught Trayshan—though if the leader was as close to her parents as she claimed, then Zanishiria knew she would not be. Quickly, she remembered her etiquettes, making a Trayshan bow, fist punched into the right hand and head bowed.

"You are truly your parents' child." The Berris returned the salute and backed away, seeing the questions form in Zanishiria's dark eyes.

The Berzén turned to follow his wife, yet he paused long enough in front of Zanishiria to say, "Someday, young assassin, we will tell you all. Someday. Skĕk reviĕ." ["Come visit us."] The retreat of the Trayshans signaled the end. The overwhelming number of supporters left the room. The injured assassin-girl sank back into her chair, exhausted and overwhelmed.

Tyracor returned to his apprentice's side and laid a steadying hand on her shoulder. "King Lapsair would have been here too had the preparations for the Assassins' Guild council not kept him away. He did wish me to pass this message on to you, though."

Zanishiria took the thin-sheet letter and read the script silently: I, too, an honored by what you have done. You have always been so strong and I respect your inner courage most of all. Remember the support of these people you see today, for, I assure you, tomorrow it will seem like many are against you. Know that, because of today, you are not standing alone. Whatever happens, there are still a great number of us who are grateful for what you did. We are no longer ruled by an emperor because of you! Now rest and leave Obseen's fate to us. You do not need to worry about anyone but yourself now (I know that has always been your wish.) I fear the council is against you, but know for certain that you are free to be yourself now—More're King Lapsair.

She held the stone tablet tightly and breathed a thought of thanks, then Zanishiria glanced up at her master to find Seircor and Anmero had joined him. "Kye mureak. I am very honored by all of this." They smiled in relief. "But, now…I would like to rest."

Seircor grinned teasingly, "I knew you'd say that."

Zanishiria rolled her eyes but refrained from punching her friend in the arm—she didn't think it would end so well for herself. "You will get what is coming to you later, Praic."

"Not until you recover, he won't. I will make sure of that.... somehow." Anmero reprimanded lightly and asked to lift Zanishiria into his arms. Though the assassins were surprised at the request, she agreed. "Seircor will go get you some food while I bring you back to your quarters."

Seircor left with the invitation, leaving the three of them alone. Master Tyracor took his own leave, knowing there was much he wanted to know about the council meeting tomorrow. "I will see you on the 'morrow, val'eya. Take it easy until then."

"Seivier." Zanishiria bowed her head and watched her master leave the room.

Anmero turned them then and started up the long stairwell back to her room. Somewhere along the way, Zanishiria began to drift, and, by the time the prince reached her bed and set her upon it, she was deeply asleep. The Royal pulled a blanket around her, careful to not wake the exhausted assassin, and brushed a soft kiss to her temple, his action by impulse. Fondly he whispered, "For one so damn unapproachable, you are so sweet, Zanishiria. I am so glad I go to meet you. Goodnight assassin. Be well."

Dawn came far too quickly and the long trail of assassins, and some Royals, began to file into the enormous council house on the northern shores of Senak'y Lake. All clan-heads from the seventy-two assassin clans of Obseen were there, the number of representatives being from two to three. The seventeen high-clans spaced themselves equally around the lower seats of the coliseum-styled bleachers. Accompanying the clans were also the dozen-count of Royal emissaries—King Lapsair and Royal Aslén Doz among them—plus the main council of the training center (numbering thirty-five after the losses in the war), and the thirteen Lakean clansmen designated to represent the Las'wa seimreal. There was barely enough room to fit the entire council in the Guild house.

Much debate had preceded the event, for two days prior, on whom should lead the council and the framework of the debates. With Sye Rainier dead, the official speaker position automatically fell to Master Teera Sabina, but, as she had been the Emperor's Honored One, there had been much opposition to her leading. Many voted for King Lapsair to take the floor, yet the aging king declined saying, "no more Royals should be the head of the Assassins' Guild; leave it to all of you." Others had called for one of the Legion of Leaders—if any would step forward and claim that they were a part of the secret faction. Some were indeed known by that time—the Berris, the Tà sharay, and Mater Quinn and his master-friends—however, these leaders were not quick to admit their positions, lest they lose the power the Legion had being in the shadows. Finally, the debate having run into the second day, the choice was cast: the blind Master Shathahel, well-respected of the Taysor representatives, would lead the proceedings.

The wise, old master humbly tapped his way to the middle of the speaker's floor and rapped his walking cane to call attention to all the gathered clans. A tense, hushed silence followed. Shathahel nodded in satisfaction. "We all know why this council has been called today," he began without preamble. "The late emperor whom oppressed many of our clans has been dethroned." An elated murmur drifted amongst some of the clans. Angered by their interruption, Shathahel rapped his cane again. "Hold your tongues, insolents! It may have been twelve years since the Assassins' Guild has been able to call a meeting but we should not have forgotten our discipline and respect! Today is a privilege, a chance for us to make a new start for ourselves, assassins and Royals alike. So….as we debate on what we are to do this day forward I ask you all to choose wisely, councilmen. Obseen's future falls to you as your task today to decide where we are headed. We must be cautious to not let happen ever again what Manscor was able to do: use our system to fight up the chain to ultimate power then take it away from us. We are assassins! We are a people who know the trials it has taken us to get as far as we have from our ancestors that fought over so much. I implore you, are we not ready to have peace?" Nods followed his question. "If we are, then I ask you think of all the ways that we have created against it and change them. And, until the time I deem this council is finished, the council doors will be closed and we will debate. Let us begin!"

* * *

Zanishiria fiddled restlessly with a leather cord on her tunic. She had been placed in a tiny room just outside of the council chambers by her master and told to wait until the Guild called on her. None of her friends had been allowed to join her, so the uncomfortable silence and heaviness of what was to come weighed on her mind. It drove her head to spinning about on the fate Zanishiria imagined the council would declare on her misdemeanors, those that King Lapsair had been able to tell her of. All killing of Manscor aside, the Las'wa knew she had killed the Senior Master of the Guild, and, she had been told, the council of the training center—headed by Master Teera Sabina— had sentenced her as a "defect". The two crimes were horrible enough that having ended the emperor's reign would not be excuse enough to hide her from the laws of the Guild. The only recourse Zanishiria knew for such transgressions was death.

Darkness was descending on the world outside the windows of the room. Zanishiria's injuries were beginning to scream at her for rest but she would not give into the impulse. Too, she had hardly let herself move all day from the chair she sat in, lost in her own head, and her body was none too happy to be left so long in one state. Only the florick moss she had in her pouches kept the pain at bay and staved off the hunger in her belly—for no one had thought to bring her food despite her having been left all day alone. Aching, hungry, and tired. Zanishiria had felt them all before; she would endure until they called her.

An hour after the final rays of sunlight had disappeared from the only window in her room, the council door creaked open. Zanishiria glanced up to see her master slipping through. She rose carefully as her seivier neared. Master Tyracor seemed slightly upset but the smile he greeted her with did not lack conviction. "The proceedings have gone more smoothly that I have ever imagined. It seems all of us are ready to have the Guild lead Obseen again; and all equalities have been preserved between our people and the Royals. I have no fear about Obseen's future now."

Zanishiria read between the lines. "On Obseen, I see you are very pleased, seivier, but something is wearing on you."

Master Tyracor frowned at his apprentice's perceptivity. "They are just starting on the final course of business."

"Myself."

Zanishiria's coolness did not seem to touch her master; his mind seemed to be worrying over some other information in his head. She waited in the now-familiar silence of her tiny room for her teacher to speak. When he finally did, Zanishiria felt herself chill inside. "Tarin Saerric is speaking against your behalf right now, val'eya." He didn't have to say more for her to know it was bad, really bad.

* * *

Her "trial" lasted two hours. There were many arguments for and against Zanishiria Novastone's actions. The injured Lakean girl stood rigidly beside her master through the whole proceeding, trying to stay outwardly stoic while internally she was reeling for the assaults thrust at and for her.

According to law, Zanishiria could not influence the trial in any way, unless asked, but she was allowed to listen to all of the debate. Some of her supporters Zanishiria knew well but other surprised her. Excluding Tarin Saerric, Teera Sabina, and some of the Honored One's supporters, most of the council from the training center (who had the most authority in her case) were supportive of Zanishiria, as were many assassins and Royals. Zanishiria felt a little hope seep through her malaise, maybe the council would not kill her, after all.

The room quieted at long last, bringing Zanishiria's attention back to the proceedings. Old Shathahel returned to the center, seeming not the least worn or vexed by the long, intense meeting. His voice was clear as he issued the final verdict. "Zanishiria Indigo Novastone, step to the center to hear your judgement." The assassin-girl came forward silently and bowed to the blind master. Shathahel cocked his head to listen but Zanishiria held herself too quiet for him to get a good read on her. She whispered for him to continue, "The Assassins' Guild has decided on your sentence, Zanishiria. Here is the basis against you: murder of the Senior Master, declaration of "defect" by the Taysor training center's council, and dis-inheritance to your home clan."

Zanishiria had to force herself to stand coolly at the last offense; she had not been warned that the Las'wa Council had made the declaration, though in hind-sight she realized she should have known it. Becoming a preshan, she had made an oath to denounce herself to her clan. They were true to their word that they had washed their hands of the assassination program. She stiffened and bit her lip to force herself to continue listening.

"The punishment for such shameful actions is…death!" The council rocked with protests. Shathahel's face hardened into a frown and he rose his hands for silence. The room stilled. "However, Zanishiria, in light of you following orders from the Renegade army regarding the late Emperor Manscor, this council has asked this penalty be waived. Your new sentence is this: as being a part of Taysor's elite training center, you are expelled unless the to-be-appointed Senior Master and the Center council agree to your return; however, your return will only be granted if you do one of two choices. The first is that you be exiled from Obseen for no less than two years; the other that you take an "Oath of Solitude" for three years here on Obseen, with only one person of your choosing to have contact with for food and medical supplies. This council gives you the freedom of this choice."

Zanishiria could hear her master suck in his astonishment at the severity of the punishment. Indeed, many were whispering their shock at the verdict. Not ever had such a long sanction been given against an assassin. Voices began to rise in opposition for the sentence to be reduced. In the middle of it all, Zanishiria felt her pulse slow and she closed her eyes to find her calm center. She realized she was relieved; death would not come to her that day. Anything less seemed to be an easier sentence—at least to her.

"I will do it." She said calmly, though many did not hear over the rising din. Shathahel heard, however, and banged his staff until the room was silent. She repeated her words. "I will do it, Master Shathahel, but it must be done here. Obseen is my home and I will not leave it. If three years is the punishment this council has seen fit to give me, I will take it."

She could feel the sadness in her master's aura as he stood behind her, but she had already accepted the task. In Shathahel, though, Zanishiria could sense his respect for her had been solidified. It was the master in front of her that gave her the deepest bow of respect she had ever received. "Very well, young assassin. From tomorrow, the count of your three years will begin."

* * *

As soon as the council was closed and the clans cleared from the building, Zanishiria collapsed. Tyracor was barely able to catch her as she fell by his side. "Zan!" He helped her to a chair and supported her as she leaned weakly against the seat. "This was too much for you. I told them to not keep you here all day but the council insisted."

"Seivier, it's okay." She replied weakly. "It needed to be done."

"No….no it didn't. They should have given you a free pass for all you did. They asked you to kill the emperor, the clan asked you—I asked you!" He cut off in anger for a moment. "And you have done all we have demanded. It is wrong for them to make the verdict this way."

"I think it needed to be the way it was." Zanishiria said, her voice distant in the thought. "For the first day of the Assassins' Guild council to pardon a student on the grounds she crossed, would not bode well for the future they wished to lay down."

"Creeshts-áet, Zan! Why do you have to cling to your parents' ideals so strongly?"

She chuckled softly at her master's anger. "They are my ideals, seivier, and we have always disagreed on them."

Her words softened Tyracor's anger. "Yes…yes, you are right."

Silence came between them for many, long minutes, then Zanishiria asked her master the question she had wanted to say since she had accepted her sentence. "Will you be the one I have contact with these next three years, seivier?"

Tyracor shifted, uncomfortable at the question. His apprentice looked at him inquiringly, confused at his hesitation. "Zan…I just can't agree with it. It is too harsh a penalty."

"But you are my master. We could train, alone, for three years."

"And you wouldn't get bored of this old man?" The skeptical eyebrow raise she cast him said she doubted it. "I mean it, Zan. I took you away from everyone but your brother and Seircor most of your life. Certainly, you have met someone better suited to keeping you company than me."

"Right." She replied, very sarcastically. "It will be like old times, seivier." She argued.

"Old times, huh?" He let himself chuckle too. "Okay, then, I guess we can come to some sort of arrangement about that. But, until tomorrow, you are still a part of all this. Go, be with friends before you forget what it feels like to be young."

"Maybe you need the reminder."

Tyracor laughed. "Trust me, val'eya, when you are my age, you won't want to."

* * *

Master Tyracor helped Zanishiria back to the training center, where she promptly fell asleep for a one-hour power-nap. Upon her waking, the young assassin took more herbal medicine and ate a light soup. Then, as she had expected, Anmero and Seircor showed up at her door to help her back to the lounge. Many students were there already taking full advantage of the excuse to celebrate the end of the war; it had been ten days of it from what her two friends told her.

"They don't seem to want to stop." Anmero had commented. Zanishiria just shook her head at the foolishness. "Come, we will clear a spot for you to sit and get you some more food and drink."

Seircor helped his younger friend to a chair near the large, bay window overlooking Senak'y Lake and settle her into it as the prince hurried away to the refreshment table. "He seems to have fit right in." Zanishiria commented as they watched the Royal.

"Crey." ["Yes."] Seircor replied. "Though I suspect some of his energy comes from not wanting to think of K'sho's death than anything else."

Zanishiria's face became solemn at the words. She nodded. "I would do similar, I suspect." She averted her eyes. "Really, I haven't had enough time to process that to mourn properly. After today," her voice began quiet, "I will have more than enough time for it."

"Zan—." Seircor began.

"Don't, Praic." Zanishiria stopped him. "I have made my choice. It is my price to pay."

"You shouldn't have to pay it. You did what was asked of you."

She chuckled without any humor. "Seivier said the same." She grabbed for his hand to hold it as if his touch could steady her from the panic he thought could be beneath her calm exterior. Her eyes were full of sadness. "Please, don't make this harder for me. I need your support."

Praic nodded at the request and bent down to her eye level. "Sy'éinen, seimie. Kye ret'aun lai eyen kye." ["Always, my best friend. I will support you any way I can."]

Zanishiria smiled wanly at him. "Kye mureak." ["Thank you."] Seircor squeezed her hand, feeling how weak her returned one was. He almost wanted to comment on it but refrained for Zanishiria's sake.

Anmero returned then, two Xsorians in tow. "Look who I found."

"I bet they found you." Zanishiria teased and head-bowed to the Torez brothers.

"Indeed, we were looking out for likes of all of you." Page replied, reaching out to take Zanishiria's hand. *"Zan, will you be all right? We just heard from father."*

"It is too soon to say, Torez." Zanishiria replied honestly.

A feeling of understanding came back to her through their mind-link. *"If there is anything we can do...?"* Page started but he heard the "no" from Zanishiria. *"I know... an "Oath of Solitude" is meant to be done alone, but I—we—still wanted to offer. You will always have a place to go in Xsenume. Remember that for the future."*

"Thank you, Page, Lap." She glanced at the other Torez, too, knowing he could at least hear that. Page smiled and released her hand, opting to be polite in the presence of those who were not telepathic. "Many are out tonight." He nodded to the crowded room. "Are there any others you wish to say good-bye to before the night is over?"

Zanishiria looked about the crowd but the one other she wished she could speak with was not present—not that he would want to see her in any case. She shook her head. "No, you few are enough for me. I am sure some masters will make their way to me before I take my leave but I have no others I wish to seek out. Really, with having just woken from a coma, this is a lot to take in in one day."

"We're sorry—or, more, I am sorry." Anmero told her. "This is the first week of my being a part of all this. I'm finding all the excitement to my liking, especially after all that time I spent alone on M2."

"This has been a very exciting two weeks for you." Lap said.

"Yeah, you can say that again. Zan gave me the full tour of Obseen before all of the fighting."

"Her type of sightseeing tours doesn't leave much to the imagination." Seircor said, his version of teasing Zanishiria.

The group laughed and Anmero nodded. "That's very true."

"Careful, seimie, I do know where you live." Zanishiria cautioned him. Seircor shrugged innocently.

"What are your plans, prince?" Page asked politely.

Anmero shrugged. "I think I will be staying here in Taysor. My uncle wants to introduce me to some masters, as I've said I want to learn more about swordsmanship and the like. I think, after recent events, that I need to learn such skills to live here."

"Wise of you." Seircor agreed. "You handled the sword well, the little Zanishiria and I taught you. Keep up your dedication and you will go far with it."

"Thank you." Anmero acknowledged. "There is so much I have to learn about Obseen and the Guild and my family's business. I'm going to be overwhelmed for some time."

"You are welcome to learn at Xsenume whenever you get around to it. Our father, the Tà sharay, has a large archive and plenty of contacts to get you around any information you may desire."

"I will keep that in mind."

The friends bantered for some time; Zanishiria joining in now and again when she found the energy to, but Seircor could see her slowly fading and finally asked to excuse themselves from the party. The two Las'wa gave final farewells and took their leave. "To your room?" He asked as he helped her walk—albeit very slowly—from the lounge. Zanishiria had been stubbornly set against being carried again, saying how it was demeaning around so many fighters when she had been the one to take down the emperor. Seircor had let her have her pride, though he had kept a steadying hand on her arm the entire way. Now alone he hoped she would relent and be carried.

Zanishiria shook her head. "There is a bench near the end of this hall overlooking the gardens and the west side of lake. I would see that sight one more time."

"Okay, but no more of this slothing around. I am carrying you."

"Slothing? Who's slothing?" She eyed him, half warning and half joking. "I thought I was doing well for being the walking dead."

"That's not entirely funny. You very nearly were dead, Zan."

"I hardly need the reminder." She replied, this time sarcastic. "You can carry me there; it is a little way—just don't get used to it."

"That's my line, I think." Zanishiria finally gave in and chuckled at Seircor's attempt to lighten her mood.

Seircor found the alcove his friend had meant. It was quiet there and secluded—just what Zanishiria had always preferred. He set her down on the stone bench and slid in next to her. They say in the silence and looked out at the night, lit faintly by the two half-filled moons. "It's beautiful here." Seircor said finally.

Zanishiria smiled softly and nodded, her eyes on the stars. "Yes. When I first saw it I stared for hours, despite it not being safe to linger so. It's so different from the caves. I've come to love the smell of the trees and the earth, the way the water looks in the daylight, the stars at night—and the breeze…" Her eyes looked more distant and somewhat sad. "One year here versus thirteen in the underworld and I find I am reluctant to leave it. Even knowing the coursa is so familiar to me, all its turns and dangers, I'm just not wanting to return to it."

"That makes sense, seeing it now." Seircor replied. "You'll lose that nice complexion you've developed from the sunlight."

"Watch it, Praic." Zanishiria warned, her eyes teasing.

Seircor chuckled. "Still, I can see what's so inciting about the surface. The Las'wa are the only clan to live in the underworld. True, it has its own beauty, but we miss out on a lot. I was ignorant to it until so recently. You, at least, got to see so much of it this past year."

Zanishiria nodded. "I see it as a gift to myself, especially when I won't have the liberty to come here for some time." Her reminder of the trial she was about to embark on had them both sobering. "I won't easily forget all this."

"I am not letting you do this alone, seimora." Seircor blurted out. Zanishiria rose her eyebrows at his declaration. "I'm not!" He reiterated. "'Oath of Solitude" my ass. I am going to see you, even if it gets me in trouble with the seimreal. You are my closest friend and I will not let you suffer alone."

"I won't be alone, Praic, seivier will be with me."

"Don't try to brush this off, Zan, like it is a trifle." Seircor warned. "I am going to help you get through it. Kye shal'aunēn." ["I promise you." Meant in a very formal way and of the highest respect]

Zanishiria frowned at her friend, her eyes bordering on a glare. She sighed unhappily and looked away. Finally, she relented. "Just don't get caught, then, seimie. I could not bear you to be sentenced with such a punishment yourself."

Seircor nodded, satisfied enough with her answer. He slipped to the edge of the bench, giving room between them and kowtowed to her. Zanishiria's eyes widened in surprise at his very deep and very formal bow. "Ai'yen slai'ey, seimora, kye sy'éinen shau'l tá'lai." ["Whatever comes to be, seimora, I will always stay by your side." This is a formal oath made to a ruler of the Las'wa; not used for intimate/sexual relationship. It cannot get more formal nor more sincere than this.]

"Seircor..." Zanishiria breathed in awe. She closed her grey eyes and absorbed the oath fully. "Sy'éinen, kye aun'laus lai. Sy'éinen, kye shau'l tá'lai-áet. Kye aun'em mar'ŭn." ["Always, I will hold you to it [the oath]. Always, will I stay by your side, too. I will make [you] proud [of me]."]

"Kye'ey." ["I already am."]

* * * Tailpiece* * *

"It is in inimitable condition, Master. I have never seen the likes of such a weapon, even from the technicians on Planet X. That it could be built with traznic and sydro-smelted steel is a wonder in and of itself. It's near-indestructible."

"I am pleased you find it to your liking, General." Master Teera turned her back to the rising suns to look at the military commander squarely. She hoped the presence of her fighting scepter at her belt made a formidable impression through his screen—at least it seemed to with every other UEF officer she had ever spoken to. The general seemed unfazed, however, sitting half a solar system away on New Earth. Sabina pushed back her annoyance. "My late Emperor Manscor was planning to use it against your people's forces. He wanted to rule all of the Abyss Solar System. But, alas, the other assassins on this planet did not see his lofty goals as fitting for them. I assume you can do better, General, from what I have heard of you."

The officer gave her a cocky grin. "I can take this weapon to heights your deceased ruler could only dream of, Master Sabina. Your "gift" gives me so many options." His arrogance leeched through the image. "Now I can do as I please beyond what my superiors give me reign to." He steepled his fingers infront of his face. "Of course, I assume such an extravagance given to me comes with a price? It doesn't seem like a probable course of action for you to work with the UEF, even one such as myself. Assassins have a tendency to hate us as much as we hate you."

Teera snarled. "I hate you crips much more than you can imagine, but you…you are not a typical UEF crit. I have read your file and selected you out of many options available to me. You have certain…items I am in need of and a means to an end that I much desire. But—do not think that I cannot take you out of the picture if I find you no longer useful, General."

"Right." He scoffed at the warning. "So, I take our deal is still a go? Or have you changed your mind, Master?"

"My plans are still as agreed, as long as you continue to keep your furtherance in the UEF and continue to supply all of my needs. If any information leaks to the Royals, I will personally slit you."

"Threats have no warrant here, Master Sabina." The general advised casually. "You will find I can accommodate you quite nicely. The Royals will never learn a thing until all you ask for is ready. And," he grinned, "The Hammerhead will be completed as scheduled. You will not be disappointed. The Abyss is as good as yours, My Empress."

Turn the page for an exclusive look at

The Cost of Redemption
(Book Two in the Assassins' of Obseen series)

Chapter One

The young man sidestepped a puddle of mineral water in disgust and continued to pick his way cautiously along the obsidian cavern he had descended into. Bending down, he placed a hand on the stone floor to assist a jump down to the next ledge barely made out in his lantern's light. The man straightened and began to stride across the spacious cavern—its girth stretching well beyond what his light emitted. Glancing around uncertainly into the oppressive darkness beyond, he wondered about the untold dangers that lurked there.

Suddenly something whooshed past his face from the dark shadows beyond, and the object, a preshair knife, burrowed its sharp point into the stone beside the man's foot. He gasped and tripped backward in fear. A chuckle of amusement from the weapon's owner resounded eerily through the cave. A moment later, a showy figure unattached itself from the cavern wall and stalked closer to the man. The young woman bent to retrieve her knife then turned to give the man a pointed glare as sharp and cutting as the weapon she has just obtained. "Why is it that my time of "Solitude" is three months over the pardon time?"

The man, a UEF scholar by the looks of him—a strange occurrence to be on Obseen, planet of the assassins—backed away from the assassin woman nervously. "Th-they sent me here to get you. I have no idea what they wanted you for...or why you are here to begin with. I'm just following their orders." Obviously, he had been given no prior knowledge to whom he had come to collect or the situation that had her living in the underworld.

The assassin woman cursed in Las'wa and turned away to walk into the darkness, not at all amused with the Guild's joke of sending a UEF scholar to collect her. The man hesitated at her dismissal and began to backtrack his footsteps, intending to leave the way he had come. "I would not go back that way." The woman warned, pausing at the end of his light. "The chreeshts will have already sealed the entrance you used." The UEF scholar glanced around nervously at the never-ending shadows, suddenly very frightened to know the large spiders native to

Obseen could possibly be lurking nearby. "You are better off following me. I just might help you get out of this place alive." She continued deeper into the cavern, ignoring the reaction her words elicited. "I know an exit that the creeshts don't web up."

The man hurried after the assassin-woman as she disappeared down a narrow tunnel. He hastened only to unexpectedly run right into her, falling backwards onto his ass on the rebound. The annoyed look cast his way did little to comfort him. The assassin pointed ahead of them. Squinting, the scholar tied to make out what the woman was pointing to but there was nothing there. She sighed and picked up a stone to throw ahead of them. A moment later, a young creeshts scuttled out of a small hole and charged the trespassers. The scholar gasped and scuttled backward as the spiderling raced toward them. Undaunted, the assassin-woman let fly her trademark whip and let it lick around the spider's large heard, to constrict itself until the body and head were snapped from each other. Glistening blue blood spilled to the floor as the corpse collapsed. "The young ones know no caution." The woman remarked as she continued on past the dead spider. "Come." She called as the scholar finally found his feet.

"Coming!" The scholar told her as he picked his way around the still-twitching body and hurried after his charge. This time, the assassin-woman waited for him to catch up—lest he run into her again.

"Odd that they picked you to come retrieve me, scholar."

"Y-yes, Princess Novastone. I was shocked myself but your uncle insisted. He thought the walk would do me some good."

"Oh, really?" A skeptical eyebrow-lift was the assassin's answer. Inwardly, she thought, they must have wanted to get rid of him to send him here unprepared. Was he that bothersome? To the scholar she said in correction, "Call me Zanishiria next time."

"Yes princess, uh…I mean Zanishiria." The man slipped over the unusual name. He scurried after the assassin as she continued on. "It's so dark down here…. how can you see so well?"

The smallest of smirks came fleetingly over Zanishiria's lips as she jumped easily from a ledge and past a pool of mineral water. "The cave walls contain a mineral called asrouc. It lights the caves when exposed to carbon dioxide." She passed the man a piece she had collected. "Breath on it and it will glow softer but longer than your lantern."

As Zanishiria expected, the scholar exclaimed, "Oh, how fascinating!"

"Yeah, okay. This way, scholar."

For nearly an hour, Zanishiria led the UEF man through a maze of tunnels. All the while, the man asked questions that were rarely answered by the woman. Finally, a thundering sound from a large waterfall drowned out the man's chatter. "Is that the opening?" He asked, coming closer to the assassin to ask the question.

Zanishiria nodded. "This is the entrance to Taysor Gulch, west of the Palace. That is where we are going, right?" The scholar nodded. Zanishiria waved him forward along the side of the cascading water and took one final glance back into the darkness that was her home. Quietly she whispered, "Oshay, Praic. Kye tai sie." ["Good-bye, Praic. I will see you again."]

The scholar looked back, hearing her speak. "What was that?"

Zanishiria shook her head. "It was of no importance to you." She walked past the man and into the sunlight. "Come, scholar, we have another half-hour to reach Taysor."

* * *

The Taysor Palace was grander than Zanishiria remembered. Its massive size stretched a full two hundred acres and four stories high, its cold surface stretching beyond what the eye could see. Zanishiria made her way to its northern entranceway, to what had originally been the Emperor Manscor's private wing. The obsidian and marble pillars that towered along the pathway to the doors gleamed a sharp ebony and pearl in the mid-morning sunshine, the years having washed away the bloodstains that had adorned them three years' past. The stones that led to the massive front entrance were engraved in Royal poems, lining the way in an intricate scrollwork; however, the tarol trees that used to line the stone walk were gone, replaced, with the tiny tarn shrubs that reminded the assassin of the webs the creeshts designed. Another new addition to the palace, she noted, were the assassin symbols that made intricate patterns across the walls.

Zanishiria frowned at the changes wondering what else she was to find inside if the outside looked so different.

Apparently, the Assassins' Guild had taken over much of the Palace. Did that mean then that were few Royals left on Obseen? She found herself hesitating on the stone steps, uncertain if she really wanted to take those last few steps forward into such an unknown. The scholar glanced her way questioningly and reached out to open the enormous right door, inviting her through. Finally, Zanishiria continued up the last flight of stairs and moved past the polite scholar.

Nothing had changed inside since Zanishiria's last visit, much to her relief. All of the walls and floors were still laid in marble and crystal and the ancient wooden furniture that lined the walls were all still in the places she remembered. Zanishiria breathed in to calm herself and motioned for the scholar to lead her onward. She fell in behind him three paces back. The UEF man continued down the main hall until he reached a large, wooden door. There, he stopped and turned to the assassin-woman. "This is where I was asked to bring you. You are to go in alone." He pushed open the door then without waiting for her nod and Zanishiria forced her feet to walk through, albeit she came cautiously.

An older man, with his dark hair laced in grey and a weathered, yet not overly wrinkled face, glanced up from his seat at a large table. A bright smile lit his face at the sight of Zanishiria. "Mora'nen, what a great surprise! Come, come in, let me see you!" [Mora'nen is familiar term for daughter, which King Lapsair considers Zanishiria despite them not being blood.]

Zanishiria hesitated, uncertain she was in the right place if the Royal king had not been the one to call for her, but the aging king was very infectious with his fondness toward her and she found herself accepting his warm hug without much trepidation. "Shayso, King Lapsair." She returned and let the man hug her for a long minute. Zanishiria was just about to comment on how good it felt to see the Royal—who had treated her like a daughter—when a movement to her right caught her attention. She stiffened and pulled from the king's embrace, her hand automatically going to the handle of the whip around her waist as she spun to face the other occupant.

"Don't, my dear." King Lapsair urged of her gently as he set his hand over hers. "He is not a threat…and this is his office now."

Zanishiria stilled her hand and eyed the robed figure skeptically. Still overly-wary, to have another in the room, she stepped so that King Lapsair was between them. "So, does that mean it was not you who called me to the Palace, King Lapsair?"

Her adoptive father looked confused at the question, confirming Zanishiria's suspicions; however, before the king could answer her, the robed figure dropped his hood on his cloak to reveal himself. "It was neither of us." Zanishiria startled as she met Tarin Saerric's sharp, blue eyes, hardened by the trials of the past three years. Her friend had grown to manhood. He towered above her in a six-foot-one frame that was lean but iron-muscled. His skin was a perfect, bronzed tan that contrasted nicely with his golden-blond hair; she had remembered it darker. To finish the effects of his handsomeness was the fact that his face had thinned to become perfectly chiseled in features seen better on a model of New Earth.

Tarin, too, was studying Zanishiria. His eyes wandered over her in a similar assessment, albeit he frowned in deep contemplation. He noted the Las'wa had grown very little in height, standing at about five-foot-five, but she had matured indefinitely. Her body was extremely lean and lithe, belying the strength it housed, but her muscles still bunched with power— and the fact that his stare unnerved her. Her eyes were still that sharp, depthless slate that had a pull of the deep emotions that were beneath the calm exterior the assassin portrayed. The eyes were just a shade lighter than the raven color of her hair, which fell now to mid-back instead of waist length. The cut, and fact that the hair was pulled tightly back, made Zanishiria's overall impression one of inviolability.

"Tarin." Zanishiria whispered. "So...this is your place now?" The Neitiege man nodded. "It explains the changes outside."

Tarin ignored the comment, as he was uncertain if was a compliment or a criticism, and instead asked his own question. "Who called you back to Taysor, Zan? Only a few masters have that power."

Her features darkened. "How would I know? I did just get done asking King Lapsair the same thing." The two once-friends stared at each other in a defiant dead-lock, Tarin believing Zanishiria was just being obstinate, while the Las'wa just didn't want to discuss anything without knowing any of the goings-ons at the capitol.

"Master Quinn called Zanishiria here to the Palace." The newcomer's voice turned their eyes to the doorway, where Scarlett Novastone, only daughter of King Lapsair, had just entered. "Quinn wants Zanishiria to join his team at the training center."

Tarin frowned. "I gave him no such authority."

"He doesn't need such, as you know Senior Master." King Lapsair stood and walked over to his daughter to put a gentle hand on her shoulder. "If Master Quinn wants Zanishiria to finish her training, what is so wrong with that? Would you deny a student whom has fulfilled her oath to the Guild a chance at finishing her training at the center?"

A dark look came over Tarin's features but he seemed to give weight to the Royal's words, for he finally relented. "I will allow her to go meet with Master Quinn." He motioned for Zanishiria to follow him as he turned his back on King Lapsair, "But, I will do no more than that—at least for the time being."

The aging king gave the retreating Senior Master's back a sad frown, not entirely okay with the answer the young man had given; however, his look was easily replaced with a fond smile when Zanishiria stopped in front of the two Novastones to bid them good-bye. "Kye rein." ["I will be fine."] She told them in reassurance. Tarin made a noise at the door, meaning her to hurry her good-byes, and bobbed his head for them to leave. Zanishiria gave a final bow and followed her once-friend at a distance as he led the way out of the Palace.

Keeping one eye on Tarin's tensed back, Zanishiria glanced around on their walk toward the center, keeping alert to any and all changes to Taysor. She felt overly exposed in the sudden light and openness of the surface—having been underground for three years and in an "Oath of Solitude" with only one person as a contact for the entire time. Too, there was something in the Neitiege man that had her hackles raised in warning; Tarin was not one she was sure she could trust anymore.

When Tarin rounded a corner ahead and disappeared, the feeling grew. Zanishiria knew the street he had taken led away from the training center, not toward it. All senses alert, she stepped farther out into the street and fingered the handle on her preshair whip. As she rounded the corner, Zanishiria readied her weapon in case it would be needed to defend herself.

Tarin stood close to the stone building. He whirled around to face Zanishiria as she neared. In his hand was a hand-gun. Its barrel came to touch the assassin-woman's breastbone as she stepped into it to make a level glare into Tarin's blue eyes. Zanishiria glanced at the gun mockingly-casual then returned her slate gaze to her one-time friend's face. "A gun is rather tasteless, don't you think, Senior Master?" She twisted the sound of his title to make is seem conceited. "Does this mean you plan to make an enemy of me?"

"You should not have come back." Tarin lifted the gun to her forehead. "You were better off staying away from Taysor. There is no place for you here."

"Think as you wish." Zanishiria shifted the gun away from her skull. That Tarin let her move it showed he lacked the vindication to take the shot. "However, it seems that someone finds a need for me at the Center."

"Master Quinn has always had a fondness for you. That does not mean that he needs you."

She almost smirked. "And you would know, Senior Master Saerric.... senior master. Now how did you pull that off in three short years?"

"One. The Guild needed someone who could pull all the factions together after the war's end. When my name came up, there were no objections."

"No, of course there wouldn't be." Tarin had been one of the most exceptional students the center had ever seen—and he had a reputation for fairness and integrity. Never had she heard of any offenses taken against the Neitiege. Zanishiria made as if to turn away, done with the conversation.

"I will kill you next time we meet."

The words made her pause, but not because she felt threatened. Zanishiria turned back. "And I believe you will not, Tarin." She replied boldly. "One thing you never were was a killer, nor would you ever take someone down without cause. Do you have a cause for taking my life?"

"Shev'ek!" [Shut up] Tarin snarled, but as he spoke his hand dropped to his side. If he was to lift it to use the gun again, Zanishiria would have the quicker reflexes to take him with her whip or a blade before he could level it properly again. That was not lost on her—or him it would seem. Tarin grumbled to himself as he turned his shoulder to Zanishiria to lay a fist into the stone wall. The look on his face was a mix of pain, confusion, and fury.

"I guess we will see if you do next time, Senior Master." Zanishiria said quietly. Slowly, as if backing from a predator one had come across, she made some distance from the Neitiege assassin. "You have no need to take me farther to Master Quinn. I will find myself to the Center without your assistance." She bowed despite the fact that Tarin seemed not to hear her anymore, and slipped away from the shadows of the building and continued on her way across the city to the training center.

Author Bio

Lindsey Cowherd lives in Salida, CO, where she was born and raised. She lives with her sweetie, Michael, who somehow tolerates her horse-craziness and love of all-things-Asian.

She started writing "novels" at a young teen; this book being one of the first she ever thought up that was beyond her normal obsession of horses. Turning to a world immersed in martial arts, codes, and "places not of this world" allowed her an outlet from everyday living and circumstances out of her control. Now, they are a place to allow her imagination to run wild.

Licensed as an acupuncturist since 2010, Lindsey still finds time for the small stuff: writing, watching almost anything Asian on Netflix, singing and playing guitar, but especially enjoying her two horses, Bricco and Tyrra, and two dogs, Ms. K and Huffington.

Connect with Lindsey:

www.authorlindseycowherd.com
Also through Facebook, Instagram, or Twitter!

Made in the USA
Las Vegas, NV
05 November 2021